TEXAS OUTLAW

For a complete list of books, visit
JamesPatterson.com.

TEXAS OUTLAW

JAMES PATTERSON
AND ANDREW BOURELLE

GRAND CENTRAL
PUBLISHING
New York Boston

Grand Central Publishing
Hachette Book Group
1290 Avenue of the Americas, New York, NY 10104
grandcentralpublishing.com
twitter.com/grandcentralpub

Originally published in hardcover and ebook by Little, Brown & Company in March 2020
First oversize mass market edition: August 2021

Grand Central Publishing is a division of Hachette Book Group, Inc. The Grand Central Publishing name and logo is a trademark of Hachette Book Group, Inc.

The publisher is not responsible for websites (or their content) that are not owned by the publisher.

The Hachette Speakers Bureau provides a wide range of authors for speaking events. To find out more, go to hachettespeakersbureau.com or call (866) 376-6591.

ISBNs: 978-1-5387-1870-4 (oversize mass market), 978-0-316-42818-7 (ebook)

Printed in the United States of America

OPM

10 9 8 7 6 5 4 3 2 1

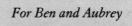

For Ben and Aubrey

PROLOGUE

SUSAN SNYDER PRESSES her foot down on the gas pedal and zooms around a curve, the headlights of her Mustang convertible cutting through the darkness and the stereo blasting the Foo Fighters into the cool June Texas air. She has the top down, and her hair whips around in the wind as goose bumps rise on her arms. Maybe from the chill. Maybe from excitement.

She knows she should slow down. She should be careful. But she can't help herself. She's giddy. She can't wait for tomorrow to come. She should probably feel more scared. That's the smart way to feel — scared and careful. But *caution* has never been a word in her vocabulary. At thirty-seven years old, she's single and successful, and she doesn't take shit from anyone.

She rounds another curve, the tires squealing against the blacktop. Up ahead, her ranch house is nestled among the sagebrush-covered hills. She races into her gravel driveway and skids to a halt, sending a cloud of dust up into her headlight beams. She takes a deep breath and sits in the car for a minute, trying to let her heart rate slow down.

It won't. She's just too excited.

She was on a dinner date tonight. At least that's what it would have looked like to the other customers at the only halfway decent restaurant in town. A man. A woman. White wine. Filet mignon for him. Crab legs for her. A shared dessert of strawberry cheesecake topped with vanilla bean ice cream.

But it wasn't a date. It was a strategy session.

Come tomorrow, the little West Texas town of Rio Lobo won't know what hit it.

Susan presses the button to raise the convertible roof. On her way up her front walk, she looks up at the moonless sky. The view is breathtaking, and she never tires of country still so untouched by light pollution that the stars look like droplets of paint sprinkled over a vast black canvas.

One of the reasons she lives here is the solitude. The simple country life. She works as a freelance web designer and makes a comfortable living. In a town like Rio Lobo, where Susan serves as one of five elected members of the town council, she might even be considered borderline rich. But her income wouldn't go nearly as far in a big city like Houston or Dallas, let alone New York or Los Angeles, where a lot of her clients are based. Besides, the town of Rio Lobo is about the perfect size for her. It has exactly two stoplights.

Susan takes her eyes off the sky for a moment and notices something on her front porch. On the rocking chair next to her door sits an object enfolded in clear plastic wrap, with a handwritten note attached. *Made some cookies for you. They're safe.* The note is unsigned, but when she sees the two snickerdoodles—her favorite cookie—she knows who left them for her.

Inside, she's already unwrapping the cookies as she

kicks off her shoes. She eats the first one and takes a drink of milk straight from the gallon. She considers saving the second one for tomorrow, but she's in an indulgent mood. She eats it and tosses the cellophane and note onto her kitchen table. She leaves her purse there next to the wrapper and heads down the hall to her bedroom.

She steps out of her dress and pulls on a pair of Victoria's Secret sweatpants and a Dallas Cowboys jersey that she sleeps in.

When she picks up her toothbrush, her fingers feel tingly, as if they've fallen asleep. She puts the toothbrush into her mouth and notices the swelling of her lips. She squints at herself in the mirror—not only does it look like someone punched her in the mouth but also her whole face appears to be swelling, as if she's suddenly gained twenty pounds.

Worse than her appearance, her breathing has become labored.

Susan tells herself not to panic. She has a known peanut allergy, and any hint of peanut oil could trigger this reaction. Her friend who left the cookies knows about the allergy—and labeled them *They're safe*—but must have accidentally baked in some trace of peanuts.

Moving slowly, trying to keep her breathing under control, Susan opens the medicine cabinet and, with fingers swollen like sausages, grabs her EpiPen. Tearing open the package, she walks over to her bed, sits on the edge, and then, without hesitation, jams the needle into her leg, right through her sweatpants.

She waits.

She knows that she needs to call 911. But her cell phone is in her purse back in the kitchen, on the other side of the house. She decides to wait a minute and let the shot of adrenaline do its job. She concentrates on her breathing. Air wheezes through her throat, like wind whistling through a desert canyon.

Her vision blurs. Her heart won't stop pounding. A wave of dizziness nearly topples her off the bed. She needs to get to her phone.

The shot isn't working.

She rises and takes a step forward, but the floor seems to tilt under her feet. She makes it to the hallway and collapses. She tries to stand, but all her muscles are cramping, shooting lightning bolts of pain throughout her body.

Over the pounding of her own heart, she hears something—footsteps.

Thank God, she thinks.

Help, Susan tries to say, but no words come out. Her lungs have stopped inflating. Her vision darkens.

There are no stars in this blackness.

PART ONE

CHAPTER 1

I PULL MY Ford F-150 into the small parking lot at the Rio Grande Bank and Trust in Waco. A big Dodge pickup, even bigger than mine, is taking up two handicapped spaces right in front. I drive around to the shady side and find an opening far from the door.

It's my lunch break, and I need to deposit a check for my girlfriend.

"Tell me again, Rory," my lieutenant and new boss says from the passenger seat, "why your girlfriend doesn't get a bank account in Tennessee."

Kyle Hendricks and I became Rangers right around the same time and have always been competitive. Up until about a month ago, Kyle and I were the same rank. Then my old boss, friend, and mentor, Lieutenant Ted Creasy, retired and Kyle got promoted. A lot of Rangers wanted me to take the lieutenant's exam, but I wasn't in the right headspace to apply for the job. I've been through hell and back in the last year.

Now that Kyle's my boss, I remind myself to be respectful of his position. After all, he's in his late thirties, a few years older than me. The Texas-bred good old boy has hair the color of straw and the long, lean body of the baseball pitcher he was back in high school and college. Since football was my sport, I thought of Kyle and me as two quarterbacks vying for the starting spot, fueled by a mix of mutual respect and distaste—then suddenly one of them became the coach.

"Coach" invited me to lunch at a local restaurant called Butter My Biscuit, which I took as a good sign that he wants to smooth this transition. But the way he's been ribbing me about Willow makes me think that maybe he hasn't changed much after all.

"Hell," Kyle says, "it's the twenty-first century. They got national banks now, you know. Wells Fargo. Capital One. You might have heard of 'em."

I ignore him. The guys at work tease me all the time about Willow, who moved to Nashville a good eight months ago. She's a country singer—a hell of a good one, too. Through most of her twenties, she played in bars and roadhouses from Texas to Nashville. But she never got her big break—until last fall, when she broke her ankle and a video of her singing on a barstool in a leg cast went viral. Suddenly producers and talent scouts were asking for demos of her songs, inviting her to fly out to Nashville for auditions. She and I had really only just started dating. But I encouraged her to go and pursue her dreams. Take her shot.

She's done well so far. A couple of songs she wrote were recorded by Miranda Lambert and Little Big Town, and are already earning her royalty checks. Her own album is due out later this summer. People are saying Willow is going to be the next big thing, but she knows every new artist is next up for fame, though fame passes most of them by.

She's been cautiously optimistic, and maybe a little superstitious. She doesn't want to open a bank account in Nashville until she feels sure this is a permanent move. Which also has a little something to do with me. The Nashville Police Department has a job opening for a detective, and she's asked me to consider applying.

I'm honored to be a Texas Ranger, born and raised in Texas, and the thought of leaving the top division of state law enforcement isn't a decision I take lightly. Times have changed since the Wild West days, but not the legendary status of Texas Rangers. The badge still carries a mystique.

"How much is that check for anyway?" Kyle says, gesturing to the sealed envelope in my hand.

I ignore this question, too. "I'll be right back," I say.

"Take your time," he says, leaning his head back and tilting his Stetson down over his eyes. "I'm going to take me a little nap."

It's early June, but already the air is hot and thick with humidity. My clothes stick to my skin. I'm wearing the typical Texas Ranger attire: dress slacks, button-down shirt, tie, cowboy hat, and cowboy boots. And a polished silver star pinned to my shirt.

I'm wearing my gun, too, a SIG Sauer P320 loaded with .357 cartridges, sheathed in a quick-draw holster. *A Texas Ranger should always be ready for anything.*

I walk into the bank head down, not paying attention to my surroundings as I open the envelope Willow sent me. I'm caught off guard by the amount of the check. I'm glad I didn't tell Kyle—I'd never hear the end of it.

Not until I hear the unmistakable click of a gun being cocked no more than a foot from my head do I sense anything is wrong. *Today I'm not ready.*

"Hold it right there, Ranger," a voice says from behind me. "One move and I'll put a bullet right through your skull."

CHAPTER 2

I SLOWLY RAISE my head and take in the scene. Besides the guy holding a gun to my head, I see only one other robber. He rises from a crouch behind the counter, where the half dozen tellers are standing. The AR-15 assault rifle he carries is equipped with a bump stock to effectively turn it from semiautomatic to fully automatic.

"No sudden movements," he yells at me, "or I'll light this place up like the Fourth of July."

The big Dodge parked out front, blocking the view into the bank, is probably the robbers' getaway car.

The guy behind me swivels around, keeping the pistol—a 9mm Beretta—leveled at my head. "Put those hands up," he says. "Slowly."

I do as he says, quickly counting the six customers standing in the bank lobby. The last thing I want is to put innocent bystanders in the midst of a gunfight.

These guys look like pros. They're wearing black tactical gear from head to toe, including masks and bulletproof vests, standard issue for law enforcement or military personnel (though your average citizen can get this stuff on the internet).

Even if these guys are professionals, I still have one question.

"Why the hell are you guys robbing a bank at lunchtime?" I say. "There probably wouldn't be a soul in here at any other time of day."

"Not that we owe you any goddamn explanation," the guy with the AR-15 says, "but the vault's on a time lock." He checks his watch. "And it's just about time."

With that, he disappears into a back room. Now is the time for me to make a move. But even if I could get the drop on the guy with a gun to my head, Mr. AR-15 would hear the gunshot and come running. He'd open fire with the assault rifle and tear the place apart. He could kill everyone in the room before he needed to reload.

The eyes of the guy with the Beretta dart to the pistol on my hip, then back up to my face. I can tell what he's thinking. He's wondering how to disarm me. If he gets close enough to reach for the pistol, maybe I can disarm and disable him. Asking me to remove it from the holster and drop it will risk putting a gun into one of my hands, even if he insists I use the left one. Or I could leave my hands right where they are, shoulder high and far from my gun belt.

"I don't want any trouble," I say to the guy. "I'm going to let you walk right out of here. You don't want to hurt anyone."

"If anyone's gonna get hurt, Ranger, it's you. I hate the fucking Texas Rangers. I might kill you just 'cause I feel like it."

The guy's voice is rough and strained. These guys might be professionals, but this one's nerves are shot. I need to find a way to keep him under control.

"Let me remind you," I say, maintaining a steady,

calm voice, "killing a Texas Ranger is capital murder. They'll give you the needle for it."

In other states, death-row inmates die of old age while their lawyers delay their sentences with endless appeals. But this is Texas, which executed more people last year than every other state combined.

The hand holding the gun trembles slightly.

"It's also capital murder," I say, "to kill someone during the execution of a robbery. If you shoot anyone today, anyone at all, that's a death sentence. Automatically."

I've scared him, which isn't necessarily a good thing.

"You and your partner are free to go," I assure him. "I don't care about the money you're stealing. Maybe you'll get caught at a later date. Maybe you'll get away with it. That's not my problem today. What I care about is that no one gets hurt."

I can't gauge the impact of my words. The guy watches as his partner lugs two loaded duffel bags, one on each shoulder. He hauls them up onto the counter and then, like a bank robber in a movie, climbs atop the marble. He stands and shoulders the assault rifle, swinging it around at the people standing in the lobby.

Some are crying. Some are shaking. All of them look scared to death.

"All right," Mr. AR-15 announces, breath heaving from carrying the bags, "since we had the bad luck of a Texas Ranger walking in on us, we're going to have to take us a hostage."

"There's no need to take any hostages," I say. "I'm going to let you walk right out of here."

"We seen you circle the parking lot," he says. "We know there's another Ranger out there. We need some insurance we won't be followed."

Mr. AR-15 looks overly confident, crazed almost. But his partner, Mr. Beretta—I can tell he's spooked. His eyes bulge in his mask. And his arm is getting tired, too. His gun hand is shaking more and more.

"If you have to take anyone," I say, "take me."

CHAPTER 3

MR. AR-15 GIVES me a look that says he's considering my request.

"I've got handcuffs on my belt," I say. "Put them on me. Get one of the tellers to give you a canvas money bag to put over my head. I won't see a thing. You can leave me wherever you want once you know you're safe."

His eyes drop from my face to the belt at my waist. The cuffs are on one side, the loaded gun on the other. He knows he won't be safe as long as I'm armed.

"Ain't gonna happen, Ranger," he says. "We're gonna take us one of these pretty little customers. The kind that they'll put all over the news, saying, 'Those damn Texas Rangers fucked up and got that little girl killed.'"

He uses his assault rifle as a pointer. "Eeny, meeny, miny, moe," he says.

Each person cringes as the gun aims at them before moving on.

"You are *it,*" he says finally, aiming the rifle at the youngest person in the room, a pretty girl who can't be eighteen. She lets out a sob, and her eyes swim with tears.

I have to do something.

And I have to do it now.

Mr. AR-15 bends his knees like he's going to hop down off the counter, but my best chance—my only chance—depends on keeping him above the rest of the crowd. It will be safer for all of the bystanders if I'm shooting upward.

"Wait!" I yell as loudly as I can.

My shift in tone has caught everyone by surprise. Let's see if I can surprise them again.

What happens next takes only a couple of seconds. Three at the most.

I drop into a crouch, reaching for my gun as I do. My cowboy hat flies off my head as if yanked by a string, and only in that split second am I aware that Mr. Beretta has pulled the trigger and filled the silence with the roar of a gunshot.

I land on one knee, in a shooting stance, and raise my pistol. Mr. Beretta is closer, but Mr. AR-15 is more dangerous. I draw a bead on the center of his black mask as he's bringing the assault rifle around. I squeeze the trigger and his head snaps back. Blood splatters the ceiling. His body leans and he starts to fall backward off the counter, but I'm already shifting, swinging my gun onto Mr. Beretta. It's only been an instant since he fired his pistol. He's moving fast, and in a fraction of a second, he'll have his gun aimed between my eyes. But I don't give him a fraction of a second. My sight is already locked on the black mask.

I squeeze the trigger.

His body hits the floor an instant after I hear the *thump* of Mr. AR-15 landing behind the counter.

The air is full of the acrid smell of gunpowder and screaming. I take a moment to verify both men are dead. Then I call out and ask if anyone is injured. People are crying, in shock—they'll be traumatized for life—but no one is hurt.

My eyes drift to my cowboy hat, lying on the floor. There's a dime-sized hole through the crown. An inch lower and the bullet would have punched a crater in the top of my skull. I'm in a trance for a few seconds, looking at the hat. Then I hear the door of the bank burst open. I whirl around with my SIG Sauer, but I pull up and point the barrel at the ceiling.

My lieutenant, Kyle, is at the door, out of breath and gun in hand. His face is a picture of absolute surprise. He takes in the scene and then adjusts his hat on his head.

"I'll be damned," he says. "What'd I miss?"

CHAPTER 4

THAT EVENING, AS the sun sits low on the horizon, I pull my F-150 into the driveway at my parents' ranch. I live here, in a separate house that's less than a year old. My place is on a small hill overlooking the spot where a bunkhouse for ranch hands used to be, back when hired cowboys lived on the property. I like the view from the little two-bedroom home that Willow and I briefly shared before she moved to Nashville.

I pass my parents' house, the home I grew up in. Mom is out working in the garden, and Dad is on the porch, whittling a block of wood.

I pull to a stop but don't get out.

"I'm okay," I say as they approach the truck, their expressions revealing they've been sick with worry. They've already heard what happened.

We talk for a few minutes as I try to set their minds at ease. I'm still numb from the deadly events at the bank, and I just want to be alone. But it can't be easy having a son who wears a tin star to work every day, so I try to reassure them.

One of the reasons I moved back to the property was that I wanted to be close so I could help out. Dad had a bout with cancer last year. He's in remission now and doing great. Most of the time it feels like Mom and Dad are helping me out and not the other way around. Tonight is no different. Mom says she made extra for supper and brings me a plate wrapped in cellophane, a venison sirloin with fried okra and mashed potatoes on the side. When I get to my place, I set the plate on the table but don't unwrap it.

I have no appetite.

I take a long, hot shower, then grab a Shiner Bock from the refrigerator and go sit on the porch. The pine boards feel good on my bare feet. It's dusk, and there's a hell of a Texas sunset in front of me. The whole landscape has a sharp golden hue, and the clouds in the sky look like they're on fire.

I take one sip of the beer and it hits my empty stomach like acid. I dump the rest over the porch railing into the grass and set the empty bottle at my feet.

This isn't my first time shooting someone, but it never gets easier. One minute, I feel like I could throw up. The next, I feel like I could break down crying. Instead, I just sit there and think. These were bad guys—identified as ex-felons with long rap sheets. Still, I took their lives to get the people in the bank out of harm's way. But I can't imagine a scenario in which I would have been okay watching those men take that teenage girl hostage.

I could not have let that happen.

I've had a complicated relationship with God— the violence I've seen can make me question God's existence—but today I say a little prayer of thanks for the safety of the innocent folks in that bank. And I say thanks for the bullet that passed through my Stetson, that its path wasn't any lower.

A faint orange glow remains on the horizon. Stars have begun to populate the darkening sky. I go inside to get my guitar, figuring if anything will clear my mind, playing will. Concentrating on the notes, focusing on the lyrics, doing something I love—that's the medicine I need right now.

But when I get inside, I see my phone is full of missed calls and text messages. Family and friends are wanting to check on me, but I'm not in the mood to talk. There's nothing from Willow. She's on tour with Dierks Bentley, and she has a show in Sacramento tonight.

There is one message that catches my eye. My old lieutenant, Ted Creasy, sent me a text that says, Call me, partner.

I do.

"I've got bad news and bad news," he says. "Which one do you want first?"

CHAPTER 5

"AREN'T YOU SUPPOSED to be retired?" I tell Creasy.

"Yeah," he says, "but I still got my ear to the floor. People tell me stuff."

As we're talking, I step out into the grass, feel the cool blades on my bare feet. Fireflies light up around me in the dark. I can hear insects chirping in the distance. I could have died today—and that perspective makes it hard to be worried about whatever Creasy has to say.

He tells me that the higher-ups in the Texas Ranger Division are happy with my performance today. From the major who oversees my company to the chief of the whole division, everyone agrees I couldn't have handled the situation any better.

"They're happier than pigs in shit," Creasy says.

"I thought you said you had bad news."

"I do," Creasy says. "While everybody's tickled pink about you, they're mad as hell at Kyle."

My stomach sinks.

"He's napping in the truck while you're in there taking on two bad guys all by yourself."

"There's nothing he could have done," I say. "No way he could have known."

What I'm saying is true. But public perception is something else entirely.

Your everyday Ranger can typically fly under the public radar, but once you're a lieutenant, you're kind of a public figure.

"What's the media coverage been like?" I ask.

The way to know if a news story is going to get airplay is if there's video of it, plain and simple. If someone took a cell-phone video of a firefighter saving a cat from a tree, that story will get a hundred times more airplay than someone saving a school bus full of children if there were no amateur videographers around to witness it.

"That's the other bit of bad news," Creasy says. "Somebody leaked the security footage of what happened inside the bank."

If my stomach sank before, now it plummets.

"It's gone viral," Creasy says. "Hell, there're half a million hits on YouTube already."

"Jesus," I mutter. "No one needs to see that."

Creasy says the news stations are warning viewers about the violent subject matter before they air the video on repeat.

"You're gonna be a bona fide media hero," Creasy says. "The switchboard at headquarters can't handle all the calls. I bet the *Today* show or *Good Morning America* tries to get you on there. No way the chief lets that happen, but it's a shit show down at headquarters, that's for sure."

I feel sick. Even more sick than I did before.

I walk back over to the porch and plop down in my chair. On the surface, this shouldn't seem like such bad news. As long as no one thinks I did anything wrong, I'm not in any danger of being reprimanded.

It might be good publicity for the Rangers. But the bottom line is, I just don't want the attention.

Last year, I was connected to a series of high-profile murders. The first victim was my ex-wife, Anne, who—up until then anyway—was the love of my life. Once the case was solved, my name was all over the papers, and the headlines weren't always good. I'd earned a reputation for being a hothead willing to bend—or even break—the rules.

Ever since, I've been trying to keep my head down, follow the rules, be the best Ranger I can be.

"I hope like hell no one's shown that video to Willow," I tell Creasy.

As if the universe could hear our conversation, an incoming call buzzes in my ear.

It's Willow.

"I gotta go," I tell Creasy.

When I pick up, Willow is crying on the other end.

CHAPTER 6

"ARE YOU OKAY?" Willow says, barely able to talk through her sobs.

I admit that I'm shaken up and a bit numb, but I assure her I'm unharmed.

Willow says that when she finished her set in Sacramento, one of the crew said, "Hey, is this your Texas Ranger boyfriend?" and shoved an iPad in her face. Without knowing what she was getting into, she watched the video of me in the standoff.

"That guy shot the hat right off your head," she says.

I apologize for not calling to tell her. I didn't want her to be an emotional wreck before she had to perform.

"I have to join Dierks in fifteen minutes for a duet of 'Long Trip Alone,'" she says. "I don't know how I'm gonna do it. I'm shaking like a leaf."

"You can do it," I say. "You're a professional."

The first time I ever saw Willow was when she was onstage. It was in a roadhouse bar, not a big concert venue, but she had a magnetism that was undeniable. She's a looker, no doubt about it, with blond hair and curves in all the right places. But what I loved about her the most was her voice. She sounds like

Carrie Underwood—and can hit the same notes—but there's also a raspy undertone to her voice that's sexy as hell.

I think I fell in love with her the first time I saw her perform. Whether it was love at first sight or love at first sound, I can't be sure.

Willow's not a fragile person—she's one of the toughest people I've ever met—but she just watched me not only come close to dying but also kill two people.

I can tell she's starting to pull herself together. I think she just needed to hear my voice.

"How was the show?" I ask, trying to divert the conversation away from death.

She fills me in on the latest in her life. After tonight's concert, there's a break in the tour, and she'll be flying back to Nashville to record the final songs for the album.

"Any chance you can come visit?" she says.

In theory, I could. I'll be on leave for at least a few days, maybe a few weeks. Any time a Ranger is involved in a shooting, there's a period of investigation. But I know what will happen if I fly to Nashville. Willow will be so busy we won't get to spend any quality time together. She'll have late-night recording sessions or be asked to visit one promotional event after another. With her debut album on the horizon, she pretty much needs to do everything she's asked these days.

I want to support her, but what I need right now is the comfort of home. I need to heal by helping Dad on the ranch, eating Mom's home-cooked meals. I'd give just about anything to have Willow fly back to Texas and spend some time here, but getting on a plane and flying to Tennessee is the last thing I want to do right now.

I try to explain this the best I can to Willow, but it turns our conversation melancholy. We talk a little more about trivial matters, but I get the impression we're both thinking about what's *not* being said.

Her career is taking off, and the long-distance thing we're doing can last only so long. If I'm not willing to take the plunge and move to Tennessee, what are we going to do?

And after today—when I almost died in the line of duty—I imagine Willow is wondering what she's gotten herself into. Can her heart really handle being in love with a Texas Ranger?

Are our careers compatible?

As great as we are together, are *we* really compatible?

"I gotta go," Willow says. "I'm due onstage."

I tell her I love her and hang up. I stand alone in the darkness, listening to the chirp of the insects and looking up at the stars. They don't shine quite as bright as they used to with all the light pollution seeping up from the horizon, that's for sure. I pick up my empty beer bottle and head into the house.

Thinking of Willow performing seventeen hundred miles away, I open my laptop and go to YouTube to find a video of her. I watch the video that made her an internet sensation—just her, sitting onstage on a barstool, with her leg in a cast and a guitar in her hands.

That's my girlfriend, I think proudly.

I catch myself smiling.

Before closing the computer, I feel a temptation. I search for my name, and sure enough a video pops up showing a grayish image of me in the bank. I press Play. There's no sound, but I can see myself talking to the robber with a gun to my head. When the one with the assault rifle climbs onto the counter, we're all three in the frame. My heart is pounding as I watch. On the screen, I drop to my knee and a flash of light takes the hat off my head—

I slam the laptop closed.

I think of Willow, what it must be like for her, seeing this and facing the reality that she could lose me at any time.

CHAPTER 7

A FEW DAYS later, Dad and I are riding horses along the perimeter of the property, looking for places in the fence that need repair. I've got my gun on my hip in case we run into any rattlesnakes. And I've got a new hat on my head. Willow had it shipped to me, a Silverbelly Stetson with a high crown, wide brim, and sterling silver buckle on the band.

The hat probably cost three hundred dollars.

It doesn't feel quite right on my head. I'm trying to break it in, but I'm sure missing my old hat.

Dad's riding Dusty, a roan he's had for a decade, and I'm riding Mom's horse, Browny, a beautiful young bay. We're supposed to be checking the fence, but my brothers and I helped Dad with a big repair just a few months ago. Really this is just an excuse for Dad and me to get out and enjoy ourselves for a few hours.

We don't talk much. Dad knows that's not what I need right now. Instead, I focus on the sound of the horses clopping along and enjoy the faint breeze blowing on our faces. It's midmorning, and the day hasn't grown oppressively hot yet.

I feel my phone buzz and dig it out of my jeans. By the time it's in my hand, I've missed the call. It was from Kyle Hendricks.

"I better call back," I say to Dad.

There's a stream up ahead with a big oak tree providing shade, so we stop there and let the horses drink. I dismount and call my lieutenant back.

"You ready to get back to work, Ranger?" Kyle says as soon as he picks up.

"So soon?" I say.

"You want a longer paid vacation?" he says.

"Just surprised is all."

"There ain't much to investigate when the whole damn thing is on video," Kyle says.

"All right," I say. "I'll be in tomorrow."

The truth is, I am disappointed. It's been good for me to spend the last few days with my family. I want to go back to work, but not in a rush.

"Don't come to company headquarters," Kyle says. "We need you for something else. You ever heard of Rio Lobo?"

"The ghost town?"

"No, that's Lobo," Kyle says. "Rio Lobo is a little town over in West Texas. Few hours from Fort Hancock."

Kyle says a town councilwoman has died under suspicious circumstances.

"All evidence suggests natural causes, but the local detective thinks otherwise. They've asked us to send a Ranger."

All of this sounds very strange to me. Not that they would ask the Rangers for help. That's what we're here for. Texas has six Ranger companies, each assigned to a geographic region. Company F, housed in the Waco office, is nowhere near this town way over on the other side of the state, close to New Mexico.

As if he can sense my confusion, Kyle says that

the Ranger covering that area recently retired, and Company E, out of El Paso, can't spare the man-power from an ongoing, enormous drug-trafficking investigation.

"They asked if we had anyone to spare, and I volunteered you. I figured you'd want to keep a low profile right now."

I sense a subtext to Kyle's words. It's true I want to keep a low profile, but this assignment seems low stakes, the kind of job they'd typically assign to a new hire in need of field experience. He might prove himself, and even if he doesn't, screwing up won't be too much of a black mark on his reputation. There are other Rangers available to do this job. Which tells me something.

My lieutenant is sending me on this job as a punishment.

"Is there a problem?" Kyle says. "You got quiet there for a minute."

"Are you really this petty?" I say, even though I know I shouldn't.

I guess everyone is right—I am a hothead.

"What did you say?" Kyle snaps. "Call you a hero and suddenly you're too good for a small-town field assignment?"

I bite my tongue. It's what I should have done in the first place.

Kyle says, "I'm giving you an order, Ranger."

I've been trying to walk the straight and narrow within the Texas Ranger Division. I've been careful not to piss anyone off lately. I need to do this job and do it to the best of my ability. And if spending a few weeks in the middle of nowhere is what it takes to mend fences with my lieutenant, that's what I'm going to do.

"I'm sorry," I say, trying to make my voice sound as earnest as possible. "I was out of line. I'm happy to do it."

"Good," he says, his voice still trembling with anger. "You leave first thing in the morning."

CHAPTER 8

THAT NIGHT, MY parents invite the whole family over for dinner. This is kind of a tradition for us. Whenever I'm going out of town on an assignment, everyone gets together. No one says it out loud, but I've always suspected they're worried they might never see me again. Of course we all know from the recent bank incident that I don't have to go to another part of the state to be in danger.

As soon as Dad told her I was leaving, Mom called my brothers and then got to work making my favorite dinner growing up, country-fried steak and gravy. It takes her a good three hours to prepare, but once you've had my mom's country-fried steak, you'll never order those frozen squares restaurants try to pass off as homemade.

My brother Chris and his wife, Heather, show up first, bringing along my nephew, Beau, who just turned three. Chris is the middle brother, the steadiest, the most reliable. The most like Dad. He helps Mom in the kitchen while Heather and I play with Beau, who is talking a blue streak these days.

My brother Jake and his wife, Holly, bring their daughter, Jess, who just started crawling. Jake's the youngest of us and the polar opposite of Chris—

impulsive, wild, temperamental. If people think I'm a hothead, they'll think Jake's hair is on fire. But he's not angry by nature. He's sentimental and will tear up watching just about any sappy romance movie. Jake joins Mom and Chris in the kitchen, and I keep myself busy chasing after Jess and playing a tickle game with Beau that he just can't get enough of. That kid's got the best laugh.

Dad adds a leaf to the dining room table to make room for everyone. At first, he sets an extra chair but then takes it away.

"I forgot Willow ain't here," he says, carrying the chair back out to the garage.

Willow's absence becomes the topic of conversation. How is she doing? When is she coming back to visit? When can I make it up to Tennessee to see her?

Everyone likes Willow; there's no doubt about that. But there are differences of opinion about a future for the two of us—and everyone feels comfortable enough to express those opinions.

"I can't believe she wants you to move to Tennessee," Jake says as he tries to get a spoonful of mashed potatoes into Jess's mouth. "Being a detective in Nashville ain't the same as being a Texas Ranger."

"You might find this surprising, Jake Yates," Holly says to her husband, "but there are other places to live in this country besides Texas. Not everyone born in Texas has to stay here."

"It's not like she's asking you to give up law enforcement altogether," Chris says.

"You really think he should go?" Heather says, surprised by her husband's position.

"I'd do it for you," Chris says, leaning over and kissing his wife on the cheek.

"She does have a heck of an opportunity," Mom says. "This is her dream. She needs to live it."

"I know," I say. "I'm not stopping her."

"But are you supporting her?"

"Rory's got a dream," Jake says. "It's called being a Texas Ranger. He needs to live it, too."

Dad doesn't say much, but after dinner he asks me to come into his study with him. The walls are lined with bookcases, but memories outnumber books on the shelves: football trophies, framed drawings my brothers and I did as kids, souvenirs from family vacations, and photographs, lots of photographs. Pictures of us kids, as babies through to adults. Pictures of the grandkids. There's a nice picture of Anne, my ex. Seeing it in here never bothered Willow because she knows how much my family loved Anne. And it's hard to be jealous of an ex who was murdered. Besides, there are pictures of Willow here, too. A couple of her next to me at family outings and another solo shot of her onstage. It was taken at the Pale Horse, the local bar where I met her, but she looks like a star playing a stadium show.

Dad and I are both staring at the picture. Dad was taken with Willow the first time he met her.

"What do you think I should do, Dad?"

"You've gotta decide that for yourself, Son. But a good woman ain't easy to find. If you got yourself one, I think you ought to hang on to her."

These words evoke the mistakes I made with Anne. She divorced me long before she was murdered. She was a good one—the best—and I let her slip away.

Am I really going to let Willow slip away, too?

CHAPTER 9

I'M ON THE road the next morning, bright and early. It's a nice day for a drive, and the F-150 makes for a smooth ride. People who live elsewhere don't always realize just how big Texas is. To drive from the Louisiana border to the western tip, over by El Paso, takes just about as long as it does to get from Ohio to Florida. Fortunately, I don't have that far to go, but I've got a long day ahead of me, that's for sure.

I pass thousands of cows, dozens of windmills, and two dead armadillos lying on the side of the road. The landscape changes around me. Texas could be five separate states. The eastern border resembles the Deep South, Louisiana or Mississippi. The Gulf Coast is a lot like Florida. Central Texas, with its lakes and rolling hills, feels like the Midwest, only hotter. And each successive mile in the north feels more and more like the Great Plains. West Texas, where I'm headed, is another world altogether. The humidity dries up. The grasslands turn to barren dirt and rolling hills of sagebrush and prickly pear cacti. And few people live in the small towns scattered across huge swaths of empty land. When I say small towns, I mean *small*—towns that make Redbud, where I grew up, look like a city. I'm heading to a county as big as Connecticut with a population less than ten thousand.

As I drive, I start to feel better about the trip. So what if Kyle is sending me on a wild goose chase as some juvenile punishment. Maybe I can actually help the folks in this town.

The Rangers bring big-city police services to the small towns of Texas. Kyle said I'm to report to a Detective Delgado. The presence of a detective tells me the police department is bigger than some. I'm sure this Detective Delgado can use the help. He's probably used to investigating robbery and vandalism. I doubt he's ever had a murder case in his life.

Besides, my girlfriend is halfway across the country, so it's not as if I'm missing out on spending time with her.

Speaking of my girlfriend, I glance at my phone and notice a text from her. Careful to keep one eye on the road, I bring the phone up so I can read the text.

I'm going to be on Bobby Bones this morning. Premiering my new single. Tune in...but don't be mad!

I don't know why on earth I would be mad at her. The fact that she's going on one of Nashville's biggest syndicated country radio shows is a huge deal. She and I have listened to the show together while making breakfast or sitting on the porch. Millions of people listen to it. I couldn't be more proud. I've heard all the demos of her songs, so I'm curious to know which one they chose for the single.

I scroll through the stations, looking for the morning show. Just my luck I'd be in a part of Texas that doesn't get it. But then I come across Willow's familiar voice, that sexy, raspy twang I've always been in love with. My heart swells as I hear her—that's my girlfriend on the radio!

She's talking about the new song, saying that she and her producer had the album nearly wrapped and decided they needed one more track.

"*I wrote it as a joke,*" she says. "*We were just goofing around. But it's got a great beat. I think people will really like it.*"

Bobby Bones asks her if the song is autobiographical.

"*Well, I am dating a Texas Ranger,*" she says. "*Everybody knows that.*"

I suddenly go from excited to nervous. Is Willow's new song about me?

"*A real-life hero,*" Bobby adds. "*He's the one who stopped that bank robbery in Texas the other day, isn't he?*"

"*Yes. And he's wonderful. Our relationship is nothing like the song. I'll tell you that. If he's listening, I hope he gets a kick out of it.*"

"*He hasn't heard it yet?*" asks Amy, the cohost of the show.

"*Nope,*" Willow says.

Everyone in the studio laughs.

"*His name's Rory, right? Rory Yates,*" Bobby says. "*This one goes out to Rory Yates in Texas. This is Willow Dawes's new single, 'Don't Date a Texas Ranger.'*"

"Oh, shit," I say aloud.

I turn up the radio to listen. It's the first time I've ever dreaded hearing Willow sing.

CHAPTER 10

WILLOW CAN WRITE slow ballads that will break your heart, and she can write fast-paced barn burners that get people up on the dance floor. This is the latter. The song starts with the sound of boots stomping on floorboards in rhythm with hands clapping, followed by a quick, heavy guitar riff. The beat is catchy. No wonder they wanted to release this right away.

My dread is momentarily washed away by pride and admiration at Willow's talent. Willow starts singing and I'm even more in awe—that voice!

> *He's a tall drink of water with a sexy Southern drawl.*
> *Your knees will go weak when you hear him say "y'all."*
>
> *With a cowboy hat, big boots, and a gun,*
> *Does he look like trouble or does he look like fun?*
> *Tall, dark, and handsome, he don't have much to say,*
> *But he'll arrest your heart and lock it right away.*

I'm feeling relieved. It doesn't sound too bad. Just good fun, as Willow said on the radio.

> *Whatever you do, don't kiss his lips,*
> *Don't slow dance with his hands on your hips.*
>
> *If he asks you to dinner, you better say no.*
> *He'll only break your heart somewhere down the road.*

Then the chorus starts.

> *You'll be dying to flirt,*
> *But don't even start.*
> *Watch him ride off into the sunset.*
> *Don't let him steal your heart.*
> *Take it from me, ladies,*
> *I should know.*
> *If you don't want to end up living with a stranger,*
> *Don't date a Texas Ranger.*

She draws out the words in that last line. There's a nice guitar solo, then she starts in with another verse.

> *He's gone for weeks while you're all alone.*
> *He's hunting bad guys and you're waitin' by the phone.*
>
> *Trust me, ladies, he's too good to be true.*
> *He'll be married to his job, not married to you.*

Willow sings through the chorus a few more times, and then she's back in the studio, laughing and basking in the admiration of Bobby Bones.

But my mind is elsewhere.

The comment about waiting by the phone isn't fair. She's gone more than I am—I could write a song called "Don't Date a Country Singer."

Really, though, it's the last line: *He'll be married to his job, not married to you.* That's the one that stings. Not because it's true in the case of Willow and me. Neither of us works nine-to-five, so we've had an unconventional relationship from the start. What hurts about the line is that it's true of my previous relationship.

With Anne.

Willow probably didn't think anything of that line when she wrote it, just looking for something that rhymed with *true,* but Anne could have written that autobiographically. In fact, she said as much in her diary, which her mother let me read after Anne died, hoping I'd find some clues to her murder.

Ever since then, I've tried *not* to be that guy. I've tried not to be the guy married to his job who lets a good woman slip through his fingers. For the first time since Willow brought up the detective opening at the Nashville Police Department, I think that I should apply.

Five minutes after Willow completes the interview on *The Bobby Bones Show,* my phone buzzes with an incoming call from her.

"Are you mad?" she says. Despite the good humor in her voice, I can tell she's anxious to hear what I have to say.

"No," I say. "I loved it."

Honestly, the song is harmless enough. But here I was keeping a low profile, and now there's a song inspired by me that a million people just heard on the radio. I can already hear the other Rangers giving me a hard time about it. And the last thing I need is some perp jawing at me during an arrest about how I need to take better care of my woman.

Willow explains that she had just been messing around during sound check one day, making up lyrics as she went along. Her producer heard it and wanted her to finish the song.

"I didn't think we'd end up putting it on the album," she says, "but once we finished, I knew it was going to be my first single."

"It's going to be a hit," I say, and I mean it.

We talk for a while longer. I hadn't told her yet about my reassignment to Rio Lobo, so I explain that I'm driving across Texas as we speak.

"They shouldn't have you back on duty this fast," she says.

I don't tell her that Kyle is punishing me.

"It will be fine," I say. "Besides, I need to get out of town for a while before everyone I know gives me shit about being in your song."

"I'm serious, Rory. Do you think you're ready to be back on duty?"

"It's a little town in the middle of nowhere," I say. "How dangerous could it be?"

CHAPTER 11

I FIND MYSELF driving on back roads that twist through the rolling hills. I go for miles without seeing another car — just sagebrush and the occasional fenced-off pump jack levering up and down, pulling oil out of the earth. Off to my left is a narrow oasis dotted with big cottonwood trees and shrubs. That's the route of the namesake of the town, the Rio Lobo, I assume. I can't see the river, but in these parts, a waterway would be the only explanation for a meandering ribbon of lush vegetation.

Around six o'clock in the evening, the road and the river converge at a little town probably no bigger than a few square miles. I drive clear through and out the other side before I realize I've seen the whole thing. There are two stoplights.

I circle back and take a second tour up and down the main roadway. The architecture is a mix of old brick with a distinct Spanish influence (picture the Alamo Mission) and New Mexico–style adobe. The houses are mostly single-story, with shallow roofs and sometimes colorfully painted walls.

I pass by the school, which likely contains every grade — K through twelve. Behind the school are a baseball diamond and a football stadium that don't look half bad for a town this small. A fenced-in lot holds several school buses, which rural kids probably ride more than two hours a day.

A handful of businesses includes a small grocery store and only a few restaurants. One is called Good Gravy and looks like your typical Texas greasy spoon. A Taste of Texas seems a little nicer. I also see a Tex-Mex place named Rosalia's. I pass a well-kept bar called Lobo Lizard. The type of place a town dignitary—or what counts for one here—could enjoy a beer alongside a day laborer or a field worker.

There's a motel with an empty parking lot and a lit-up VACANCY sign with a couple of letters burned out. A tiny adobe post office stands next to a gas station with a mechanic's garage. I spot a couple of churches, both built in the Spanish style of the early settlers. A pharmacy—a little mom-and-pop place, not a chain—stands next to a small medical center with twenty-four-hour urgent care. The public library is located next to a park with some new-looking playground equipment. I spot a newspaper, the *Rio Lobo Record,* housed in one of the bigger buildings in town.

I see a McDonald's, of course, but otherwise the branded world seems to have left the little town alone. The one exception is banks. I count at least five: Wells Fargo, BBVA Compass, Prosperity, PlainsCapital, and Rio Grande Bank and Trust, where Willow and I share an account. There might be more banks than restaurants, which seems odd for a town this size.

Rio Lobo is small, but it's clean and well maintained. I spot instances of graffiti on fences but no abandoned eyesores. No vacant lots. The occasional man-made arroyo splits off from the river corridor, feeding irrigation throughout the community. The canals are lined with well-worn dirt walking trails. There are plenty of trees, and the lawns are green. For whatever reason—probably oil—Rio Lobo doesn't seem as cash-strapped as the typical small Texas town.

It's easy to find the police station, which isn't much bigger than my two-bedroom house. It shares a gravel parking lot with other municipal buildings: a community center, a senior center, the volunteer fire department.

I pull into the surprisingly busy parking lot. People are filing out of the community center, heading toward their cars. Some of them are dressed up with button-down shirts and bolo ties and sport jackets. A man wearing a tan police uniform with a pistol on one hip and a radio on the other spots me right away and walks over. He probably knows every vehicle in town—and that my truck isn't from around here.

"I'm John Grady Harris," he says. "Police chief."

I open my mouth to introduce myself, but he interrupts me.

"I know who you are. You're the Texas Ranger we don't need."

CHAPTER 12

WHEN A RANGER reports to a town like this, there are two ways things can go. This isn't the open-armed welcome, the red-carpet roll. This is the resentful, jealous, resistant reaction of small-town officers who think they can do their job as well as anyone and don't like the idea of a Ranger coming in and taking the credit.

I want to remain professional. I don't want to give Chief Harris an indication his comment bothered me.

"Rory Yates," I say and extend my hand.

When I say my name, he gives me a look of recognition. He knows who I am — the Texas Ranger who stopped the bank robbery. He takes my hand grudgingly.

Harris is in his early thirties, a few years younger than me. He has muscular arms accentuated by his tight short-sleeved uniform. In a lot of rural Texas areas, the police chiefs and sheriffs are good old boys. Big hats and big beer bellies hanging over Texas-shaped belt buckles. Some of them get the job because of who they know, not because they're qualified. But Harris looks different. He has short-cropped hair, no cowboy hat, and muscles like an amateur weight lifter. If I had to guess, I'd say he's ex-military.

"There are only two nights a month when this parking lot fills up," he says. "When the council meets and on bingo night at the senior center."

I say, "If you didn't want me to come, Chief, then why am I here?"

"My detective keeps nagging me that there might be more to this than we realize. I called the Rangers to appease her. Don't worry. I'll play nice. I'll co-operate."

"I appreciate that," I say, trying to be diplomatic.

"But I know what you're going to find," Harris adds. "Susan Snyder died of natural causes. There hasn't been a murder in Rio Lobo in a decade."

It's easy to say there hasn't been a murder in a decade if you close the book right away on every suspicious death.

"My detective spends her days investigating graffiti and shoplifting," Harris says. "She's got a hair up her ass that this might be something more just so she'll have something else to do."

I notice he says *her* and *she*. I was given the name of a Detective Delgado, but I didn't realize the detective would be a woman.

"Here she comes now," the chief says.

A young Latina in well-worn cowboy boots strides toward us from the community center. Her tall, slim body is dressed in blue jeans and a white T-shirt, and her dark hair is pulled back from her face in a ponytail that highlights sharp cheekbones. She has a pistol on her hip and the unmistakable no-nonsense air of a cop.

"Ariana Delgado," she says, extending her hand.

Her arm is muscular and her grip firm. She doesn't smile.

I introduce myself, and she has a better poker face than her chief does. She shows no hint of recognition at my name.

Even without makeup, she has long, naturally dark eyelashes that most women would kill for. The eyes themselves are intensely big and beautiful, with deep coffee-colored irises. I can't take my eyes off them— or her.

No, I hadn't expected Detective Delgado to be a woman—and I damn sure didn't expect her to be so good-looking.

CHAPTER 13

AS I STAND talking to Chief Harris and Detective Delgado, I notice a graying man in his late fifties leaving the community center for the *Rio Lobo Record* building. He's studying me with the intensity of a reporter on deadline. He's carrying a small reporter-style notebook in his hand, but with the staff limitations on a local weekly, he might be the editor or even the publisher.

I'm relieved that he doesn't stop to talk. I've always had a frosty relationship with the media.

Harris waves over four other men who are also leaving the community center.

"This is the Texas Ranger you were telling us about," one of them says.

The men, all good old boys over the age of sixty, introduce themselves as members of the town council. Prominent community members.

Big fish in a little pond.

There's Fred Meikle, who owns the restaurant Good Gravy and looks like he eats every meal there, with extra gravy. Troy Sanchez, a Mexican American with salt-and-pepper hair and mustache, owns the gas station I passed. Kirk Schuetz is a retired rancher whose son runs the family business now, though his strong handshake and callused hands signal that the oldest of the four could still put in a long day of work. Council chairman Rex Kelly is a redheaded Irishman who runs a construction business in town but doesn't look like he's swung a hammer himself in years.

"You had a long drive today," Fred says to me. "You hungry?"

"I could eat."

"Well, all right, then, let's all go over to Good Gravy and get this boy some supper."

"There's a quorum of you present," Ariana says to the men.

She's citing the open-meeting law. If the four of them hang out together outside of a posted place and time, they'll be violating it. The whole point of the law is to keep elected officials from doing backdoor dealings out of the public eye.

Troy Sanchez looks like an unruly middle schooler who's just been reprimanded by his teacher. Fred Meikle looks tempted to lecture Ariana on the importance of showing a Texas Ranger some hospitality. His expression says that surely a reasonable Ranger would know she's making something out of nothing. Schuetz, the rancher, has turned his hateful glare from me to her.

"She's right," Rex, the chairman, finally says, breaking the awkwardness. "I've got to get home anyway."

"I'm not hungry," Schuetz says in a tone that suggests he'd rather go shovel horseshit than eat a meal with the likes of me.

"That leaves two of us," Fred says. "That ain't against no laws. Let's get something to eat. We'll tell you everything you need to know about our beloved little town."

Ariana excuses herself, saying she'll brief me first thing in the morning. She heads toward a motorcycle parked over by the police station, fires up the bike, and rumbles out of the parking lot.

The truth is, I'd rather be sitting down with her and learning about the case than going to dinner with these guys, but sometimes you've got to play nice with the locals.

CHAPTER 14

THERE ISN'T ANY music playing inside Good Gravy, but when we walk into the dining room, the imaginary movie soundtrack scratches to a halt. As a Ranger, I'm used to stares of awe—*Holy crap, that's a Texas Ranger!* But the restaurant patrons are locals wordlessly letting a stranger know, *We don't want you in our town.*

Fred Meikle leads us to a table by the front window with a RESERVED placard on the checkerboard table-cloth. The restaurant walls are adorned with mule deer mounts and sports memorabilia of various Texas teams, both college and pro. A row of arcade games stands next to the restrooms, where a couple of kids are playing Big Buck Hunter.

When Fred Meikle tells me to order anything I want, on the house, I insist on paying for my meal.

"It's the Rangers' rule," I say, and that seems to alleviate some of his obviously hurt feelings.

They all order beer, but I drink a Dr Pepper. I don't want to get too chummy with these guys.

Over dinner, Troy and Fred talk almost nonstop about Rio Lobo. The chief sits quietly and eats a plate of barbecue ribs while they chatter on and on—about the star high school quarterback, a Main Street side-walk repair, the local market's overpriced groceries—never once mentioning the reason I'm here.

The woman who died was also a member of the town council.

Before I question them about the dead woman, I need to gather my own facts. Besides, I don't want Ariana—who single-handedly brought me here—to think I'm going behind her back. I don't want to do anything to piss her off.

At least not yet.

One of the most difficult tasks of being a Ranger is determining how you fit into any particular investigation. As we *range* across the state, every place is a little different. Sometimes you'll co-lead an investigation with a local detective. Sometimes they want you to pretty much take over. I find it best to proceed with a little bit of caution until I get a sense of what they need and what I can do.

As we're finishing dinner, Troy says, "I'm sorry Carson couldn't come out to meet you, but he's out of town on business."

Who is Carson? I think.

"Mr. McCormack," Harris says, as if to clarify.

I really do need to do some homework about this town and this case.

I say good night to the men and thank them for their hospitality. I tell the chief that I'll see him tomorrow. Then I climb into my truck and drive two blocks down the street to the empty motel. I choose the room farthest from the road.

I pull off my boots and stretch out on the bed. When people think of the life of a Texas Ranger, they probably don't think of the lonely nights in crappy motels.

I pick up the John Grisham novel I brought and try to clear my head by reading. But something is bothering me, something I saw in town, so I put my boots back on and climb into my truck. I drive up and down Main Street, looking more closely at the signage.

MCCORMACK COMMUNITY PARK, reads a sign in the park next to the library. The football and baseball fields are called McCormack Sports Complex. The urgent care is housed in the McCormack Medical Center.

His name is everywhere, but not on any actual business. There's no McCormack's Garage, no McCormack Café. Only community-type properties, the kind that might not get built without sizable donations.

Who the hell is this Carson McCormack?

CHAPTER 15

I GET MY answer when I wake up in the morning. There's a copy of the *Rio Lobo Record* on the welcome mat. I sit on the porch in front of the room and drink a cup of instant coffee and flip through the paper.

The main story—under the byline of Tom Aaron—is about a planned addition for the library, passed unanimously at yesterday's town council meeting. Apparently this was a pet project of Susan Snyder's, and Fred Meikle is quoted as saying that the new wing should be called the Susan Snyder Children's Library in her honor.

There's another small story from the meeting, below the fold, that mentions Carson McCormack, owner of McCormack Oil. That's why everything in town is named after him. He's an oil baron—probably the richest guy in town, and the biggest community fundraising donor.

Tom Aaron's article states that McCormack asked the town council for an easement to drive his oil tanker trucks through the southern part of the town's jurisdiction. There was no opposition from the public, and the decision passed unanimously as well. The town council probably figured they owed it to the guy.

After skimming through the paper, I drive, not walk, over to the police station, in case I need my truck later. I arrive promptly at eight o'clock. Ariana's Harley-Davidson Sportster is already there. When I enter the lobby, she comes out to meet me, wearing jeans and a T-shirt like she was the day before—and looking just as beautiful.

Ariana escorts me through the station and introduces me to everyone on duty.

Liz, a fifty-something woman who works at the dispatch terminal and has a voice like a chain smoker, seems very excited to meet me. She says she heard Willow's song on the radio and loved it.

"I hope y'all don't break up," she says, giving me a wink. "But if you do, I'm single. You know where to find me."

When it comes to the patrol officers, however, the three who are on duty greet me with the same disdain Harris did the night before. The message is clear: *We don't need you here*.

I can see Harris through the glass window of his office. He's on the telephone, with his boots kicked up on his desk.

There's not much to the police station: a single jail cell, a small conference room, a dispatch terminal, and an evidence room that's not much bigger than a closet. The small supply room houses everything from road flares and traffic cones to a gun safe and bulletproof vests. Ariana's desk is wedged into a corner next to a kitchenette area with a microwave, mini fridge, and coffeepot.

The jail cell holds prisoners overnight. Holds longer than twenty-four hours are taken to the sheriff's office in the county seat. That's where all the court proceedings happen, even for misdemeanors.

The department consists of Harris, Ariana, and a handful of patrol officers who work overlapping shifts so at least one person is on the clock from five a.m. to midnight. After midnight, I'm told, all calls go through to the county sheriff's office.

Ariana and I head to the conference room, where we can talk privately about the case. Before we close the door, I see across the station that another private conversation—about me—is about to get under way. The three patrol officers are stealing glances my way as they enter Harris's office. I shake it off. I'm here to do a job, and I aim to do it right, regardless of whether I'm wanted or not.

I expect the conference room to be converted into a makeshift investigation room, with boxes of paperwork, dry-erase boards, photographs taped to the wall.

Instead, Ariana pulls out a single, thin file folder.

The investigation hasn't even begun.

CHAPTER 16

ARIANA EXPLAINS THAT Susan Snyder was found dead in her home a week ago. The councilwoman appeared to have had an allergic reaction after consuming peanuts. There was a discharged EpiPen on the scene, but it must not have worked. She shows me crime-scene photographs of a woman lying on the floor, her face swollen and purple. I ask for a picture of Susan Snyder before she died, and Ariana hands me a flyer from her election campaign. The woman I'm looking at is much younger than I expected. The four council members I met last night are all retirement age, but Susan Snyder was in her thirties. She certainly didn't fit the mold.

She was pretty, too, with a vibrant smile.

Ariana explains that a medical examiner from El Paso did the autopsy since the county doesn't have its own. He listed the cause of death as anaphylactic shock.

An accident.

Ariana seems slightly more at ease today. She's still professional, still guarded, but she's been asking for help on this case for days and is excited to finally have it. The conference room is hardly bigger than a

king-sized mattress, and I can smell her perfume—
just a hint of it—in the tight quarters.

I ask if they know what food she ate, where it came
from. Ariana says there was nothing on scene that
she could find. No suspicious wrappers. No crumbs.
Susan Snyder had dinner that night at A Taste of
Texas, but the owners said there's no way it came from
them. They were well aware of her allergy and were
always very careful.

"Besides," Ariana says, "Susan's allergy was so
severe that she wouldn't have made it home if she'd
eaten peanuts in the restaurant. She lives out of
town. Whatever caused the reaction, she ate it at
her house."

I look through the autopsy report.

"Did they look in her stomach?" I ask. "I don't see
anything in here about that."

She shakes her head and agrees that it seems like
an oversight.

"Where's the body now?" I ask.

"Cremated," Ariana says.

I give her a hard stare. *That* seems like an oversight. On her part. It was a mistake to release the body
to the family before a comprehensive autopsy was
performed—and the report I'm looking at doesn't
seem comprehensive to me.

Ariana looks at the glass door to make sure no
one is close enough to the conference room to hear
us talking.

"I couldn't get the chief to declare this a murder
investigation," she says. "She was already cremated
before John Grady finally gave in and agreed to call
you guys."

I nod, letting her off the hook. Obviously she's been

alone in this from the start. I want her to know I'm here to help. And in a situation like this, with a seemingly obvious cause of death, it's possible they would have skipped the autopsy entirely. So we should consider ourselves lucky to have any information at all.

"I think the examiner hung on to some blood samples," she says.

"So why do you think this wasn't an accidental death?" I say, sitting back in my chair and giving Ariana my full attention. "Aside from the fact that she never would have knowingly eaten anything with peanuts, what's so suspicious?"

Again, she looks toward the door as if she's afraid someone might be listening.

"Let's drive out to the crime scene," she says. "I'll tell you on the way."

CHAPTER 17

I OFFER TO drive, and we climb into my truck. For a second, I almost go around to the passenger side and open the door for Ariana. But I wouldn't think to do that for a male cop, so I don't do it for her.

She tells me where to turn, and within a minute of leaving the station, we're heading out of town on a curvy back road. The landscape is quite pretty. Coming from Waco, which is much greener, I appreciate these rolling brown hills, rocky buttes, and zigzagging slot canyons. There is a beauty to the barrenness.

A few minutes out of town, Ariana says that she found Susan Snyder's body the morning after she died.

"What were you doing at her house?" I ask. "Were you friends?"

"Not really."

She seems nervous to go forward with what else she wants to say. Sometimes silence is the best motivator, so I remain quiet.

"I went to her house because she'd called me the day before," Ariana says. "She said she had something important to tell me. She wanted to talk to me about a crime. I'm sure of it."

"I see," I say. "You get a call that says she's got something important to tell you. Then she winds up dead. I'd be suspicious, too."

Susan Snyder owned a nice ranch-style house that we can see from a long way off. We pull into the gravel driveway, and Ariana takes me inside and shows me around. She points to where the body was lying on the floor and where the used EpiPen had been left, but there isn't much else she can tell me. If this had been declared a crime scene from the start, forensic investigators could have examined the house from top to bottom, looking for fingerprints, DNA, anything suspicious. But there have been dozens of people in and out of the house since then, obliterating the evidence. Her family came in from Florida and hosted a memorial service in the house.

Ordinarily in a murder case you look at the evidence on the scene first. And it can usually tell you a lot. But we've got nothing to go on this time.

"The family said they'd return in a few weeks to take care of the house," Ariana says. "Clear out all the stuff. Put it on the market. They were upset, as you might imagine. I don't think they were in any shape to go through her things."

We look in Susan Snyder's office, which contains a desk with two large-screen computer monitors. Inside a filing cabinet are loads of paperwork—town council agendas, news clippings, various reports from county agencies. There are also files and files of work-related information: invoices for clients, folders full of graphic design samples, notes about design projects, etc. And that's just what's been printed— I'm sure the computer itself has a whole world of information on it.

"It will take forever to go through all this stuff," she says.

"Box it up," I say. "We don't know what's going to be relevant."

We fill file boxes and evidence bags with anything that seems like it might be useful later. I have a feeling that most of what we're doing is a waste of time, but this is part of the job. You have to be thorough.

When we're finished, we sit on the tailgate of my truck under the shade of a mesquite tree. The temperature is blazing hot, but the air lacks the oppressive humidity I'm used to in Central Texas. I take a couple of warm bottles of Ozarka spring water from the cab, and we each drink one. Ariana's demeanor seems friendlier now. More relaxed. I think she's just happy to be doing something on this investigation. Anything at all.

"What I don't get is why the chief wouldn't declare this a murder investigation," I say to her. "Or at least take a good close look before ruling that out. The phone call she made to you seems like enough cause to raise suspicions."

Ariana fixes me with her big brown eyes. She looks vulnerable right now, scared.

"There's something else," she says.

I can tell she's deliberating whether to trust me. Again, I let silence do its magic.

"The truth is," she says finally, "I never told the chief she called me. He doesn't know that part."

"What?"

"That was the other part of what Susan told me," Ariana says. "She said she had something important she needed to talk to me about. And she said don't tell the chief. Her exact words were 'I'm not sure he can be trusted.'"

CHAPTER 18

WHEN WE GET back to the police station, I can feel Ariana's nervousness. Am I going to tell Harris? Am I going to report him to my higher-ups?

A big part of what the Texas Ranger Division does is investigate instances of suspected corruption of public officials. Ariana could have contacted us and asked us to look into Harris, but instead she gave him the benefit of the doubt and asked him to be the one to call for help. That suggests to me that she still believes—or wants to believe—that Harris is trustworthy. So I want to tread carefully here. I don't want to let him know I'm suspicious of him, but it's also too soon to open a full-fledged investigation of him.

"Got the case solved yet?" the chief says, smirking at the evidence boxes we're bringing into the station.

"Looks like it's probably just an accidental allergic reaction," I say, taking a suggestive tone. "We're just going to dot all the i's and cross all the t's. I should be out of here in a couple of days. You've got a zealous detective over there." I nod toward Ariana. "She wants to be thorough."

He laughs, enjoying the condescending way I'm talking about Ariana. This seems to satisfy him, and he heads out the door.

Ariana looks at me and mouths the words, *Thank you*.

I give her a nod, and then I catch Harris walking back into the station.

"I forgot to tell you," he says, "I told the local newspaper guy you're helping us out with something. I didn't want to say what until I okayed it with you."

I appreciate the chief deferring to me. He might not have wanted me here—and maybe he can't be trusted—but so far he hasn't given me any resistance.

"Can you put him off for a while?" I say. "I don't want to talk to him if I can help it."

"Will do," Harris says. "But I know this guy— he's going to keep calling and calling until he's able to interview you."

"If you can stall him for a few days," I say, "maybe we'll have this whole thing wrapped up by then."

I'm stalling, too. It might not hurt to do an interview with the local newsman—the media could be used to our advantage—but I still need to learn more before I say anything.

When the chief is gone, Ariana and I discuss our plan of attack for the next day. Susan Snyder had recently gone on dates with two men—Ariana had asked around enough to find this out—and one date was on the same night she died. We'll try to interview both men tomorrow.

Before we call it a day, I ask Ariana why the chief finally gave in and agreed to call the Rangers.

"Did you threaten to quit?"

She says she did, but that isn't what made the difference.

"He wouldn't have cared if I'd resigned," she says. "I threatened to go before the town council and tell everyone *why* I was resigning. Then I'd go straight to Tom Aaron, the editor of the paper, and I'd tell him. He thought about it for about twenty-four hours and then decided to call the Rangers."

"We'll figure this thing out," I tell her, but truthfully I don't feel any closer to understanding what's going on than I did yesterday. "Good work today," I add as we head to the door.

I want her to know the condescension I used in front of Harris was just an act.

"Thanks for your discretion," she says.

I think about asking Ariana to join me for dinner at one of the restaurants in town—not a date, just two colleagues who both have to eat. But I figure it's probably best not to blur any lines in our relationship. Besides, I'm not sure she would accept the invitation.

We can work together without being friends, her demeanor says.

Maybe that's a good thing. I do have a girlfriend, after all.

CHAPTER 19

AFTER I EAT a quick plate of tacos at Rosalia's, I head back to the motel as the sun is going down. I try to call Willow but don't get an answer. I grab my guitar and sit on the porch outside my room and start plucking at the strings. I place on a chair in front of me a little notebook of songs, with lyrics and chords. I know a lot of songs by heart, but this helps me practice new ones.

My guitar is a Fender acoustic-electric, which lets me practice quietly by myself, but it can also be plugged into an amp if I ever have the occasion to play on a stage, which hasn't happened since high school. It's a nice intermediate guitar, a step up from a beginner's instrument but not quite what a pro would use. Willow has offered to buy me a fancier, more expensive guitar, but this one suits my needs. And it's a pretty instrument, with a body made of laminated spruce and basswood, and a neck of mahogany.

One of the great things about being with Willow is playing together. I sang and played guitar in a band in high school, but I wasn't ever good enough to take a shot at making a career of it. It was just fun. Willow and I will sit on the porch of the house and play and sing duets. Her talent blows me out of the water, but she humors me and seems to have a good time. Playing tonight makes me miss Willow even more.

I practice playing the Kenny Chesney song "Better Boat." It's a mellow song—just an acoustic guitar and vocals—about a guy riding the waves of life, with a guitar part that's just tricky enough to be a challenge for an amateur like me. On Kenny Chesney's version, Mindy Smith sings backing vocals, so it's a fun song for me to do with Willow.

Tonight, though, the lyrics make my mood worsen. The words suggest the narrator is starting over after a significant loss. He has friends, but he's mostly alone. I can't help but think of myself, starting over after Anne's death and all the events surrounding it. I've got friends and even a girlfriend, but here I am, alone on the porch of an empty motel in a town where I have no friends.

I try to switch gears and play Cole Swindell's "Break Up in the End." This is another slow song, another combination of vocals and acoustic guitar. But this one's about a guy ruminating about the girl who got away. He'd go back and do it all over again, even though he knows they break up in the end.

I can't help but think of Willow. Are we going to break up in the end?

When I've managed to put myself in a thoroughly bad mood, I set down the guitar and sit back in the silence. The sun has gone down, and I watch the cars pass under the streetlights and let my mind wander.

I notice a black truck with white lettering painted on the door pass by the motel. I swear the same truck passed a few minutes ago. I pick up my guitar and play, but this time I only pretend to look at my notebook. Really, I've got my eyes on the street. Someone is watching me.

A few minutes later, the truck passes again from the other direction. It slows down in front of the motel. Because I took the room farthest from the road, I can't make out the words on the door. The reflection of a streetlight makes it impossible to see in the window.

When it passes a third time, I'm ready. I pretend to be looking at my phone, like I'm sending a text, and I snap a series of photos. Once the truck is gone, I scroll through the images, trying to find the best one, and when I do, I use my fingers to zoom in on the words on the door.

McCormack Oil

Next to the stenciled words is an illustration of an oil derrick.

I already solved the mystery of who Carson McCormack is, but now I've got a new question.

Why does he have someone keeping an eye on me?

CHAPTER 20

"DID YOU EVER have sex with Susan Snyder?"

The guy sitting in front of me, Alex Hartley, looks stunned at my question. We've been interviewing him for an hour, and so far we've played pretty nice, but now I want to make him uncomfortable.

"Do I really have to answer that?"

"The more clearly we understand your relationship with Susan," Ariana says, "the easier it will be to clear you from our investigation."

Alex told us that he dated Susan on and off for the better part of six months. Nothing serious. Nothing exclusive. Sometimes they'd go a month or six weeks without seeing each other. To me, that doesn't sound like two people who want to be dating. It sounds like two people who hook up every once in a while.

Still, he seems genuinely upset by her death. She wasn't his girlfriend, but he liked her. He came into the office today willingly. At one point, describing how he heard the news of her death, his voice became choked and I thought he might cry.

Alex is the football coach at the high school, where he teaches woodworking. He's a good-looking guy, forty years old. He has a solid alibi for the night Susan

Snyder died. He was in El Paso at a convention for football coaches and gave us about a dozen names of people who could verify he was there. But in a case like this, that doesn't free him from suspicion. Someone could have given her food with peanuts in it before going out of town.

"All right, look," the coach says. "I'll tell you if you turn that off." He gestures to the camera we've set up to record the interviews.

I give Ariana a nod, and she turns off the recorder.

"I don't want a wife. Susan didn't want a husband. We both liked being single. But we both liked having sex every now and then. We're human. This town's too small to use Tinder. We had a nice little arrangement. Nothing serious."

He says that people don't care if the football coach sleeps around, but a town councilwoman?

"If it gets out and people call her a slut, I'm going to feel bad. I don't want to smear anyone's name."

We question him for a while longer, with the camera back on, but he honestly doesn't seem like our guy. I can't figure out what he'd gain by poisoning Susan Snyder. He's right—it wouldn't hurt his reputation one bit if people found out he was sleeping with her. In fact, I suspect everyone already knew.

As we're walking Alex Hartley out the door, I spot a black truck in the parking lot with the same lettering on the door as the one I saw last night.

A man in jeans and a blue work shirt steps out and heads our way.

"I'm Skip Barnes," he says to us. "Chief said you wanted to talk to me."

Skip Barnes—the other name on our suspects list. He'd been dating Susan Snyder on and off, too. He's the one who went out with her the night before she died.

We bring him into the conference room, the closest thing this police station has to an interrogation room. We ask if we can record the interview, and he consents.

He looks nervous, a sharp contrast to the football coach. Skip fidgets and asks if he can smoke a cigarette. When we tell him he can't, he squirms in his seat even more. We go through some softball questions—how did they meet, how long had they been dating—and we get pretty much the same impression as we did from Alex Hartley. They'd dated for a few months, going out every couple of weeks.

"Did you ask her out or did she ask you?" I say.

"I asked her," he says. "Look, she's got a reputation. She don't go out with every guy who asks. But if she thinks you're cute or whatever, she'll go out with you. I figured it was worth a shot, and lo and behold, she said yes."

Skip is more forthcoming with information about their sex life.

"Hell yeah, we had sex," he says. "That was the point. She didn't want nothing serious. She just wanted a good fuck every now and then."

It's hard to understand what Susan Snyder would have seen in the guy. He wasn't the good-looking jock type that Alex was. He was wiry, with a ruddy complexion and greasy hair. His teeth were yellow from smoking.

"Most of the time," he says, "we just skipped dinner and met up at her house."

He seems looser now, bragging about his sexual exploits.

"But you went out to dinner the night she died," I say. "Her treat."

"Was it?"

"We got the receipt from the restaurant."

"Yeah, I guess she paid."

"And did you go back to her house that night?"

"No."

"But you said that was the whole point. 'She just wanted a good fuck every now and then.' That's what you said. But on this night, you had a romantic dinner—crab legs, steak, wine, a nice dessert. All that and no sex afterward?"

Skip twists in his seat like a fish at the end of a hook. I can't tell exactly what he's hiding, but there's something he doesn't want us to know.

CHAPTER 21

"I DIDN'T FEEL like it," Skip says.

"You didn't feel like it?" I say. "What man doesn't want to have sex with an attractive woman?"

"I mean she didn't feel like it. I mean..."

He freezes for a minute.

"I didn't kill her," he says, and the fear in his voice that we would think he did makes this seem like the most honest statement he's made since coming in.

Ariana steps in, playing the good cop. "Skip, we're just trying to get a clear picture of what Susan did that night. We want to get all the facts. Can you help us do that?"

He opens his mouth to say something, then he stands up out of his chair.

"Y'all are trying to twist things around," he says, angry. "I ain't talking anymore without a lawyer." Then, hesitantly, he says, "Am I free to go?"

I rise and approach him.

"You may leave. You are not under arrest. We will reschedule once you've consulted with a lawyer."

He nods with a jerk, as if to say, *You're damn right I'm free to go.*

"Skip," I say, getting closer to him. He backs up

against the wall, but in this tiny room, there's nowhere else for him to go. "Don't you dare think about leaving town. I don't care if you had anything to do with Susan Snyder's death or not. If you leave without talking to us again, that's obstruction of justice, and I will move heaven and earth to find you."

Skip looks like he believes me.

After he leaves, Ariana and I watch the truck pull out of the parking lot, clearly in a hurry, driving at least fifteen miles over the speed limit. The license plate says MC 9.

"I thought he was going to piss his pants there for a minute," Ariana says.

She cracks a smile, and we have a good laugh together. It's nice to see her laughing. She's a pretty woman when she's stone serious, but when she looks happy, she's absolutely stunning.

"What do you make of Skip?" she asks. "You think he had something to do with it?"

"Honestly, no. But he's hiding something."

"That's the way I feel."

I don't think either of the guys we interviewed today is our man, but that's just a hunch, and I'm certainly not ready to cross either of them off our suspects list. Alex seemed to genuinely like Susan Snyder. And Skip doesn't seem quite bright enough to concoct a plan to poison her.

"That truck Skip was driving," I ask Ariana, "do all McCormack's employees drive them?"

"Yes. There are at least a dozen of them."

Skip was driving one with an MC 9 license plate. I pull out my phone and look at the photos I took last night. In one of the pics, I can make out the plate: MC 1.

"You know who drives this one?" I ask, showing her the picture.

"Why?" When she senses I might not tell her, she

says, "I've been open with you about everything. Don't keep anything from me."

I tell her I saw the black truck driving by several times last night and thought maybe I was being watched. Now that I know there are multiple trucks that look the same, I can't be sure it was MC 1 that drove by each time.

"Carson McCormack's son, Gareth, drives MC 1," Ariana tells me.

"Tell me about him," I say, picturing a sixteen-year-old kid spoiled by Daddy's money.

"Ex-military," she says. "Army Ranger. Sniper. Iraq and Afghanistan. Rumor is he has a dozen confirmed kills."

My eyes widen. That certainly isn't what I was expecting. "Do you think he had anything to do with Susan Snyder's death?"

"I have no idea," she says, glancing, as she often does, toward the door to make sure no one is listening. "But he and the chief are pals."

"Could be why Susan Snyder didn't want you to tell him."

"Maybe."

I can tell by the look on her face that she's skeptical.

"What are you thinking?" I ask.

"Honestly, I bet it was him, driving up and down, getting a good look at you. But I doubt it had anything to do with Susan Snyder. If he murdered her, he'd be keeping a lower profile."

"So why was he spying on me?"

"Gareth McCormack is the alpha dog in these parts," she says. "Even the chief, who's about as tough a guy as you'll find, doesn't measure up. I think Gareth McCormack heard a Texas Ranger is in town and he's sniffing around to see if you're any threat to him."

CHAPTER 22

THAT EVENING, I'M back on the porch of my motel room, but instead of plucking my Fender, I've got Susan Snyder's case file in my hands. Tonight, I've brought out my pistol and set it on the chair next to me, covered by my cowboy hat. I'm probably being paranoid, but Ariana's words about Gareth McCormack have me on edge.

As the alpha dog, he can come sniffing around all he likes. But if he wants to try to mark his territory, I'll be ready.

Besides, the hat still doesn't fit me very well. I'd just as soon have it on the chair as on my head.

It's a clear night, with the moon high in the sky. The streetlights obscure my view of the stars. There are hardly any cars rolling up and down Main Street, and the parking lot of the motel, like always, is empty. I'm alone with my thoughts.

I'm thinking about a conversation Ariana and I had late in the afternoon, before we called it quits for the day. I asked her to give me a clearer picture of who Susan Snyder was.

"You mean was she a slut?" Ariana asked, sensing my question was motivated by the two men we'd interviewed claiming to have had sex with her.

"I don't care how many people she slept with," I said. "I just want a better idea of who she was."

What I didn't say is that from my experience, reputations aren't always accurate. I've been accused of being a womanizer, but the truth is I can count all the women I've slept with on one hand. Every one of them was someone I cared deeply about.

But Susan Snyder is a bit of an enigma to me. The rest of the council are a bunch of good old boys, probably stuck in their ways. Susan Snyder was young and vibrant. In a town like this, a woman would be expected to marry, settle down, have babies. Susan Snyder hadn't done any of that, apparently by choice.

Susan went to college at UT and stayed in Austin for a few years afterward, working as a graphic designer. When she was in her late twenties, she came back. She'd apparently built up a big enough client base to go freelance and could live just about anywhere. Even though her parents had retired to Florida, she chose her tiny hometown of Rio Lobo.

She was always busy in the community, Ariana said, volunteering at the library, organizing fundraisers for the Kiwanis Club, chaperoning dances for the high school kids. About five years ago, when a seat opened up on the town council, she ran. Her opponent was just like the others—an older guy who'd been in the community for a million years. But people seemed taken with Susan's enthusiasm and charisma. She was elected narrowly.

Ariana said that the election was controversial—briefly—but the other members of the council seemed to embrace her. They treated her like a daughter—in both good and bad ways. If she had an idea they didn't agree with, they'd talk to her like she was a young, silly girl who didn't know any better. But she got her way more often than not. She was reelected without opposition.

"Enemies?" I asked.

"None that I know of."

"What about the person she beat out in the election?"

"He's on the council now. Fred Meikle. He ran for an open seat in the last election. As far as I heard, there were no hard feelings. I saw them interact in the meetings and he seemed fond of her."

With any public figure, there's the image they present to the world, and then there's the real person—and the two aren't always the same. People in Rio Lobo might not know about the sexual activity, or they might not care, but otherwise, the Susan Snyder I pictured in my mind felt like a portrait she wanted people to see.

I could see the image everyone else had of her, but I was going to have to dig deeper to find the real Susan Snyder. When you have abundant physical evidence or witness accounts or even motive, you may not need that picture of a murder victim.

I need to understand her to understand why someone would kill her.

If anyone killed her.

As I sit on the motel porch with my legs stretched out in front of me, there is someone else on my mind that I have an unclear picture of. Two people, actually: Carson McCormack and his son, Gareth. They are mysteries to me as well. I've already developed a dislike for the two of them, which is unfair. I haven't even met them.

McCormack is probably the reason this town doesn't

look like half the insolvent little towns in rural Texas. He pays taxes, employs residents, and, as I've seen, makes donations to community projects. But as much as people speak about McCormack in this town, I haven't yet heard anyone speak highly of him. I have no idea if McCormack or his son had anything to do with Susan Snyder's death, but I'm going to find out.

As if on cue, one of McCormack's trucks rolls down the street. Without using a turn signal, the truck whips into the parking lot of my motel and rolls toward my cabin. I sit up and reach my hand toward my hat, pretending I'm going to pick it up. What I'm really doing is reaching underneath to grab my SIG Sauer.

The truck rolls to a stop right in front of me. Two men are sitting in the cab. The driver reaches for something on the seat between them. Something I can't see clearly, something bigger than a pistol— maybe a shotgun.

Then he pushes open the door.

I slide my hand under my hat and wrap my fingers around the grip of the pistol.

CHAPTER 23

"HOWDY, FRIEND!" THE guy says as he comes around the door of the truck.

My heart is galloping, my muscles tensed and ready to swing the gun out.

"Mind if we jam with you?" the guy says, and he raises the object in his hands: an acoustic guitar.

I exhale loudly and let go of the gun.

"Excuse me?" I say, trying to keep my voice steady and not give any indication that my body is racing with adrenaline. "You want to do what?"

"We heard you was sitting out here picking on a guitar last night," the guy says, grinning widely as he approaches. "We thought we'd stop by and see if you wanted to jam with us."

The man seems to be about thirty, give or take a few years. He wears a Dallas Mavericks ball cap and the same blue work shirt Skip Barnes wore earlier today. He has strong worker's hands and a beer belly that strains the buttons of his shirt.

"Who told you I was playing?" I say, thinking of the black truck that seemed to be keeping an eye on me the night before.

"Norma," he says, gesturing toward the office of the

motel. "She owns the place. You can't do anything in Rio Lobo without half the town hearing about it."

The man introduces himself as Dale Peters. He says that he and his friend, Walt Mitchell, used to be in a band that played one night a week at Lobo Lizard, but their lead singer left town and now they just play together for fun.

Walt gets out of the truck and shakes my hand. He's a middle-aged black man with graying hair. He has a pleasant smile and wears a plaid shirt, new jeans, and a clean pair of tennis shoes.

"I play bass or rhythm guitar," Dale says. "Walt here teaches music at the school and can play just about any instrument God created. But neither of us can sing worth a lick."

I'm not really in the mood to play with a couple of strangers, but it occurs to me that I might be able to use this to my advantage. Today we interviewed two men, one who works at the high school and one who works for Carson McCormack. Maybe I can get some information on our suspects.

"Sure," I say. "Let me just go get my guitar."

I pick up my hat, careful to keep the gun concealed, and walk into my room. When I come out with my guitar, Dale is sitting down, trying to tune his instrument, and Walt is walking from the truck with a banjo in one hand, a small snare drum in the other, a fiddle case wedged under one arm, and a harmonica tucked into the breast pocket of his shirt.

I bring a chair over from the porch of the neighboring unit, and the three of us sit down in a triangle. I ask why they want to play with me. Rio Lobo might be small, but there have to be other people here who can pick a guitar.

"We ain't never jammed with a Texas Ranger before," Dale says.

"Or someone who has a hit country song written about them," Walt adds.

I chuckle. "So you know all about me, I guess."

"Not everything," Dale says, grinning. "We don't know if you can sing worth a damn, but we aim to find out."

CHAPTER 24

DALE STARTS PLAYING the recognizable opening chords of Johnny Cash's "I Walk the Line." Walt
plays the snare drum with a wire brush to keep the
same scratchy background beat you hear on Cash's
version. I join in on guitar. Dale sings the first verse.
He was right—he's not much of a vocalist. When it
comes time for the second verse, he nods to me, and I
sing it. He defers to me and lets me sing the rest. In the
original recording, Cash changes the key of his vocals,
and the last verse is almost a full octave lower than the
first. I don't sound anything like Johnny Cash, but I do
my best to lower my voice as the song progresses.

Dale and Walt both notice and appreciate the effort.

"Hot damn, boy," Dale says. "You ain't half bad."

I sing the rest of the night. We play George Strait,
Tim McGraw, Blake Shelton, and Eric Church. We
don't just stick to guys' songs, either—we play a
couple of Dixie Chicks tunes and have a good laugh
rolling through Dolly Parton's "9 to 5."

Dale is a heck of a guitar player, much more than
just the rhythm guy he made himself out to be. And
Walt, as Dale said, can play pretty much anything.
Through the two hours we spend playing together,

he rotates among guitar, banjo, fiddle, and drum. He even breaks out the harmonica when we play Willie Nelson's "On the Road Again."

As personalities go, Dale is gregarious and fun to be around, with a comfortable air and an infectious laugh. Walt is much more demure, letting his instruments do the talking for him.

They're both talented musicians, but I hold my own with them. I sing and play and feel like a kid again practicing in my buddy Daryl's basement after school. I'm surprised by how much fun I have and forget that I wanted to ask them some questions until they're putting their instruments back in their cases.

"So what did you guys hear about me?" I ask them, trying to make it sound like small talk. "Why I'm here?"

Dale says he works with Skip Barnes, and Walt works with Alex Hartley, the football coach. Both have heard what I've been investigating.

"You're a lucky man," Dale says to me.

"Why's that?"

"'Cause you get to work with Ariana Delgado," he says and whistles through his teeth. "Man, I've had a crush on her since high school."

"He's dating Willow Dawes," Walt chimes in. "Have you seen a picture of her?"

"You're doubly lucky," Dale says to me.

"Did either of you know Susan Snyder?" I ask.

"Sure." Dale shrugs. "Hell, everybody knows everybody in this town. But I didn't know her well."

"I voted for her," Walt says, "but I never actually talked to her."

"What do you think of the guys who were dating her?" I say. "Skip and Alex."

"I don't know if I'd use the word *dating*," Dale says.

There it is, I think. *Confirmation that people knew she was sleeping around.*

"She and Alex was just friends is all," Dale says. "And I don't know what she was doing hanging around with Skip. He's a buddy of mine, but she was way out of his league."

I'm not sure how far to push this, but I say, "He claims they were sleeping together. Friends with benefits, I guess you'd call it."

Dale laughs. "I doubt Skip Barnes has been with any woman outside a Juárez brothel."

"What about Alex?" I say. "He made the same claim."

Dale and Walt exchange a look that I can't read.

"Like I said, I always thought they was just friends. What they did on their own time ain't none of my business."

With that, the two pack up and climb into Dale's truck.

"That was fun," Dale says out the window. "Let's do it again sometime."

I give them a wave as they pull out of the lot and then I stand on my porch, thinking.

Earlier today, I thought Skip Barnes was hiding something. Now I think Alex Hartley might have been as well.

And when I think of the look they gave each other, I think my new friends, Dale Peters and Walt Mitchell, are hiding something, too.

Does everyone in this town have secrets?

CHAPTER 25

I'M DREAMING. I know I am.

But I can't wake myself up.

I'm back in the bank, with the robber standing on the counter with the AR-15 and the other holding a handgun to my head. Just like before, I drop to my knees as my hat is blasted off my head. I raise my SIG Sauer, aim it at the robber on the counter, and squeeze the trigger. But this time nothing happens.

I miss.

The robber squeezes the trigger of the AR-15 and begins cutting down the customers in the bank. There is no sound. Not from the bullets jumping from the gun barrel. Not from the men and women collapsing in mists of blood, their mouths open in silent screams.

I know I should shoot again.

I have to stop him.

But I'm panicking.

I turn my head slowly—everything seems to be in slow motion—and look at the other robber. His gun is aimed at my face. I stare into the black hole of the barrel.

I should move. I should shoot. I should do something.

But I don't.

He squeezes the trigger, and I sit up in bed, my chest heaving, my body slick with sweat. I throw a hand to my face, half expecting to find a bullet hole in my forehead.

When I've convinced myself that I'm okay, I rise out of bed and walk to the bathroom. I leave the light off, but my curtain is cracked and there's enough light coming in from the parking lot to see. I splash water on my face. I cup my hands and take a drink.

I walk back to my bed and check the time on my phone. It's two o'clock in the morning. I wish I could talk to Willow, but there's no way she'll be awake. And maybe that's not the best idea anyway. She's already worried about me. She didn't like the idea of me going back to work so soon after the shooting.

Now I'm starting to agree with her—maybe I'm not ready.

This case has been a little more trying on my nerves than I anticipated. A few days have passed since I jammed with Dale and Walt, with Ariana and me working long hours and making almost no progress. We've interviewed all the town council members as well as all the people who saw Susan Snyder in her final days. We've done a million phone interviews, talking to her family members and her clients in faraway cities. Sometimes motive is irrelevant—the evidence is what matters. But in this case, we have no evidence.

I'm sitting in my bed, in my dark room, thinking about all this, when I hear something outside my door. Voices talking low, trying to be quiet. The fact that I can hear them at all tells me they're very close. I hear a sound like someone spraying an aerosol can.

Maybe spray paint.

I creep over to the window and peek through the crack in the curtains. Two men stand next to my truck. One is kneeling by a tire. The other is standing next to the driver's side, spraying the door with paint. As far as I can tell, both are wearing masks, just like the guys in my nightmare.

I grab my pistol and unlatch the safety chain on the door as quietly as possible. I'm wearing boxer shorts and nothing else, but I don't have time to get dressed.

I throw open the door and point my gun.

"Freeze!" I say, my voice raised but not yelling.

My body is inside the room, but my gun hand is sticking out. This is a careless mistake because I haven't anticipated that there might be a third guy with them, hiding next to my door.

A tire iron swings down from behind the door jamb. I pull my hand back but not fast enough. The iron connects with the barrel of my SIG Sauer, and I feel the vibrations up to my shoulder.

The gun tumbles out of my grasp.

CHAPTER 26

BEFORE I CAN reach for my gun, the assailant kicks the pistol, and it goes sliding off the porch and onto the gravel. But this leaves him exposed, standing right in front of me with his legs spread at an unbalanced angle.

I burst out of the motel room like a defensive tackle going after the quarterback, and I slam the guy down onto the wooden porch. He's bigger than me, stronger, but I'm on top of him, and that gives me an advantage. He flails with the tire iron, but I grab his wrist, twist his arm, and pin it down against the wooden planks of the deck. He swings his free fist into my ribs, but he's fighting from a bad position and can't put much behind the punch.

I drive my fist into the center of his mask, just below the eyes. The cartilage of his nose crunches audibly, and the back of his head crashes against the porch. His muscles go weak. He's not unconscious, but he's stunned.

The guy with the spray paint charges toward us. I catch a glimpse of the other guy pulling a knife out of my truck tire.

The one with the paint can presses the dispenser

and a cloud of red fills the air. I close my eyes and throw my arms up to shield my face. I can feel the cool mist around me. I roll away in the direction of my pistol, then scramble onto my hands and knees. I risk opening my eyes and spot my gun lying in the gravel. I grab it and spin around, the gun raised, my knees sliding on the rocks.

The three men are running away.

They're not stupid—three on one might be good odds, but not when I have a gun.

I sprint after them. The gravel digs into my bare feet. The men hop a waist-high, chain-link fence at the back of the property. I launch over the fence like an Olympic hurdler. I cross a street and look around. We're in a residential area now. There isn't much moonlight, and no streetlights, so it's hard to see. I spin around, looking, listening.

An engine fires up a block away. Headlights ignite the darkness, and tires squeal. I can make out the shape of a truck, but I can't see it clearly. The truck heads toward Main Street, and I run back through the parking lot of the motel. If it turns right on Main Street, I might be able to cut it off.

But when I get to the sidewalk, the truck is heading the other way. It's too far away to get a good look at it. I can't see the license plate. I can't tell the make and model. It could be one of McCormack's trucks, but I can't be sure. It's not like there's a shortage of pickup trucks in Texas.

I watch until its taillights disappear from sight. Then it occurs to me I'm standing on the sidewalk on Main Street holding a pistol and wearing nothing but my underwear. Luckily, there are no cars on the street at this time of night.

As I walk back toward my room, I hear the hiss of air wheezing out of my punctured tire. There's enough ambient light to read what's been written on the side of my truck:

GO HOME LAW DOG

CHAPTER 27

I WALK BACK inside my motel room and flip on the light. I pick up my phone and call Ariana's cell.

"It's three in the morning," she says. "What the hell's going on?"

"Can you come to my motel?" I say.

She hesitates, and I realize maybe she thinks I'm propositioning her.

"Three thugs just assaulted me," I say.

"I'll be right over."

I catch a glimpse of myself in the mirror and see red paint freckling my face and frosting my hair.

"Also," I say, before she hangs up, "do you have any mineral spirits?"

I manage to pull on a pair of sweatpants and a T-shirt before she shows up five minutes later, riding in on her motorcycle and wearing jeans and an AC/DC T-shirt. She pulls off her helmet, and her hair falls down around her shoulders. Although the jeans and T-shirt she normally wears aren't exactly formal dress, the concert T-shirt and free-flowing hair is a look that I haven't seen before.

I like it.

"I would have been here sooner, but I had to look

through my garage for this," she says, handing me a metal container of paint thinner.

I show her the damage to my truck and explain everything that happened.

"You're lucky," she says.

"*They're* lucky," I say.

She gives me a look that says, *Don't be so macho*. I can't help it, though. My adrenaline has finally settled down, but I'm still damn mad.

The truth is, I was lucky, but so were they. There are a whole lot of other ways it could have gone down that would have ended up much worse for either side. If the tire iron had connected with my wrist, it would have broken bones. And if I had been able to hold on to the gun, I might have ended up shooting the guy.

Ariana and I take photographs of my truck—it's a crime scene now—and I get out my fingerprint kit and dust the door and the hubcap. We look around for blood droplets, hoping for some DNA evidence. I'm sure I broke the guy's nose, but the mask must have kept the blood contained.

When we're finished documenting the crime scene, I change the flat tire. I don't ask for her help, but Ariana gives it anyway. Afterward, as we're wiping the grease off our hands, we notice the black sky has started to turn blue, and a faint orange glow emanates from the horizon to the east.

"Ready to get to work?" Ariana says.

"Hell yes," I say. "It's not a good idea to piss off a Texas Ranger."

Ariana heads home to get ready for the day, and I stand in the gravel parking lot rubbing paint thinner on my arms and in my hair. Afterward, I go inside and take a shower, scrubbing myself with soap and water to get rid of the solvent smell.

I'm skinned up in various places: the bottoms of my feet, my knees, one elbow. I spend a few minutes rinsing the worst of the scrapes with peroxide and putting on Band-Aids.

As I get dressed—tying my tie, pulling on my boots, positioning my hat, and pinning the star to my chest—I feel like a knight putting on his armor for battle. The last piece is my gun, which I holster at my waist like I'm sheathing a sword into a scabbard. I don't want to sound melodramatic, but as I'm getting ready for the day, I feel like a lone samurai in a Kurosawa film. The difference is in those films, the samurai or knight or western gunfighter is steely-eyed and ready, determined to overcome the obstacles in front of him.

But me?

I'm just weary.

Part of it, I think, is that the jolt of adrenaline has worn off, and my body feels like it's ready to crawl back into bed rather than head off to work. But the other part, I realize, is that I just don't feel ready for this. It's been less than two weeks since the bank, and this assignment in this supposedly sleepy town might have seemed like a walk in the park at first, but it's turning out to be anything but.

There's something wrong in this town.

Something rotten.

When I'm finally ready to start the day, I step out onto the porch, squinting my eyes against the sunrise. It's as if my senses are on high alert and can't handle the bright, harsh glare of morning.

My phone buzzes.

It's Willow.

I love her. I do. But I don't want her worries about me to fuel the fires of self-doubt I'm feeling.

If I'm honest with myself, she's the last person I want to talk to right now.

CHAPTER 28

I THINK ABOUT not taking the call—I'm anxious to get to the police station—but I decide I should answer. I wouldn't like it if she was blowing off my phone calls, and I want to treat her as I'd like to be treated.

"I'm glad I caught you," she says, her voice full of excitement.

She tells me that Dierks Bentley added an extra date to the tour, making up for a show he canceled last fall when he had the flu.

"It's in Albuquerque," she says. "How far is that from you? Any chance you can come?"

"It's a good five hours away," I say. "Maybe six."

"Boy, you really are in the middle of nowhere, aren't you?"

I debate whether to tell her about what happened this morning. Part of me doesn't want her to worry. But the other part of me knows that a healthy relationship is built on open, honest communication.

No secrets.

"I don't want to alarm you," I say, "but I had some excitement this morning."

She can't believe it. She says she thought this was

supposed to be an easy assignment. I can hear the worry in her voice. I don't mention my nightmare or the way I'm feeling. She'll worry enough even if she thinks I'm clearheaded and capable of handling myself. If she knows I'm having a crisis of confidence, that will take her anxieties to a new level.

"Enough about me," I say. "Tell me the latest with you. How's the song doing?"

She seems thankful for the distraction. "Don't Date a Texas Ranger" is getting all kinds of airplay, she says. Her producer has told her that when her album drops, listeners are going to snatch it up. Buzz about her success is already spreading. She played last night at the Bluebird Café, a famous Nashville music venue, and Kathy Mattea was in the audience and introduced herself afterward. The night before that she was invited to a dinner party at Jennifer Nettles's house.

"Wow," I say. "You're really rubbing elbows with country music royalty, aren't you?"

"Regardless of how the album does, Rory, I really think I could have a life here. Whether I'm the next big thing—like my label keeps saying—or I'm a songwriter for hire, I feel like I belong here in Nashville."

With this statement, a moment of silence hangs in the air—a moment full of questions. If she belongs there, what does that mean for us? Even though a few days ago I'd all but made up my mind to apply for the detective job in Nashville, I never mentioned my decision to Willow, and now, with this case, I'm feeling some reluctance to make that commitment.

"Oh, Rory, what are we going to do?"

"We'll figure it out," I tell Willow. "Just let me get this case resolved and we can have a good long talk about our future."

We end the conversation by saying we love each other. Then I drive over to the police station.

When I walk in the door, the chief says, "I'm still getting calls from that newspaper editor. Honestly, I'm surprised he hasn't camped out in the lobby."

"Not now, Chief. I've got more important things on my mind today."

"Like what?" he says, and when I brush past him into the station, I know he senses I'm on to something.

When I get to the conference room, Ariana holds up a piece of paper.

"This might be our first break in the case," she says.

She got a copy of Susan Snyder's phone records from her cellular provider.

"Right after Susan called me," Ariana says, "she made one other call. It was a very brief conversation."

"To who?" I say.

"Tom Aaron."

The name sounds familiar, but I can't remember why.

"He's the newspaper editor," Ariana says. "The one who's been trying to talk to you ever since you came to town."

CHAPTER 29

ARIANA AND I walk out to my truck to go find Tom Aaron.

I hear a group of cars coming down the road from the north. My ears, trained by years with the highway patrol, tell me these engines are going way past the speed limit. Three black vehicles come into view—one of McCormack's pickup trucks, followed by a brand-new Cadillac Escalade, with another of McCormack's trucks bringing up the rear.

"That's Carson McCormack in the middle," Ariana says, gesturing to the Escalade. "Heading out of town on business. He doesn't usually bring his entourage into town."

These vehicles are moving in the tight, protective formation the motorcade of a high-profile politician might utilize.

Who the hell does this Carson McCormack think he is?

"When he gets back into town," I say, "I think it's time to pay him a visit. At the very least, I'd like to take a look around his oil field and see if any of his employees have broken noses."

We have no real idea if Carson McCormack or his son had anything to do with Susan Snyder's death—

or what happened to me this morning. Hopefully Ariana is right: this call to the editor might be our first lead.

When the receptionist at the paper tells us Tom Aaron isn't in yet today, Ariana says we'll go to his house. Back in my truck, Ariana gives me directions. In a town like this, not only does everyone know everyone but they also know where everyone lives.

As we're driving through the north edge of town, Ariana points to a nice little ranch-style house with a well-kept yard. "That's where I live," she says.

There's a Prius sitting in the driveway.

"So you do have another vehicle," I say, "besides the Harley."

"Sometimes it rains," she says and flashes me a smile.

Tom Aaron's large house is two blocks away, right at the edge of the development. From where we park, we can see the property borders the arroyo that limits the town's expansion—and the rolling brown hills beyond it. The backyard contains not only an elaborate flower and vegetable garden but two additional out-buildings—a greenhouse and a two-story structure with a garage on the lower level.

A woman works in the garden. In the garage, the reporter type I saw walking out of the town council meeting is leaning under the hood of what looks to be a sixties-era Mustang. What appears to be a tarp-covered jeep is parked next to the classic car.

The woman looks up from a flower bed and sees us. There's a radio playing in the garage, and as fate would have it, Willow's song is on.

"Morning, Jessica," Ariana says.

"Well, I'll be damned," she says, beaming. "Rumor has it this song is about you."

She hurries over to us, then pumps my hand and gives me the friendliest greeting I've had since arriving in town.

"I sure am happy to meet you," she says. "I'm going to buy your girlfriend's album as soon as it comes out."

Jessica Aaron has the tan, muscular arms of a dedicated gardener. Her short hair is streaked with silver, which suits her.

Tom Aaron approaches, wiping grease off his hands with a rag.

"I've been trying to reach you," he says.

"Sorry, Tom," Ariana says, "we're not here to answer your questions. We're here to ask *you* some questions."

There's a moment of tense silence. I brace for a confrontation, a citation of the First Amendment.

"I wasn't calling to interview you," he says to me. "I have something to tell you."

"Okay," I say. "So tell me."

He glances uncomfortably at Ariana.

"Not in front of her," he says.

CHAPTER 30

I HAVE A feeling I know what Tom Aaron's going to say, so I take a chance.

"Let me guess," I say to Tom Aaron. "Susan Snyder called you the day before she died and said, 'I've got something important to tell you. Don't mention it to anyone. I don't know who can be trusted.'"

He looks at me, surprised. "I was scheduled to interview her the next day," he says. "But then I found out she died."

"She made the same call to Ariana," I say. "That's why I'm here."

Tom exhales loudly. "Susan said not to trust anyone, but you're a Texas Ranger from out of town. If I couldn't tell you, who could I tell? Sorry," he says to Ariana, "I just didn't know who I could trust."

"I know the feeling," she says.

Jessica invites us inside their beautifully decorated home. Joanna Gaines from *Fixer Upper* could have designed the interior (Willow likes to watch that show because Chip and Joanna Gaines are from Waco). The wood-textured walls are accented with vintage mirrors and oversized clocks. Open shelves display candleholders, old books, and framed photographs of

Tom and Jessica with two good-looking kids, a boy and a girl.

A decorative list of life lessons—ALWAYS TELL THE TRUTH, SAY YOUR PRAYERS, HAVE COURAGE, HELP OTHERS—hangs above the kitchen table, where Jessica serves prize-worthy pecan pie and sweet tea.

As we talk, I get to know Tom and Jessica a little. They're good people. Jessica grew up in Rio Lobo and met Tom when she was studying for a pharmacy doctorate at the University of Houston. He was a rising crime reporter for the *Chronicle,* but after they got married, they decided to raise their kids in her small hometown.

"I'm sure Houston is no different from other big cities, but I saw the evil that people are capable of. I didn't want my kids growing up there."

"When we moved to Rio Lobo, he was a weekend stringer," Jessica says. "Now he's running the paper."

"I *am* the paper," Tom says. "I've been running the *Rio Lobo Record*—from selling ads to writing stories and headlines—for twenty years. I know this community better than anyone."

"What about you, Jessica?" I ask. "Do you work at the pharmacy on Main Street?"

"We own it," she says. "I started as a pharmacist, but Tom and I bought it when the previous owner decided to retire to South Padre Island."

I ask her if Susan Snyder filled her EpiPen pre-scription at the pharmacy. She says yes, looking sad, as if she somehow failed Susan because the medicine she provided didn't work.

"In about twenty or thirty percent of cases," she says, "a second dose from an auto-injector is required. The second dose is almost always administered at a hospital. You're supposed to call 911 as soon as you've injected the epinephrine. Susan knew that."

Ariana and I trade a look about a detail we won't share, that Susan Snyder's phone was on the other side of the house. If nearly a third of people who use EpiPens need a second injection, and Susan Snyder simply couldn't make it to her phone, then it's quite plausible her death was accidental. Either that or someone with knowledge of the severity of her allergy tainted her food with peanut oil.

To Susan Snyder, an ordinary recipe could be as dangerous as any deadly poison.

CHAPTER 31

TOM AND JESSICA walk us out to my truck.

"Oh, wow," Tom says when he sees the graffiti on my pickup. "We've been having problems with kids vandalizing town property. Looks like you're the latest victim."

I play it off like it was probably just kids.

"Are you staying at the motel?" Jessica asks. "You should stay with us. We've got a studio apartment over the garage. It used to be the kids' playroom, but they're both off at college now."

I thank them for the offer and tell them I'll think about it.

"We've got an alarm," Tom says. "And there's a video camera on the front porch. No one could vandalize your truck without being caught red-handed."

"You've got that kind of security?" I say, surprised. You always hear about small-town folk not bothering to lock their doors, let alone having an alarm system.

"Most Texans' idea of home security is to sleep with a .45 under their pillow," Jessica says. "But I loathe guns."

"And I used to work the crime beat," Tom says. "I know the world's not as safe a place as most people think it is."

As a member of law enforcement, I can't argue with that.

When we arrive outside the police station, I say to Ariana, "Did you say the medical examiner kept some blood samples?"

"You want him to do more tests?" she says.

"Not him," I say, pulling out my phone and scrolling through my contacts list.

"What's up, amigo?" says Freddy Hernandez, a high school friend who is now the medical examiner for the county that includes my hometown. "Rumor has it you've been banished to the middle of nowhere."

I glance at Ariana and tell him that Rio Lobo is a lovely place to take a needed break from home.

"That's good because all anyone in Redbud is talking about is Willow's song. The local station plays it at least once an hour and mentions you by name every single time."

"Just what I want to hear."

I see the chief walk out of the station and toward the town offices, where Kirk Schuetz, the rancher on the council, is waiting for him outside the door. They glance our way when the chief reaches the door, and their body language suggests they're making some kind of joke.

Freddy says, "I also hear that some of the Rangers keep teasing your lieutenant about what happened at the bank."

Freddy not only is a brilliant medical examiner but also knows every detail—official and unofficial—of law enforcement in a two-hundred-mile radius of his office.

"I heard someone set up a cot in his office with a sign that said NAP ZONE."

"If they keep that up," I say, "I'll never get to come home. I might as well buy a house here."

I get to the reason I called. I ask if I can send him an autopsy report and have him take a look.

"The body's been cremated, but we have blood samples," I say. "Can I send them to you?"

"You think something fishy is going on with the medical examiner out there?" he asks.

"Not necessarily," I say. "I just think he was quick to stamp NATURAL CAUSES on this thing, and I want a discerning eye to take a second look. I trust you."

I tell him about Susan Snyder's death.

"It's hard to find poison in the blood," he says, "unless you have an idea of what to test for."

"What I want you to do is look for the *absence* of something," I say.

I tell Freddy that Susan Snyder used an EpiPen, but it hadn't saved her life. "Is it possible the EpiPen was tampered with?" I say. "Can you test the blood for epinephrine?"

Ariana gives me a look. She mouths the word *Jessica?*

"Theoretically the injection of adrenaline should raise the levels of certain compounds in the blood," Freddy says. "There's no way the lab would check for that unless you asked for it specifically."

I tell him I'll have the samples sent to him.

When I hang up, I ask Ariana how well she knows Tom and Jessica Aaron.

"I've known Jessica since I was a teenager going in and picking up prescriptions for my parents," she says. "But I can't say I know either of them well."

"In a town this small," I say, "everyone's on the suspects list until we're able to cross them off."

As Ariana and I head into the station, my phone buzzes. I don't recognize the number, but the area code is local.

"Hey, buddy," Dale Peters says enthusiastically. "Want to jam again?"

I think about it. I started my day at two a.m. with a fistfight, and I'm already dragging. But I had fun last time, so it might be a nice way to unwind.

"Okay," I tell him. "You guys want to come back to the motel?"

"I was thinking we should jam over at Lobo Lizard."

"The bar?" I say.

"Yeah, I got us a gig. We'll be playing to a live audience."

CHAPTER 32

WHEN I SHOW up to the bar at six o'clock, Dale and Walt are setting up. I have only my guitar, but they have loads of other equipment: Walt's various instruments, Dale's guitar and bass, electrical cords and amps.

Dale shakes my hand and says, "I was afraid you might stand us up."

"I thought about it," I say. "It's been a long time since I played in front of an audience."

Lobo Lizard is about half the size of Pale Horse, the Redbud bar where Willow used to play, but there is a decent crowd filling the tables and barstools, though the small dance floor close to the stage is empty.

A waitress brings me a Sol that I didn't order.

"The gig doesn't pay," Dale says, "but the beer is on the house."

Dale and Walt have their setup routine worked out, so I pull out my guitar and act like I'm tuning it.

If this isn't a hostile audience, I don't know what is.

The door opens and Ariana walks in. She gives me a bright, friendly smile. Her hair is down, and she's wearing a little bit of makeup. She's also wearing a black skirt—the first time I've seen her in one—and a Def Leppard T-shirt.

"Thanks for coming," I say, feeling even more nervous now. I have to work with her tomorrow whether I make a fool of myself or not.

"Oh, I wouldn't miss this," she says.

I nod to her shirt. "I take it you're not much of a country music fan."

She smirks. "I prefer rock and roll."

Dale comes over, struggling to maintain his gregarious personality in the presence of Ariana. When she walks away to get a beer, Dale says, "How do I get her to marry me?"

I clap him on the back and laugh. "You could start by talking to her."

We begin our sound check, and my nerves are a mess. I tell myself I've been involved in high-speed chases, I've faced men armed with shotguns and assault rifles, and my Stetson has been shot right off my head—I should *not* be scared to play some music in a little bar in the middle of nowhere.

But I am. I can't deny it.

I try to picture Willow, going from playing bars to performing in huge venues. As the opening act for Dierks Bentley, she'd step out onstage to face an indifferent crowd eager to see the headliner, not someone with one single on the radio. She'd have to win over the audience with her energy and her talent. If she has the courage to step onto a stage like that, I need to match it.

"Ready?" Dale asks.

"As I'll ever be."

Our rendition of "I Walk the Line" earns polite applause, but no one gets up and starts dancing. When I glance at Ariana, sitting alone at the bar, she raises her beer to me and nods.

Not bad, she seems to say.

I feel better, looser, and we keep going.

A successful cover band plays songs the audience can't resist. Songs they'll dance to. Songs they'll sing along to. Songs they already know by heart. Next we surprise them with "Take Me Home, Country Roads" by John Denver. I change the lyrics, switching in "West Texas" for "West Virginia," "Guadalupe Mountains" for "Blue Ridge Mountains," and replacing "Shenandoah River" with "Rio Lobo." The crowd loves it, and by the time we sing the second chorus, pretty much everyone in the bar is singing along with us.

Then we hit them with Garth Brooks's "Friends in Low Places." The crowd sings practically the whole song with us, and the dance floor fills up.

I find myself smiling, having a great time.

I see people on the phone, telling their friends to come catch the show, and soon the place is packed, standing room only. When we're playing the last song in our first set, I notice a group of guys walk into the bar. They're all muscular and tough looking. All wearing pistols on their hips. This isn't all that unusual. Open carry is legal in almost every state, but Texans seem to take advantage of it a lot more than most.

Chief Harris is with the group. He stands close to a guy who is even more muscular than he is. The guy has long dark hair pulled back into a ponytail, a thick beard, tattoos covering both his arms. He's wearing sunglasses that he doesn't take off, and he crosses his arms and stares at me, as if appraising me.

One glance and I know who he is.

Gareth McCormack.

The alpha dog.

CHAPTER 33

WE TELL THE audience we'll be back after a short break. As we're setting down our instruments, Dale throws an arm around my shoulders and says, "Hot damn. That went better than I expected."

"Is that your boss's son?" I ask, nodding toward Gareth McCormack and his men, who have moved to the pool table, displacing players who had been in the midst of a game.

"Yeah, that's Gareth," Dale says. "He thinks his shit don't stink, but he ain't a bad guy to work with."

"Are all those guys your coworkers?"

"The chief ain't—obviously. But the rest of 'em is."

"No offense, Dale," I say, "but you don't quite look like you fit in."

While Dale doesn't look completely out of shape, he has a beer gut, and his biceps probably haven't felt the weight of a dumbbell in a long time. In contrast, the men in Gareth's entourage look like out-of-uniform soldiers.

Dale explains that when Gareth was discharged from the military, he and his old man slowly began hiring his army buddies. People like Dale and Skip Barnes are the old guard, the longtime roughnecks who've been working the fields for a decade or more.

"It's not like they're running us out," Dale says, "but whenever someone leaves town, like our singer, they replace him with somebody who looks like an extra from a *Mission: Impossible* movie."

I scan the faces of the men, looking for anyone with a broken nose, but none of them look like they've been punched recently.

"Do they know anything about working in the oil business?"

"Eh." Dale shrugs dismissively. "I'm going to get a beer. Want one?"

I tell him I'll pass. I notice Ariana on her way over with a second beer in her hand.

"I'm impressed," she says, handing me one of the two bottles. "If the Texas Rangers ever fire you, you've got a good backup career."

"Very funny," I say.

"Seriously," she says. "You were good up there."

I thank her and then, speaking low, ask her if she noticed who walked in.

"I saw," she says, glancing over toward the table. "You figured out who that was, I take it."

"I think I'll go introduce myself," I say.

She takes my arm. "I don't think now's the time, Rory. He's over there with all his army buddies, carrying sidearms like they're cowboys in a goddamn John Wayne movie. Wait till you've got your badge on. It will give you the upper hand."

"It's okay," I tell her. "Nothing's going to happen."

I push through the crowd, nearly everyone I've met in town, and I get several compliments about my playing. Alex Hartley, the football coach we interviewed, gives me a nod. I don't see Tom and Jessica Aaron or Skip Barnes, but I spot two of the town council members and Norma, the woman who runs the motel where I'm staying.

Gareth McCormack is bent over the pool table, sliding the cue back and forth over his hand. The balls are racked, and when he breaks, the sound is like a rifle shot. The balls slam around the table, two sinking into pockets.

"Gareth," the chief says, "let me introduce you to Rory Yates."

Gareth comes around the table and inflicts a bone-breaking handshake.

"I seen that video of you in the bank," Gareth says, a wad of tobacco in his cheek. "That was badass."

Badass is not a word I would ever use to describe people dying—but I let it go. My handgun is locked away in my truck right now, but he has a gun on his hip, a SIG Sauer like mine.

"Thank you for serving our country," I say.

"And thank you for your service to Texas."

I try to be sincere in my gratitude, but I don't like his implication that serving Texas isn't as big a responsibility as serving the country.

"We're both Rangers," he says. "Texas Rangers and Army Rangers. No offense, but I'd take my Rangers over yours any day."

Gareth McCormack is my height, but he has at least thirty pounds on me—all muscle. He's taken his sunglasses off, locking his gray eyes on mine. He doesn't look away. His intimidation tactic, I hate to admit, is working on me.

"John Grady says you're looking into the death of Susan Snyder," he says. "You really think she was murdered?"

"Sorry," I say, "I can't talk about an ongoing investigation."

I give the chief a look that says, *And neither should you*.

"Did you know Susan?" I ask Gareth.

He laughs and looks away from me for the first time.

"I'd met her," he says, "but I didn't know her well. She's one of the few pieces of ass in these parts that I haven't tapped."

He turns his gray eyes back on me, gauging whether his crude comment has shocked me.

I'm struck speechless.

"Come to think of it," he adds, nodding across the bar, "I never fucked your partner, either. She's a sexy little thing. Have you hit that yet?"

The chief stands idly by, and I ask myself, *Will I let Gareth get away with this?*

"Where I come from," I say, "we don't talk about women like that."

Gareth's eyes harden. All of his friends are grinning as they watch their alpha dog show the new pup who's the boss.

"Is that right?" Gareth says, standing up straighter and stepping forward, so we're chest to chest, eye to eye. "How do you talk about women?"

"Same way we talk *to* women," I say. "With respect."

CHAPTER 34

GARETH MAKES A *pfft* sound with his lips. He looks over at the chief and laughs.

"If you're so respectful of women," he says to me, "how come your girlfriend doesn't want to date a Texas Ranger?" He spits a stream of tobacco juice on the bar floor. "Maybe she'd like to date an Army Ranger."

I'm burning inside, ready to erupt like a volcano, but I give him another hard stare, then I reach up and tip my hat to the chief and then to Gareth. "You gentlemen have a good night," I say.

"Nice to meet you, Rory," Gareth says sarcastically. "Give Ariana my best."

I turn back. "By the way," I say, "when does your daddy get back into town, Gareth? I might have some questions for the two of you."

He clearly doesn't like the sound of that but keeps up his tough-guy act.

"Not till next week," he says. "Y'all come with your questions. We ain't got nothin' to hide."

Working my way back through the crowd, I can see Ariana looking my way, but I also see a back exit. I push through it, hoping it won't set off an alarm, and step outside, startling two guys huddled together by the Dumpster. I'm not sure what they were about to do. Smoke a joint maybe? Deal drugs? Maybe something more innocent.

"Sorry to interrupt," I say. "I needed some fresh air."

"No problem," one of them says, and I realize it's the football coach, Alex Hartley. "We were just headed back inside."

When I'm alone in the dark night, I try to calm my fury before I take the stage again. I'm a Texas Ranger. But the truth is, I'm no match for an Army Ranger trained in lethal hand-to-hand combat—not without my gun.

The back door pushes open, and Ariana steps out.

"You okay?" she says, her face genuinely concerned.

"You were right," I tell her. "I shouldn't have gone over there."

"What happened?"

"Nothing," I say. "He just got under my skin is all. The Rangers have an official name for guys like him."

"What's that?"

"Asshole."

She and I share a good laugh. Before she can ask any more questions, Dale pokes his head out the door.

"Hey, cowboy, we got one more set. This crowd's getting restless."

CHAPTER 35

WHEN WE START playing again, I'm not feeling it, and neither is the audience. My musical mistakes and dropped lyrics are emptying the dance floor.

"You all right?" Dale says to me between songs. "We're losing the crowd."

I tell him I'm fine, but I'm not. Then I see Gareth standing in the back, watching me, his arms clasped behind his back like he's standing at attention all the while, as my dad would say, *grinning like a possum eating shit*. I put my hand over the mic and tell Dale and Walt I want to try something a little different.

I pluck at the guitar and start singing the country-and-western classic "Big Iron" by Marty Robbins. In the original recording, released as a single in 1959, the beat is fast under Robbins's signature melody. The year before he died, Johnny Cash recorded a slow, haunting cover, and that's the version I attempt.

The crowd goes quiet and listens—it's that kind of song. The lyrics tell the story of a vicious killer named Texas Red and the gunfighter who rides into a small town to bring in the outlaw, dead or alive. The original lyrics describe the stranger as an "Arizona Ranger," but I switch Texas for Arizona, which gets a few whoops and whistles from the crowd. Otherwise, they're caught up in the performance, listening to the story, waiting to see what happens next.

Modern country songs typically repeat a chorus around a couple of verses, but old songs like this tell full narratives in several verses with a lot of lyrics to remember. But as a kid I used to listen to this song with my dad, and I know it by heart.

When I get to the part in the story where the two gunfighters face off, I turn my gaze to Gareth McCormack, who spits and stares back at me. In the song, the townsfolk expect Texas Red to kill the stranger, but the gunfighter is so fast that Texas Red is dead on the ground before he can "clear leather."

I don't stop staring at Gareth until I strum the last notes. The crowd goes wild, clapping and whistling.

"I'll be damned," Dale says. "You got 'em back."

I grin and say, "I've got another idea."

I tell them I want to try a song that none of us has ever played.

"You think they'll go for it?" Dale says. "This don't seem like that kind of crowd."

"I think we can pull it off," Walt says. "I'll play drums. Rory, you play lead guitar. Dale, you just try to keep up."

I turn back to the audience and find Ariana in the crowd.

"This one goes out to a friend of mine," I say.

Then we dive into an impromptu country version of Def Leppard's "Pour Some Sugar on Me."

The audience loves it. People dance and throw their hands into the air, singing along so loudly that no one notices when I mess up the lyrics a few times. Ariana sings along, too, smiling ear to ear and holding her beer up like she's at a rock show.

I'm having so much fun that I don't realize until the song is over that Gareth and his goons have left.

Whether the Marty Robbins song got under his skin or he just couldn't stand to see the people in his town rocking out to my music, something drove him out of here.

It's not much, but I consider it a moral victory.

CHAPTER 36

THE NEXT FEW nights I have trouble sleeping. Every time I hear a noise, I jump out of bed, grab my gun, and look out the window to make sure no one is vandalizing my truck. When I do sleep, I dream some twisted variation of what happened inside the bank.

I miss the shot.

Or I'm too slow.

Or I'm paralyzed with fear.

In the most recent dream, the man with the AR-15 isn't some masked robber.

It's Gareth McCormack.

That morning Ariana and I sit in the conference room, looking for suspicious details in Susan Snyder's business invoices. She catches me yawning.

"You getting enough sleep?" she says.

"The bed in that motel isn't very comfortable," I say.

Which is a lie. I can sleep on the hard ground on a bedroll if my mind is clear and I feel safe.

"I notice you haven't taken up Tom and Jessica Aaron on their offer to stay in their studio," she says.

I shrug.

We've done some discreet investigation into Tom and Jessica. We checked with the Texas State Board of

Pharmacy to make sure there were no red flags in Jessica's history. We asked around to see if there was any kind of bad blood between Tom and Susan Snyder. So far, nothing has stood out. But I'm still waiting to hear from Freddy about the blood test. Plenty of people in town knew about Susan Snyder's allergy. The only reason Jessica makes sense as a suspect is if the EpiPen was faulty.

"Let's go get some lunch," Ariana says. "Maybe that will wake you up."

For our first lunch together, Ariana and I pick up deli sandwiches to go. The counter girl greets us with a friendly smile and asks when I'll be playing at Lobo Lizard again. Maybe I'm starting to win this town over.

When our food is ready, we walk down to the park. The day is hot, but there's shade under a big bur oak, and we sit on a rock at the edge of the wide, clear river. Downstream, kids play on a rope swing, taking turns launching themselves out into a deep spot. Upstream, a man in waders is fly-fishing.

Ariana and I are quiet for a few minutes as we navigate the implied break from talking about the case.

"So," I say, "how did you end up a detective in Rio Lobo?"

Ariana says that after studying criminal justice at Angelo State, she went to work for the highway patrol. The chief in Rio Lobo, who remembered her from high school, encouraged her to apply for an open detective position. The town council, however, was pushing for an outside applicant with more experience: John Grady Harris.

"The chief found the budget to hire two detectives in a town barely big enough to support one," she says.

"So you were partners?"

"For a while."

"How did you get along?" I ask.

"Just fine," she says. "He flirted with me a bit until he realized I wasn't interested, and then we developed a mutual respect. Up until recently, that is."

She says the former chief, who was well past retirement age, drowned in the river a little over a year ago.

"He liked to canoe in the afternoons after work," she says. "It was spring, so the current was pretty swift. I guess the canoe flipped. He wasn't wearing a life jacket."

Both she and Harris applied for the police chief job.

"We interviewed before the council in an open meeting that Tom Aaron covered for the paper, but the deliberations were closed. They picked Harris."

"Was it unanimous?"

"One or two of them may have preferred me, but as a group, they decided not to go on record with any dissent. They made a public show of support for the new chief. Or maybe none of them thought I was qualified, and they were nice enough to keep quiet about it."

"I doubt that's the case," I say.

I think she'd make a good Ranger.

We sit for a few minutes and watch the river. A red-tailed hawk flies down and takes perch on a yucca stalk, and in the water a raft of ducks swims around, dunking their heads and looking for food.

I'm about to ask Ariana if she has ever considered applying to the Texas Ranger Division—but my phone buzzes.

It's Tom Aaron's number.

"Can you come to the paper?" he says when I answer. "I found a couple of items of interest."

I tell Ariana, "Looks like our break is over."

CHAPTER 37

TOM'S OFFICE IS full of newspapers, notebooks, file folders—and maps. A US Geological Survey topographic one is pinned to the wall behind his desk, along with a street map of Rio Lobo. His Texas Press Association awards for community service are nearly obscured by even more piles of paper.

Tom tells us that he's discovered two pieces of town council history.

"I tracked Carson McCormack's contributions to town council campaigns over the last twenty years," Tom says. "Every candidate he backed won, with the exception of one person who was elected without his support."

"Let me guess," Ariana says. "Susan Snyder."

"This proves she was different," I say, "but we already knew that."

"And we don't know of any bad blood between her and the council," Ariana says. "Or her and McCormack."

"That brings me to my other discovery," Tom says.

Since Susan Snyder was elected, he explains, every item that came before the council passed—or was voted down—unanimously. There were differences of opinion, of course, but the council members always found a compromise.

"People were worried that Susan Snyder might not fit in, but really the group was highly functional."

"I'm sensing there's a *but* coming up," Ariana says.

He asks if I read the recent article about Carson McCormack filing for an easement to move his trucks through an area designated as open space.

"This didn't go to a vote until after Susan was dead," Tom says, "but the town clerk let me take a look at the full file." He pulls out a printout of email correspondence and holds it up. "Susan planned to vote no."

Tom is providing us with this information about Carson McCormack unprompted. He doesn't know about the attack on my truck, or my encounter with Gareth McCormack.

But it's far from a smoking gun. In fact, it's almost inconsequential.

"Correct me if I'm wrong," I say, "but all Mc-Cormack needed was three votes. Had Susan lived to vote against the measure, it still would have passed four to one."

"What we need to figure out," Ariana says, "is *why* she was going to vote no."

I ask Tom to explain the easement that Carson McCormack requested. Tom stands up and focuses on the US Geological Survey map behind his desk.

"Here is the town proper," he says, pointing to a small cluster of black squares. Then he uses his finger to trace a much larger area, extending into undeveloped hills and valleys. "But *this* is the town's incorporated area."

Tom identifies a huge section of the map as McCormack's property.

"Years before I moved here," Tom says, "McCormack began buying up property and drilling it for oil. Carson's late wife was still alive, and Gareth would have been a little boy."

This is the first I've heard about a Mrs. McCormack, and I ask how she died.

"I don't think an autopsy was ever performed," Tom says. "From what I hear, she complained of a bad headache and an hour later she was dead."

Ariana and I exchange a look — another unusual death.

Getting back to the easement, Tom explains that almost twenty years ago McCormack asked the council to designate a chunk of land in the southern part of the town's incorporated area as open space.

"I'm no expert about oil," Tom says, "but the terrain out there is pretty rugged. I figure he didn't want anyone else to drill there because their pumps would compete with his."

"So what changed?" I ask. "Why does he want access now?"

Tom shrugs. "Maybe his shipping routes are different."

"Maybe it's time we go ask him," I say to Ariana.

I thank Tom for his help and discretion, and at the front of the building, we say good-bye.

As I'm about to climb into my truck, I get a call from Freddy Hernandez, who has the results of the blood test. He starts going on about blood glucose, fatty acids, adrenergic receptors, and vasoconstriction — whatever those things are.

"Freddy," I say. "Remember, you were the valedictorian in high school while I was the quarterback of the football team. Break down the test results for me."

"Bottom line?" he says.

"Yes. Bottom line."

"The EpiPen worked," he says.

"You're sure?"

"Yep. I can explain why in court if you need me to. But to analyze the blood any further, I need to know what I'm looking for," he says.

"That's the problem," I say. "I don't know. I need you to work some magic here, Freddy."

He says there's enough blood left for one more test. "I'll see what I can do," he says. "But don't hold your breath."

When I hang up, I tell Ariana the news.

"I told you it wasn't Jessica Aaron," she says.

"On that note," I say, "hang on a sec."

I leave her on the sidewalk next to my truck and I head back into the newspaper building.

"Where are you going?" she asks.

"I'm going to ask Tom if his offer to stay in their studio still stands."

CHAPTER 38

I'M NOT SAD to say good-bye to my little motel room. Norma, the woman who runs the place, comes out to see me off.

"I'm going to miss sitting in the lobby and listening to you play that guitar," she says as I carry my guitar case out of the room and set it in the passenger side of the truck next to my duffel bag.

"If you don't mind my asking," I say, "how do you stay in business?" Since I came to town, I've been her only customer.

She pops a cigarette into her mouth and lights it, then mumbles through her closed lips, "McCormack."

"McCormack?"

She says that when Carson McCormack's business associates are in town, he usually rents out every room. That income keeps her afloat during the lean weeks.

"Ask around," she says. "I bet he subsidizes just about every business in this town in one way or another. Rio Lobo would crumble and blow away without him."

"A regular Robin Hood," I say.

"Or a necessary evil," she says, taking another drag. Then she nods toward the road and says, "Speak of the devil."

McCormack's Escalade rolls down Main Street, preceded by one of his trucks and followed by another—McCormack coming back from his business trip. The cluster of vehicles drives the same tight pattern, at speeds way over the limit, as they did on their way out of town.

On my way to Tom and Jessica Aaron's place, I call Ariana on Bluetooth.

"Guess who just got back into town?" I say.

"I saw the convoy from the parking lot here at the station," she says.

"We're on for tomorrow," I say. "Let's go ask a few questions of Rio Lobo's most famous father and son."

When I pull up in front of Tom and Jessica's, I find Jessica in the garden, where she proudly shows me her flowers and vegetables, and even an orchard with pear, peach, and fig trees, as well as an enormous pecan tree.

"No wonder your pecan pie is so good," I say.

"I heard your girlfriend's song again today," Jessica says. "Any chance we'll get to meet her while you're staying with us?"

"I wish," I say. "She's pretty busy right now."

She leads me around the side of the garage. The walkway to the stairs is overgrown with bushes laden with ripe berries.

"I need to get out here and pick these berries and prune the bushes back," she says as we squeeze past the overgrowth. "When Tom called, I changed the sheets, but otherwise we haven't been up here in months."

The apartment itself isn't much—just a bed, a couch, a kitchenette area, and a bathroom. The vintage, rustic decorations, with the same touch as the house, make it feel homier than the motel room felt. A window air-conditioning unit exhales cool air into the room.

"There's no TV," she says.

"I've got a book," I say.

Jessica points to a cabinet that contains a small metal safe and tells me the combination.

"If you want to keep your gun in there, you can," she says, and I get the impression she wants me to.

I don't expect full bed-and-board service, but an hour later Tom knocks on my door with a dinner invitation. The chili con carne is delicious and so, of course, is the pecan pie we have for dessert. My earlier suspicion of Jessica tampering with the EpiPen hasn't completely left my mind, but as we talk, my feelings of unease ebb. I tell myself to welcome their hospitality but keep my eyes open.

After dinner, Tom shows me his garage.

"The garden is Jessica's pet project," Tom says. "The garage is mine."

In one bay is the 1965 Mustang I saw days earlier. In the other, he pulls off the tarp to reveal a 1960 Land Cruiser J40.

"Does the Cruiser run?" I ask.

"Yeah," he says. "There's no power steering, no power brakes. It will give you a workout just shifting gears."

I tell Tom he has a very nice home, and I appreciate him letting me stay.

"It's the least I can do," he says. "I love this little town. If Susan Snyder was murdered, I want you to make it safe again."

"I will," I say, but the truth is, some cases are never solved, and right now, this one looks like there's no light at the end of the tunnel.

CHAPTER 39

COYOTES OUT IN the hills sing me to sleep, and I get my first decent night's rest since I caught the guys vandalizing my truck. Shortly after eight o'clock the next morning, Ariana and I are heading out of town to McCormack's place in the hills. We pull off the pavement and take a gravel road parallel to a riparian corridor full of mesquite trees, yucca plants, and cholla cacti. Jackrabbits and roadrunners take turns zipping across the road in front of us.

After a few miles, the land levels out and we start passing fields of pump jacks, networks of pipelines, and the valve stations—what the roughnecks call Christmas trees—that regulate the oil flow.

My parents own a big cattle ranch, but its size pales in comparison to this spread.

"You haven't seen half of it yet," Ariana says.

The road drops into a valley, and we spot an eighty-foot-tall oil derrick standing next to a ribbon of lush vegetation. The metal structure is purely decorative, stamped with the McCormack Oil logo, with creeping vines entwining its metal framework.

The road winds to the ranch entrance, surrounded by hurricane fencing topped with razor wire, the kind of fence you'd see along the perimeter of a prison, not a Texas ranch. The main house is huge, probably ten thousand square feet, and surrounded by big oak trees and smaller Texas mountain laurels. Nearby is a man-made pond, a tennis court, and a guest house bigger than the home my parents live in. Horses and longhorn cattle graze in separate pastures and shelter in separate barns.

We approach a wooden archway stenciled SADDLE-BACK MESA. It's a security gate manned by two guards armed with TEC-9s. We roll to a stop, and they approach the driver-side door.

One of the men has a metal splint secured to his nose with white medical tape. The skin around his eyes is the yellow of bruising that's begun to heal—the consequence of a broken nose.

"Can I help you?" the other guy says.

I ignore him and stare at the one with the bandaged nose.

"Hello again," I say.

"Have we met?" he says, his voice nasal.

"*You* should recognize *me*," I say. "I wasn't the one wearing a mask."

"Mister," he says, trying to sound tough, "I don't know what you're talking about."

"Don't call me mister," I say. "It's Ranger to you."

With that, I turn to the other guy, the one closest to me, and tell him that we're here to see Carson McCormack.

"Do you have an appointment?"

Instead of answering, I nod toward the walkie-talkie on his belt and say, "Just call him and tell him we're here."

"And what's your name?" he asks as he reaches for the radio.

"Don't act like you don't know," I say and face forward to wait.

The man with the walkie-talkie turns and walks away, but we can still hear him.

"The Texas Ranger is here," he says. "He's got that other cop with him. You know, the girl."

A few seconds later, the guy tells us to follow him. As the gate opens, he climbs onto an ATV and zooms off.

Before I pull away, I wave the broken-nosed guard over to my door.

"Just listen to me for a second," I say. "You don't have to say anything that will incriminate you. Just listen."

He takes my advice.

"You need to think about what you're doing here," I say. "What happened the other night, if that had gone a different way, one of us could have gotten killed."

"I did two tours in Iraq, Ranger. I ain't afraid of you."

"Then maybe you should be afraid of what you're doing here—whatever you're doing." I sweep my hand toward McCormack's spread. "Serving our country in Iraq is something you ought to be proud of. But sneaking around, vandalizing cars, taking a swing at a Texas Ranger with a tire iron, I don't see how you could take much pride in any of that."

He smirks.

"Be all you can be," I say and point to my driver-side door, which still has the *Go home law dog* message on the side. "Is *this* all you can be?"

His smirk disappears, but he still doesn't say anything.

"I'm not trying to threaten you," I say. "I can see

you're not scared of me. I'm saying you could still do the right thing."

"What was all that about?" Ariana says as I'm driving away. "You really think you can get that guy to flip on McCormack and tell us if he had anything to do with Susan Snyder?"

"Probably not," I say. "But I figured it was worth a try."

CHAPTER 40

THE ATV IS idling on the shoulder. When the guard sees us coming, he roars forward again, leaving us to follow in a cloud of dust.

I take my time—I want to look around.

The road winds over a small hill, and we enter a work area the size of a football field full of metal buildings, valve stations, heavy equipment—a backhoe, bulldozer, dump truck, plow, tow truck—and a fleet of oil tanker trucks. I spot Dale working on one of the tankers with Skip Barnes, both of them standing on the bumper and leaning inside the open hood. I give my horn a soft beep, and when Dale looks up, I wave. Dale waves back, but Skip Barnes looks away, as if the sight of me hurts his eyes.

I decide that I need to apply some pressure to Dale. If I can get any of McCormack's men *to flip,* as Ariana said, it's going to be Dale.

As we drive away from the work area, we hear the crack of a rifle. I get a feeling we're approaching Gareth McCormack's shooting range.

And I feel certain that's him taking target practice.

The ATV stops in a pullout next to a dense copse of trees along the creek. One of McCormack's trucks is already parked there. We climb out of the truck and follow the guard through a narrow, overgrown path onto McCormack's gun range. It's a country club for gun enthusiasts, nothing like the flat stretch of land with an earthen backstop my dad built on our property. Here, a long concrete pad marks the firing point, covered by a shade roof. Tables beside each shooting station serve as rifle rests.

All of the shooting bays are empty except for one on the far right, where Gareth is seated, looking through a riflescope, and Carson McCormack, seated also, is looking through binoculars.

The silhouette target is so far away I can't see it.

Both men wear ear protection, and the ATV driver calls out to them to let them know we're here.

Carson McCormack pulls the protective earmuffs off his silver head and rises out of his seat, a big smile on his face. In his sixties, he looks a lot like his son; if not as muscular, still in good shape.

He's dressed informally, jeans and a T-shirt, but for his bright silver python-skin cowboy boots and politician's smile.

"Here he is," McCormack says. "Ranger Rory Yates. It's so nice to finally meet you."

He shakes my hand vigorously.

"I've been hearing so much about you," he says. "And Gareth showed me the video of you in the bank. Very impressive. Texas is lucky to have you as a Ranger."

He seems completely full of shit, but I act polite and appreciative of his praise.

He turns to Ariana and says, "Ms. Delgado."

"You can call me Detective Delgado," she says.

"Of course," he says dismissively.

Gareth, now standing, approaches and gives my hand a shake like we're old buddies. Like before, he has chew in his lip and a pistol on his hip.

"Sorry about giving you a hard time at the bar the other night," he says, almost sincerely. "I get competitive when I know there's a badass around."

I tell him it's no problem, but then I see Carson McCormack has a strange twinkle in his eye.

"Speaking of competitive," he says. "When we heard you were coming to see us, we had an idea."

"Who told you we were coming?" Ariana asks.

"Oh, the chief might have mentioned it."

"What did you have in mind?" I say, trying to hide how pissed I am that John Grady Harris tipped off McCormack.

McCormack smiles devilishly.

"How about a little shooting contest?"

CHAPTER 41

I TELL McCORMACK there's no way I'm going to compete in a shooting contest with his son.

"That's too bad," he says. "There's no way we're going to talk to you without a lawyer present. Unfortunately, my lawyer is in Houston, so it might take a week or so to get him out here."

The message is clear. If I play along, they'll answer our questions today. If I don't, they'll use all their legal power—and McCormack probably has a lot of it—to stonewall us for as long as they can.

"Don't do it, Rory," Ariana says. "This is stupid."

I know I'm playing right into their hands, but I want answers today, not next week.

"Sure," I say. "What the heck?"

I can feel Ariana's disapproval in her stare. Carson tells the ATV driver that he's excused, and a minute later, we hear his ATV fire up and whine away.

The father and son lead Ariana and me over to the shooting tables. McCormack opens a cooler and offers me a bottle of TexaCola, which I decline. There are a few empties standing on the table with the cooler and an ammunition box. A bumblebee buzzes around the mouths of the bottles.

Gareth takes a bottle, drinks, and says, "Let me show you my baby."

On the table sits an M24 rifle, the military version of the Remington 700. It has a telescopic sight and is mounted on a bipod to keep the barrel steady. The stock is covered by a sleeve with narrow sheathings to hold the cartridges.

Gareth slides back the bolt and opens the breech. He takes out one of the cartridges, which is almost three inches long, and slides it into the chamber.

"You ever shot an M24?" he says.

"No."

"Well," he says, sounding disappointed, "this won't be much of a competition, then."

Carson hands me the binoculars so I can see what we're shooting at. Way out in the range, they've set up a folding table with a line of milk jugs. A couple have already exploded from Gareth's earlier practice, but two remain untouched.

"That's a thousand yards," Carson says.

Ten football fields.

A bullet travels faster than the speed of sound but not faster than the speed of light. That means, at this distance, if you were on the other end of the range, you'd see the muzzle flash first. Then at least a second later, maybe a fraction more, you'd feel the bullet hit you. Only a full second after that would you actually hear the gun go off.

That's how far away the milk jugs are.

Gareth goes first. He sits in his chair, pulls the rifle against his shoulder, and snugs his eye close to the sight. His body goes as still as a statue.

When the rifle goes off, the report is muffled by the ear protection we're all wearing. In a moment like this—waiting for a bullet to fly one thousand yards—you understand just how long one second can be.

Then one of the jugs explodes, sending white liquid splattering all over the table. Dust bursts from the berm behind the target.

Carson applauds.

"Nice shot," I say.

That's an understatement. I've seen videos of men doing milk jug challenges. Someone who's a good shot, a great shot, might need ten tries to hit a milk jug at this range, and that's with spotters advising him where each shot goes—high, low, left, right—and how to make adjustments.

Even though Gareth was practicing this morning, the fact that he hit a bull's-eye the first time he squeezed the trigger is nothing short of incredible.

"Your turn," Gareth says, ejecting a round and reloading.

I sit down and bring the rifle to my shoulder. I'm being set up to fail. We all know it. The rifle hasn't been sighted for me. If they gave me ten shots, instead of just one, I might have a chance. Even then, someone who is a practiced sniper would probably need more than that to adjust the gun to his own eyes and body—and then he might need ten more to actually hit the target. I've never taken a shot at longer than half this distance.

Still, I'm going to give it my best shot—literally.

The cheek rest and length of the stock are adjustable, and I ask Gareth if I can move them. I take my time, making adjustments so the rifle feels right in my arms. They wanted the theater of a shooting competition, so I'm giving it to them.

When I'm finally ready, I settle in and try to slow

my breathing and my heart rate. The scope magnifies the sight by ten, but the jug still looks tiny. The crosshairs float all over and around the target. At a thousand yards, the slightest movement on my end could throw the bullet five feet off course.

I'm able to still my body and line up the crosshairs. I steady my breathing so it won't move the sight. I'm locked on the target.

I squeeze the trigger.

CHAPTER 42

THE RIFLE KICKS against my shoulder. As the bullet soars through the air, I have time to reorient myself in the scope to see where it hits. A puff of dust bursts from the dirt mound about a foot high and to the left of the target.

"Not bad," Gareth says. "Not bad at all."

He shakes my hand. Now that he's proven he's better than me, he doesn't seem to feel the need to be such a jerk. It's as if he genuinely respects me for my attempt.

"In all fairness," Carson McCormack says diplomatically, "a sniper rifle isn't really your specialty, is it, Ranger?"

He points to Gareth and me with both hands, aiming his fingers specifically at the pistols on our hips.

"How about one more contest?"

Ariana gives me a look that says, *Don't do it,* but Carson starts in again about how he won't talk without his lawyer. I tell them I'll do it, and Carson clasps his hands together with enthusiasm.

At this point I'm not participating to get Carson and Gareth to talk. I have a feeling what they tell us won't be all that useful anyway.

But I'm anxious to shoot my gun after having it knocked out of my hand the other night. I've taken it apart, cleaned it, and reassembled it. But I won't really feel that it's undamaged until I get a chance to fire it again. And if I'm honest with myself, there's another reason I'm participating.

I'm curious to see how good Gareth McCormack is with a pistol.

Gareth and I move the long folding table that held the cooler and the bottles about twenty feet out into the range. Carson puts two empty bottles on the table, about five feet apart. The bumblebee that had been circling the bottles earlier reorients, then finds its way to the bottles and begins buzzing again.

Gareth and I stand facing the table, with Ariana and Carson behind us, off to the side so they can see the bottles. Carson says he'll drop an empty shell casing on the concrete flooring. When we hear it ding against the concrete, that's our signal to draw.

I ready myself, my hand at my side, inches from my SIG Sauer. Carson was right. Shooting a sniper rifle isn't my specialty.

But this *is* my specialty.

I was raised by my dad to think of a gun as an extension of my hand. I should be able to hit any target as easily as reaching out and knocking it down with my fist, he told me. And on top of that, I went on to train in law enforcement, even studied under quick-draw experts and became just as fast as them. My brother Jake says I am with a pistol what LeBron James is with a basketball. Or Serena Williams with a tennis racket.

Or Michelangelo with a hammer and chisel.

It's hard to describe how I feel as I get ready

to draw against Gareth. There's a song by Charlie Daniels called "The Devil Went Down to Georgia" in which Satan challenges a young fiddle player named Johnny to a competition. After Johnny has won, he calls the devil a son of a bitch and declares, "I'm the best there's ever been."

That's how I feel.

That confident.

"Ready?" Carson asks.

Neither of us says anything—which tells him his answer. Everyone is silent. Time stands still for a moment. Then I hear the ding of the shell casing as it hits the concrete.

My hand flies to my pistol.

Draws.

Fires.

Gareth's gun goes off, the shots so close together that it's impossible to tell who fired first.

Gareth's bottle detonates in an explosion of glass.

My bottle stands upright, not even wobbling.

CHAPTER 43

"HOT DAMN," GARETH says, thrusting his fist in the air like a pitcher who just struck out a batter in the ninth inning of the World Series.

"Good shot," I say, trying to be as genuine in my sportsmanship as I can.

I glance at Ariana. She replaces the disappointment on her face with a mask of indifference, pretending that she doesn't care who won and doesn't support this whole charade anyway.

Carson and Gareth are in good spirits after the contest, and they seem friendly and forthcoming as we sit in the shade and talk. Carson admits that he convinced the town council to buy the land and designate it as open space simply because he didn't want to buy it himself.

"I didn't need to drill on it," he says. "But I didn't want any competitors to drill on it, either."

There is an old access road that runs from his property to the highway, bisecting the open space, and he admits that his drivers had been using it for a few months when someone—he doesn't know who—spotted them and complained to the town.

"So I put in a request to use the road, make it official. Hardly anyone goes out there."

When I ask him if he was aware of Susan Snyder's objection, he says he was.

"She wanted an environmental impact study done," he says. "Which would have cost me and wasted a bunch of time. I'm a businessman, and if I can get what I want without spending extra money, I do it.

"But," he quickly adds, "the other council members supported me, so the study wasn't necessary. It certainly isn't something I would kill someone over. I liked Susan Snyder."

By the time we're finished with the interview, it's almost noon. Carson offers to make us lunch back at his ranch house, but Ariana and I decline.

On the drive back through his property, she sits silent and sullen in the passenger seat.

"You're disappointed in me for losing?" I say.

She takes a deep breath and says, "No. I wish you hadn't been roped into their bullshit game to begin with."

"You're right," I say. "Honestly, I was curious how good Gareth was."

"Now you know," she snaps, showing more emotion than she probably wants to. "He's better than you."

"He's good," I say. "I'll give him that. If we'd been squaring off in the Wild West, we'd probably both be dead."

As I say this, I can't hide a roguish grin. She stares at me, her disappointment turning into admiration.

"You let him win, didn't you?" she asks, unable to hide the pride on her face.

"Let me put it this way," I say. "Afterward, did you see any sign of that pesky buzzing bee?"

Her mouth drops open. She stares at me. Dumbfounded.

"Are you saying you shot that bee out of the air?"

I shrug playfully and keep on driving.

CHAPTER 44

"HOW ABOUT 'WAGON WHEEL'?" Walt asks, positioning his fiddle in the crook of his neck.

"Let's give it a try," Dale says.

We play the song that was made famous by Darius Rucker but was first recorded by the string band Old Crow Medicine Show. When we finish, our audience erupts with applause—our audience of two, that is. Tonight we're sitting in lawn chairs at Tom and Jessica's house. They let us play here on the condition that they get to listen.

With the flowers, vegetable plants, and berry bushes in Jessica's garden, and the sun lighting up the clouds to the west, this is about as pleasant a place as I can imagine practicing music—much better than the porch of my old motel room. It's especially nice because before we even started playing, Jessica brought us all a slice of pecan pie, and Tom brought out a six-pack of Fire Eagle IPA from Austin Beerworks.

As much as I enjoy playing with Dale and Walt, I had an ulterior motive for inviting them here tonight. Once Tom and Jessica call it a night, I plan to question Dale and Walt about Alex Hartley and Skip Barnes, the two guys who were seeing Susan Snyder.

When we got back to the police station that afternoon, Ariana checked with the town clerk, and it
turns out that Alex Hartley, the football coach, was
the one to complain about McCormack's trucks driving through the open space. Ariana and I decided we
need to bring him—and Skip Barnes—in for another
round of questions, but we did some checking and
found out Hartley's in El Paso for a few days.

For now, I'm trying to enjoy the music we're
creating. But I'm having a difficult time. As we play,
I notice an itching, burning sensation on the fingers
of my right hand. I scratch my fingers between songs
and try to keep going, but then I take a good look and
notice tiny red bumps crawling from my fingertips up
to my wrist. I've got some kind of rash that itches like
the dickens.

I tell the guys I can keep singing but I can't
keep playing the guitar. Jessica takes a look and
fetches a tube of cortisone anti-itch cream from inside
the house.

"You've had an allergic reaction to something,"
she says.

I explain that Ariana and I were in the woods on
McCormack's land.

"Try not to scratch it," Jessica says. "You'll only
make it worse."

"It's on my right hand," I say. "It's going to be hard
not to irritate it."

With their own personal concert now over, Tom
and Jessica head inside while I sit with Dale and Walt,
finishing our beers. The night air is cool, and out in
the desert hills we can hear a coyote yipping. I know
now is the time.

"Are we friends?" I say to Walt and Dale.

"Hell yeah, we're friends," Dale says. "I'm trying to figure out how to convince you to move to Rio Lobo so we can keep the band together."

"If we're friends," I say, "why are y'all holding out on me?"

CHAPTER 45

DALE AND WALT stare at me, surprised by my change in demeanor.

"The reason crimes go unsolved," I say, "is because people who know something don't speak up. I know you two know something about Alex or Skip or both of them."

They exchange glances. Dale seems at a loss for words, which is unlike him (except when he's near Ariana, that is).

"I don't know nothing," he says finally, "and I think you're barking up the wrong tree looking at McCormack. The guy's got an ego the size of the Gulf of Mexico, him and Gareth both, but I really don't think they had anything to do with Susan Snyder's death."

"What about Skip?" I say.

"He ain't the brightest bulb, but he sure as hell ain't no killer."

"What about Alex Hartley? His name keeps coming up in this."

Dale looks to Walt again. Walt shakes his head subtly, as if to say, *Don't do it*. My instinct tells me not to push, and it turns out I'm right.

"Coach has a secret," Dale says, "but it ain't what you think."

Walt takes a deep breath, resigned to the revelation of Alex's secret—whatever it is. "Alex Hartley wasn't sleeping with Susan Snyder," he says. "Alex is impotent."

The two explain that Coach Hartley is diabetic and consequently suffers from erectile dysfunction. Susan went out on friendly dates with Alex to keep up the pretense that he was a socially active single man.

"Don't they have Viagra for that?" I ask.

"Doesn't work for everyone," Walt says.

"This is West Texas and he's the football coach," Dale says. "He's supposed to be tough. Manly. He didn't want people gossiping, saying, 'Coach can't get it in the end zone.'"

"It's nobody's business," I say. "Why would people even wonder about that?"

"He's a good-looking guy and this is a small town," Walt says. "If he's not married or getting some, people start to talk."

"You know how people are about football in this state," Dale says. "Lose one game you're supposed to win, and people look for any cruel thing to say behind your back."

"I think what he worried about most is the locker room," Walt says. "Kids say mean things they grow up to regret. He didn't want to put them in a position to do something stupid."

"How do you know all this?" I ask.

"His classroom's right next to mine," Walt says, then nods to Dale. "Plus, the three of us play poker every other week. We're a close group."

"Who else plays?"

They list some names I haven't heard before—
more people Ariana and I probably need to interview.
Before this case is over, we might have a statement
from everyone in town.

"Now, Rory," Walt says, "don't go thinking that
Alex Hartley murdered Susan because she was going
to blow his cover. They were *friends*. Alex's secret is
not one worth killing someone over."

I thank them for their honesty. But what I'm thinking is that, for the first time, I've found someone who
seems to have a motive to keep Susan Snyder silent.

If Hartley was willing to lie to our faces during our
interrogation, what else is he willing to do?

CHAPTER 46

THE NEXT MORNING, Ariana comes to work an hour late. This adds to my impatience at playing the waiting game.

We find out Alex Hartley is in El Paso seeing a diabetes specialist and won't return for a few days. Skip Barnes is delivering a load of petroleum and won't be back until tomorrow. We still don't know if he's talked to a lawyer.

"I've got an idea," I say to Ariana. "Let's drive out to the open space."

As we're about to head out of the station, the chief asks us where we're going.

"Why do you want to know?" I snap. "So you can keep Carson McCormack informed?"

"As chief of police," he says, "I need to be kept in the loop of this investigation."

Ariana stands in silence as everyone in the station turns to look at us. When this case is over and I drive off into the sunset, she's still going to have to work with the guy.

"Either you start cooperating," Harris says to me, "or I'll call your lieutenant and tell him you're out of line. I'll request a different Ranger."

I'm burning mad, and I can't stop myself from directing my frustration over the case toward the chief.

"You want to be kept in the loop?" I say. "Here's the loop. Before Susan Snyder died, she made two phone calls. One was to Tom Aaron telling him that she had a big story for him—and not to trust anyone. The second was to Ariana." I gesture toward her. "Susan told Ariana the same thing. Only she gave a specific name of who not to trust. Can you guess who that person is?"

Harris looks around, hyperaware of all of his employees staring at us.

"In my office," he says, his voice simmering. "Now."

Ariana and I follow him inside. None of us sits. But as he paces behind his desk, his anger seems to deflate by the second.

"Is that true?" Harris says to Ariana. "She said not to trust me?"

"She said she wasn't sure if you could be trusted," Ariana admits. "That's why I pushed so hard to bring in the Rangers."

Harris's office is as sparse as Tom Aaron's was disorganized. A Texas state flag hangs on one wall, and a mule deer mount flanked by two good-sized trout mounts decorates the wall space above his chair. A framed photo of George H. W. Bush rests on the desk.

"I'll be honest with you," Harris says. "Susan and I dated when I first got to town. Not really dated. Just, you know, hooked up."

I don't say anything, but what I'm thinking is that after debunking one person of interest's story about sleeping with Susan Snyder, it's unlikely that the chief's would hold up any better under scrutiny.

"Susan didn't want people to know," Harris says. "Neither did I. We thought it might give the appearance of a conflict of interest, especially later when I became chief."

"You said this was when you first got to town," Ariana says. "You weren't chief yet."

"I was thinking of my future," he says. "Chief Múñez was nearing retirement." He locks eyes with Ariana. "And if you're thinking I had one vote in my pocket when we were both up for the job, you're wrong. Kirk Schuetz told me that Susan Snyder wanted you for the job. She only ended up voting their way to keep it unanimous, show unified public support for the new chief."

"So there was bad blood between you?" I say.

"No," Harris says emphatically. "Susan was objective. Rational. She thought Ariana was the better candidate. Let's be honest: those other four were never going to vote for a woman to be police chief."

He looks at Ariana, his expression pleading and—to my eyes—honest.

"We work well together," he says to Ariana. "I respect you. I think you respect me. When I became chief, you might not have liked it, but you behaved professionally, and I never rubbed my success in your face."

I can relate to what Ariana went through, seeing her peer promoted to her boss. From what I can tell, Harris and Ariana have handled their situation better than my lieutenant and I have.

"We did work well together," Ariana says. "Until you refused to investigate Susan Snyder's death."

"Put yourself in my shoes," he says. "I didn't know about these phone calls Susan made. Now I understand."

The tension in the room seems to be subsiding.

"Keep investigating," he says. "I give you free rein."

I know why he's changing his tune, and it's not to find justice for Susan Snyder. He knows that one phone call is all it would take to bring in our Public Corruption Unit. No one, no matter how innocent, wants that kind of scrutiny.

"Keep digging," he says to me. "I want my name cleared of any suspicion."

CHAPTER 47

WE GRAB A couple of deli sandwiches and head out of town. I tell Ariana I'm sorry I revealed her secret to Harris.

"It's okay," she says. "We all needed to get that off our chests."

We drive south into hillier country. Ariana directs me onto a gravel road. Unlike the one to McCormack's ranch, this one is strewn with rocks the size of basketballs and potholes twice that big. As I navigate, I'm glad I purchased a new spare tire.

The road cuts into a ridge, with rocky outcroppings above and a steep slope below us. At the bottom of the ravine is a creek bed overgrown with brush. Up ahead, two mule deer spring from hiding and bound through the canyon, their antlers still in velvet.

The terrain opens onto a spacious view of the Rio Lobo winding through the canyon. Ariana was right—it's beautiful out here. Some of the prettiest country I've seen in West Texas.

We're tucked deep into the hills. I check my phone and see that I have no service. The police radio in my truck has gone to static, and I turn it off.

The dirt road splits from time to time, but Ariana always knows which fork to take. Finally, we cross the river on a wide and sturdy wooden bridge.

"This is the road from McCormack's place," Ariana says.

The route is wide and graded enough to support a tanker truck, and by the look of the tread marks in the dirt, they've been doing it regularly for a while now.

"No wonder McCormack wanted this designated open space," I say. "The only decent way to get here is from his property."

The sun is high in the sky, and I can feel sweat running down my skin inside my shirt. I ask Ariana if she wants to find some shade and eat lunch, and she tells me to keep driving. Twenty minutes later, we stop at a spot that's worth the effort. Next to the river, there's a flat patch of shore where the water makes an S-shaped bend. The roots of a big bur oak jut out the side of a cut bank.

"I used to come out here to swim when I was in high school," Ariana says. "The water is deep enough to dive."

We sit in the shade of the oak and unwrap our sandwiches, our second lunch along a riverbank. I decide to ask Ariana what I wanted to ask her the first time.

"Have you ever thought of applying for the Texas Rangers?"

When she doesn't answer right away, I explain how she'd meet the qualifications. Beyond her experience in Rio Lobo and with the highway patrol, she would need only a job with the Department of Public Safety, which oversees the Ranger Division, before she could take the entrance exam that precedes an in-person interview. There are six Texas Ranger companies, and even fewer female Rangers. We need more of them, in my opinion.

"It sounds like a long shot," she says.

"I'd vouch for you," I say. "That will count for something."

She gives it some thought, looking out over the river. We can hear insects chirping and the trickle of the river as it works its way past us, but otherwise the landscape is silent.

And peaceful.

"The truth is," Ariana says, "I'm not sure I'm up to the task of being a Texas Ranger."

"You've got a knack for investigation," I say. "I've worked with good detectives and bad detectives, and you're one of the good ones."

"It's not that," she says. "It's the other part of the job. The physical part."

She says she's not strong like the chief and can't shoot a gun like me. "I've never been in a situation where I had to draw my gun, let alone shoot it," she says. "I'm not sure how I'd handle a situation like you faced in that bank."

I'm crushing on this vulnerable new side of her, maybe even falling for her.

"Listen, Ariana," I say, resuming a professional dialogue. "It doesn't matter how big your muscles are. It doesn't matter how fast you can draw a gun. What matters is what's in here." I point to my head. "And here." I point to my chest. "A Ranger needs to be smart and good-hearted above all. And you have those qualities in spades."

She smiles brightly and genuinely, touched by my words. "Thanks, Rory."

After we finish our sandwiches, I ask if she's ready to head back to town.

"Is there any reason to hurry?" she asks.

"I guess not," I say. "What do you have in mind?"

Ariana gives me a sly grin I haven't seen before.

CHAPTER 48

"CLOSE YOUR EYES," Ariana says, "and don't peek."

I do as she asks. I hear her strip off her jeans and drop them in a heap. I don't hear her take off her shirt, but I assume that's what she's doing.

"Now you can look," she says.

I glance up in time to see Ariana in midair, suspended over the river—wearing only a bra and underwear—and then she's gone in an explosion of water. She comes up laughing, throwing back her wet hair.

"You coming?" she says.

I want to encourage this intriguing new side of Ariana, so I undo my gun belt and hang it over a branch that's broken off about six inches from the trunk. Then I loosen my tie and unbutton my shirt and hang them over the gun. I pull off my boots, set them aside, and strip off my undershirt and pants. I stand at the cut bank in my boxer shorts, looking down at Ariana in the water.

I watch Ariana's face, the way her eyes drift down to my chest, the way one corner of her mouth curves slightly into the hint of a smile. I can't believe it—she's checking me out!

"How deep is it?" I ask.

"Seven feet maybe."

I dive headfirst, stabbing the water with my hands and sinking down into the cold. I pull up quickly, and when I surface, Ariana and I face each other, treading water and smiling like kids playing hooky from school. With her wet hair slicked back and rivulets of water running down her skin, Ariana looks amazing. We find a slightly shallower section of the river and stand. I can see her bare shoulders and make out the blurry form of her body below the water.

The way she's looking at me, I feel like I could swim up to her, take her in my arms, and kiss her, and she wouldn't stop me. She'd kiss me back.

As much as I'm tempted to, I know I shouldn't.

Can't.

I lean back and float on top of the water, drifting away from her.

When I right myself again, farther away, she says, "Feels good, doesn't it?"

"Amazing."

I'm not sure if she's talking about the refreshing chill of the water or how it feels to finally take a break from the case, but my answer works for either. We know we can't stay in for long. We can't postpone our responsibilities for the whole day. Even an hour. I've had my share of time off since I arrived in town—jamming with the guys, the gig at Lobo Lizard—but the person in Rio Lobo I like spending time with the most is Ariana. And this is the first time we've ever done anything fun together, just the two of us.

It feels great.

But it also feels a little inappropriate.

I ask myself how I would feel if Willow was

swimming in Nashville's Cumberland River right now with a handsome man.

"You okay?" she says.

I tell her I am, but she can sense that something is bothering me.

"I'm sorry," she says. "This was a stupid idea."

"No," I say. "I'm glad we did it. Even a Texas Ranger and a police detective deserve a break every now and then."

We climb out of the water. Ariana abandons her previous modesty, making no request for me to keep my eyes closed. I try not to stare at her, but I can't help take in an eyeful. Her body is long and slender, muscled and toned. Like a runner or a swimmer.

"Hang on a sec," I tell her, and I unlock the large storage box in my truck bed.

I dig past the rifles, shotgun, body armor, evidence kit, and other equipment, and I pull out a couple of musty shirts I keep in there in case I ever get dirty in the field. We use them as towels, doing the best we can to dry off before we get dressed. I also have an extra pair of underwear, but I don't change. It doesn't feel fair since Ariana has to keep her wet underclothes on.

Before driving away, I reapply the cortisone cream to my hand and fingers.

"I noticed you've got a rash," Ariana says.

"Some kind of allergic reaction from when we were at McCormack's. You didn't get anything, did you?"

She shakes her head.

The rash itches like hell. What makes it worse is that it's on my right hand, which I use constantly, so I'm always re-irritating the red bumps.

Ariana's bra has made wet spots on her T-shirt,

and my underwear has done the same thing to my pants. So as we're driving back, we open the windows to let the hot air dry our hair and clothes. Ariana has her elbow out the window and a peaceful look on her face as she gazes at the canyon. Her hair is down and whips in the wind.

My heart swells as I look at her, and I can't help but wonder what a life with her might be like. Willow is amazing, but we spend most of our time eight hundred miles apart. What if Ariana moved out of Rio Lobo and became a Texas Ranger? What would it be like to be with someone who works in law enforcement?

My thoughts are interrupted when we reach the turnoff to the main highway and our phones start buzzing with voice- and text-message alerts. I check my phone and immediately feel guilty when I see a missed call from Willow.

When Ariana looks at her phone, she gasps.

"I got four missed calls from John Grady," she says. "And he sent a text."

"What's it say?"

She holds the phone so I can see.

Where the hell are you? There's been another murder.

CHAPTER 49

I PULL THE truck onto the dirt road leading to McCormack's ranch. Down by the trees, a few hundred yards from the oil derrick, multiple cars are parked, with red and blue lights flashing. Several of McCormack's black trucks and ATVs are there, and I also recognize Tom Aaron's Land Cruiser.

"Damn it," Ariana says. "We're the last ones here."

The chief stomps up to the truck and growls, "Where the hell have you two been?"

"Ariana took me down to the open space to see the easement," I say. "There was no cell service. We told you."

He looks at Ariana and does a double take at her noticeably damp ponytail.

"Follow me," he says, and he leads us through the chaos.

This is by far the worst-maintained crime scene I've ever been involved in. Harris's patrol deputies are trying to put up police tape around the perimeter, but McCormack's men have already stomped through and aren't respecting police requests to step back. A couple of paramedics stand idly. And Tom Aaron, who shouldn't have been allowed this close, is right next to the body, holding a handkerchief to his mouth and looking as pale as a sheet.

I spot Carson McCormack and his son near the body, too. Carson looks put out at the inconvenience. Gareth looks bored.

Dale Peters stands back from the group, head down, hat in hand, looking like he either is about to throw up or already has.

I spot a stump about a foot tall, and I step up onto it.

"Listen up!" I shout. "We need everyone who isn't law enforcement to vacate the scene."

McCormack's men seem disappointed.

"Mr. McCormack," I say, "please take your employees to your ranch and have them stay there until Detective Delgado and I collect your statements.

"Tom," I say, quieter now, "go home. Your deadline isn't for a couple of days."

"Something like this," he says, almost choking, "I need to write up and put out over the AP wire."

"Go back to the office, then," I say. "One of us will call you soon. Me or Ariana or the chief. We'll tell you everything we can."

He nods and starts to walk away with McCormack's men.

Harris gives me a nod as if to say, *Thank you*.

I whisper to him, "As soon as your men get this area taped off, send one of your guys up to the house to make sure no one leaves."

He sets off to give the orders.

Finally, Ariana and I approach the body. We're at the edge of the woods, where the tree growth is thin. A small, old shack stands at the top of an embankment sloping down to the creek.

The body is about ten feet from the shed, slumped

against a tree, the head nearly resting on the chest. The wiry man is in a McCormack uniform, but he's not the burly soldier type. I kneel down and confirm my suspicion.

It's Skip Barnes.

And he has a bullet hole through his head.

CHAPTER 50

"MEDICAL EXAMINER'S ON his way to pick up the body," Harris tells us.

"How far out?"

"I bet he's still an hour away," he says. "Maybe more."

The hole in Skip Barnes's forehead is about the width of my pinky finger and has emitted a single stream of blood—now dried. The exit hole is about the size of a golf ball, and the back of Skip's skull is matted with blood, some of which is still wet. Flies buzz and crawl around the face wound, and the body is beginning to stink from the heat.

"The longer he takes to get here," I say, "the harder his job is going to be."

I can't be sure, but I suspect the bullet was a sporting round, not a full metal jacket like Gareth and I were shooting yesterday. A sporting round would mushroom as it passed through the skull, making a bigger mess on its way out than a full metal jacket bullet, which is designed to pass through and keep on going.

Whatever kind of round it was, it did the trick. Skip Barnes would never tell us what he knew. He'd never work on a truck with Dale Peters again. He'd never visit another Juárez brothel.

"Gareth found him," Harris says. "He heard a rifle shot and drove an ATV over to the derrick to investigate. During deer season, Gareth uses the derrick as the ultimate tree stand, and apparently poachers sometimes come and try to use it, too."

He explains that Gareth decided to drive up and down the tree line to see if he could spot anything.

"When he saw the body, he called me," Harris says and quickly adds, "then I called Ariana."

"What about the guards at the gate?" Ariana asks. "Did they see anything?"

"I asked the same question," Harris says. "There weren't any stationed at the gate at the time. They're not always there. I know that for a fact."

"Only when they know a Texas Ranger is on his way," I say.

I'm still kneeling, and I look at him over my shoulder. We cleared the air this morning—my comment is a cheap shot.

"I thought we moved past that," he says finally.

"You're right," I say, rising to my feet. "Truce."

Lying at Skip's feet is an unlit cigarette and a Zippo—as if he was in the act of lighting a smoke when the bullet came. He has a pack of cigarettes in the breast pocket of his shirt and a wallet in his pants pocket, but no cell phone that I can see, not on his body or on the ground.

I examine the tree the body is slumped against. Blood—lumpy with brains—is splattered on the wood about five feet off the ground. In the middle of the red stain, a fresh chunk of bark is missing.

"We got lucky," I say.

The bullet hit the tree, which means we can recover it. Another six inches either way and we probably never would have found it. After going through a skull and slamming into wood, the slug will be mangled as hell, but hopefully it will tell us something important.

I walk to my truck and pull out my evidence kit. I take out a trajectory rod and insert it into the hole in the tree. The rod points directly at the oil derrick. The angle is actually high, pointing over the top of the tower, but that makes sense because the bullet would have dropped over the hundreds of yards it traveled. The actual path of the bullet would have been a slight arc.

"Ariana, can you handle this crime scene?" I say. "I'm going to check out the sniper's nest."

CHAPTER 51

I WALK TO the derrick so I can get a sense of the distance. I pace off four hundred seventeen yards to the base. I might be off by a few yards, but it's close. Before climbing, I have a good look around. Vines have been scaling the scaffolding for some time, and the weeds underneath are overgrown. I duck beneath a metal beam and walk below the structure. The four legs of the base are about twenty-five feet apart, making it a big area for one person to search.

But I spot something twinkling in the sunlight and look closer to find a rifle shell casing. If Gareth shoots from the derrick with any regularity, there might be more shells around here. But this one, the way it's sitting on top of the weeds, not down in the dirt, couldn't have been here long. I take some photographs of its location. Then I slip on a pair of rubber gloves and use an evidence bag to scoop up the shell without ever touching it.

I lift the bag and inspect the casing through the plastic. On the bottom, WINCHESTER 30-06 SPRG is pressed into the metal. If this is the shell to the bullet that killed Skip Barnes, that rules out Gareth's M24. The bullet itself is the same width as a .308, but the casing is too long to fit his rifle. Still, plenty of rifles shoot a 30-06 round—I have no doubt Gareth owns at least one.

A metal ladder ascends one side of the derrick, and I start to climb. The metal is hot to the touch. I take my time, looking as I go. The ladder is rusted, and I expect it will be difficult to get fingerprints. But if we're lucky, there will be prints on the shell.

My fingers sweat inside my gloves, which makes the itching worse as I climb. I try to ignore the discomfort.

When I get to the top, I pull myself onto a small metal platform that runs around the edges of the structure. It's about eight feet from corner to corner but the path around is only a few feet wide. A metal mesh railing runs around the outside, giving me some minor sense of safety, but in the center of the derrick the platform is wide open, a straight drop to the ground, where the drilling machinery would go if they were using the derrick to bore into the earth.

I feel unsteady on my feet. Eighty feet might not seem that high from the ground, but once I'm up here, the whole world looks different. I can see for what seems like miles: the ranch house, the tank yard, and fields and fields of pump jacks. Everything looks small, like someone built miniature replicas for a model train display.

Standing this high, looking around, I get a strange feeling. I don't think McCormack built this scaffolding for decoration. Nor do I think they put it up so Gareth could have the *ultimate tree stand,* as Harris described it.

I get the odd feeling they erected it for security. From here, a sharpshooter like Gareth would have a clear shot along a huge stretch of fence line. The ranch house is probably around a thousand yards away, which I've seen for myself is well within Gareth's range. The tank yard is farther away, probably two thousand yards, but someone like Gareth could conceivably make a shot from that distance.

And the tower is located along the ribbon of vegetation that runs clear through McCormack's property, making it accessible. Or escapable.

The question is why they might have fortified their property. Has Gareth really positioned the tower according to his military-trained brain? Or is there a verified threat?

Oil is valuable, but it's not a commodity that thieves can easily steal.

I visually retrace the road that Ariana and I drove in on yesterday. If Gareth had been here instead of on the range, he could have easily put us in his crosshairs. He could have put a bullet through my brain before I even heard the shot.

From this vantage point, I look over the crime scene. I grab binoculars from an outside pocket of my evidence kit, and through them, I clearly see the body of Skip Barnes, as well as Ariana and Harris searching the scene for evidence.

I'm anxious to climb down from the unshaded metal emitting heat like a cast-iron radiator. But I kneel and then lie prone, as a sniper would, on top of the hot platform. Whoever it was—Gareth or maybe one of his men—would have been hidden mostly from view by the metal mesh railing.

That's where something else catches my eye. A long strand of dark hair hangs from the metal mesh, as if it became snagged when someone was in this very position.

I rise to my knees and take out another evidence bag, then insert the hair inside. I hold it up in the light, looking at the strand, now curled inside the plastic.

The strand looks like the long hair Gareth McCormack keeps tied back in a ponytail.

CHAPTER 52

IT'S AFTER DARK when I pull up in front of Tom and Jessica's house. The light in the garage is on, and I see Tom tinkering with his Mustang.

"You okay?" I say as I approach.

He nods, but he looks upset. Tom picks up an open can of Texas Lager from the workbench and offers me a fresh one. The radio is tuned to a classic country station, and an old Ronnie Milsap song is playing.

"Get your article sent off to the Associated Press?" I ask, cracking my beer.

He nods again, leans against the fender. His hands are dirty with car grease.

"I don't know how you get used to it," he says. "I feel like I've had a heck of a long day, but I only had to write about it. You have to figure out who did it."

"It's not an easy job," I say, "but someone's got to do it. Just like your job." I put a hand on his shoulder. "I'll admit to having had my share of conflicts with the press, but people need to be informed."

Jessica comes out in a nightgown and puts an arm around Tom. "You ready to come in?" she says.

He finishes the last of his beer and pulls down the garage door. The lawn chairs from the other night are still sitting out, and I tell them I'm going to relax for a few minutes and finish my beer.

I'm alone, perched at the edge of Jessica's garden, listening to the chirp of insects. The sky is full of stars, bright and beautiful. Sitting here is peaceful, but it's hard for me to enjoy it. My fingers itch, for one, like there are fire ants crawling over my skin. More than that, though, there's simply a lot on my mind.

After the medical examiner arrived, Ariana and I went on to the ranch house and interviewed Carson and Gareth McCormack. Gareth had a smug expression on his face the whole time. We didn't tell him we had a strand of hair, the bullet casing, or the bullet slug itself recovered from a tree. I'm not sure he would've been so self-assured if he'd known.

He consented to be swabbed for DNA and gunshot residue. And he showed us his gun collection, which took up an entire room of the house, every wall covered in corkboard and displaying rifles, shotguns, handguns, military rifles, muzzleloaders, crossbows, compound bows, and everything else you could think of. There were a few items—two machine guns, a short-barreled shotgun, some suppressors— that require a permit to own, but he had the proper paperwork.

In the stockpile were a Remington Model 783 and a Winchester Model 70, both of which will fire a 30-06 round. McCormack agreed to let us take those so we could compare the rounds fired. Every rifle barrel has lands and grooves that leave unique markings on a bullet, kind of like a fingerprint, and as long as the slug from the tree isn't too mangled, we'll know if either of Gareth's guns fired the bullet. He agreed to let us take the guns so readily that I'm sure neither of them will result in a positive match. Which means that if it was him, he used another gun he's not sharing.

"Don't leave town, Gareth," I said as we were leaving.

"Don't worry," he said. "I'll stick around so you can give my guns back with a big fat apology."

We also swabbed Carson and all of his men for gunshot residue, including Dale Peters and Mr. Broken Nose. But we ran out of time before we were able to properly collect statements from everyone. When I had a moment alone with Dale, I gave him a good hard stare and said, with just a touch of anger in my voice, "You still think we're barking up the wrong tree?"

He lowered his eyes, his skin pale. He'd just lost a friend to murder—but if he was hiding something, I wanted him to feel guilty for it.

We'll have the fingerprint results soon, and through the Rangers I can get the DNA testing fast-tracked. But there's still loads of work to do. We need to have the ballistics tested on Gareth's guns. We need to properly interview every one of McCormack's men, setting up a timeline of where people were, what they heard, what they saw. We need to search Skip's residence and see if there's any clue why someone would want to kill him. And we need to find and notify Skip Barnes's next of kin.

And even if this isn't related to the death of Susan Snyder—which I think it is—we can't stop looking into that case. We need to interview Alex Hartley when he gets back to town. We need to continue combing through Susan Snyder's background.

The one thing the murders have in common is that both victims were planning to talk to the police soon. Susan Snyder *wanted* to talk to the police. Skip Barnes was being compelled to talk to us. But both of them ended up dead before they could.

Sitting by Jessica's garden in the dark, I feel overwhelmed. This thing is getting too big for Ariana and me to handle ourselves. We need help. And there's only one place to get it. I pull out my phone to call the last person I want to talk to right now.

The lieutenant who banished me to this little town in the first place.

CHAPTER 53

"WELL, IF IT ain't everybody's favorite Texas Ranger," Kyle says upon answering. "Rory 'Guns Blazing' Yates, as I live and breathe."

With that one sentence, I can tell he's been drinking. By the sound of the background, I bet he's in a bar right now.

"Sorry to bother you so late," I say. "I can call back tomorrow."

I'm dreading this conversation as it is. I definitely don't want to have it while he's drunk.

"No, no," he says. "I'm glad you called. I'm celebrating. We made an arrest today in a big case—no thanks to you," he adds.

He tells me that the Rangers continued to investigate what happened at the bank robbery I stopped. Just because the two robbers were dead didn't mean the case was closed. It turns out one of the bank tellers was in cahoots with the men. That's how they knew to rob the bank at the precise moment when the time lock on the safe would open. They arrested the teller today.

"That's great news," I say, impressed. "Good job, Kyle."

"I do know how to do my job, you know."

"I know," I say.

It's true. Kyle and I were never friends, but he's always been a good Ranger. I feel a swell of respect, and I think maybe this conversation won't go so badly after all.

"So you got the case solved in that little town yet or what?" he asks.

"Not even close," I say. "In fact, there's been another murder."

I explain what evidence we obtained and who the chief suspect is, but I also tell him how much work is ahead of us. All the interviews we need to do. If the fingerprints or DNA link to Gareth but the guns don't match, we'll need to get a search warrant and take a look at every inch of McCormack's property. And it's a big property.

"We need help, Kyle," I say. "Can you spare us a couple of Rangers? Maybe the El Paso office has a few guys they can free up."

"You want help?" Kyle says, exaggerating his disgust. "Hell, Rory, there ain't but a hundred sixty-six Rangers in the whole damn state. You *are* the help."

He starts on a rant about how we don't even know if Susan Snyder was murdered, and in the case of Skip Barnes, it seems like there is plenty of evidence to make an arrest.

"For someone who shoots first and asks questions later," he says, "you sure are taking your sweet time."

I'm burning up inside. Kyle is way out of line. He could deny my request—I figured it was about a fifty-fifty chance he would—but there's no need for him to be an asshole about it.

"I've spoken to the chief down there," Kyle says.

"He says you're working with a pretty little *chica*. Is something going on with her? I wonder if you're taking your time on this thing so you can cozy up to her. What would Willow think, Rory?"

I'm up and out of my chair, as if Kyle is in front of me and not on the phone talking from a bar five hundred miles away.

"Listen here, you son of a bitch. You have no right to talk like that to me. You're a lieutenant in the Texas Ranger Division. Act like it."

I could get in big trouble for talking to my lieutenant that way, but he's behaving unprofessionally, too. I prepare myself for a fight. He just laughs at me from the other end of the phone.

"Looks like I pressed the right button," he says. "Sounds like you've got a guilty conscience, Rory."

He hangs up on me before I can say anything else. I take a deep breath and flop back in the chair, trying to calm down in the silence. After a while, I head to the side of the garage to climb the stairs to my room. Jessica pruned back the berry bushes like she promised, so the path is easy to navigate in the dark.

Once I've showered and climbed into bed, I pull out my phone and consider calling Willow. But I don't want to worry her—*Another murder!* she would say—and she's probably busy anyway, hanging out at the Grand Ole Opry or going to a dinner party at Kacey Musgraves's house.

If I'm honest with myself, I don't really feel like talking to her right now anyway.

The person I *want* to call is Ariana.

But I don't. I turn out the light and try to sleep. It's been a long day. Any day you see a dead body is a long day, but this one seemed especially long. The open space, the oil derrick, the shit show at the crime scene, the tension with the chief and later with Kyle. My mind should be reeling. But really I'm only thinking about one thing.

I can't get the image out of my head of Ariana, treading water, her hair slicked back, smiling for just a moment like she didn't have a worry in the world.

CHAPTER 54

THE NEXT DAY, Ariana and I are sitting in the conference room, going over everything we know. The tiny room, which was empty when I arrived, has since been transformed into our investigation center. We have boxes and boxes of paperwork, maps, and poster-sized diagrams on the walls, plus a dry-erase board that we're constantly writing on and wiping clean.

As of right now, the medical examiner hasn't given us a precise time of death. The heat of the day made the temperature of the body an unreliable indicator. As for eye dilation, the bullet that traveled through Skip Barnes's brain filled his eye sockets full of blood. The examiner said some of the other determining factors—skin condition, settling of the blood, contents of the stomach—had to wait until the body was in his lab.

We can be sure the death was yesterday morning, but beyond that, we don't have any more specifics.

McCormack provided us with some security footage from over in his tank yard that shows Gareth being there most of the morning. But he disappears from the cameras late in the morning. This is the time period he claims to have been at the house and heard the gunshot, but it's plausible that he could have gone to the derrick, taken the shot, and then pretended to discover the body.

There are enough people who live and work on the ranch that someone certainly would have seen him drive over there on an ATV. If we had a team of Rangers, we could have people interviewing McCormack's men right now. But it's just the two of us, and we're hoping to get some more information before we really start interrogating. The tests of gunshot residue and DNA, as well as the ballistics comparisons on the gun, will take a while. But, at the very least, we should find out soon if there's a match on the fingerprints found on the shell casing.

I feel nervous as we wait, and I'm not sure why. I tell myself it's just anxiety—I want to get on with this. But there's something else to it, some growing sense of dread I can't quite put my finger on.

Then it hits me: we have too much evidence.

We were lucky enough to find the bullet, the casing, and a strand of hair. Any one of those by itself would be a fortunate discovery, but I found all three without even looking that hard. I've been assuming Gareth is the shooter, but I haven't focused on the unlikely carelessness. It's conceivable his hair could get snagged without him knowing, and it could just be his bad luck that the bullet hit a tree after passing through Skip Barnes. But military shooters are trained to police their brass. Collecting his shell casings would be second nature to a sniper like Gareth.

I remember Gareth's smug expression. I originally took it for ego, but now I think it might be something else. Did he want us to find the shell?

The chief comes in, looking grim, and my heart

sinks. I've been waiting for bad news, and here it comes.

"Got the fingerprint results," Harris says.

His eyes are locked on Ariana.

"Is there something you want to tell us?" he says to her.

"What do you mean?" she says, clearly confused.

He looks at me and says, "You collected the shell casing. Before you fingerprinted it, was the shell ever compromised?"

"I wore gloves on the scene," I say. "And when I fingerprinted it. I never touched it."

"Did Ariana touch it?"

"No," she says. "Never."

He stares at Ariana, his expression unreadable.

"The fingerprints are yours, Ariana."

CHAPTER 55

I SHOOT TO my feet.

"This is a setup, Chief."

I explain how I was afraid of something like this. The abundance of evidence felt like a trap.

"That may be," Harris admits, "but we have to take this seriously."

I say nothing. I can't argue with that.

Ariana looks pale. I've seen the same expression before on people I knew to be guilty, but I'm sure she's feeling something else.

Defeat.

We've been working on this case, fighting against some faceless opponent, and she's just realized how outmatched we are. We've underestimated our adversary, whoever he is—or whoever they are—and now the score is so imbalanced there's no way we're going to climb back in this game. At least not Ariana. She's out, as of right now. For Ariana, the best-case scenario is that she gets pulled off this case.

The worst is that she goes to prison.

Actually, the worst is that she gets the death penalty, but I won't even let my mind go that far.

"You still have your granddaddy's rifle, don't you?" Harris asks Ariana.

She nods her head gravely.

"What am I missing?" I say.

Ariana opens her mouth to speak, and her voice comes out in a hoarse croak. Seeing she can barely talk, Harris answers for her. He says that Ariana owns an M1 Garand, a semiautomatic rifle used during World War II. Her grandfather used it in the Pacific and later gave it to her as a college graduation present.

I nod my head in understanding. The Garand fires a 30-06 round.

And as a semiautomatic, the Garand ejects its shells automatically. The shell could easily have gone tumbling down from the tower without the shooter being able to grab it.

I don't say any of this to Harris, even though he's probably thinking the same thing.

The three of us ride in Harris's patrol car over to Ariana's house. I ride in back because I don't want Ariana to have to do it. I don't want her to feel like a criminal. When we get to her place, she unlocks the door and takes us to her bedroom.

"It's under there," she says, pointing to her bed.

The chief puts on rubber gloves and kneels down to retrieve it. The gun is probably eighty years old but looks in good condition, the wooden stock oiled and the iron barrel polished. The rifle has no telescopic sight, just the original rear-aperture sight that adjusts for distance based on hundred-yard increments.

The head shot that killed Skip Barnes would not have been easy with this gun. It would take a good shooter.

"Do you keep it loaded?" Harris asks Ariana.

"Yes," she says, her voice still dry. "There's an eight-shot clip, and I keep it full."

Harris ejects the clip, and we all count the 30-06 rounds inside.

Seven.

CHAPTER 56

"CHIEF," I SAY, "she's obviously being framed. If Ariana shot Skip Barnes, she wouldn't have come home and put the gun back under her bed—and then led us here right to it." I tell him that someone obviously came, stole the gun, and then replaced it, all while Ariana and I were at the open space. I say we need to conduct interviews of people in the neighborhood and see if there were any witnesses who saw someone coming in or out of the house.

"We'll do all that," he says. "But first we need to check the ballistics on this gun. See if it matches the bullet fired. We've got a bullet and a shell casing from the scene. We'll be able to tell if this rifle fired the shot or not."

I don't object. He's right. But I already know what we'll find. The bullet and shell casing will have similar marks.

This is the gun.

And I suddenly realize that the hair we found is probably Ariana's as well. Gareth, or whoever set her up, could have easily stolen a strand when he was in her house taking the gun.

Harris seems to think this as well because he says to

Ariana, "If one more piece of evidence comes in link-ing you to the murder—the ballistics test, the DNA results, anything—I'm going to have to arrest you."

Harris takes a cheek swab for DNA evidence, and he swabs Ariana's arm for gunshot residue. Even though it's been a day since the shooting, he's trying to be thorough. He also asks for the clothes she was wearing yesterday.

"You shouldn't be handling that evidence," I say to the chief. "You could be compromised."

"Bullshit," he snaps, losing his cool.

"It's no coincidence all this happened while Ariana and I were out at the open space," I say, also getting angry. "You were one of the few people who knew we'd be gone."

"I'm not going to listen to this shit," he says, practically yelling. "*You* could be compromised."

"Me?" I say.

"Yeah, you," he snarls. "You claim to have been with Ariana at the time of the shooting. You could have been in on this."

"That makes no sense," I say, but he's caught me off guard. The anger in my voice subsides as I try to defend myself. "I'm not from around here. What motivation would I have to kill Skip Barnes?"

"I'm not saying you had anything to do with it," Harris says, his voice also calming slightly. "I'm saying your loyalty to Ariana might be clouding your judgment."

I smirk to indicate my disbelief in what he's saying, but he has planted a seed of doubt in my mind. Is my affection for Ariana obscuring my thinking? How would I handle this if it weren't her?

"Were you two really out at the open space that

whole time?" the chief asks. "You were gone longer than you needed to be. What were you doing?"

I open my mouth to give him an honest explanation of our whereabouts, including our time eating lunch together and swimming in the river, but Ariana stands up and says, "You don't need to defend me, Rory. I'm sure this is all some big mistake."

In my opinion, there's no use hiding what we did, not when there's so much at stake, but I can tell Ariana doesn't want it to get out that we were splashing around in our underwear. No one would believe that's all we were doing. And this is a small town. She doesn't want the reputation of being some badge bunny sleeping with the visiting Texas Ranger when she should have been investigating a murder.

"You don't trust me," Harris says to me, "and I don't trust you. So that means we're both going to keep a close eye on this evidence and make sure it gets handled on the up and up. Got it?"

I nod, not sure what else to do. If my lieutenant was supportive, I'd call him to bring in the cavalry, let the Texas Rangers come in and take over the whole damn investigation. But the way things went with Kyle last night, I'm on my own here.

We're all quiet for a moment, and then Ariana asks, "Can I stay on the Susan Snyder case until the results come in?"

Harris stares at her, shocked that Ariana doesn't fully realize the level of danger she's in.

"As of this moment, you're on paid leave," he says. "I need your badge and your gun. And I'm going to put a patrol officer outside your house to make sure you don't try to run."

"You're putting me on house arrest?"

"Not officially," Harris says. "I'd need a court order for that. But effectively speaking, yes. I don't want you leaving this house. If you so much as set one foot out your door, I'll have you arrested, and you'll stay in our little jail until we get all this sorted out. Understand me?"

She unfastens her holster from her belt. Then she pulls out her badge. She stares at the gun and the badge—her hands trembling, her eyes brimming with tears—and hands them over to the chief.

"As of this moment," Harris says to Ariana, "you're no longer a cop."

Which means, as of this moment, I'm on my own to find out who killed Susan Snyder and Skip Barnes.

PART TWO

CHAPTER 57

GARETH McCORMACK STARES through the M24's riflescope at his target. He slows his breathing, gets his heart rate under control. His body is completely still. The only movement is his right finger, slowly squeezing the trigger.

The rifle kicks against his shoulder. Fire spits from the barrel. A second later, the bullet zips through a milk jug one thousand yards away and plunges into the mound of dirt acting as the backstop for the range. Milk glugs out of the punctured jug like white blood.

"Good shot, Son," Carson says, sitting next to Gareth with binoculars.

Gareth sits up and says, "It's just not as much fun when you're not shooting at a living thing."

The sun is setting to the west, spectacular and red.

Before Gareth loads another round into his M24, he notices his phone buzzing. When he answers, he listens more than he speaks. It's his source from town—one of them—filling him in on the latest.

When he hangs up, he packs a can of Skoal against his palm and puts a plug of snuff into his lip before talking.

"Everything's working out," he says to his father, then spits tobacco juice into an empty Dr Pepper can.

Carson sits back and props his python-skin boots up on an empty chair. He notices a clump of mud on the bottom of the boots and takes out a pocket knife to pry it off.

"Let's not underestimate the Rangers," Carson says.

Gareth laughs. "That Rory Yates. He ain't nothing."

"I'm not talking about Yates," Carson says. "I'm talking about the whole Texas Ranger Division. We need to get rid of Yates and make sure no one else comes snooping around." He folds his pocket knife and slides it into the breast pocket of his shirt. "Or if they do send another Ranger, we need it to be someone who will wrap things up quick."

"No shit," Gareth says.

If it was as simple as getting rid of Yates, Gareth would just kill him. But killing a Texas Ranger would only bring more Texas Rangers, so their plan requires nuance.

There is some tension between father and son. They haven't quite been on the same page about how to handle their latest problems. They disagreed about how precarious their situation was, how much of a threat Rory Yates actually was. Gareth was the confident one, sure that everything would work out in their favor. Carson was more cautious, giving the Rangers more credit than Gareth thought they deserved.

He wanted his father to trust him in this situation. His father knew about the business side of things—the laws of supply and demand, how to cut costs and make a profit, when to abandon one business model and start another. That's where Gareth thought the old man should keep his attention focused. As for these new developments, Gareth knows how to handle them. He's been in war zones before.

The brilliant crimson clouds above the horizon, like cotton balls soaked in blood, begin to fade and become a subdued purple.

The clouds look a little like brains, Gareth thinks.

Skip Barnes's brains.

He can't help but smile. His father doesn't notice — his eyes are fixed on the horizon as well.

They hear the whine of an ATV approaching, then parking on the other side of the nearby copse of woods. A few seconds later, Dale Peters comes walking up the path.

"Howdy," he says, adjusting his ball cap on his head. "Y'all wanted to see me?"

Gareth can tell Dale is nervous. He's acting like his normal, good-humored self, but it's a show. He has a tremble in his voice. He can't quite keep his hands still.

"We wanted to call you here to thank you," Carson McCormack says to Dale.

Dale can't hide his relief. "What for?"

"Wearing the recording device the last time you hung out with that Texas Ranger."

"Oh," Dale says. "No problem. I never would have gone and played with him in the first place if I thought he was going to poke around in your business. Walt and I was just looking for someone new to play with since Charlie left town."

Carson says he is glad that Dale has become friends with Rory. That way he can do a little spying for them.

"I didn't expect him to ask me about y'all," Dale says. "That's why I told him all that about Alex Hartley. Throw him a bone, you know, send him off sniffing somewhere else."

CHAPTER 58

"DO YOU MIND making tomorrow's run by your-self?" Carson asks Dale. "Since, you know...?"

He doesn't need to complete the sentence. Dale usually made his runs with Skip.

"Course," Dale says. If he goes alone, that means he's earned back Carson and Gareth's trust.

"Or do you want us to send one of the boys with you? I want to keep them all close with everything that's going on. But we could probably spare one."

"That's not necessary," Dale says. "I can handle it."

Dale's not stupid. *Don't cross us, Dale, or the same thing that happened to Skip will happen to you.*

"It's a tragedy about Skip, isn't it?" Carson says. "I know you two were friends."

"Yes, sir," Dale says, nodding his head. "It's a damn shame."

"What do you think happened?" Carson asks.

Dale stares at him. All three of them know what happened. They're just pretending they don't.

"Poacher, I imagine," Dale says, the tremble in his voice giving away his lie. "That Ranger will probably try to make some bigger deal out of it, but I figure it's a freak accident. Just one of them things."

"That's what we thought," Carson says, "but we hear they've already got a suspect in mind."

Dale, going along with the pretense that none of them has any idea who committed the murder, says, "Is that so?"

"You won't believe it," Gareth says, speaking up for the first time since Dale arrived. "They think that female detective did it. Ariana Delgado."

Dale is unable to hide his surprise. His head recoils and his eyes widen.

"They haven't arrested her yet," Gareth says. "But we hear it's just a matter of time."

Gareth knows Dale has always had a crush on the detective, so he delivers the news with relish, like twisting a knife when it's already buried to the hilt. He likes to make people squirm.

"Hopefully they lock her up soon," Gareth says, his eyes boring into Dale. "Before anyone else gets hurt."

Dale gulps. He takes off his hat, adjusts it, puts it back on.

"That's too bad," he says. "I guess I'll never marry her now." He grins, trying to make it sound like he's joking but unable to keep his voice from cracking with heartbreak.

He tells them good-bye and starts back toward the trees. Gareth lets him make it all the way to the edge of the trees before he calls and asks Dale to do a favor before he leaves.

"Sure thing," Dale says. "What you got in mind?"

Gareth leads him about ten feet out into the range.

"Give me your hat," Gareth says.

Dale hands him his cherished ball cap and runs his hand through his sweat-soaked hair.

"Balance this on your head," Gareth says, handing Dale an empty Coke can.

"You're not gonna do what I think you're gonna do," Dale says, trying to sound calm. "Are you?"

"What's the matter?" Gareth says. "Don't you trust me? We trust you with millions of dollars of our property."

"Sure, I trust you," Dale says, but as he raises the can to his head, his hands shake.

Gareth backs up like a gunfighter getting into position. He finds a good place about ten feet away and puts his hand five inches from his pistol's grip. Carson comes and stands near him, a few paces back. The old man has a grin on his face like he's walked into a cockfighting arena—he knows he might see bloodshed and can't hide his pleasure at the prospect.

The sun has almost disappeared beneath the horizon. The light is dim. Dale's knees wobble wildly. The aluminum can on his head teeters.

"Now, hold still," Gareth says. "If you move too much, you might make me miss."

Dale tries to stand still, but his legs are shaking so badly that he can't.

"You count down from three," Gareth says.

"You want me to count?" Dale says.

Gareth spits tobacco juice onto the ground. "Yes, you count."

"It's getting pretty dark," Dale says. "You sure you can see?"

"Trust me," Gareth repeats, but the way he says it sounds vicious, not trustworthy.

Dale closes his eyes, knowing that he might be counting down to his own execution.

"Three," he says, his voice rough.

He opens his eyes and sees Gareth, statue-still in the twilight. He looks like a predator, a wolf, eyeing his prey before striking.

"Two," Dale croaks.

His whole body trembles.

"I don't want to die," he says, tears streaming down his cheeks. "You don't have to worry about me. I'll do anything you want."

"Say 'one,'" Gareth growls.

Dale takes a deep breath. He says a prayer inside his head. "One."

Gareth's hand flashes to his pistol. Dale hears the zip of the bullet flying toward him, and then the clang as the can catapults off his skull. He drops to his knees and throws his hands over his head.

Gareth and Carson both laugh like they've just heard the funniest joke of their lives.

Dale rises to his feet and approaches them on numb legs. He tries to smile, like all of it was a big joke, but he notices a large patch of wetness in the crotch of his jeans. He thinks for a moment that it's blood and he's been shot after all.

He realizes what happened.

He pissed his pants.

"Go clean yourself up," Gareth says, his face transforming in an instant from jolly to grim. "And if you ever forget where your loyalties lie, the next one will be six inches lower."

CHAPTER 59

I PULL MY truck to a stop in front of Ariana's house. One of Harris's patrol deputies, sitting sentry out front, sees me and jumps out of his car.

"You can't go in there," he says.

"Yes, I can."

"Chief Harris says—"

"She hasn't been arrested," I snap, freezing him in his tracks. "You can't put her on house arrest without a judge's order. What you're doing here is borderline illegal, and if you want to test me on that, I have no problem cuffing you and making you spend the night in jail in your own police station."

I push past him. I'm carrying a small paper bag with the name of Jessica's pharmacy stenciled on the outside.

"I'm going to tell the chief," he calls after me.

"Go right ahead," I say.

I've had a long day, and my patience is all used up. After Harris took Ariana's gun and badge, he and I went back to the station with Ariana's rifle. We argued for a while about how to handle the evidence. Neither of us wanted to let the gun or DNA sample out of our sight until we got them to the crime lab in

El Paso, so we rode together in near silence during the five-hour round trip.

Now we just have to wait. Fortunately, we might not have to wait very long. The technicians at the Department of Public Safety lab in El Paso have given us their word that our requests will bypass the backlog and move to the top of the queue.

As early as tomorrow, a technician will fire Ariana's grandfather's rifle into a special water tank and then use a microscope to compare the undamaged bullet to the slug found in the tree. At the same time, technicians will be looking at the DNA of the hair strand, comparing it to the DNA obtained from the cheek swabs of Ariana and Gareth.

This time tomorrow, Ariana could be exonerated.

Or in jail.

Which is why I need to talk to her tonight.

Ariana opens the door before I knock. Her big beautiful eyes look terrified.

She leads me into her living room and asks if I want anything to drink. I tell her I'll take a beer if she has one, and she disappears into her kitchen. I wait, lingering in her living room. She has a nice home. Small. Nothing too fancy. But she takes good care of what she has.

In one corner is a record player that's probably older than I am next to a rustic wooden shelf holding an impressive collection of vinyl albums. I browse through the bands. Guns N' Roses. Led Zeppelin. Pearl Jam. The occasional classic country artist is present—Emmylou Harris, Kenny Rogers, Hank Williams—but the rock albums outnumber country ten to one.

On one shelf are framed photographs of a Mexican man and woman I assume are her parents.

Ariana comes back with two bottles of Bud Light, and we sit at opposite ends of the couch. I take my hat off—I still don't like the way it fits on my head—and set it on the floor. I set the pharmacy bag beside it. I run my hands through my hair, damp with sweat, and point to the pictures on the shelf.

"Are those your parents?" I say.

She nods and takes a drink.

"Do they still live in Rio Lobo?"

"My dad's in prison over in Fort Stockton," she says. "My mom moved back to Mexico after I graduated from high school. Said she couldn't stand to be here anymore after my dad was arrested."

I ask what he did, and she explains that he was a janitor at the high school and one day the principal found a stash of marijuana hidden in his supply closet. The amount was enough that they believed he was selling drugs to kids, and a few of them testified to that effect.

"He always claimed he was innocent," she says. "I believed him for a while. That's one reason I became a cop. I thought I could help him somehow. But by the time I was out in the world, working as a cop, I started to think differently. I wasn't so naïve anymore."

"The former police chief, the one who hired you, was he the one who arrested your dad?"

"Yeah," she says. "I think that's why he wanted to give me a chance. He saw that I was trying to be a better person. And once I saw him on the job, doing everything by the book, I knew Dad was guilty."

She blinks back tears and adds, "Now I might end up in prison just like my old man. Makes me wonder if he was telling the truth all along. Maybe he was framed just like I'm being framed."

She turns to me, her eyes hardening. "You know it's a setup," she says. "Right?"

I do…except there's a small seed of doubt in my mind. The videotapes of Gareth show him off camera long enough to have committed the crime, but no where near long enough that he could have driven to town and stolen Ariana's gun, made the shot, and then driven back to replace it.

If it was Gareth, someone was helping him.

And if it wasn't Gareth, then could it have been Ariana?

"I need you to tell me something," I say, hating myself for asking the question. "Why were you late to work yesterday?"

CHAPTER 60

ARIANA GLARES AT me, feelings of betrayal evident across her strained features.

"I have to ask," I say. "You're never late. But on that day, of all days, you were."

"You think I drove out there and shot Skip Barnes before coming into work?" she asks. "That's outrageous."

"We don't have a firm time of death yet," I say.

She shakes her head in disbelief and then answers. "I went for a run. We've been working on this case day and night. I thought I deserved a break." She says she ran on the arroyo behind her house, which also passes behind Tom and Jessica's place. "I actually ran by your apartment. I thought about stopping, but I decided to just keep on running. I was going to see you in an hour anyway."

She looks embarrassed. She was going to drop in and see me for a friendly visit, and now here I am questioning her like she's a criminal. But I have to be professional about this. I have to ask the same questions I would ask anyone.

"Any witnesses see you?"

"I don't know," she says. "The path on the arroyo is pretty hidden."

We're quiet. She's probably thinking what I'm thinking. If the DNA, ballistics, and fingerprint tests all point to her, a witness who *might* have recognized her won't make much difference anyway. Eyewitness testimony isn't always reliable. But ballistics, fingerprints, and DNA—not to mention all three put together—would be hard to argue with.

"None of this makes any sense," Ariana says. "Why would I kill Skip Barnes?"

She's right—it doesn't make a lick of sense that Ariana would want to kill Skip Barnes. But motive is often speculation. In a courtroom, the DA could spin theories about why she would commit the crime. It wouldn't matter how far-fetched the theories were if there was abundant physical evidence.

"I believe you," I say. "I know you didn't do it. There's no question in my mind."

She lets out a sigh of relief.

"I think the only question," I say, "is whether I'm going to let them arrest you or whether I'm going to help you escape."

I pick up the bag from the pharmacy and pull out the item inside.

A burner cell phone.

I purchased two when Harris and I got back into town. Having kept one for myself, I now give this one to Ariana. I tell her to keep it close. When Harris and I get the results, I'll text her. The patrol officer out front isn't keeping a very close watch. She could sneak down the arroyo.

"And do what?" she says, stunned. "I won't have a car. I'll only get so far."

"I'm working on that," I say.

She rises from the couch and paces in front of me.

"I don't think this is a good idea," she says. "This isn't the way to fight. If I run, it will be like announcing I'm guilty. And you," she adds, "you're putting your badge on the line. Your life. Imagine a Texas Ranger being sent to prison—those inmates would kill you within the first two hours."

"They could try."

She gives me an exasperated look. "This isn't the time to act tough, Rory."

I stand up. It's my turn for an impassioned speech.

"Listen to me," I say. "Whoever is behind this, they're not playing by the rules. They're fixing the game in their favor. They didn't *just* kill Skip Barnes. They're getting you out of the picture, too. Who knows what they've got in store for me? Something bad is going on in this town. We've got to figure it out."

"It doesn't feel right to fight the people breaking the law by breaking the law ourselves. Isn't this the kind of thing that's gotten you into trouble in the past?"

She's right. When I started this case, all I wanted to do was follow the rules, investigate the case by the book, be the best Ranger I could be. No cutting corners. No stepping outside the lines of the law.

"You have to solve this case without me, Rory. The *right* way."

"The right way to solve this case," I say, "is *with* you. You're the one who suspected foul play from the start. This is your case. I'm just helping you."

"I'm scared, Rory," she says, her big eyes full of fear. "I don't know what to do."

"I'm not sure, either," I say, "but the one thing I know for certain is I can't let you go to jail for a crime you didn't commit."

CHAPTER 61

I TOSS AND turn all night, hardly sleeping. The rash on my fingers itches, but that's the least of the reasons for my sleeplessness. I keep thinking about a plan that would allow Ariana to escape arrest—and whether I should actually go through with the plan or not. When I was talking to Ariana in her house, I felt confident that it was the right thing to do. But in the darkness of night, alone with my thoughts, I can't be sure. Is this just another of my impulsive shoot-first, ask-questions-later solutions? Have I really thought this through?

When the sky starts to turn blue and the sun is on the verge of rising, I'm already up, dressed, and staring out the window at the arroyo and the hills behind Tom and Jessica's property.

I'm taken for a moment by how beautiful the country here is. This land is different from my hometown—browner, drier, more desolate—but it's all Texas.

I love this state and the people in it. I don't want to betray this land I've sworn to protect.

I've stepped over the line before, not doing things by the book, but I've never so blatantly or egregiously broken the law. A Texas Ranger helping a suspected murderer escape from justice—any judge in the state would toss me behind bars and throw away the key.

I consider myself a lawman.

If I go through with this, I'll be an outlaw.

I walk down the stairs, past Jessica's berry bushes, and stand at the back gate of their property. Outside, in the peaceful morning air, I watch the sun peeking up from the horizon and igniting the hills in a brilliant gold light.

I pull out my cell phone.

In the last twenty-four hours, I've missed several calls from Willow. I know I should call her back, but I don't want to talk to her right now. I don't want to lie to her and tell her nothing's going on. But I don't want to worry her, either, so I justify silence as the best strategy.

But there is someone I do want to talk to.

"Hey, Dad," I say when my father picks up. "Did I wake you?"

"Hell no," he says. "Somebody's gotta get up and feed the horses."

He's delighted to hear from me and wants to know when I'm coming home.

"Not any time soon," I say, and I tell him I'm having trouble on the case in Rio Lobo.

I don't get too much into specifics—that might take all day—but I tell him I'm at a crossroads, split between doing what I feel is right and doing what I'm bound to by the law.

My father is quiet for a minute and then he speaks.

"Rory, a Texas Ranger is more than just a government official. More than just a badge and a fancy title. A Texas Ranger is an idea. A higher standard.

A Ranger swears an allegiance to Texas. Not just the state government but Texas itself."

My heart pounds as he puts into words my own thoughts and feelings about the job. It is more than an honor to be a Texas Ranger.

It's a duty.

"A Texas Ranger isn't above the law," Dad adds, "but when the system is broken, when the law isn't working, you have a duty to do what's right. You have a duty to this state and its people. You can't stand idly by and watch a miscarriage of justice. A Texas Ranger *is* justice."

"Thanks, Dad," I say, my voice choked. "That's what I needed to hear."

"I'll be praying for you, Rory. I love you, Son."

"I love you, too, Dad."

My throat feels thick. His words inspire me, but they also make me realize the depth of the trouble I'm about to wade into. I've never been this far over my head. As I say good-bye to my father, I realize I might never see him again.

Or if I do, it might be through three inches of bullet-proof glass in the visiting area of a Texas prison.

CHAPTER 62

BEFORE HEADING TO the police station for the day, I stop over at Tom and Jessica's. Tom is drinking coffee in the kitchen, scrolling through the latest news from the *El Paso Times* on his laptop. Jessica has gone to work already.

He offers me a cup of coffee, but I don't take it. I don't even sit down.

"I've got a favor to ask," I say.

"Sure," he says. "Anything."

"No," I say. "A real favor."

When I explain what it is, he looks as pale as paste.

"That could be dangerous," he says.

I nod.

"And illegal."

"You'd have plausible deniability," I say. "I doubt they could get any charges to stick."

"That may be," he says, "but I happen to believe in *this*." He points to the decorative sign on the wall. His finger is aimed specifically at the life lesson ALWAYS TELL THE TRUTH. "I'm in the business of uncovering the truth, not lying about it. And I'm certainly not in the business of lying to police. Or a jury."

I think about letting it go, telling him to forget

I asked. But I need him. This won't work without him.

I point to the two messages HAVE COURAGE and HELP OTHERS.

"Ariana needs your help, Tom. You said you wanted to get to the bottom of the trouble in Rio Lobo. This is the way. I need you to be brave here."

He runs his hands through his hair, thinking hard about what I'm asking him to do. Finally, he nods and says, "Okay, I'll do it."

"This is the right thing to do," I say. "Even if it isn't legal."

He tries to force a grin. "Tell that to Jessica when she's bringing me pecan pies in prison."

CHAPTER 63

WHEN I GET to the station, the chief and I eye each other suspiciously. Both of us try to look busy—him in his office, me in the makeshift investigation room—but no further work can be done until we get word from the crime lab. I kill time until late morning and then tell the chief I'm heading out to eat some lunch.

I step into Rosalia's—which I've determined is not only the least expensive restaurant in town but also the best—and I spot Alex Hartley, back from El Paso, sitting alone and reading an issue of *Texas Football*. I planned to push off a second interview with him until Ariana's situation is resolved, but seeing him here, I can't help myself.

I sit down across from him without invitation.

"Ranger," he says, looking uncomfortable.

"You lied to me," I say, loud enough for other patrons to hear. "Either you cut the bullshit or I'm going to arrest your ass right here." I lean in closer to him. "You're worried about your reputation in this town. When I walk you down Main Street in handcuffs, what do you think that will do to your reputation?"

"Okay," he says, putting his hands up. "I'm sorry." He looks around at all the eyes on us. "Can we go outside?"

Out in bright sunlight, with the heat coming up off the blacktop parking lot, I say, "You've got erectile dysfunction. You didn't want people to know, so Susan was nice enough to act like an on-again, off-again girlfriend. Right?"

"I've got diabetes," he says. "Pretty bad. Most people don't even know that."

"You were the one who reported McCormack's trucks going through the open space. Why did you do that?"

"I noticed them is all. Why? Does that have something to do with her death?"

"I'll ask the questions," I say.

He stares off down the street. A car goes by and the driver waves to him. That's how it is for the football coach in a Texas town. Everyone knows you.

"Look," he says, contrite. "I'm sorry I wasn't forthcoming. I didn't have anything to do with Susan's death, so I didn't figure it would hurt to lie about my personal details. I swear to God."

The irony isn't lost on me that earlier this morning I was asking someone devoted to the truth to lie and now I'm asking someone comfortable with lying to finally tell the truth.

I have a flash of memory from when I saw him outside Lobo Lizard the night I played there with Walt and Dale.

"What were you doing that night at Lobo Lizard?" I say. "I came outside and you and that other fella looked like you'd been caught with your hands in the cookie jar."

He lets out a long exhale, as if resigning himself to honesty.

"I was buying pot."

"Pot?"

"Yeah," he says. "I buy marijuana for my diabetes. It helps with the pain. I've got a prescription, but there aren't any dispensaries around here."

He tells me he doesn't like to use it at his house. There's no telling who might stop by—assistant coaches, his principal, some of his players—and he doesn't want anyone thinking he's a stoner getting high all the time. He drives out into the open space and uses his vape pen in solitude. That's when he spotted McCormack's trucks, which he didn't think were supposed to drive through there, and he mentioned it in passing to Susan.

I could arrest him for his admission of buying marijuana—as well as obstructing justice by lying to me—but I've got bigger problems on my plate. And what's he really guilty of? Worrying too much about what people think of him.

"The last guy to pretend he had a relationship with Susan Snyder ended up dead," I say to him. "So don't go keeping any more secrets from me."

I head back toward the restaurant, but before I make it through the door, I get a call from Liz at the dispatch desk.

"Come on back. Chief says he's got the lab results."

I climb into my truck. Before starting the engine, I send two text messages from my burner phone. One to Tom Aaron. One to Ariana Delgado. With those two texts, I'm now breaking the law.

It's official.

I'm an outlaw.

Even if no one knows it yet.

CHAPTER 64

I WALK INTO his office without a word. He doesn't tell me the results, just hands the papers to me so I can see for myself. I scan the reports without sitting down.

There's no equivocation about what the tests revealed, nothing inconclusive.

Everything points to Ariana.

The 30-06 round that passed through Skip Barnes's head was fired from Ariana's M1 Garand. The hair strand I took from the top of the oil derrick is also a genetic match for Ariana. With her fingerprints on the shell casing, that makes three significant pieces of forensic evidence that all point to Ariana as the shooter who killed Skip Barnes.

I set the papers down on Harris's desk. He stares at me. I know he's ready for me to argue. He's known since we found the gun that this moment would come, and I'd argue until I was blue in the face that this is a setup.

Instead, I take a different tactic.

"Do you really think she did it?" I say, my voice as calm and submissive as I can make it.

The tension in his posture seems to lessen.

"I don't know," he says. "But what would you do if this wasn't Ariana? If this was someone you didn't know?"

I act like I'm thinking about his question. I sit down in the chair across from his desk, and he does the same on the other side.

"Under ordinary circumstances," I say, "I would arrest her. This is enough evidence to keep her in jail while we try to fill in the gaps in the investigation."

If Ariana is arrested, it's not as if the work on the case would be finished. We would need to look for witnesses, conduct interviews, continue looking for evidence. Ariana said she went for a run that morning. We would need to find witnesses who could contradict her statement—or verify it. This is a small town. Someone probably saw her running. Or, if she did drive out to McCormack's ranch, then someone probably saw her in a vehicle.

If this was anyone but Ariana, I would assume the person is guilty based on the evidence we already have. I would continue to work to make sure the case is as solid as possible. But I would like to think that if I found holes in the case, if witnesses did claim to see her running on the arroyo, I wouldn't ignore the possibility that Ariana might be innocent. I wouldn't cherry-pick my facts and use only the ones that support a case against a suspect.

I explain all this to Harris as clearly as I can, how I would ordinarily arrest the suspect at this point because I would be confident that our continued investigation would not weaken our case, only make it stronger.

"In this case," I say to Harris, "I feel certain that once we really dig into this thing, we'll find holes.

We'll find problems. We'll get to the bottom of the setup. We're going to end up letting her go. So let's just skip the part where we look like jackasses a week from now or a month from now. Let's refrain from making a bad arrest."

To Harris's credit, he doesn't get angry with me. We talk about this like two professionals, weighing the pros and cons, discussing what the best next step is. In the end, he finds the flaw in my argument. Essentially, I'm saying that if this was anyone else, I would arrest the person, and the only reason I don't want to arrest Ariana is that I know, in my heart, that she didn't do it, despite all evidence to the contrary.

"Do you hear yourself, Rory?" he says. "We can't just ignore the facts and say, 'Oh, but I know her. She would never do this.' I don't like the idea of arresting her any more than you do. She's my detective, for Christ's sake. But we can't let her walk around free when everything points to her being a murderer."

"All right," I say. "But before we go arrest her, Chief, let me make a promise to you. I know this is a setup. You're either a pawn or a participant. If it turns out you're a pawn, that's forgivable, I guess, but it means you're inept as a police chief. If it turns out she's innocent—and it *will* turn out she's innocent—then you're signing your own fate. When the smoke clears on this thing, no one in Rio Lobo will ever trust you again."

He's simmering mad, but I don't stop. All amiability between us is gone.

"That's the best you can hope for," I say. "If you turn out to be a participant—and therefore corrupt—I'll make sure you live in prison until you're a very old man."

He glares at me.

"A month from now," I say, "you're going to be either out of a job or in jail."

"You Texas Rangers," he snarls. "You don't know what it's like to maintain the peace in a town like this, to earn the respect of the people. You bounce from place to place, acting like you're better than everyone. But this is my town, not yours. I was here long before you showed up, and I'll be chief of police here long after you're gone."

"We'll see," I say.

"Yes, we will."

We sit in silence, the hostility between us heating the room like a furnace.

"Okay," I say finally, rising out of my seat, "let's go arrest our girl. We'll do it together."

This was an argument I was never going to win. But I knew that going in. It wasn't my real intention to persuade Harris. What I was really doing was stalling.

Giving Tom and Ariana some time.

Hopefully it was enough.

CHAPTER 65

ARIANA PEEKS BETWEEN the blinds at the police car sitting in front of her house. The officer behind the wheel is Hank Humphreys, a young kid and nice enough guy. He and Ariana have always been friendly to each other, but he'll arrest her in a heartbeat if that's what John Grady Harris wants.

If she snuck out the back door, she might be able to make it, but she doubts it. Hank has his window rolled down, and even if he couldn't see her, he might hear her. Her back door always squeaks, and the fence gate at the rear of the lot is even worse.

Rory told her to wait for the distraction.

Whatever that is going to be.

She spots Tom Aaron walking up the street with a reporter's notebook in hand. He heads toward the police car, and Hank Humphreys steps out. Tom holds his notebook in front of him, ready to write. Ariana can't tell what's being said, but she can get the gist from their actions. Tom is asking Hank questions, which the officer is refusing to answer.

This is it, she thinks. This is the distraction.

She heads toward the back of the house and eases

out the door. It squeaks, but she doesn't think Hank notices—she can hear him in a heated discussion with Tom. At the back of her property is a short wooden fence, separating her yard from the arroyo. She's afraid to open the gate—it's even more noisy—so she puts one hand on a post and vaults over it, landing deftly in the dirt path on the other side.

She walks quickly down the trail. The water in the ditch next to her is brown and slow-moving. When she gets to a point where she can see around her house, she spots Tom and Hank talking furiously.

"So you are not denying that Detective Delgado is a suspect in the murder of Skip Barnes?" Tom says, sounding more aggressive in the interview than she's ever heard him.

"I ain't denying nothing," Hank says, flustered. "I ain't confirming nothing neither. I'm saying you need to talk to Chief Harris."

Ariana loses sight of them when she steps behind her neighbor's house. She takes off running. She moves at the same pace she would if she was out for a morning run. If anyone sees her, they might not suspect anything is amiss. She doesn't usually run in jeans and boots—and not at noontime on a summer day when the temperature is so high—but hopefully no one will notice anything unusual.

A few blocks away, she arrives at the back of Tom and Jessica's house. Her body is slick with sweat, her jeans and T-shirt sticking to her skin.

She lets herself in the gate and approaches the outbuilding that houses Tom's garage and Rory's apartment. She creeps around the side next to the berry bushes and arrives at the garage bays. The Land Cruiser and Mustang sit inside. She checks the Land

Cruiser, and sure enough the keys are in the ignition just like Rory said they would be.

She fires up the engine, applies the clutch, shifts it into gear, and tries to ease the Cruiser forward. The engine stalls, and she has to start over. Everything about the vehicle is tough. There are no power brakes, so she feels like she's working out her calf muscles pressing down on the pedal. And there's no power steering, so she has to wrestle with the wheel.

Finally, she pulls the Land Cruiser around the house and stops at the edge of the street. Not fifty yards away, Chief Harris's cruiser is headed her way, with Rory in the passenger seat.

"Oh, shit," Ariana says, ducking down.

After the cruiser passes, she peeks up over the dash. It begins to slow down as it approaches her house. Ariana puts the Land Cruiser in gear and turns onto the street, heading the other way.

Her hands tremble as she shifts gears.

She's a fugitive.

"Rory," she says aloud, "I sure hope you know what the hell you're doing."

CHAPTER 66

CHIEF HARRIS ROLLS his police cruiser to a stop in front of Ariana's house. Tom Aaron is on the sidewalk, engaged in an argument with the patrolman stationed out front.

When we exit the car, Tom approaches the chief, hammering him with questions.

"Chief, is it true that Detective Delgado is a suspect in the murder of Skip Barnes? Is she also a suspect in the death of Susan Snyder? Are you here to arrest her? What kind—"

"Tom!" Harris says, practically shouting. "What the hell are you doing here? How did you hear about Ariana?"

"So it is true," Tom says, making a note.

"You didn't answer my question," Harris says.

"You haven't answered mine."

Harris huffs. "Answer mine and I'll answer yours."

"I'm a journalist," Tom says. "I have my sources. You know I can't reveal them."

Harris glares at me, accusing me without saying a word.

"Don't look at me," I say, holding my hands up.

It feels weird—wrong—to lie to a member of law enforcement, but compared to what I've already done, this is a small transgression.

The chief turns back to Tom. "Yes, Ariana is a suspect in the murder of Skip Barnes. No, she is not a suspect in the death of Susan Snyder—which we still believe was accidental," he adds.

"Are you here to arrest Ariana?" Tom asks.

The chief nods toward the point-and-shoot camera hanging around Tom's neck.

"Get your camera ready," Harris says. "Maybe you'll find out."

With that, Harris and I approach Ariana's front door. He knocks forcefully. No noise comes from inside the house. It's the kind of silence that feels like absence. You can tell no one's home.

"Shit," Harris snaps, drawing his gun.

"I'll go around back," I say, and before he can agree or disagree with my plan, I take off.

A minute later, I hear Harris kick in the front door with a loud bang. The back door is unlocked, and I let myself in. Harris and I meet halfway in the house, in the living room where Ariana and I sat last night. When we've cleared every room and found no sign of her, Harris holsters his gun and stares at me.

"Let me see your phone," he sneers.

"Why?"

"I want to see if you warned her."

I hand over my cell. Not the burner phone—that one is hidden under the seat in my truck. He scrolls through my calls and texts, seeing the only call I made today was early in the morning.

"Whose number is this?" he says.

"My dad."

He thrusts the phone back to me and then gets in my face.

"Did you have something to do with this?" he says, his teeth clenched. "You're in some serious shit if you did."

Instead of answering, I say, "We better call the highway patrol. There aren't but a handful of ways out of this part of the county. If we hurry, they can get roadblocks up."

He doesn't stop glowering at me.

"She could still be on foot," I say, acting like his glare isn't bothering me. "You ought to get your patrol officers doing sweeps around town. We've got work to do, Chief. Let's get to it."

Finally, he looks away and storms out of the house. I follow, keeping back far enough that when Tom starts snapping pictures of the chief walking out looking furious, I won't get in the frame.

"Go home, Tom!" Harris roars, pointing his arm down the street toward Tom's house.

An hour later, back at the station, Harris and I have reported the fugitive to the highway patrol and the county sheriff's office, and we've got the local patrol officers searching the Rio Lobo streets and neighborhoods. Harris took a break at one point to go into his office and make a private phone call. I assumed he was calling to update McCormack. Afterward, he seemed in better spirits, and I noticed out the window that suddenly several of McCormack's trucks were driving up and down the road.

I have a feeling that McCormack, or whoever Harris talked to, told him that this might be good news. Putting Ariana on trial would always have been problematic. It might have called attention to the crimes and could have blown up in their faces—whoever *they* are. But if McCormack's men can find her before the police do, then Ariana might not live long enough to face trial.

It dawns on me that we might have done exactly what they were hoping. Ariana fleeing arrest might have been part of their plan all along.

Harris and I are talking by the front desk—pretending as if we trust each other and are on the same side—when Tom Aaron walks into the front lobby.

"Go away, Tom!" Harris shouts. "I'm not telling you any more information."

"It's not about the article," Tom says, looking embarrassed. "I'm here to report a crime."

Harris frowns.

"My Land Cruiser has been stolen."

This was always a part of the plan, a way for Tom to keep his involvement hidden. If Ariana took his vehicle and he never reported it, that would signal Tom's involvement. But if he reports it stolen, that makes him look a little more innocent.

Unfortunately, reporting the theft has its drawbacks for Ariana.

Harris looks at me and can't hide a grin.

"Now we know what she's driving," he says.

CHAPTER 67

ARIANA SITS AT the bank of the river where she and Rory went swimming. It was only three days ago that she and Rory stripped off their clothes and dove in. Now, sitting under the same oak tree where Rory hung his gun belt, Ariana is cold, alone, and scared.

She's also ashamed. She took an oath to uphold the law. Now she's broken it—both the law and her oath.

It's after midnight, and the desert air has grown cold. She thought about building a fire, but she didn't want to risk anyone seeing it. It's not unheard of for high schoolers to come out here and party or make out. There is no sense drawing attention to herself.

But the darkness sure makes the experience of being a fugitive even more lonely. She didn't think to pack herself a sleeping bag or change of clothes, not even a long-sleeved shirt. She didn't bring any food, either, and now her stomach rumbles.

A beam of light cuts through the blackness, and Ariana spots a vehicle making its way toward her on the bumpy dirt road. She hides behind the tree and listens as the vehicle pulls up just on the other side of it.

"Ariana!" a voice calls out. "It's Rory."

She comes from around the tree, and Rory climbs out of his F-150. She throws her arms around him—she can't help herself—and he holds her in a tight hug. She wants to sob into his chest, but she holds back the tears. This is Rory, the guy who thought she would make a good Texas Ranger. She doesn't want to behave like a scared little girl.

"I brought you some food," he says. "Hungry?"

"Starving."

The two of them sit down to eat in the same spot where they had lunch. Rory brought her a sandwich from the grocery store in town. She can tell on the first bite that he ordered the sandwich just the way she does. She's surprised he could remember the specifics. That attention to detail must be what makes him a good detective.

"Where's the Land Cruiser?" Rory asks.

She hid it in a canyon about a half mile away. It's a little more out of sight than here, and she thought it was a good idea not to stay too close to it. When Rory texted her that she should sneak down the arroyo and steal Tom Aaron's Land Cruiser—the keys would be in it—he'd asked her to meet him tonight at their place. He hadn't been specific, but she'd known what he meant.

Now he fills her in on the results of the lab tests, as well as all the efforts within a hundred miles of Rio Lobo to make sure she doesn't escape.

"You think they'll come looking out here in the open space?" she asks.

"I bet McCormack will send his men out here," Rory says. "Tomorrow, during daylight, you'll want to keep your head down."

The moonlight reflects on the water. Rory's face

is illuminated just enough to reveal the worry in his expression.

"What have we done, Rory?"

"We did what we had to."

"What are we going to do now?"

She can't hide the desperation in her voice. She can't believe she's in this situation.

Rory tries to reassure her by saying he's going to report to the station tomorrow like it's business as usual. He's going to keep investigating, and Ariana just needs to stay in hiding long enough for him to find a break in the case.

"You know it's just a matter of time before they try to get you out of the picture, don't you?"

"I hope they do," he says. "That might give us the break we need. If McCormack sends some guys after me, like he did at my motel room, maybe I can capture one of them this time."

"That's a dangerous game, Rory."

"I need something to convince a judge to give us a search warrant for the ranch. I'm sure we'd find something useful if we could just get out there and look around."

"I appreciate you saying *we,* Rory, but you're on your own now."

"Just hang in there, Ariana. We'll get through this."

Rory opens up the storage box on his truck and pulls out a sleeping bag for Ariana. Inside the cab of his truck, he has a grocery bag of canned goods and water bottles.

"This ought to last you a couple of days," he says, "but I plan on coming out again tomorrow night."

"Can you stay a little longer tonight?" Ariana asks, hating the sound of fear in her voice.

They sit back down, and Ariana wraps the sleeping bag around her shoulders. She's shivering, but she thinks it's more from fear than the cold. Still, Rory scoots closer to her and puts an arm around her shoulders—to warm her or comfort her, or both. Being so near him makes her heart speed up and her stomach do flips. She leans her head into the crook of his neck. She can feel his stubble on her forehead. She wonders what he would do if she tried to kiss him.

Would he kiss her back?

She tried to maintain her professional distance from him when he first arrived in town, but the more she got to know him—as a detective and a man—the more she liked him.

She tries to push away her feelings. He has a girlfriend. It wouldn't be appropriate. But at a moment like this—with her whole world on the verge of collapse—who can say what's appropriate and what isn't?

They might both be going to jail before this is all over.

They might both be killed.

If they're going to die tomorrow, what harm would it do to kiss him today?

CHAPTER 68

I CAN FEEL Ariana's warmth against my body, feel her hair on my cheek, smell her natural, intoxicating scent. I know our lives are in complete turmoil right now, but I can't help but think about what it would be like to kiss her. I even picture us stripping down, like we did two days ago at this same spot, only this time we wouldn't dive into the water. We would dive into each other, the moonlight dancing on our skin.

I know I have a girlfriend, but not only does she seem a million miles away but our relationship seems like it happened a lifetime ago. I feel so incredibly distant from Willow, so removed.

There's no way Willow and I can survive her living in Nashville and me living in Texas. And if I'm finally honest with myself, there's no way I'm moving to Tennessee to work in law enforcement there. I'm a Ranger. Texas is where I belong. As long as I can draw breath into my lungs, I want that air to be Texas air.

The right thing to do is to tell Willow that I'm interested in someone else. I need to break things off before I start anything with Ariana. The problem is Ariana and I might be dead before I ever get that chance.

If I don't kiss her now—or soon—I might never be able to.

But still, it doesn't feel right. Willow deserves better.

"I should go," I say.

She sits up and looks at me, her big eyes as beautiful in the moonlight as they are in the daylight.

"You're probably right," she says. "You better go before we do something we might regret."

I stare at her, take in what she's saying. She does like me the way I like her.

"When this is all over," I say, "I'm going to sit down with Willow and—"

She shakes her head and interrupts me. "Don't tell me," she says. "Let's just focus on getting out of this mess. If we're not dead or in jail when this is all over, then we can talk about it."

I lean forward and kiss her gently on the forehead.

"Take care of yourself," I say. "I'll try to visit again tomorrow night."

To get back to town, I take a meandering route. I did the same thing when I drove out to the open space. At that time, I didn't want to be followed. Now I want to misdirect anyone who might spot me on the road. I end up coming back into town from the opposite direction of the open space. I pass a patrol car and one of McCormack's trucks, and I feel certain that the people inside are immediately calling their bosses to report where they saw me driving.

I tell myself that I'll need to have an excuse ready for Harris tomorrow. My explanation will be simple: I couldn't sleep, so I wanted to drive around looking as well.

He won't believe it, but hopefully my misdirection won't tip my hand that Ariana is out in the open space.

When I finally climb the stairs to my apartment, it's not far from dawn. I'm dog tired, having hardly slept in days, and I crash down on the bed still wearing my clothes and boots. I tell myself that I'll just rest for a moment before getting undressed, but before I can get up, I'm adrift in a sea of blackness.

Out of the darkness comes a dream.

I'm back in the bank. This time, the robbers are Gareth McCormack and his father. And this time they take a hostage. It's Ariana. Carson holds his gun to her head while Gareth, up on the bank counter, aims the AR-15 at me.

When he opens fire, I jerk awake in a cold sweat.

Bright daylight floods in from the window. My mouth is dry, as if I'm hungover. I feel like I can still hear the *bang, bang, bang* of the rifle, but then I realize it's someone pounding on my door.

"Rory," Jessica Aaron calls, her voice tense. "Open up. I want to talk to you. You had no right to rope Tom into your troubles."

CHAPTER 69

AS I OPEN the door, Tom is running up the stairs to intercept Jessica.

"Now, Jess," he says, "leave Rory alone. It was my choice. If you want to be mad at someone, it should be me."

She ignores him and scowls at me. But there's something in what she sees that takes some of the anger out of her expression.

"You look like hell," she says to me. "Did you sleep in those clothes?"

"It's been a rough couple of days," I tell her. "I'm sorry about asking Tom to get involved. I just didn't know what else to do."

She exhales loudly. It seems she came here ready to fight, but my apology preempted her. More than that, my haggard appearance—which I'm certain includes puffy eyes, unshaven cheeks, unwashed hair—seems to give her a level of understanding of the pressure I'm under that no words could convey.

"Come in," I say. "We can talk if you'd like."

"No," she says. "You get yourself cleaned up and ready for the day. Then come down and I'll make you breakfast. We'll talk there."

As she walks back down the stairs, Tom says softly, "Sorry. I had to tell her. We don't keep secrets from each other."

"I would never ask you to lie to your wife," I say, thinking about what I'm keeping from Willow.

I take a quick shower, run a razor over my stubble, and put on clean clothes. I pin my star to my shirt, wrap my gun belt around my waist, and position my Stetson on my head. I was groggy when I woke up, but now I'm awake and ready.

I've got to get to work and get this case solved. No one else is going to do it. The responsibility falls on my shoulders.

When I walk into Tom and Jessica's house, Jessica sets a plate of huevos rancheros on the table and tells me to sit. I didn't realize how hungry I was until I saw the food. I brought Ariana a sandwich last night, but I forgot to eat dinner myself.

Tom has already begun eating. He seems more demure than normal, but I know he's in the hot seat and doesn't want to upset his wife more than he already has. As for Jessica, her anger seems to have dissipated.

"So," she says, "is our girl okay?"

"You really want to know?" I ask. "The more you know, the more trouble you could get into."

"I was mad before," she says, "but Tom's right. Helping her was the right thing to do. There's no way she killed that roustabout Skip Barnes, may he rest in peace. It doesn't make a bit of sense why she would."

As she talks, she goes to the oven and pulls out a tray of warmed sopapillas. She places them on the table with a jar of honey.

"To tell you the truth," she says, "I think I was more upset that y'all went behind my back. Y'all didn't include me. I wish there was something I could do to help Ariana, too."

I swallow my bite and tell her there is something she can do. "I was going to ask Tom, but if you're willing, you two can do it together."

I explain that I need to go to the station and pretend like I'm working with Chief Harris. Business as usual. But I need someone to go up and down the street that Ariana lives on—the same one Tom and Jessica live on—and ask the neighbors if they saw anything suspicious the day Skip Barnes was shot.

"Someone stole Ariana's rifle, killed Skip with it, and then returned the gun. I need to find a witness who spotted something unusual going on. A strange car in front of her house. A person walking to the door or going around back. Something. Anything to go on."

I suggest they do it together, but Tom says that he has something he wants to look into at the office.

"What?" I ask.

"I don't want to say yet," he says. "It's probably nothing. Just a wild idea. But if Jessica can handle canvassing the neighborhood, I'd like to do some digging."

I tell Jessica that if anyone from the police department asks what she's doing, she should tell them that she's acting of her own volition, trying to understand what Ariana was arrested for.

"Don't say I sent you," I say. "It's for your own protection. If I end up getting arrested for all this, the last thing I want is for you two to get into any trouble."

When we're finished talking, I thank Jessica for the meal—delicious as always—and, more importantly, for her help.

"I'm sorry to get you two involved in this," I say, "but there's something rotten in this town, and I'm going to find out what it is."

"You better," Jessica says. "We're in it now, too. There's a lot more on the line than just your badge, Rory."

CHAPTER 70

"YOU'RE LATE," HARRIS says when I walk into the police station.

He's standing at the front counter, waiting for me. When I open my mouth to make an excuse as to why I'm arriving to work at almost noon, he cuts me off.

"You're out, Rory. Pack up your things and get out of my police station."

"What?"

All of the employees in the station are staring at us. Harris is relishing this. If he was going to try to kick me off the case, he could have done it in his office. He wanted an audience.

"I talked to the Rangers," Harris says. "You're off the case. They're sending in someone to replace you."

My stomach sinks. So this is how McCormack—or whoever is behind all this—is going to take me out of the equation. They killed Skip Barnes. They framed Ariana for murder. But me? They simply had Harris call the Rangers and complain.

It makes the most sense, actually. If they killed me, the full power of the Texas Rangers would descend onto this little town. But now they will only have to contend with one Ranger, someone who might wrap up the case quicker.

"You're making a mistake, Chief."

"The only mistake I made was ever allowing you into my town in the first place. You've been stirring up trouble since you got here."

I shouldn't say what I'm about to, but I want everyone in this station to hear it.

"I wasn't sure if you were in on it, Chief. Not until now. You should be in that jail cell over there instead of wearing a badge."

"Listen here, Yates," Harris says, approaching me and staring me down. His muscles bulge in his tight uniform. "I want you out of this town by sundown. I don't ever want to see you again."

I say nothing, just let my stare do the talking for me. But it's not working. He's not intimidated. He's got me. Or at least he thinks he does.

"And if I find out you're aiding and abetting Ariana," he says, "I'll make sure you never wear this again." With that, he flicks the tin star on my chest.

I turn to leave. When I'm at the door, I stop and ask, "Who are they sending to replace me, Chief? Tell me that much."

"They're sending in the big guns," Harris says. "Your lieutenant, Hendricks, volunteered to come clean up your mess."

I should have known. Kyle sent me on this fool's errand in the first place. Now he's going to make sure I play the fool. He'll declare Susan Snyder's death an accident, and he'll put his stamp of approval on Harris's decision to arrest Ariana for the murder of Skip Barnes.

End of story.

Kyle Hendricks isn't corrupt, but he's the perfect puppet to bring in to put an end to this investigation. He won't be in town twenty-four hours before he declares the cases closed and heads home. And life in Rio Lobo will be back to normal.

Which is just what the person —or people—who killed Susan Snyder and Skip Barnes want.

"Oh, and Rory," Harris says as I'm about to leave, "if I see you in Rio Lobo after sunset tonight, I'm going to arrest you for interfering with a police investigation. I'll put the cuffs on you myself. You'll never wear that tin star again."

CHAPTER 71

ARIANA HEARS THE whine of four-wheelers making their way through the desert hills.

Those are McCormack's men, she thinks. *Looking for me.*

She spent most of the morning trying to hide the Land Cruiser by throwing tumbleweed and other kinds of brush on top of it. The camouflage wouldn't bear close inspection, but from the vantage point of an ATV cruising by, the vehicle might be pretty well hidden.

Now she does the same with her possessions, tucking her sleeping bag and canned goods into a hiding spot in a clump of sagebrush. She hides behind the oak tree next to the river as she hears the four-wheelers get closer. They are so near she can make out voices.

"Where to now?" someone calls, shouting to be heard over the idling motors.

"Let's go down by the river."

"Shit," Ariana whispers.

She's hidden from view where she is, but if they come closer, she doubts she can stay out of sight. She looks around, frantic to find a hiding spot.

The only place she can think of is the river itself.

She creeps to the water's edge. Fully clothed, she

lowers herself over the cut bank that she and Rory jumped off a few days ago. The cold water embraces her, and she drops down out of sight just as the ATVs pull up next to the tree.

The cut bank creates an overhang, and she backs as far into its shadow as she can. Tree roots twine into the water around her and she grabs one to stay afloat without kicking her feet. The smell of moist earth fills her nostrils. A spider crawls through her hair, and she fights the urge to brush it away. She can't afford to make any sudden movements.

"These tire tracks look pretty fresh," a man says.

"Probably kids coming out here to go swimming," another replies.

"You guys want to take a smoke break?" someone says, and then they shut off the engines.

It sounds like there are two ATVs, maybe as many as four guys. Ariana can hear them setting objects down on the ATVs or leaning them against trees— metal objects that she imagines are guns.

One of the men approaches, so close to Ariana that when a clump of dirt falls into the water from his boot step, it passes only inches from her face. She hears a zipping noise, and a few seconds later, a jet of urine comes down from above, splashing into the water.

Ariana turns her face in disgust.

"You ever seen this girl we're looking for?" the man urinating says.

Some of the others have, some of them haven't.

"She's a knockout," the guy says, finishing and zipping up.

Ariana's arm is starting to cramp. She feels another insect crawling on her forehead. She closes her eyes, breathes through her nose.

The men smoke for a few more minutes, talking about what they'd like to do to Ariana if they find her. Hearing the disgusting things they say makes Ariana appreciate Rory even more. He's as tough as they come, but she's sure he would never talk about a woman this way, not even if he was in the company of only men.

Ariana feels something against her neck, and she glances down to see the head of a snake making a tunnel through her hair as it slithers out into the river. Her body goes cold from head to toe, and she bites her lip to keep from screaming. She nearly faints with relief as the tip of its tail slides out of her hair.

The snake, about three feet long and the texture of rough bark, is an olive-green color with dark vertical bars along its sides. The snake glides atop the water, its undulating body propelling it forward.

"Hey, check out this snake," one of McCormack's men says.

Another one laughs and says, "Watch this."

The air is filled with explosions of automatic gunfire. The sound is deafening, and Ariana nearly shrieks in surprise. Spouts of water burst into the air as the bullets rain down into the river. The snake disappears, leaving only a trace of blood in the water.

The men howl with laughter. Gun smoke hovers over the surface of the river like morning mist.

"All right," one of the men says finally. "Fun's over. Let's go find that pretty little cop and see if we can't make her disappear like that snake."

McCormack's men start pitching their cigarette butts into the water, each one making a hissing noise as the water extinguishes the embers. Ariana exhales in relief as she hears the ATVs come to life. The engines whine loudly as they drive off into the hills. She waits until she can no longer hear them before she swims out into the water and finds a place to climb out that isn't so steep. She lies on her back in the dirt, taking deep breaths and trying to calm her nerves.

Her wet clothes cling to her body as she sits up to pull her boots off and dump the water out. She's in the midst of pulling her socks off and wringing them out when she hears something and freezes. She stares toward the hills, alert.

It's the whine of the four-wheelers.

They're coming back this way.

CHAPTER 72

I STOP MY truck down by the river at the park in Rio Lobo where Ariana and I once had lunch. I stare out at the water, glimmering in the sunlight, and try to think. A father with two toddlers is having a picnic on the grass. A woman fly-fishes out in the water.

My heart keeps racing, and I don't know how to slow it down. I'm up to my neck in some serious shit, and I don't know how to find my way out. Getting kicked off the case—getting kicked out of town—isn't something I was expecting. Now I don't know what to do.

My phone buzzes on the passenger seat, and I see that it's Dale Peters calling. I don't answer. The last thing I need right now is to explain to him why I can't jam tonight or play another gig at Lobo Lizard.

I've already made up my mind that I'll head out to the open space tonight and camp with Ariana. Then I'll really be a fugitive, hiding out with a wanted murderer. But after that, what happens next? How can we possibly solve these crimes if we can't show our faces in town?

My phone buzzes again, and I expect it to be another call from Dale. But it's not.

It's Willow.

I pick up. I've ignored her calls long enough, and I don't know when I'll be able to talk to her again.

"Where've you been, Rory?" she asks. "You've got me worried sick."

"I'm sorry," I say. "Things aren't going so well here."

"Tell me what's going on."

"It's a long story."

"I've got time."

I debate about how much to tell her. I remember Tom Aaron saying that he and Jessica don't keep secrets. I don't want to lie to Willow, but I also don't want to worry her. And then there's the issue of Ariana. How I feel about her. How she feels about me.

I don't want to lead Willow on. But I sure as hell don't want to break her heart over the telephone.

"I don't want to keep you," I say. "I'm sure you need to get to a meeting with your publicist or a last-minute recording session or something."

"I've got all the time in the world, darling. My schedule's clear today. You're my number one priority."

Hearing her say this makes my heart ache. Do I really want to break up with Willow? As I ask myself the question, I realize there are two answers. The first is no, I don't *want* to break up with her. The other answer, though, is that I *need* to break up with her.

Living apart isn't working. We can't be each other's priorities. I can't be the boyfriend Willow deserves. Maybe I'll find happiness with Ariana and maybe I won't, but either way, I need to let Willow go so she can follow her dreams.

"Look, Willow," I say, "when I get everything straightened out here, I think we need to sit down and have a long talk. About us."

I half expect her to make a joke and defuse the tension by saying, *Are you breaking up with me?* But she doesn't, which is even worse. It means she knows what's coming and it's no laughing matter.

"You're right," she says. "We need to figure this out."

The tone in her voice tells me she's thinking what I'm thinking—this relationship just isn't working anymore.

An awkward silence hangs in the air, and it occurs to me that if I'm going to break the law and go into hiding with Ariana, it might be a long time before Willow and I can have this conversation. And the truth is I could be killed before I ever get to see Willow again. I don't want our last conversation to end this way, with both of us feeling uncomfortable knowing that we're not right for each other.

"Willow," I say, "what I've got to do over the next day or two might be pretty dangerous."

"You're scaring me, Rory."

"I'm sorry. But if anything happens to me, I want you to know how much I love you."

She tells me she loves me, too, but I'm not finished with what I have to say.

"You met me at a difficult point in my life," I say. "But you aren't just some rebound girl I've been using to get through a hard time. I think we both know where this relationship is headed, but if something happens, if I don't live long enough to have that conversation with you, please know I love you with all my heart and soul. I honestly can't imagine loving anyone more than I love you."

I can hear her crying on the other end. She knows what my ex-wife, Anne, meant to me before she died. For me to admit that I love Willow as much as or more than her is a surprise even to me.

But it's the truth.

I realize it as I'm saying it.

It's just that maybe soul mates don't always get to live happily ever after.

Maybe some soul mates only get a brief, burning romance as they pass in the darkness, like two shooting stars going in opposite directions.

CHAPTER 73

I PULL INTO the parking lot at the *Rio Lobo Record* and go inside to see Tom Aaron. I find him sitting behind his desk, with a handful of hardback books open around him, each page filled with black-and-white pictures.

"Find anything?" I say, startling him.

He closes the book he's looking at with a snap.

"Sorry," I say. "Didn't mean to catch you off guard."

He asks me to sit and starts to tell me about the hunch he's been following.

"At a small-town paper like this," he says, "it's common practice to keep each consecutive school yearbook. They can be a consistent resource for background information about people."

I page through one of the open books, noticing that the volume contains information about students from kindergarten through grade twelve.

"Your hunch was to look at old yearbooks?" I say, surprised. "What were you looking for?"

"I wasn't sure," he says. "But Susan Snyder went to school here. So did Skip Barnes. And Gareth McCormack. Even Carson McCormack grew up in this town back in the day. Most local people have contacts that well predate my arrival."

His logic is sound. In fact, I wish I'd thought of it. You never know what you might find browsing through old records like this.

"Did you find anything?"

"Maybe," he says, "although it isn't what I was expecting."

He opens one volume to a page of black-and-white photos. The heading at the top of the page says HOME-COMING, and the photos all show high school kids hanging out at a dance. Their clothing and hairstyles seem about ten or twelve years old. Maybe a little more recent than when I went to high school, but not that much.

"Recognize anyone?" Tom asks.

My eyes scan the pictures from top to bottom, and when I reach the last photo, I feel an instant recognition. A young Ariana Delgado is pictured dancing with a handsome young man. She looks younger, not quite as tough as the Ariana I know, but she is every bit as pretty as the woman she's grown up to be.

She has a smile on her face and is looking up into the eyes of a boy. She's obviously smitten.

"You recognize who she's with?" Tom asks.

"No."

The view of the boy isn't quite as clear. The picture shows more of Ariana's face than his. Just some small-town boy.

"That's Gareth McCormack," Tom says.

I pick up the book for a closer look.

"I'll be damned."

The long hair is gone. The beard. The boy in the picture appears fit but not nearly as muscled as Gareth. Though if I examine the face in profile, I can see the resemblance. The boy in the picture exudes confidence. Ariana is looking up at him dreamily, but the boy isn't looking at her with quite the same affection. He has a cool air of indifference. He likes her, I can tell that, but not in the way she likes him.

She looks like a girl in love.

He looks like a guy trying to get laid.

Or maybe I'm just trying to project meaning onto his long-ago expression based on who I now know him to be. I feel sick to my stomach. Not just to see her dancing with him. But to see the way she is gazing at him.

"Did she ever mention that they dated?" Tom asks.

"Were they dating?" I say. "Or did they share one dance and the photographer happened to get a good picture?"

He points to the text along the side of the page, a list of the Homecoming Court. Ariana Delgado and Gareth McCormack were the Homecoming queen and king.

"This doesn't mean anything," I say. "This was more than ten years ago."

"You're probably right," he says. "But these details are worth your attention."

I sit back in the seat and flip through the book. Gareth looks to have been a star athlete in football, basketball, and baseball, as well as student body president. Beyond the Homecoming photo, Ariana's presence at the school is undetectable—except for her listing among students with NO PICTURE AVAILABLE. I flip back to the picture of her and Gareth. It's stupid to feel jealous, but when you meet someone you really like, you can't believe she could ever have been interested in someone completely unlike you.

And there couldn't be two people more different than me and Gareth McCormack.

And why would Ariana not mention to me this past connection?

From the start of this investigation, Ariana asked me always to be honest with her, never to keep her in the dark. But she was keeping something from me all along.

Tom Aaron looks at me gravely. "How confident are you that Ariana isn't caught up in this somehow?"

CHAPTER 74

AFTER TALKING TO Tom, I climb into my truck and see another missed call from Dale Peters. I ignore it and head over to Tom and Jessica's house, where I find Jessica in the garden, pruning rose bushes.

"I went up and down the street," she says. "I knocked on every door. No one saw anything."

"Damn it," I say, flopping into one of the lawn chairs and taking off my hat.

I feel like that was my last chance to find some viable information before heading out of town. I run my fingers through my hair.

"How's your rash doing?" she asks.

I look at my hands. The rash hasn't spread, but it hasn't gone away, either.

"Still itches," I say. "My mind's just too preoccupied to notice."

"Any luck getting to the bottom of what's going on?"

"No," I say. "In fact, I've been kicked off the case. The chief's running me out of town. I just broke the news to your husband."

"You're not leaving, are you?"

Jessica's concern is palpable and reconfirms that I

need to answer her question—by staying and getting to the bottom of this.

When I first arrived in town, the people here treated me with distrust. Some of them were openly disrespectful. But since then, it seems like the community has warmed up to me. People are nicer in restaurants. Some wave when I drive by. And a few of them, like Jessica and Tom, I've gotten to know pretty well. Good people who just want what's best for this community.

"I'm not going anywhere, Jessica," I say, rising from my seat. "But I can't stay at your place anymore."

"Where are you going to sleep tonight?"

"Better you don't know."

It doesn't take me long to pack up my belongings. When I come back down carrying my duffel bag and guitar case, Jessica gives me a hug and hands me a paper sack full of food.

"Share that with Ariana if you see her," she says.

"Will do."

"And stay alive," she adds. "I expect you to bring that pretty girlfriend of yours by to visit someday."

I smile and tip my hat to her.

Back in my truck, I drive, but I'm not sure where to go next. Before nightfall I can be easily spotted or followed, so I don't want to head out to see Ariana before then. My phone rings with another call from Dale Peters, and this time I decide I've got time to talk. He's been a good friend. I'll miss playing with him and Walt.

"You avoiding my calls, partner?" he says when I pick up.

"Can you blame me?" I quip as I pull my truck over to the side of the road. "Your last singer ditched town completely to get away from you."

He chuckles.

"I've got bad news," I say. "I'm not going to be able to play with you tonight. Or any other night. I'm leaving town."

"Leaving town?"

"The Rangers are sending my replacement," I say.

I expect him to wonder aloud if the new Ranger can sing and play guitar. Instead, he's quiet for a moment.

"Rory, I ain't calling so we can get together and play music. I'm calling about Skip."

My stomach lurches. This could be the break I need.

"Do you know something about Skip's death?" I ask.

"Hell, Rory, I know everything there is to know. I'm ashamed I ain't said nothing till now, but I aim to make it right."

Dale tells me he's driving one of McCormack's tankers back to Rio Lobo now. He asks me to meet him at the easement through the open space and gives me exact GPS coordinates.

"Bring Ariana if you can," he says.

"Why?"

"What do you mean *why*? 'Cause I got the keys to her freedom, and I want to see the look on her face when she knows. She ain't never gonna date me, but I like to see her smile, and trust me, bud, she's gonna be smiling big."

I urge him to tell me what he has to say over the phone. In this town, witnesses have a tendency to die before they can speak.

"It ain't just what I got to say," he says. "It's what I got to show you."

CHAPTER 75

WHEN DALE HANGS up, I put my truck into drive and take off. Dale could be setting a trap for me—and Ariana. He works for McCormack, after all. I could be leading us both into God knows what kind of trouble. Gareth and his soldier buddies could surround us out there in the desert canyons and force us to surrender at gunpoint.

Or kill us.

But I'm not sure I have much of a choice. Dale might be my last hope.

I pull onto Main Street. The harsh glare from the late afternoon sun reflects off the cars parked along the road. Up ahead, I see a pickup truck driving into town.

I recognize it.

It's just like mine.

I pull over and my lieutenant, Kyle Hendricks, pulls over, too, parking his truck nose to nose with mine. He climbs out, and so do I. We stand in the middle of Main Street, two Texas Rangers with cowboy hats and sidearms, staring at each other like a couple of gunfighters in an old western.

There won't be any shooting today, but this is a showdown nonetheless.

"Yates, you sure fucked up this time," he says. "Every Ranger in the state, from the rookies picking their noses at their desks all the way up to the company commander, knows you screwed the pooch on this one. My lord, how the golden boy has fallen from grace."

"Kyle," I say, "I've had about enough of your bullshit."

"Fine," he says. "I'll take your gun and badge right now. You can sign your resignation papers tomorrow at headquarters. Otherwise, you're going to have to keep taking my bullshit."

"I'm not resigning," I say. "If anyone should turn in his star, it's you. You've been acting like a damn baby ever since the shooting in the bank. Grow up. Act like a Texas Ranger, for Christ's sake."

"Act like a Texas Ranger? That's rich coming from you. Hothead Rory Yates always bending the rules to suit his needs. Your old lieutenant gave you too long of a leash. I'm just trying to keep you in line."

I can see I'm getting nowhere, so I try to shift gears.

"You don't know what you're getting into here in Rio Lobo. This thing is a lot bigger than it seems."

"It seems simple enough to me," he says. "One woman died of an allergy. Case closed. And the local detective you been running around with shot and killed an oil worker. Case closed. I'll be out of here by this time tomorrow."

"That's exactly what they want you to do." I point to the graffiti on my truck door. "You see that? They've been trying to get me out of this town since I got here. You're just playing into their hands."

"They?" he says. "Who exactly is *they*?"

"I'm not sure," I say, "but I think the local oil baron—"

He silences me with a wave of his arm. "Chief Harris told me all about your wild conspiracy theories. But I think the truth is a lot simpler. Carson McCormack's son beat you in some kind of shooting match, and now you're out to get him."

"That's ridiculous," I say. "And the chief's probably in on it."

He shakes his head to dismiss my harebrained suspicion, but the anger in his demeanor is flagging. He feels like he's won the fight and now he can play the role of a tough mentor, instead of the jealous peer that he is.

"Go home, Rory. The media loves you for that quick-draw maneuver in the bank. You've still got a decent career ahead of you if you play your cards right. Messing around with some female detective who turned out to be a murderer could be just a blip on your record. That is, if you don't pursue this any further."

"She didn't do it," I say, although after I saw the picture of Ariana dancing with Gareth McCormack at their high school Homecoming, I'm less sure than ever.

If I had seen that picture two days ago, would I have helped her escape?

"Do you know where she is?" Kyle asks. "You better not be hiding her, Rory."

If I tell Kyle where she is, maybe I can get back into his good graces and help figure this thing out from within the lines of the law. This might be my last chance to save my future with the Rangers.

But I just can't do it. I can't sell out Ariana.

"You win," I say to Kyle. "I'll leave town. I'll go crawling back to Waco and let you finish things here."

He nods his head as if to say, *You're damn right you're leaving*.

"But before I go," I say, "I've got just one thing to say."

He waits. I step close to him and stare him down.

"It's not your fault you were sleeping in the truck that day," I say. "If I'd have known something illegal was going on inside that bank, I would have told you. You came running as soon as you heard the shot. You did everything right. But you're sleepwalking on the job *right now,* and I'm telling you to wake the hell up. If this all comes crashing down, that's on you. You'll be a laughingstock all over again, and this time it *will* be your fault."

"Get out of here, you son of a bitch," he barks. "That's a goddamn order."

I climb into my truck and pull out into the street. I stop when my window is right next to him. I reach out and point to the star on his chest.

"It means something to wear that badge," I say. "Don't you ever forget it."

Then I hit the gas and take off before he can get the last word in.

CHAPTER 76

I DRIVE OUT to the spot on the river where Ariana and I met last night, but she's nowhere to be seen. There are fresh ATV tracks all over the place. When I walk closer to the river, I spot shell casings lying in the dirt.

I put on a pair of gloves and pick up one of the casings. WINCHESTER 223 REM is stamped on the bottom. The rounds could have been fired from an AR-15, and there are enough shells to suggest that it was equipped with a bump stock or had been converted to fully automatic. Whatever was on the receiving end of these shots, it would have been turned into swiss cheese.

I just pray to God it wasn't Ariana.

I scan the hills for blood or any sign of bullet holes, but I don't see anything.

Did they take her?

But then I have another thought. What if this is just some elaborate trick? Are they making it look like Ariana was shot when she's actually in on it?

I spot something in a clump of sagebrush and investigate. It's my sleeping bag and the sack of food I brought to Ariana, hidden away. But there's nothing else, no sign of her.

I look around, my heart pounding. Above me, a hawk screeches as it glides through the blue sky. Otherwise the whole area is silent. The sun is still a couple of hours from setting, but shadows have already fallen across the canyon.

I don't want to draw attention to myself—not if McCormack's men are nearby—but I don't know what else to do but call out to her.

"Ariana!" I shout, just loud enough to hear an echo calling back to me through the canyon.

I hear splashing in the river and look down to see Ariana wading out from under the cut bank.

"Rory?" she gasps, looking up at me. "I thought it was them again. They've been crisscrossing this area all day."

She swims over to the bank and climbs out of the water. Her hair is mud slicked and her once white T-shirt is now the color of chocolate milk.

I throw my arms around her in a big hug. Her body is ice-cold, her trembling arms covered in goose bumps.

"Thank God," I say, feeling guilty for thinking that she might have been double-crossing me. "What the hell happened?"

She says McCormack's men have been patrolling in ATVs. They finally left for good about an hour ago, but when she heard a vehicle coming, she thought they were trying again, this time in a truck.

"I hadn't expected you until after dark," she says.

As she talks, she tries to catch her breath and can't.

I give her a minute to breathe and then ask, "What about the rifle rounds?"

"They shot a snake," she says. "They said they'd do the same to me if they found me."

I get an old shirt out of my lock box and give it to her to try to dry off and wipe away some of the mud.

"I must be a sight," she says, wiping dirty water from her face.

"You're as beautiful as ever," I say, and I mean it.

I'm still trying to get my emotions under control after fearing she was dead—or that she might have betrayed me.

"What are you doing here?" she says, dumping water out of her boots. "What's going on?"

"I've got bad news and what I hope is good news," I say.

I explain to her about being replaced by my lieutenant, how he and Harris both warned me to get out of town.

"I was told in no uncertain terms that if I step foot in Rio Lobo, I'll be arrested."

"Damn it," Ariana says, "they've really got us, don't they?"

"Maybe not," I say.

I tell her about Dale Peters and how he has something to show us that will help the investigation.

"The GPS coordinates are about a mile and a half from here, over along the access road McCormack and his men have been using."

"Are you sure you can trust Dale?" she asks. "McCormack is the one who signs his paychecks."

"My gut tells me we can trust him," I say, "but I've been wrong before."

CHAPTER 77

"WHAT ARE WE waiting on?" Ariana says. "Let's go see what Dale has for us."

She's right. We should hurry. We have only about an hour or so of daylight left. But there's something I want to get off my chest before we drive out there.

"What is it?" she says, sensing something is on my mind.

"Why didn't you tell me you dated Gareth McCormack?" I ask.

A wave of emotions rolls across her face.

First confusion.

Then embarrassment.

Then anger.

"You're still not sure about me, are you?" she says, her voice trembling with betrayal. "You're still wondering if I'm somehow involved in this?"

She steps away from me and walks in a circle, shaking her head incredulously.

"I can't believe this," she says, clenching her hands into fists. "Do you have any idea what I've been through today? And you think that I have something to do with all this?"

My patience cracks.

"I helped you escape," I say, raising my voice. "I put my badge on the line for you. I'm putting my life on the line. For you."

"You're the one who convinced me to run," she snaps. "I'd be better off in jail than I am out here."

Her words hit me hard. I think about what kind of danger I've put her in. If she gets killed, it's on me.

"Besides," she says, "it's no one's business who I've dated."

"You've been keeping a secret from me," I say, trying to calm my nerves. "Gareth McCormack is at the top of a very short suspects list. You can't tell me it's not relevant that the two of you were Homecoming king and queen."

Ariana turns away, walks to the water's edge. Her clothes and hair are still soaked. I hate that I've confronted her with this when she's been hiding all day from people who would kill her. But this is the only time I have to ask. I can't wait.

"I was afraid you'd take me off the case," Ariana says, her voice subdued now. "If you found out I'd dated Gareth, you might say there was a conflict of interest. I didn't want to risk that. This is my case. I'm the one who believes Susan Snyder was murdered. To be barred from the investigation because of some stupid high school romance wouldn't have been fair."

"Sometimes life isn't fair."

"Tell me about it," she says, throwing her arms up in a gesture to her current situation.

"Did you think I would never find out?"

She whirls around and faces me. "Gareth never talks about it. He acts like it never happened. Like I was nothing to him. Maybe I was. I thought it would be okay to act like it was unimportant to me because that's the way he acts."

I lean against my pickup, trying to be as relaxed as possible with my body language. I want this to be a discussion, not a fight.

"Was it serious?" I ask.

"It was to me."

"Do you want to tell me about it?"

She leans against the truck as well, her anger over my betrayal mostly replaced with exhaustion.

"It's what you might expect," she says. "Rich popular kid asks out the poor girl from the wrong side of town. Rumors fly."

She explains that she was head over heels for Gareth. Carson didn't approve. Gareth defied his father. But when Ariana wouldn't sleep with him on Homecoming night, Gareth broke up with her.

"He was going against his father just long enough to get laid," she says. "When I wouldn't put out, he tossed me aside."

She says she was heartbroken. She had really fallen for him. A few months later, her father was arrested, making her final year of high school even more stressful.

"That's the other reason I didn't say anything," she adds. "I was embarrassed. Not because he threw me aside like I was trash. I was embarrassed because I fell for him to begin with."

Looking at her now, I can see how the events of that year of her life stole the carefree happiness from the pretty girl in the photo.

"I've had trouble opening myself up to people ever since," Ariana says, looking at me, her eyes glossy with tears. "Which is why it hurts so much to know you still don't trust me."

As an answer, I pull out my truck keys and open

the storage box in the bed of my F-150. I reach in and grab the two rifles I keep inside: a standard-issue .223 M4 and a heavier caliber LaRue .308.

"I trust you," I say, holding a gun in each hand. "Which is why I'm going to give you one of these rifles to cover me when I go see Dale Peters."

"I thought you said you trusted him."

"Let me put it this way," I say. "I have a hell of a lot more doubt about him than I ever had about you."

CHAPTER 78

ARIANA OPTS FOR the .223 M4, which is an accurate gun even at long ranges. Nothing like Gareth McCormack's M24, but still a damn fine weapon.

We drive toward the rendezvous in silence. The tension between us has dissipated, but it's left a lingering effect. We're both tired, our nerves ragged from too much happening in the last few days.

I let Ariana out of my truck one ridge over from the GPS coordinates Dale gave me. She scrambles up the hill to find a good vantage point.

The truth is, if this is an ambush, she won't be able to do much good. If Dale is in cahoots with Gareth McCormack, the sharpshooter could be anywhere. He could be farther away and, with his shooting skills, far more accurate than Ariana. There is no way Ariana could protect me.

But covering me isn't my only reason for asking her to hunker down in the hills while I drive out to see Dale. I also want to keep her hidden. That way, if a bullet sails a thousand yards through my skull, Ariana may still be able to get away.

Maybe.

As I round a bend, I spot one of McCormack's tanker trucks parked in the ridged valley below. I scan the hillside for Ariana and don't see her among the sagebrush and gnarled tree snags. I drive slowly, looking around for any sign of an ambush. With McCormack's range, there are dozens of places he could be hiding, especially now as the sun is lowering and casting shadows in every hollow in the hillsides and every crevice in the rocky outcroppings.

I approach the tanker truck and see Dale sitting on the tank with some kind of box in his lap. The truck is a single unit, with the cylinder of the tank connected to the truck itself—an eight-wheeler instead of an eighteen-wheeler, but still an enormous vehicle. There's a metal ladder on the passenger side of the rig, which Dale must have used to climb up there.

I park my truck and shut off the engine. I leave the keys in the ignition in case I need to make a quick getaway. As I approach Dale on foot, my heart is racing. My nerves are on high alert.

The air is still and silent except for the crunch of my boots on the rocks.

"Howdy, partner," Dale says, smiling down at me with the big grin I've come to expect from him.

The box on his lap appears to be a pizza box. Dale is chewing a slice.

"Want a piece?" he says. "It's cold, but it's still damn good."

"Maybe later," I say.

"Suit yourself."

"Why'd you bring me out here, Dale?"

"All business, huh?" he says, grinning with a piece of pepperoni stuck in his teeth. "No time for bullshitting today?"

"Sorry," I say. "It's been a long day."

My body is tense, my hand ready to fly to my pistol and draw.

"Where's Ariana?" he asks.

"I don't know," I say. "She's a fugitive."

"That's too bad," he says. Then he adds, "Climb on up. The surprise is up here."

I feel nervous about this. Is he asking me to climb on top so Gareth can get a better shot? I'll be in full view for a thousand yards in any direction. But I've come this far.

I set my boot on the bottom rung of the ladder and pull myself up. I keep my eyes on Dale as I do. When I get to the top, I stand, my feet unsteady on the narrow, flat walkway atop the cylinder.

There appear to be two hatch openings on top, each with a hinged steel strap across it and a clamp securing the strap. I don't know enough about tanker trucks to be sure, but I assume one hatch is where oil is pumped in, and the other is where it's pumped out.

Dale kneels before the closest hatch and releases the clamp.

"Move slowly," I say, knowing he could have a weapon stashed inside.

"I ain't gonna shoot you, Rory," he says, looking back at me. "I seen that video of you. I ain't stupid."

I watch him closely.

"Ready?" he says, giving me a big shit-eating grin.

"For what?" I say.

Dale swings back the metal strap and opens the hatch door, about the diameter of a basketball. He steps back to let me look inside.

I expect to see an opaque ocean of oil.

Instead, there is a compartment full of bricks and bricks of white powder vacuum-sealed in plastic wrap.

"Holy shit," I say. "Is that what I think it is?"

"Well," Dale says, grinning, "it ain't baker's yeast."

CHAPTER 79

I WAVE FOR Ariana to come down from the hill-side. When Dale sees her start to make her way down from the rocks with my rifle slung over her shoulder, his grin widens even more.

"Didn't trust me, did you?" Dale says, although he doesn't look the least bit disappointed that I didn't.

"What the hell are you doing carrying thousands of dollars in drugs in your truck?" I say.

"That ain't thousands of dollars in drugs, Rory." He points to the cache. "That's millions."

I can't tell how large the compartment is, how deep it goes into the tank. But if each brick is a kilo, that means they're probably worth anywhere from ten to thirty thousand dollars apiece. If there are a hundred bricks, that means the pile of them could be worth one to three million dollars.

Carson McCormack's oil business, Dale explains, is a front for a more lucrative drug business.

"His wells are going dry," Dale says. "Most of the pumping you see is just for show. Whenever you see his tankers going up and down the highway, they're more likely to be carrying coke than oil. And I ain't talking about the carbonated beverage."

As he talks, everything I've seen in Rio Lobo starts to make sense. The fact that most of McCormack's employees look more like mercenaries than oil workers. The way his ranch is fortified with hurricane fencing and razor wire and a guard station. The way he travels with an entourage, driving together like a military convoy.

Dale says he picked up the drugs from a location over by the Mexico border earlier in the day. McCormack owns land out there, with a single pump jack that's just for show, housed inside a securely fenced area. Someone from McCormack's team takes a trip out there two or three times a week under the guise of filling a truck with oil when in reality what they're doing is picking up drugs.

The location is close to the border but otherwise in the middle of nowhere, with hills and rocks and no easy way for trucks to travel between the countries. But there's a trapdoor at the pump station that opens to a twenty-foot shaft. At the bottom is a tunnel equipped with metal tracks, similar to a mine passage, with a pulley system to move a cart back and forth.

"I don't know how long the tunnel is or where it goes," Dale says. "It's a quarter mile from the Rio Grande, and I wouldn't be surprised if they got it rigged to go under the river somehow and into Mexico. All I know is whenever I show up, there's a big pile of drugs waiting to be picked up."

Dale says there's even a makeshift elevator they use to bring the drugs up, similar to a dumbwaiter. The only slightly difficult part of the job is carrying the kilos up the ladder of the truck to stash in the hidden compartment on top.

"That's why you need two people most of the

time," Dale says. "Skip and I used to make the run pretty regular."

In recent years, Dale says, Carson McCormack's whole operation has transformed from oil drilling to trafficking in illegal drugs. Mostly cocaine, but also heroin and methamphetamine. The operations center on McCormack's land, with all the buildings once associated with oil production having been converted to drug refineries. They bring in the cocaine, cut it with laundry detergent or boric acid, repackage it, and ship it throughout the Southwest.

Dale explains that Carson McCormack sat down with all his oil workers a few years ago and gave them a choice: either they get with the program and start working in his drug business or he buys them out.

"That's what happened to the guy Walt and I used to play with," he says. "Carson bought him out and he started a new life somewhere else."

Dale says he considered moving, but he's lived in Rio Lobo his whole life. He didn't want to leave. And by staying, he was making better money than ever. He didn't think about the people the drug trafficking might hurt—on either side of the border. When Susan Snyder died, he honestly thought McCormack had nothing to do with it. But when Skip was killed, he knew Carson and Gareth were responsible for both murders.

"I'm ashamed to admit I still might not have said nothing," Dale says, "but when they tried to pin it on Ariana, that was the final straw. I couldn't stay quiet anymore."

Ariana arrives just as the sun disappears behind the horizon. She is out of breath with a healthy dose of sweat mixed into her river-soaked clothes. She looks exhausted, but when she climbs up onto the truck and I shine a flashlight into the hidden chamber in the oil tanker, her expression lights up with amazement. Dale begins explaining to her what he's already told me.

When she realizes what this means—that he does in fact have the keys to her freedom—she throws her arms around Dale and gives him a tight hug. She kisses his cheek.

He looks as happy as I've ever seen him.

"Before we celebrate," I say, "we need to figure out what the hell we're going to do next. This is far from over."

CHAPTER 80

AS THE SKY darkens, the three of us discuss our options.

Out here in the hills, we have no cell service and no radio signal. And while McCormack's tanker is able to navigate the thoroughfare from his property to the highway in the south, there's no way it could make it over the roads I drove in on. They're too narrow and several skirt hillsides with steep embankments below. Driving the tanker truck, which probably weighs twenty thousand pounds, might collapse the slope and send the truck rolling downhill.

And even if we could make the drive, Dale says that McCormack's men will be positioned at all the roads going into and out of the open space. On the drive today, before he went into the hills, he'd been privy to all the radio chatter among the men.

"It might not be but two or three guys at each place," he says, "but they're going to have AR-15s and TEC-9s and God only knows what else. I know you're good with that peashooter of yours, Rory, but I don't think you've got the firepower to go up against a couple of guys with fully automatic weapons."

With my pistol, two rifles, and the shotgun still in

my storage box, that's a pretty good portable arsenal a Texas Ranger hauls around. But the last thing I want to do is get into a firefight with some ex-military mercenaries, especially with the lives of Dale and Ariana at stake. There has to be another way. Bloodshed should be a last resort.

It's tricky. McCormack and his men don't know where we are—at least not precisely—but now we can't leave the open space without running across one of their traps.

"They don't figure you made it out of the Rio Lobo area," Dale says to Ariana. "So now they're going to tighten the noose and see if they can squeeze you out."

"If Chief Harris is in on it," I say, "he'll tell law enforcement to keep an eye out for my truck. They'll know soon enough I haven't left town, either."

To further complicate our problems, Dale says that if he doesn't show up at McCormack's ranch soon, he'll at least need to find a place with cell service so he can call and give him an excuse.

"I'll tell him I've got a flat tire and that I won't be there till morning."

"What about tracking devices?" I say. "Are there any on the truck?"

"Not that I know of," Dale says. "But it ain't gonna be hard to figure out where I am. If they ain't able to get me on the radio or the phone, there ain't but one place I can be."

As we talk, I feel claustrophobic. We're standing in wide-open country, but I feel like walls are closing in around us.

"If we can't get out," I say, "we're going to have to bring someone in to help us."

"You think Tom and Jessica can help?" Ariana asks. "You think they can get in here without arousing suspicion?"

I don't want to involve the Aarons. It's too dangerous, and I've already put them at risk enough.

Unfortunately, the person I have in mind is someone I don't trust nearly as much as Tom and Jessica Aaron.

My lieutenant—Kyle Hendricks.

CHAPTER 81

I USE A flashlight and do my best to look for a tracking device of some kind on the tanker. When I'm satisfied there isn't one, Dale and I leave Ariana to guard the tanker truck. I hate to abandon her, but both Dale and I need to make phone calls and she's the only one left to keep an eye on the truck and the evidence inside.

We drive south, heading the way Dale came in. I haven't been this direction in the open space yet, and before long the hills start to flatten and the roadway smooths out. I turn my lights off and do my best to drive by moonlight. The desert hills are pale in the darkness, and the roadway is a clear corridor through the sagebrush and cacti.

Dale says we have about one more mile before we get to the highway—and McCormack's roadblock— and I feel anxious that we're not going to get a signal before his men see us. But we keep checking our phones and finally discover we have one bar.

I park the truck and let Dale make the first call.

"Hey, boss," he says. "I've had some bad luck."

He tells McCormack the elevator in the tunnel was malfunctioning, and he had to climb down via ladder and carry up the whole load, just two or three kilos at a time.

"Then I'll be damned if I didn't blow a tire as soon as I got on the road," Dale says.

He looks nervous in the moonlight, but he is able to keep his voice calm.

"I think he bought it," Dale says afterward. "Your turn."

I try to mentally prepare myself for this call. Kyle and I have been butting heads since the day in the bank. Somehow I need to get through to him. I could go over his head, call Company E in El Paso. But they'd be wondering why I was going outside the chain of command. The first thing they would do is check with Kyle before sending anyone. Then he would tell Harris, and Harris would tell McCormack.

And then it would be over—his men would descend on us and we'd fall in a hail of bloody gunfire, like a reenactment of *The Wild Bunch*.

I need to get Kyle to come out here without tipping off McCormack.

The best way to do that, I figure, is to lie to him. He wouldn't believe me if I told him there was an oil tanker full of cocaine. But there is one thing he might believe.

"Yates," he says when he picks up, "you better be calling me from Fort Stockton by now."

"I've got a proposition for you," I say, cutting to the chase. "A way for us both to walk away from Rio Lobo looking pretty good."

If Kyle's anything, he's opportunistic. If I can convince him that I want to play ball, work out some kind of deal with him, then he might agree to what I'm asking.

He takes a breath and says, "I'm listening."

"I know where Ariana Delgado is," I say.

"Then you better tell me where," he says. "Right now."

"Hear me out first."

I tell him that I don't trust Chief Harris, so I want the Texas Rangers to handle the arrest without the help of local law enforcement.

"You and me," I say. "We're going to bring her in together. That way we know she gets a fair shake."

The other end of the line is quiet as he's thinking.

"I could just bring her in myself," I say. "Take all the credit. But I'm trying to show you that I'm a team player. I want to patch things up and move on."

"All right," he says finally.

"I don't want Harris involved," I say. "He can't know."

When he agrees to this condition, I give him the GPS coordinates and tell him to meet me there at first light. It makes me nervous to wait until then, but if Dale is right, then the entrance used to access the open space is going to be guarded by McCormack's men. If Kyle drives in at night, they'll be awfully suspicious. If he drives in during the day, that would be more understandable, maybe even expected.

I tell him that if he sees any of McCormack's men at the entrance of the open space, he should tell them that he's just going out there to poke around and look for the missing fugitive.

"You sound paranoid, Rory."

"I don't trust the folks around here," I say, "but I'm trying to do the right thing. You convinced me that bringing her in is the best course of action."

"How do I know I ain't walking into a trap?" Kyle says.

"I don't trust you, and you don't trust me," I say. "But I know you're no criminal, and I hope you know the same about me. We're Texas Rangers. We're going to have to put our differences aside and trust each other on this one."

"That's gonna be hard after what you said to me," he says, "about not being fit to wear this star on my chest."

"You said pretty much the same thing to me," I say. "Let's prove to each other we're fit to wear these badges."

CHAPTER 82

WHEN DALE AND I return to the tanker truck, we find Ariana digging into the box of cold pizza.

"Sorry," she says. "I was starving. I saved a couple of slices for y'all."

I suddenly realize how ravenous I am, so I finish what's left. The bag of food Jessica Aaron gave me is still sitting in the cab, but I figure we ought to save that for breakfast. We've got a long day ahead of us tomorrow.

The three of us don't want to risk building a campfire, but we sit around the pizza box as if it's a fire ring. Out here without light pollution, the sky is filled with stars. The Milky Way is visible, the stars so dense and copious that it makes me feel tiny in the grandness of the universe.

Ariana's clothes are now mostly dry, and under the glow of the moon and stars, she looks more relaxed than I've seen her in days. I think she can finally see a safe way out of this mess. I hope I can give that to her.

Dale looks like a man who's been carrying the weight of the world and has finally let someone shoulder the burden with him. He did the wrong thing for a long time, but now he's trying to do the right thing. God knows how many lives he might be saving, starting with Ariana's.

As for me, I doubt I look as stress-free as my companions. My mind is reeling. Here I've been waiting for a break in the case, but this is like a dam exploding. Like looking on the ground for a penny and finding a pot of gold—a whole mine full of gold!

I never dreamed something this big was going on. But the murders of Susan Snyder and Skip Barnes make more sense now. Susan must have caught wind of what was going on. She'd convinced Skip to go public so she could expose McCormack's big secret. Skip Barnes must have sold her out, and as a result, someone on Carson's team poisoned her with peanuts to make it look like an accident. Then when it looked like Skip might talk to us, they killed him.

I don't have all the details figured out, but that's my working theory, and it seems plausible given what I know now about McCormack's operation. I just have to survive long enough to bring in the cavalry—the Rangers, the DEA, the FBI—to help me fit in all the missing puzzle pieces.

"Hey, Rory," Dale says, shaking me from my thoughts, "you didn't bring your guitar, did you?"

When I tell him I did, he encourages me to pull it out. My first impulse is that playing the guitar right now, out here in the middle of nowhere, seems like a terrible idea. But it might do me some good to take my mind off what's happening.

Dale and I take turns, passing the guitar back and forth, playing and singing. We play quietly and keep our voices low. We figure if anyone is out looking for us, we'll hear their vehicles or see their headlights long before they would hear us strumming on an acoustic guitar. But still we don't want to push our luck, so we play slow, mellow songs. Ballads, not barn burners.

Dale plays a couple of George Strait rodeo tunes— "Amarillo by Morning" and "I Can Still Make Cheyenne." His vocals leave something to be desired, but his guitar skills are spot on. I try my hand at Kenny Chesney's "Better Boat," which I last practiced at the motel in Rio Lobo what seems like a million years ago. And I play the folk song "Clay Pigeons," my version a little bit more like John Prine's than Blaze Foley's original. "Better Boat" and "Clay Pigeons" are songs about starting over, but the funny thing is that playing these types of songs doesn't make me sad the way it did when I first arrived in Rio Lobo.

It might be the possibility of something happening with Ariana that makes starting over feel okay. But it also might be simply that I'm in serious danger here in Rio Lobo. The thought of starting over isn't nearly as scary as the thought of dying at the hands of Gareth McCormack or one of his soldiers.

I hope I live long enough to start over.

Ariana is a good audience, smiling and telling us how talented we are. She refrains from applauding, but only because she doesn't want to make much noise. I try to think of a rock ballad she might like, so I do my best playing Poison's "Every Rose Has Its Thorn" for her. I look up as I'm playing and see her smiling brightly, her face aglow in starlight.

When I put the guitar away, we settle in for the night. The air is cool, but none of us feels like sleeping inside the vehicles. Instead, we opt for the hard ground. Dale has one blanket, and we decide— against her objections—that Ariana should have it.

Dale and I at least have long-sleeved shirts, and Ariana's clothes are still a little damp.

I lie awake for a long time, looking up at the stars. Dale begins to snore and Ariana appears to be asleep, her face relaxed, her breathing regular.

I tell myself that all I want is for Ariana and me to make it through the next twenty-four hours so I can see that smile on her face over and over again in the future.

It doesn't seem like too much to ask.

CHAPTER 83

MY SLEEP IS restless, jumbled with conscious thoughts and unconscious fears. I dream that I hear ATVs in the distance, and this jolts me awake.

But the land all around us is as silent as a cemetery. The horizon to the east is just starting to turn blue. The chill of the night air has seeped into my bones, making my body ache. I rise to stretch my muscles and warm up. I hike away from Ariana and Dale, who are both still asleep, and relieve my bladder on the other side of the tanker truck. The landscape is changing from gray to brown, and I'm struck again by the stark beauty of these desert hills.

When I walk back, Ariana is sitting up, blinking sleep from her eyes.

"What's the plan?" she asks.

"I want you on that hill with the rifle," I tell her. "Just like yesterday. Only this time, take Dale with you."

I explain to her that if we see any vehicle except for a Ford F-150 identical to mine, then she needs to stay hidden.

"No matter what happens to me, do not come out," I say. "If I'm arrested, or worse, you need to stay alive.

And keep Dale safe. Find a way to get back into town and go ask Tom Aaron for help. Tell him to put this thing on the AP wire, to at least get the story out before they have a chance to arrest you."

Thirty minutes later, as the sun is breaking over the hills, Ariana and Dale start to climb a nearby hill and hide behind a rock outcropping. I climb up onto the tanker and watch and listen. My stomach rumbles and I regret not eating the food in my truck that Jessica made for me.

I hear Kyle's truck before I see it. When it comes around the bend, I wave my arm in an exaggerated arc so he'll see me. Not that he could miss the tanker. It's thirty feet long with a stainless-steel drum reflecting in the morning light.

He guides his truck toward me, taking his time just like I did yesterday afternoon. He's looking around for an ambush. I know where Ariana and Dale are hidden, but I don't move my head in that direction. I don't want to tip him off.

When he parks, he steps out of the truck and looks up at me. He looks like a Texas Ranger should— his slacks and shirt wrinkle-free, his face shaved and smooth, his hat clean enough you could eat off the brim, and the star on his chest polished and gleaming. I must look the opposite. I slept in my clothes, in the dirt, and I haven't shaved in days. I'm sure my badge has lost its luster, and the hat Willow bought me could use a good scrubbing.

"I don't see the girl, Yates," Kyle says. "This better not be some kind of joke. I'm bringing someone back to town in handcuffs. If it ain't her, it's gonna be you."

"She's in the tanker," I say. "You've got to come up here to see for yourself."

Kyle squints at me in disbelief. What I'm saying doesn't make a bit of sense. There's no way for a human to get inside the tanker. The openings aren't that wide. But maybe he doesn't know that.

"You've got to see for yourself, Kyle. If you don't like what you see once you're up here, I'll put the cuffs on myself."

He gives me a skeptical look, then glances around to see if anything else seems suspicious. Finally, he resigns himself to what I'm asking, and he starts to climb the ladder.

When he arrives on top, I can't help but think what a strange sight we must be. Two Texas Rangers standing atop an oil truck with nothing around but sagebrush and rocks.

"Thanks for coming," I say.

"Don't thank me yet," he says. "You're going to be under arrest in about five seconds if you don't show me where Ariana Delgado is."

I step over to the first hatch, which is closed.

"Ready?" I say. I can't help but grin.

"Christ, Yates, get to it already."

As I swing open the hatch, I have a moment of panic. What if it's empty? Dale and I left Ariana with the truck last night—what if she took the drugs out?

Then sunlight illuminates the cache of cocaine bricks, and I feel guilty for—once again—doubting Ariana. I vow not to do it again.

Kyle kneels down to take a closer look at the cocaine. Then, still kneeling, he swings his head and gives me a confused look, as if to say, *What's going on?*

"Carson McCormack is working with the cartels to bring drugs over the border," I say. "His whole oil business is a front for a major drug network that supplies dealers all over the Southwest. What you're looking at there has a street value of at least a million dollars. Maybe two or three. And once he cuts it and repackages it at his plant, there's no telling how much he'll get for it."

Kyle stands up and stares at me. His expression is unreadable. As he opens his mouth to speak, I honestly have no idea what he is going to say.

CHAPTER 84

"RORY," HE SAYS, his face still expressionless, "I'm very disappointed."

"Disappointed?" I say.

"Yes," he says, nodding gravely.

I don't know what to say. I'm about to argue, but if what I'm showing him doesn't speak for itself, I don't know what will.

"I'm disappointed," he says again, then adds, "with myself."

His stone-cold expression breaks into a smile.

"I've been a horse's ass," he says. "You've done good work here, and I'm sorry I haven't helped you. A lieutenant is supposed to help his Rangers, not stand in their way."

He extends his hand, and I take it, surprised and relieved.

"I'm going to make it up to you," he says.

He claps me on the shoulder. I feel like Dale must have felt last night. I've been carrying a heavy burden on my own, and now I finally have help. With Kyle on board, we can bring the full power of the Texas Rangers down on Rio Lobo, not to mention a handful of other state and federal agencies.

But there's still the question of how to make that happen.

"What do we do next?" I say.

"You've been doing all right on your own up till now," he says. "I defer to you. What's our next step?"

I start by waving Ariana and Dale down from the hill. As they make their way toward us, Kyle and I climb down the ladder to the ground and discuss what we should do. We're still trapped in the open space, with McCormack's men guarding the exits. The difference now is that Kyle is here on official police business, whereas Ariana and I were—and technically still are—fugitives.

We might be able to drive the tanker to the highway and have Kyle talk our way through. But I'm afraid they might very well start shooting, especially if they see us taking one of their tankers, no doubt full of drugs, with us.

Another possibility is that Kyle drives back on his own, like nothing has changed. He could act like he didn't see anything—no sign of me or Ariana—but as soon as he gets a cell phone signal, he could call in the cavalry. But this is risky because that leaves Dale, Ariana, and me out here with the tanker. Now that it's daylight, I imagine McCormack's men will be scouring these hills. Besides, once Dale doesn't show up this morning with a truckload of drugs, McCormack will start to suspect something, if he hasn't already.

Ariana could hide Tom Aaron's Land Cruiser, but there's no way we can hide Dale's tanker.

Once McCormack gets wind that we have this truck—and the millions of dollars of evidence inside—along with a witness who will tell us everything about the trafficking operation, he could move heaven and earth to try to cover his ass before we can get a warrant to bring an army of detectives to his property. Given enough time, he could move all the drugs off his property, start destroying evidence, maybe make a run for it himself. All he and Gareth would need to do is get across the border and hook up with their cartel buddies and we might never see them again.

All of this is why I think our best course of action is strength in numbers. Kyle, Dale, Ariana, and I should all take the tanker south together, not splitting up. As soon as we get into cell phone range, Kyle and I will start making calls. We'll bring in reinforcements from Company E in El Paso. We'll work on getting search warrants. We'll notify the DEA. We'll call the sheriff's office and highway patrol and tell them that the roadblocks set up for Ariana should now be on the lookout for any and all vehicles associated with Carson McCormack.

We'll put as many wheels in motion as we can, as fast as possible.

"Sounds good to me," Kyle says.

When Dale and Ariana arrive, they look unconvinced of Kyle's trustworthiness, but he quickly wins them over.

He shakes Ariana's hand and congratulates her on a job well done.

"You started this investigation all by yourself," he says. "There are about to be a hundred detectives on this from half a dozen agencies, but no one will forget that you're the one who started it all. I'll see to that."

When he meets Dale, Kyle claps him on the back and says, "Coming forward must have been very hard, but you've done the right thing. I'll do everything in my power to make sure you're a protected witness through the whole legal process."

Dale, embarrassed, smiles and adjusts his ball cap.

For a moment, it feels like everything is going to work out. We've finally broken the case open and it's just a matter of time before all the bad guys are in jail and all the good guys are safe.

But then Dale opens his mouth to speak and instead of words coming out, blood and teeth explode from his lips. His body collapses into the dirt, blood spilling out of a hole in the back of his skull.

His Dallas Mavericks cap lies in a growing pond of gore.

As I stare in disbelief, I finally hear the shot, trailing at least two seconds behind the bullet that killed Dale Peters.

CHAPTER 85

I SCAN THE hillsides, looking for the sniper, but all I can see is sagebrush and rocks and the occasional desert tree.

Gareth could be anywhere.

I feel panic around me—Ariana and Kyle are shocked and unsure what to do—and I tear my eyes away from the landscape.

"Take cover!" I shout at them. "Underneath the tanker!"

Ariana and Kyle move in that direction, and as I'm backing that way myself, I let my eyes dart back to the hillsides.

I spot a tiny spark of light on a hillside at least a thousand yards away. And then it's gone.

My brain has time to process that it's the muzzle flash from Gareth's rifle, but my body seems to be frozen in place. I have a second or two to act—it will take the bullet that long to get here—but I can't move.

Just like in my nightmares, I'm paralyzed.

Strong hands grab my shoulders, hauling me downward. I hear the whine of the bullet soar just over my head as I'm falling. My hat flies off my head.

The next thing I know I'm lying in the dirt, with Ariana on top of me.

"Come on," she says, pulling my arm.

We hear the report of the rifle as we crawl into the shelter of the oil tanker. Kyle is there, kneeling, with his gun drawn. We crowd underneath the tanker, trying to catch our breath and orient ourselves. My eyes spot the rifle lying next to Dale's body. Ariana must have dropped it when she grabbed me. Then my eyes catch something else: my Stetson. There's a bullet hole through the crown of the hat, almost identical to the one shot off my head in the bank.

I came *that* close to dying.

Again.

The only difference is this time it was someone else who saved my life. But there's no time to thank her. We have to figure out what the hell we're going to do.

"Did you tell anyone where you were going?" I ask Kyle.

"No one," he says. "I swear."

That means there must be a tracking device on the truck that I couldn't find. Or there might be another possibility. Maybe McCormack figured all along that Dale would betray them. Maybe they knew him better than he knew himself and they sent him on the drug run by himself so he could unknowingly set a trap for us.

"I saw the muzzle flash," I say. "I have a rough idea where the shots are coming from."

But this information doesn't do us much good. Between the three of us, we have two SIG Sauers and nothing else. The .223 M4 is lying in the dirt, and Kyle and I both have more guns in our trucks—if we could get to them—but they don't have the kind of range Gareth's M24 does. Even if we knew Gareth's precise location, we could never hit him.

The good news is that we have a ten-ton tanker truck to take shelter beneath.

A bullet zips into the ground next to the tanker, puffing a cloud of dirt into the air, followed a couple of seconds later by the sound of the gunshot.

"Think we can make it to the truck?" Kyle says.

His truck is closest, about fifteen feet away. If we could run to it and start the engine, we might get away. Gareth would probably fill it full of holes—and one or all of us could end up hurt or dead—but it might be our only chance.

As if Gareth can read our minds, the next bullet punctures one of the truck's tires. Then another. He shoots a series of holes into the hood of the truck—firing as fast as the bolt action will let him—and soon oil and radiator fluid start to bleed into the dirt underneath.

When he has completely disabled Kyle's truck, he does the same to mine, puncturing two of the four tires and pumping bullets into the engine. Each one hits the hood, making a *plink* sound, followed by the rifle reports rolling over us.

He finally stops shooting, and the air is silent.

The smell of sagebrush is tinged with the odor of oil and gasoline.

"He's letting his barrel cool," I say.

"There's nothing left for him to shoot at anyway," Kyle says. "We're at a stalemate."

He's right.

Gareth can't get to us where we're hiding. But we can't move. And we sure as hell can't get to him.

"Where are the keys to the tanker?" Kyle asks.

I don't know. They're probably in Dale's pocket, which means they're no good to us. Gareth would kill whoever stepped out to get them. And it wouldn't much matter if they were in the ignition. The truck is facing the direction where the bullets are coming from. As soon as one of us climbed into the cab, bullets would come raining through the windshield. This isn't a pickup—it would be a slow process to start it, shift it into gear, and get the vehicle moving. Whoever was in the driver's seat would be a sitting duck and would certainly be dead before the vehicle ever hit five miles an hour.

"What do we do?" Ariana says.

"The only thing we can do," Kyle says. "Wait."

As awful as that sounds, he's right. We have no play here. None at all. Our only hope is to stay alive a little longer and hope our situation somehow changes.

But then, now that the air is silent, I hear something in the distance. It's what I heard this morning, waking me up: the whine of ATVs. The noise must not have come from my dreams after all. McCormack's men were getting into position, staying far enough away that I could barely hear them in the morning silence.

As the ATVs get closer, I risk a glance around the edge of the truck. I spot two ATVs climbing up over the top of distant hills, so far away they look like insects. Kyle crawls under the truck and looks at the other side. He says he sees another ATV. That makes three.

This changes things. The four-wheelers will descend on us, their occupants armed with automatic weapons. With only a couple of pistols to fight them off, we don't stand a chance.

A minute ago we had a stalemate.

This is checkmate.

CHAPTER 86

KYLE, ARIANA, AND I hunker in the dirt next to the tanker truck's wheels.

"We need that rifle," I say, pointing to the .223 M4 lying over by Dale's body. "That will give us a fighting chance when the ATVs get close."

All of us look over at the gun, which is a good ten feet away. Dale's body, with his head in a swamp of red mud, serves as a reminder of the high risk of going out there.

"I'll go," Ariana says. "If I keep moving, he won't be able to get a good shot."

There's truth to what she's saying. Hitting a target at such a long range is hard enough—hitting one that's moving is just about impossible.

It would be like shooting a bumblebee out of mid-air with a pistol.

The sniper would have to be as good with a rifle as I am with a pistol. The problem is I've seen Gareth in action. He might just be that good.

"No," I tell Ariana. "I'll go. I'm faster."

This is an arguable claim—Ariana runs regularly and is just as athletic as I am. But I want to keep her safe. She saved my life already today. It's my turn to risk my life to save hers.

The whine of the ATVs is getting louder. I peek in their direction and see that soon they'll be close enough to start shooting. Each vehicle has two men, one to drive, the other behind him armed with an AR-15.

I shift into a runner's stance, ready to burst into a sprint.

Kyle puts a hand on my shoulder.

"You stay," he says. "I'll go."

Kyle and I were both athletes once upon a time—his sport of choice was baseball, mine football—so it's questionable who might be faster. There's no good reason for him to go instead of me.

"No, Kyle, I'll do it. You and Ariana—"

"I'm giving you an order, Ranger."

He grins, an expression that says, *I know I've been a jerk. I'm going to make it up to you right now.* Then, before I can object further, he bursts from cover and darts out toward the rifle. He scoops it up with one arm and turns around. Before I realize what Kyle is doing, the rifle is soaring through the air toward us. I reach out to catch it, then hunker back down in the cover of the tanker.

I expect Kyle to run back, but he doesn't. Instead, he takes a few quick steps to his truck and pulls his keys from his pocket. He jams a key into the storage box. I know what he's doing: trying to get the rifles inside.

But he's a sitting duck.

I throw the rifle to my shoulder, step out from cover, and start launching bullets in the direction where I saw the muzzle flash earlier. The bullets might fly that far, but not with any real accuracy. And I'm not aiming at a specific target anyway—just throwing bullets in a general direction. All I want is to get close enough that Gareth will keep his head down and not take aim at Kyle.

Shots start coming from the ATVs, puncturing the truck and puffing dirt from the ground. They're just tossing lead around, like me, but with this many bullets flying, you never know where one could land.

Kyle flips open the storage box and reaches inside. He yanks out his .223 M4, then reaches in with his other arm and pulls out an ammo can and some kind of satchel. He starts running back toward us. He has a grin on his face like he's on the baseball field about to steal home plate.

He's almost made it when he winces and pitches to the side. He falls onto his knees. I'm unsure of what happened, then I hear the shot finally catching up to the bullet that knocked him down.

He tosses the ammo can over to us, his face in agony. I catch the canister before it hits the ground, never taking my eyes off Kyle.

Blood trickles from two bullet holes—the entrance wound under his armpit and the exit on the other side of his body at the bottom of his rib cage. The bullet would have passed through both lungs, probably clipping his heart along the way. Blood gurgles from Kyle's mouth.

Kyle growls through bloody teeth and uses his last bit of strength to throw the rifle our way. It doesn't quite make it to us, but Ariana darts out, grabs it, and hurls herself back behind the cover of the truck.

Kyle looks at me as if he wants to say something, but when he opens his mouth, he can only cough up blood. He hunches over and collapses face-first in the dirt.

As I stare at him, I regret every unkind thought I ever had about him. He redeemed himself in the end. And then some.

He died a hero—a Texas Ranger—more than worthy of the star on his chest.

As more bullets start to rain down around us, I only hope he hasn't died in vain.

CHAPTER 87

I DON'T HAVE time to mourn. The ATVs are closing in fast.

Ariana and I hunker down in the shelter of the tanker. I yank open the ammo can and reload my rifle. She loads Kyle's.

"Aim for the ATVs," I say.

My thinking is we need to slow their advance. And the four-wheelers will be bigger targets than individual people, easier to hit.

Ariana crawls underneath the tanker and lies prone, aiming up the hill. I stay in a crouch and shoulder my rifle. I'm tucked back, partly underneath the tanker, out of sight for the sniper a thousand yards away. But one of the ATVs is taking a wide flank. I find the ATV in the scope and follow it as it slaloms down the hill around clumps of sagebrush. I don't recognize the driver—just one of McCormack's faceless mercenaries—but the man on the back has a splint on his nose.

It's the guy I tussled with outside my motel room and then talked to at the gate to McCormack's property.

I know I told Ariana to shoot for the ATV, but I

figure the ATV will be useless if there's no one alive to drive it. I put my crosshairs on the driver, lead him in relation to his speed, and squeeze the trigger as I keep my rifle moving.

The bullet smashes through his skull. The ATV runs directly into a rock the size of a microwave, and the passenger and dead driver fly headfirst over the vehicle. As Mr. Broken Nose rises, I put the crosshairs on him. He climbs aboard the ATV and tries to start it again. I could have killed him already, but I'm hesitating. It's not panic. Not like in my dream. It's something else. Just a feeling.

He pauses what he's doing, as if he can sense he's in my sights, and he looks my way. Even though we're separated by a good two hundred yards and there's no way he can see me with any clarity, I feel like we're staring eye to eye.

I line the crosshairs directly over the splint on his nose. One squeeze of the trigger and I would spray his brains over ten feet of sagebrush and rocks.

When I confronted him at the gate and encouraged him to do the right thing, he didn't say anything to suggest I made a dent in his armor. But I can't help but hope I made some kind of impression. Maybe he's not completely lost.

I lower my rifle, and instead of killing him, I put two rounds into the engine block of the ATV. Mr. Broken Nose darts for cover behind a cluster of boulders.

His retreat breaks me from my trance. I hope my mercy doesn't come back to haunt us.

Ariana fires on her side.

"One ATV down," she shouts. "The men are taking cover."

"I took out one ATV, too," I say, my voice hoarse and rough.

That leaves one more ATV. From where we are, we can't see it. We can only hear it. The motor has slowed, and it sounds like it's taking its time descending the hill. The two that were flanking us were easy targets, so whoever is driving this one has moved into a more direct line. That means if we step out to shoot at it, we'll be exposed to Gareth on the hill with his sniper rifle.

"When he gets down here," I say, "it's going to be a close-quarters gun battle. Get ready."

But the ATV doesn't come. Instead, when it's closer, within a hundred yards or so, it sits and idles. There is no talking among the soldiers, but I get an idea of what they're doing. The men on foot are making their way down the hill following a more direct line between the tanker and the sniper, gaining some cover.

"Can you get a shot on anyone?" I ask.

"No."

I peek my head out to try to find Mr. Broken Nose, but a bullet zings past me from the idling ATV. I lean back to a safer position.

We have slowed their descent, but we haven't stopped it. They're on a path we can't get to without exposing ourselves. When they get to the bottom of the hill, they'll try to rush us.

It will be two against five.

Semiautomatic weapons versus automatic weapons.

And those odds don't take into account Gareth, looming a thousand yards away with a gun so powerful and accurate that he can reach across that space with a high-velocity bullet and kill us before we even hear the report of the rifle.

Bullets start flying into the dirt in automatic bursts, creating dust clouds around us.

They're not trying to hit us—they just want to keep us pinned down. I huddle under the tank and try to breathe. I need to calm my frayed nerves. Ariana crawls over and we crouch back to back.

"Should we surrender?" Ariana asks, her voice full of fear.

"They won't let us live," I say. "We know too much."

I glance over at Kyle and Dale lying dead and bloody in the dirt. We will be joining them in another minute or two.

Something catches my eye.

When Kyle was running toward us, he was carrying the gun and the ammo can, but there was something else, a satchel of some sort. I squint through the dust cloud and realize what it is.

"Thank you, Kyle," I say aloud, slinging my rifle over my shoulder and preparing to run. "You're not only a hero—you're a goddamn genius."

CHAPTER 88

AS SOON AS there's a lull in the AR-15s firing, I sprint from my hiding spot. I don't even take the time to explain to Ariana what I'm doing. I'm just up and gone.

I snag the satchel without breaking stride. Bullets strafe the dirt behind me as I dive behind Kyle's F-150. They fire into the truck, and a metallic symphony fills the air. Jewels of glass explode from the windshield.

I make myself as small as possible, curled up and head down like I'm in elementary school during a tornado drill. Hollywood will have you believe a bullet can't pass through a vehicle, but that's far from true. A round from an AR-15 could enter a driver-side door and fly right through and out the passenger door on the other side. Fortunately, I'm at the front of the truck and they're shooting from the back, at a slightly downward angle from the hill, so there's a whole lot of metal to go through to get to me. They have to practically shoot through the whole truck lengthwise.

Finally, the firing stops. The silence in its aftermath is overwhelming.

I dig into the satchel, trying to be quiet so they'll think I'm dead. I glance over at Ariana. She has a terrified, confused expression on her face, but when

I pull out a bundle of road flares from the bag, a different look comes over her features.

A look of hope.

I'm hiding behind Kyle's truck—or what's left of it—which means I'm halfway between the tanker and my truck. My truck has a large colorless puddle underneath, and the air has reeked of gasoline since the sniper first shot it up, so I assume the gas tank's been punctured.

I pull the cap off the flare, exposing the igniter button on the end. I hold the sandpaper surface on the igniter, ready to strike. Watching from the tanker, Ariana gives me a nod.

As soon as I scratch the rough surface against the flare, brilliant, burning light bursts from the stick and the air is filled with the smell of sulfur. Molten chemicals spray onto my shirtsleeve.

I rise to my knees and lob the flare up into the air toward my truck, like I'm back on the football field making a short pass over a line of defenders to a receiver across the goal line. Only instead of my tight end, I'm throwing to a puddle of gasoline.

The flare lands right where I want it, and the effect is instantaneous: flames erupt around my truck. A column of thick black smoke rises into the air.

When Kyle was digging into his storage box, he must have had the realization that if we could light one—or both—of the trucks on fire, we might create a wall of smoke that could cover our retreat.

McCormack's men seem to realize what's at stake because they spring into action. The ATV motor roars, and I risk a glance to spot the gunmen charging down the hill. They're not far away at all—fifty yards from the tanker, maybe closer.

"Run!" I yell to Ariana, and I light the second flare.

I back away from Kyle's truck and give the flare a sidearm toss to squeeze it between the bumper and the ground. The gasoline underneath the truck ignites with a *whoosh,* and suddenly the air around me is twenty degrees warmer. I run, keeping the wall of smoke between me and the sniper on the hill. Bullets from the M24 come sailing through the cloud, but Gareth is firing blind. Without even discussing it, Ariana and I meet up and race toward a rocky ravine up ahead that bisects two hillsides and looks like it will be out of Gareth's sight.

The ATV roars around the tanker, carrying two of McCormack's men, the driver gripping the wheel with both hands and another guy on the back trying to steady his AR-15. Before he can get his bearings, I draw my pistol and spin and shoot, all in one fluid motion. The gunman on the back tumbles off, his flaccid body like a sack of dead weight.

The driver skids to a stop and reaches for the TEC-9 strapped to his chest. He swings the gun toward us, but I don't give him the chance to pull the trigger.

He slumps over the steering wheel, one of his eyes replaced by a bullet hole.

Then Ariana and I continue to sprint toward the cover of the ravine. The AR-15s start up like chain-saws, ripping the air apart. Bullets fly through the smoke, tearing giant clumps of dirt from the ground. But the shooters can't see us and don't realize that we've already retreated from the spot where they're concentrating their fire.

We arrive in the ravine but don't stop running. It's a tight corridor choked with brush and cacti, but we barrel through it all, ignoring the thorns tearing our clothes and needles stabbing into our skin.

As the ravine narrows into a slot canyon that might provide an escape route, I risk a look back. Through the chaos, I spot two of the men using fire extinguishers on the flames. These guys are fearless, getting right up on the vehicles, determined to get the fires out before the gas tanks explode. I'm not sure where the extinguishers came from. Maybe the cab of the tanker. Another might have come off the ATV.

A wildfire would bring a whole army of firefighters to this area, something McCormack definitely doesn't want. His men know they need to get the fires out as badly as they need to catch us. And it looks like they're doing a good job. The initial exposed gasoline has burned off, and neither vehicle ever became fully engulfed. The vehicles are still smoking terribly, though, which I'm thankful for. We need the cover.

While the two men fight the fires, they've sent one man ahead to keep pursuing us. I spot him at the mouth of the ravine, walking on foot through a thin veil of smoke and scanning the brush with his AR-15 shouldered and ready.

I recognize our pursuer immediately.

It's Mr. Broken Nose.

CHAPTER 89

ARIANA AND I slip farther into the slot canyon. The sides aren't high at first, but quickly they rise around us until we're standing in a canyon that's twenty feet deep but only three or four feet wide. The sandstone walls narrow at points where we have to squeeze through sideways. I'm over six feet tall and this kind of passageway wasn't built for someone my size. Our rifles make it even harder to maneuver through the tight passages.

Fortunately, Mr. Broken Nose is even bigger—not taller, but more muscular—and he'll have a hard time getting through. That he's coming, I have no doubt. He'll see the entrance to the canyon and know where we went.

Part of me thinks I should send Ariana ahead while I wait in hiding, ready to take him out. But a gunshot—even just one—will alert everyone else to where we are.

Our best bet is to make it out of the canyon and into some kind of hiding spot.

When the canyon widens, Ariana and I hurry as fast as we can. The silt-covered ground is loose and difficult to move through, like running on sand dunes.

Rays of sunlight shine down from the opening above. Dirt clouds float in the beams.

The passage forks from time to time, but we stick to the largest corridor. The smaller forks might narrow to a point where we can't get through.

I let Ariana lead the way, as I spend most of my time looking behind us, with my gun at the ready. I expect Mr. Broken Nose to come around a corner at any moment, spraying bullets.

"Shit," Ariana says, her voice barely more than a whisper.

I turn to see what the problem is. The passage we're in narrows to a point where the gap is no more than four to six inches. Not even Ariana can fit through it.

We're stuck at a dead end. The only way out is to go back the way we came or to look for another route through the labyrinth. Either option will bring us face-to-face with our pursuer.

I put my finger to my lips, and Ariana and I wait in silence. We can hear Mr. Broken Nose's footsteps, not far away. He's moving in spurts, which tells me that at each curve he's hiding and then bursting from cover with his gun ready, like a soldier clearing an abandoned building.

I aim my pistol at the curve he'll come from. It's only ten feet away. Close quarters. I'll have a split second to kill him before he pulls the trigger and fills the whole cavern with ricocheting lead.

Down here in the canyon, the temperature is ten degrees cooler than out in the sun. The silence is overwhelming. I can hear my own heart, my own breathing.

Distance is hard to judge in the canyon, but it

sounds like the footsteps are on the other side of the curve. I need to fire at the perfect moment. Too soon and I'll alert him. Too late and he'll open fire first.

In a blur, he bursts from cover, his rifle aimed directly at us. I lock my sight on his face.

I hesitate.

So does he.

He and I are frozen, each with the other in his sights. If he squeezes the trigger, maybe I can get a shot off. If I fire, all he has to do is tense his finger and Ariana and I are both dead.

But neither of us shoots.

"Hey, McQueen," a voice calls from far away, maybe the entrance of the slot canyon. "Any sign?"

Without taking his gun off me, Mr. Broken Nose shouts back, "No. It's a dead end in here. They must've gone another way."

"Get your ass back here, then. We need to report to Mr. McCormack."

"Be there on the double."

With that, Mr. Broken Nose—or McQueen— lowers his rifle.

I lower my pistol.

We stare at each other and have a moment of understanding. He knows I could have shot him on the hillside. So he's letting me live now.

He owed me one.

But now we're even.

I have no doubt that if he has me in his sights again, he won't hesitate to kill me.

I nod as a way of saying thank you. He turns and disappears into the canyon.

As we hear his footsteps retreating, Ariana and I collapse onto the canyon floor, exhausted and in shock.

My limbs are suddenly jelly as the adrenaline empties out of me. I feel faint. The sandstone walls spin. Ariana throws her arms around me and sobs, and I hug her back like I've never held anyone in my life.

Holding on to her is the only way I can believe that we're still alive.

CHAPTER 90

WE DECIDE TO hide in the slot canyon until night-fall before moving.

We have nowhere to go.

No plan.

No good options.

But we can hear what's happening outside. More ATVs have arrived, and they seem to be crisscrossing the hillsides, looking for us. We hear the engine of the tanker truck start up and the sound of it pulling away. More trucks arrive, which, by the sound of them, are tow trucks picking up the two destroyed F-150s.

"They're trying to get rid of all the evidence," I say.

What I don't say is that they're certainly picking up all the bodies, too, including Dale and Kyle. It makes my heart hurt to know that these men—both of whom died trying to do the right thing—might never get a proper burial.

Which reminds me how close I came to being with them.

"You saved my life," I say to Ariana. "Thank you."

She nods. She seems shell-shocked, crouched in the shadows with her arms wrapped around her legs. I move to sit next to her, my back against the sandstone wall, and try to offer some comfort.

"You did good today," I say. "You handled yourself under incredible pressure. You'd make a good Texas Ranger."

"If we survive," she says, "I'll give it some thought."

Her tone is cynical, but her lips curl into the hint of a smile. She may be accepting my compliment or realizing her own strength. The crucible we faced today was unlike anything I've ever experienced and should have dispelled any doubt Ariana had about how she would handle herself in the line of fire.

As the sun moves across the sky, the beams of light coming from the top of the canyon move to new angles, changing the hue of the sandstone walls. The surface of the rock looks like brushstrokes of a painting, a mixture of orange and brown and, as sunset approaches, a bloodlike crimson. In our hideout, there isn't much to do but sit in the shadows and think. What happened keeps playing through my mind in blurry, confused images. The chain of events seems fuzzy now—everything happened so damn fast—but I get flashes of thoughts that tie everything together.

Dale's mouth exploding with blood.

My hat lying in the dirt with a hole through it.

The look on Kyle's face right before the bullet knocked him down.

Neither of us have eaten anything since having a few slices of cold pizza last night. We're hungry and thirsty. We were both soaked with sweat from the gunfight, and now we feel dehydrated. I smell of gunpowder, and I'm filthy from head to toe. Having discarded my long-sleeved shirt, the remaining T-shirt is sweat stained and grubby. I've got a dull headache spreading from the back of my skull to my temples, and my face feels hot. I probably have a thermal burn from being too close to Kyle's truck when it went up in flames.

Ariana leans her body into mine, and I put my arm around her shoulders. She rests her head against my chest. A few minutes later, I can feel her body loosen, and I can tell she's fallen asleep.

I'm sure there's no way I will sleep, but I'm wrong. I try to think of what our next steps should be. But exhaustion worms its way through my body, and before I know it, I'm diving into the black cavern of sleep, too.

CHAPTER 91

THE SUN HANGS low on the horizon as Carson McCormack drives his pickup along the dirt road leading through his property. He arrives at the main tank yard, full of metal buildings and valve stations, and turns onto a field that abuts the mini village of structures. Ordinarily, the field is empty except for maybe a few horses allowed to graze there. Today, the field is erupting with activity.

A plow is running up and down the field, churning dirt beneath its blades. Meanwhile, a backhoe is digging a school-bus-sized hole in the soil at the edge of the field. Two tow trucks stand idling, their raised beds holding the burnt, bullet-riddled remains of the Texas Rangers' pickup trucks. Tendrils of smoke still radiate from the melted tires.

Dale Peters's tanker truck is nearby, with a crew of men unloading it. Despite being at the center of a firefight, the tanker looks okay. Some of the paint on one side blistered a little from the heat, but Gareth and the boys were careful not to put any bullet holes in it.

Carson parks and steps out. His son, who is overseeing all of the work, waves for his father to come over to the tow trucks. As Carson approaches, Gareth climbs up onto one of the flatbeds and extends a hand down to help his father up. The trucks reek of burnt metal.

Once Carson is on the flatbed with his son, he can see inside the bed of the truck. There's a pile of bodies. They've been tossed in, not laid neatly, and it's hard at first to count them. Carson notices there are two Stetsons in the pile, but only one of the Rangers they belonged to.

"I'm not happy," Carson says, stating the obvious to his son.

Gareth was supposed to take the men out this morning, using the tracker hidden on the tanker truck, and ambush Yates. If they could have hauled the bodies of Yates and Ariana Delgado back to the police station, they would have been heroes—catching the fugitive and her Texas Ranger accomplice.

Instead, Yates and Delgado are still alive, and Gareth ended up killing the new Texas Ranger instead, which could bring all kinds of attention to Rio Lobo.

"It's all under control, Dad," Gareth says, speaking loudly to be heard over the backhoe and plow. "Everything's gonna be okay."

"Like hell," Carson says. "I just got off the phone with Harris. You're lucky he was able to stop the fire department from investigating the smoke. They were halfway out there before he was able to call them back."

Gareth says that as soon as they drop the trucks into the hole, they'll cover them over and plow the whole field as a way to camouflage the new excavations.

"We've got corn," Gareth says. "We'll go ahead and plant a new crop. Everything will look normal."

"It's awful late in the season for planting," Carson says.

Gareth shrugs. "Late, but not *too* late. It's a good disguise. Who gives a shit if the crop is worth a damn."

"Someone's going to come looking for that missing Texas Ranger, Son. It doesn't matter how well we hide the trucks. There's other stuff on this property we don't want anyone to find."

Carson has always been a careful businessman, a planner who thinks ahead. That's why he's been so successful. He takes risks—transporting drugs throughout the Southwest is a risk—but they've always been controlled risks. He's never reckless.

They've buried bodies on the property before but never whole trucks.

"What if they bring in a plane and use infrared to find the buried trucks?" Carson asks. "They can do that, you know."

Gareth says that once the field is plowed, they'll park some equipment over the spots where the trucks are buried. To the naked eye, it will just look like a couple of pieces of heavy machinery are parked at the edge of a newly planted cornfield. To an infrared camera, the equipment will distort any images of whatever is under the ground.

"There's still a problem," Carson says. "Yates and Delgado are out there."

Gareth explains that once they're dead, then Harris can make up any story he wants. Pin the missing Texas Ranger on them.

"People already think she's a murderer," Gareth says. "And they think Yates is helping her."

Gareth explains that every dirt road from the open space is blocked with their men. At first light tomorrow, they'll redouble their efforts to search the open space. Half the team has been preoccupied today with cleaning up the mess. Tomorrow they'll be able to do a proper search.

And even if Yates and Delgado somehow make it out of the open space, there are roadblocks every conceivable way out of West Texas.

"We don't want them arrested," Carson reminds his son.

"Harris has at least one friendly at each roadblock. Accidents happen all the time transporting prisoners to jail."

The holes are ready. Carson and Gareth climb down to watch as the tow trucks begin to lower the burnt corpses of the F-150s into the ground. The one with the bodies goes first. It's Yates's truck—they can tell by the graffiti on the door. Instead of rolling, the malformed tires slide down the angled bed. When both vehicles are finally in the hole, the backhoe uses its front bucket to push the mound of dirt onto them. In a matter of minutes, the trucks—and the bodies— are gone.

Now the plow moves toward the disturbed dirt, ready to make the area of excavation indistinguishable from the rest of the field.

Before Carson heads back to his pickup, he says to his son, "The Ranger's star was gone. Where is it?"

Gareth, still wearing the desert camouflage he had on this morning in his sniper's nest, reaches into a cargo pocket in his pants and pulls it out.

"Souvenir," he says.

He also pulls out a crumpled ball cap that Carson recognizes as once belonging to Dale Peters.

Carson knows his son always takes trophies from the people he's killed.

"Don't worry," Gareth says. "I'll hide these real good. No one will find them."

Gareth has a pleased look on his face, as if he's brought home a football trophy to show off to his father.

"Don't be so fucking proud of yourself," Carson barks, his patience with today's fiasco finally snapping. "By my count, Yates got three to your two. You think you're better than him? Prove it."

Gareth goes red, his anger boiling just under the surface of his skin.

Carson knew this would piss him off. But he wants his son pissed. Gareth is the most competitive person he's ever known. Carson wants him angry and ready to destroy whatever stands in his way.

It's time for this game to come to an end.

"Don't worry, Dad," Gareth says, his eyes icy in the fading light. "That Texas Ranger won't live another twenty-four hours."

CHAPTER 92

I AWAKE TO moonlight coming down through the canyon instead of sunlight. My body is stiff. I try to rise without waking Ariana, but my shifting disturbs her. We both stand and stretch and try to get our bearings.

I feel weak, my stomach in knots. We haven't eaten in almost twenty-four hours. What I wouldn't give to have that sack of food Jessica gave me. But it was inside my truck and must be ashes now, along with everything else. There wasn't much of personal value in there, except for my guitar. I feel a pang of sadness knowing the source of so many good memories—especially memories with Willow—has been destroyed.

It's silly to feel sad about a musical instrument when what was really lost today was Dale and Kyle.

I can buy a new guitar.

But Dale and Kyle are gone forever.

A flame of anger rises inside me like an ember glowing with renewed life. I feel a growing resolve to keep pushing on. Earlier today I felt completely defeated. But now I'm getting mad. I'm not going to give up. I have to make sure Dale and Kyle—not to mention Susan Snyder and Skip Barnes—didn't die in vain.

I don't know what our long-term plan is, but I know what our first step is.

"We need to go to the river," I say. "There's that stash of food I brought you. We need to eat. We need to drink. We need strength."

We sling our rifles over our shoulders and make our way through the twisting corridors of the slot canyon. We walk to the place where the trucks burned. In the moonlight, we can see the ground is scorched, and some broken glass remains, but otherwise, there's no real evidence of what happened. The dirt with blood on it has been shoveled up. The tanker, of course, is gone.

We hike toward the river. The air is cool, and the desert hills look blue in the moonlight. We don't say much on the walk. My mouth is drier than I can ever remember it feeling. My muscles are sore from what I've put my body through in the last twelve hours. Inside my boots, my feet burn with blisters. My arms are scraped up from running through brush and cacti, and even though it hadn't been bothering me too much lately, the rash on my right hand seems to be flaring up, particularly on my trigger finger. I probably scraped it on a rock during our escape. Or it might simply be that the act of shooting so much was comparable to me scratching my finger over and over.

Whatever the reason, the hand and finger itch irritatingly.

I have no doubt Ariana feels as bad as I do—minus the rash—but to her credit, she never complains.

We arrive at the river and find Ariana's stash of supplies. We open cans of soup and choke them down cold. We've been starving all day, but now that we have access to food, neither of us feels particularly hungry. We have no appetite, but we certainly have thirst. We gulp from water bottles until our stomachs feel bloated.

Finally, when we have some energy back, Ariana says, "Rory, what the hell are we going to do?"

We're sitting at the riverbank where we went swimming, which feels like a hundred years ago.

"I've been thinking about that while we walked," I say. "You know that greenbelt that runs through McCormack's property? That little tributary with all the vegetation growing around it?"

Ariana knows what I'm talking about—the ribbon of oasis outside the fence line that passes the shooting range and the oil derrick.

"I'm assuming that waterway comes from the open space somewhere, right? Do you think you could find it?"

Ariana knows right where it is. When she was in high school, Gareth would drive a four-wheeler parallel to it and meet her in the open space.

"They've blocked every dirt road out of here," I say, "but I bet they won't expect me to walk right onto their property."

"It's a hell of a hike," she says. "Maybe ten miles."

Once the land begins to flatten out, she says, that means I'll be on McCormack's land.

"And at that point, I'll be able to get a cell phone signal, right?"

"Rory," she says, "what have you got in mind?"

I tell her my plan.

When I'm finished, she says, "That sounds like suicide."

"What other options do we have?" I ask.

She can't think of any.

CHAPTER 93

GARETH McCORMACK CAN'T sleep. He rises from his bed and paces through the ranch house, anxious for dawn to come so he can mobilize the men to hunt down Yates and Ariana. He can't wait to get his hands on them.

When he was in high school, he started a trophy box, keeping souvenirs of all the girls he slept with.

When he was in the army, he started a different trophy box—one that held souvenirs from all the people he killed.

Ariana avoided making it into his first trophy box. He's glad he'll have the chance to put her in the second. And as for Yates, Gareth doesn't think he's ever wanted to kill someone so bad.

He hates that fucking Texas Ranger.

His father thinks Yates is a worthy adversary, and Gareth can admit the guy is good—for a civilian. But Gareth has no doubt that in any contest—fists, knives, rifles, pistols—he could take the Texas Ranger. There is no scenario in which Rory Yates could best him.

Gareth steps out onto the front porch. The moon and stars provide some light, but most of the property is hidden in darkness. He can make out the gate and some of the fence line, white in the blackness, but the oil derrick a thousand yards away is completely invisible.

The land is silent, the air chilly.

A light comes on in his peripheral vision, and he turns his head to see a dull glow coming from his father's study. Gareth takes a plug of snuff and stuffs it in his lip. He spits into the grass, then heads back into the house.

"Can't sleep?" Gareth says, seeing his father behind his desk. "Me neither."

"I was just thinking about your mother," Carson says, leaning back in his plush chair.

The only light in the room is a desk lamp. They call the room a study, but it's bigger than some houses, with a vaulted ceiling and a picture window that a school bus could drive through. The wood-paneled walls are lined with animal mounts—a bear, an elk, a lion taken on an African safari—that Carson killed when he was younger and still interested in hunting.

"What about Mom?" Gareth asks.

"Just how glad I am that she's gone," he says and smiles widely.

Carson has a bottle of scotch and a tumbler with two fingers in it. He pulls another glass out of a desk drawer and offers Gareth a drink. By way of answer, Gareth takes the empty glass and spits tobacco juice into it.

He doesn't drink, doesn't use drugs. Shooting is his drug. Especially when a person is in the crosshairs.

There is no high that compares to killing a human being.

"What's that noise?" Carson says, annoyed.

Gareth doesn't know what he's talking about but

then realizes it's a phone buzzing. He checks his own pocket and finds that his phone is the one ringing.

"Who the hell is calling at this hour?" Carson says.

Gareth looks at the screen and sees that it's a Waco number.

Yates.

Gareth answers and says, "Did you decide to turn yourself in?"

The other end of the phone is quiet, and for a moment Gareth thinks there's no one there. Then Yates speaks.

"I let you win," he says.

"What?"

"Not with the rifles," Rory says. "You won that fair and square. Of course, you and I both know that contest was rigged because I hadn't had time to sight the gun for my eyes."

"What the hell are you talking about, Yates?"

"But with the pistols," Rory says, acting as if he wasn't interrupted, "I threw the game. I let you win."

"Bullshit," Gareth says, his stomach turning to acid. He's remotely aware of his father staring at him.

"You're pretty good," Rory says. "I'll give you that. But you're nowhere in my league. Not with a pistol anyway. Especially not in a real gunfight."

Gareth's heart is racing. He wants to reach through the phone and tear that arrogant asshole's throat out.

"You think 'cause you shot a couple of guys in a bank robbery that you know what it's like to kill?" Gareth says. "I've killed more…"

Gareth stops himself. He doesn't want to admit to all the murders he's committed, so many more than the twelve confirmed during his time in the army.

"You ever stood face-to-face with a man holding a

gun?" Rory says. "Ever shot anyone who had any real chance of fighting back?"

He hates to admit to himself that he hasn't. His army kills were all long-range sniper shots. Skip Barnes was, too. He also killed Rio Lobo's former police chief, making way for Harris to take over, but he'd hit him in the head with a rock and drowned the old man in the river. And all their old employees, the ones who were told they would be bought out, to start over somewhere else, he'd slashed their throats while they slept and buried their bodies out among the pump jacks.

Sure, he's killed a lot more people than Rory Yates has.

But not one of them knew what was coming.

Not one of them had any chance of shooting back.

"I'm happy to make you the first," Gareth snarls into his phone.

"Good," Rory says, "because I'm calling you out. No beer bottles this time. You and me, face-to-face. Two cowboys with two pistols. Nothing else. An old-fashioned showdown. A duel—to the death."

CHAPTER 94

"IS YOUR FATHER with you?" Rory asks.

"Yes."

"Put me on speakerphone."

Gareth does, setting the phone on top of his father's desk so both of them can hear.

"How much faith do you have in your son taking me down?" Rory asks.

"All the faith in the world," Carson answers, grinning.

"Okay, then here are my conditions."

Rory says that he'll show up to the ranch two hours after sunrise. He and Gareth will have a duel. Winner takes all. If Gareth kills Rory, then it's over, the McCormacks have won. But if Rory wins, Carson has to give his word that he'll surrender. Turn his operation over.

"This used to happen on ancient battlefields," Rory says. "Instead of two armies massacring each other, they sent in their best warriors—knights, samurais, whatever—to decide the outcome."

"The difference," Carson says, "is that you don't have an army."

"Not true," Rory says. "I've got a bigger army than

yours. I've got the whole Texas Ranger Division. And behind them I've got the DEA and the FBI and Homeland Security. They're not here yet, but they'll be coming if you're not careful. You might be able to stop me before I can bring them all in, but then again, maybe you can't. Do you want to take that risk? Or would you rather gamble on your son to end this once and for all?"

Carson is quiet for a moment. Gareth mouths the words, *Do it*.

"What about Ariana?" Carson says.

Rory changes the tone of his voice. "You didn't find her body?" he asks.

Carson and Gareth look at each other but say nothing.

"She took a bullet while we were running away," Rory says. "I stayed with her until she stopped breathing, but then I had to leave her behind. Your men were all over the area. I thought they would find her."

"Who got her?" Gareth asks. "Me or one of my guys?"

"I don't know," Rory says. "But I blame you. That's why I'm doing this. I want *you* to pay. I just need your daddy to give me his word that he won't gun me down afterward."

"You have my word," Carson says. "A duel. Winner takes all."

"I'll see you two hours after sunrise," Rory says and hangs up.

Gareth and his father stand in his office, grinning like hyenas.

Gareth says, "I'm going to kill that son of a—"

"Yes," Carson says, interrupting him, "you are, but not in any stupid duel."

Gareth glares at his father.

"I want you on that tower," Carson says, pointing at the darkness on the other side of the window. "When he shows up, I want you to put a bullet through his brain. You got it?"

"I can take this guy," Gareth says, his voice furious. "I'm not afraid of him."

"This isn't the fucking Wild West, Son," Carson snaps. "I'm not risking my whole operation on some dick-measuring contest between you and that Texas Ranger."

Gareth opens his mouth to argue, but Carson cuts him off. "You'll still get to kill him, Gareth. Just my way. Not his. He doesn't get to make the rules."

Gareth seethes.

Carson says that at first light he wants Gareth to walk out to the derrick and get into position. At the same time, he'll send out some teams into the open space to see if Yates was telling the truth about Ariana Delgado.

"I'm not sure that son of a bitch wasn't bluffing," Carson says. "This might be some trick. If he doesn't show and we can't find Delgado, it's time to pack all the merchandise and get ready for a raid. We'll haul out what we can, burn what we can't."

Gareth says that he doesn't believe Rory was lying. "He's a fugitive who aided and abetted a known felon," Gareth says. "He knows this is his only option. If he could call in the Rangers, he would have done it already."

Carson argues that what Gareth says would be true if the other Ranger was still alive. But if one Ranger has gone rogue and the other has gone missing, more Rangers will come. Which means the McCormacks need to resolve this today.

And the only way they can is by bringing the bodies of Yates and Delgado in on a platter.

"I still think I could take him in a shoot-out," Gareth says.

"Look at it this way," Carson tells his son. "Put the first bullet in his kneecap. And then put one in his balls. Torture him a little. Have fun with it. If you face off with pistols, you'll have to kill him too quick. I'd like to see the bastard begging for mercy, wouldn't you?"

As much as Gareth wants to prove his mettle against the Texas Ranger in a one-on-one duel, he likes even more the sound of making him suffer.

CHAPTER 95

WHEN I HANG up the phone, I check my battery and see that it's almost dead.

I take a deep breath and look out at the stars, which feel incredibly close this high off the ground. It feels like I'm floating in outer space.

I'm not.

I'm sitting on top of the oil derrick overlooking McCormack's property.

I spent most of the night walking through the green growth alongside the river with only the moon and the sound of the water to guide me. When I arrived at the derrick, sweaty and tired, I climbed to the top as quietly as I could. Through the blackness, I can see a few lights at what I assume is the ranch house. But otherwise, the whole landscape is dark.

When I proposed my plan to Ariana, I felt certain of two things.

First, I could bait Gareth into agreeing to the duel.

Second, his father would break his word. He would send Gareth out to the derrick to kill me from up here. Which is why, as soon as the sun starts to rise, I'm going to lie down behind the metal railing and wait for Gareth.

When he gets to the top, I'll arrest him and hand-cuff him to the derrick.

And then I'll have his rifle. I'll be outnumbered on his property, but the roles will be reversed from the situation I was in yesterday. I'll have the gun that can reach across a thousand yards. They won't be able to get to me, especially in the open expanse of the ranch. There's even less cover here than what we had yesterday.

I won't be as good a shot as Gareth would be, but I'll be good enough to hold them off until help arrives.

Which brings me to the second part of the plan.

Ariana.

She has to find a way to sneak past McCormack's men guarding the exit of the open space. Then she's going to hightail it to town, find Tom Aaron, and tell him everything she knows.

If he can get word to at least the Rangers in Waco, tell them what happened to Kyle, and back that up with something put out over the AP wire, we'll hopefully have a handful of law enforcement agencies converging on Rio Lobo by noon.

As long as I'm still alive, up here with a sniper rifle and Gareth as my hostage, I should be able to disrupt McCormack's plans long enough for help to arrive. If I'm dead, maybe McCormack will be able to clear out his operation. Take the drugs off his property. Clean up all—or at least most—of the evidence.

The sky is starting to turn from black to blue, the stars disappearing. In the distance, I can make out the shape of the ranch house and the barns and corrals.

I have one more play before I lie down and wait for Gareth. I pull out my phone. My battery is in the red. I waited to send this message until after I got off the phone with Gareth and Carson. I wanted to make sure I had at least enough juice for that call.

I type a message to my former lieutenant, Ted Creasy.

I'm not sure what my reputation is within the Rangers right now, if Kyle really has soiled my name and made it so they won't take a message from me seriously. Or, worse, if they think I'm an outlaw now, aiding a fugitive.

But Creasy will believe me.

And he'll do everything he can to send in the cavalry.

I write,

Multimillion-dollar drug ring operating out of Rio Lobo. Kyle Hendricks has been murdered. They've murdered at least three others. Primary suspects are Carson and Gareth McCormack. Rio Lobo police chief is compromised. Send reinforcements to the ranch of Carson McCormack.

I think for a moment and then add,

If I don't make it, tell my parents and brothers that I love them.

And Willow, too.

As I send the message, the screen goes black. The battery is dead. I don't know if the message went through or not.

CHAPTER 96

ARIANA SNEAKS THROUGH a copse of trees to get a closer look at the roadblock McCormack's men have set at the exit of the open space. The men are about two hundred yards away. The landscape is still gray in the morning light, but she can see well enough.

One of McCormack's black pickups is parked there along with an ATV. Two men sit in camp chairs next to a fire. One of the men is sleeping, but the other is alert.

Ariana drove Tom Aaron's Land Cruiser to a nearby ridge and walked the rest of the way. She has a plan to siphon some gas from the tank, put it in an empty water jug, and then set a fire somewhere else in the open space. When McCormack's men go to investigate, she'll race the Land Cruiser out of the open space as fast as she can.

It will take a lot of work because she needs to set the diversion far away from the Cruiser but close enough that she'll be able to get to it and escape without alerting the men.

She realizes that another, easier solution is available. She has the .223 M4 with her. She could probably kill both men before they knew what hit them.

She dismisses the idea. That isn't the way a police

officer conducts herself. They might deserve it. They might do it to her if the roles were reversed. But she can't bring herself to shoot them in cold blood.

She is about to sneak back to the Land Cruiser when she sees one of the men get a call on his walkie-talkie. They're close to the edge of the highway and must be able to get a radio signal. Ariana checks her phone and sees that in this canyon she has no bars.

"Damn it," she mutters, cursing her luck.

Who could she call anyway? She is a wanted fugitive.

But her luck takes a turn for the better.

"Come on," the one who answered the walkie-talkie says to the other, waking him up. "McCormack called. We've got a job to do."

The mercenary sits up, alert in an instant.

"We're supposed to go search for the Delgado woman. McCormack says she might be dead out there."

The men grab guns and supplies and mount the ATV. They fly off, leaving a cloud of dust in their wake.

Ariana gets ready to hurry back to the Land Cruiser, then has a thought. Did they leave the keys in the truck?

She refused to kill the men in cold blood, but she doesn't have any problem with stealing their truck. It would be a lot faster. When she runs over to their camp, she finds that her luck continues: the key is in the ignition.

Ariana fires up the truck and kicks up dust when she stomps on the gas. She races in the opposite direction from where the men went. When she hits blacktop, she floors the accelerator. It doesn't take long to arrive in town. The sun is just breaking the surface of the horizon. The town is quiet, the streets empty.

Ariana turns down the street that she and the Aarons live on. She pulls into the Aarons' driveway and immediately spots Jessica kneeling in the garden, no doubt getting an early start on her work before the heat of the day makes gardening unbearable.

"Is Tom here?" Ariana shouts.

"He's at the paper," Jessica says, rising from a crouch.

Ariana can't believe he'd be at work this early. As if she can read Ariana's confusion, Jessica says, "Today is deadline day. He always goes in early to get a jump on things."

Ariana says thanks and backs the truck out of the driveway, leaving Jessica with a confused look on her face. She races over to the paper. She wonders for a moment if she should park behind the building. There's no parking lot back there, just a sagebrush-filled area. The truck would be better hidden but not completely out of sight. She opts for the parking lot in plain sight. McCormack has a dozen of these trucks. She hopes it won't raise any suspicions.

She goes to the front door and finds it locked. There's no receptionist in the lobby. It's too early.

She pounds on the door as hard as she can, trying to make enough noise that Tom might hear it from his office. Twenty seconds later, he comes out from the newsroom. His expression changes from irritation to alarm when he sees Ariana.

"Ariana," he says, swinging the door open. "What the hell happened? Are you okay?"

Ariana smiles and says, "Are you ready to win the Pulitzer Prize?"

CHAPTER 97

THE ENTIRE NEWSROOM is empty, but Tom closes the door to his office anyway. He has a few employees who show up early on deadline days, and he wants to ensure that his and Ariana's conversation remains private.

"Tell me everything," he says. "Start from the beginning."

She does. It's an elaborate story, and it's taking longer to tell than she'd like, but she wants Tom to understand each detail. He needs to be able to convince the Rangers in Waco of everything that's happened, convince them not to trust the Rio Lobo police chief. Plus, Tom needs to keep her name out of it, because if the Rangers think this info came from Ariana Delgado, wanted fugitive, they'll discount it all and simply come after her. The more solid information Tom can convey, including about Lieutenant Hendricks's death, the more likely it is the Texas Rangers as well as the federal agencies will rush into Rio Lobo. Even if Rory doesn't survive—which she doesn't want to think about—the drug ring will be exposed.

"Okay, I think I got it all," Tom says as he looks over his notes.

Then he and Ariana hear something.

Footsteps.

They look through the window of the office door and see Chief Harris standing outside the window, gun drawn. One of his patrol officers, Hank Humphreys, is with him.

Ariana rises in a protective stance, but she has no weapon. She left the rifle in the truck. She didn't want to make Tom feel uneasy.

Speaking of the truck, she curses her stupidity for not parking it out back. Rory wouldn't be so eager to invite her into the Texas Rangers if he saw her now, she thinks.

Harris could easily open the door—it's not locked—but he opts for a more dramatic entrance. He slams the butt of his gun against the glass, exploding shards into the office. Then he steps back and kicks the door at its handle. The wood around the latch splinters, and the door bangs open, knocking more glass down onto the carpet.

Tom Aaron tries to get in front of Ariana, but she holds him back with her arm so they stand side by side.

"This is outrageous," Tom shouts. "You have no authority to walk in here and—"

Harris slams the butt of his pistol against Tom's nose, sending him flying backward onto the floor.

"Here's my authority, you son of a bitch."

Ariana moves to intervene but freezes when she sees Humphreys's pistol pointing at her chest. Harris grabs Ariana by the hair and yanks her head back. He places the barrel of the pistol under her chin.

"You couldn't just leave it alone, could you?"

"You're a disgrace to that badge," Ariana says.

Harris throws her into a corner and tells her to put her hands against the wall. He places the gun in the small of her back and begins searching her. His hand lingers on places she doesn't want him to touch.

Humphreys grabs Tom and pulls him to his feet. His nose is clearly broken. Blood cascades over his mouth and chin. He blinks back tears and looks woozy.

Humphreys shoves him over the desk and cuffs his hands behind his back. Tom's face is pressed against his notebook, blood dripping onto the pages. Harris picks up the notebook, glances at the notes, and flips it closed. He shoves it into his back pocket.

"What's wrong, Chief?" Ariana says. "Don't like what you see there?"

"This is a violation of the First Amendment," Tom says, his voice nasal and hoarse. "My lawyer—"

Harris pulls his gun back and jams the barrel against Tom's nose. Tom winces in pain and turns away from the barrel.

"You can take your lawyer—and your First Amendment—and shove them up your ass."

Ariana thinks of what Rory might say in this situation.

"It's not too late to come out on the right side of this, Chief."

Harris grabs her by the hair again and shoves her against the wall. He leans his body against her and places the gun against her lower back. His mouth is by her ear. She can smell the coffee on his breath.

"Keep talking and I'll smash that pretty face of yours," he says, his voice barely more than a whisper.

Ariana doesn't respond. She knows that won't get her anywhere.

Harris looks at Humphreys and says, "Take Tom

to the station and wait to hear from me. Lock him up. Don't let him make a phone call. Not to his lawyer. Not to his wife."

"What about Ariana?" Humphreys says, pulling Tom by his cuffed wrists.

"The Rio Lobo Police Department is about to have an opening for a detective," Harris says. "If you want the job, shut your goddamn mouth and don't ask any more stupid questions."

CHAPTER 98

I TRY TO stay hidden, but I position myself to watch McCormack's ranch through the scope of the .223 M4. The telescopic sight doesn't have the magnification Gareth's M24 does, so I can't see much. But I see enough.

A trio of ATVs peels off from the house and heads in the direction of the open space. No doubt going to look for Ariana. One of my reasons for making up the story was so they might do that. That's six fewer of McCormack's soldiers I have to worry about right now.

I'm beginning to wonder if Gareth isn't going to come out here after all. If he doesn't climb up on the tower, I've already decided I will climb down and walk over to the ranch.

We'll have that showdown.

It will be suicide, of course.

Even if I shoot Gareth in an honest-to-God duel, there's no way Carson McCormack will stick to his word. His men will gun me down within seconds.

But I'll do it.

As long as he doesn't double-cross me, I won't double-cross him. That's just the way I was raised.

When I'm almost convinced he's not coming, I spot a figure leaving the ranch house and heading this way on foot. I focus the sight. The person is Gareth, and he has his sniper rifle slung over his shoulder and his SIG Sauer holstered at his hip. He's dressed in black clothes, no doubt so he can stay hidden atop the derrick, where I'm hiding now.

The platform is a square with a hole in the middle. To one side of me is the metal mesh railing, which will keep me from rolling off. But in the center, where the drilling equipment would be if the derrick was operational, there is nothing but a straight drop to the ground.

I lie flat on my back to stay out of sight. I keep the rifle at my side. I don't pull my pistol out of its holster.

Not yet.

I don't want my hands to sweat on the grip.

Gareth has half a mile to walk. I try to calm my nerves, slow my breathing. I stare at the sky—blue from horizon to horizon without a single cloud.

I think of Willow.

I think of Ariana.

I think of my father telling me, *A Texas Ranger is justice*.

When Gareth gets close, I can make out the sound of his pants moving through the overgrown weeds. When he's below, I hear the crackle of a walkie-talkie.

"Gareth, come in," Carson says over the walkie-talkie.

"Yeah, I'm here," Gareth says.

I'm eighty feet above him, but the air is so clear and silent that I can hear every word of the exchange.

"Harris has the girl. Delgado. She's alive."

"Copy that."

"Yates lied to us. He's up to something."

My heart pounds. Fear flows through my veins. *Please, God, don't let them hurt her.*

"What do you want me to do?" Gareth asks. "Come back?"

Carson tells him not to return to the ranch house. He wants Gareth to go ahead and get into position in case I show up.

"If Yates isn't here by the deadline, I'll send someone to pick you up. In the meantime, Harris is bringing her to the ranch. We'll get her to talk. I told McQueen to get the blowtorch."

"Don't kill her," Gareth tells his father. "I want a lock of that bitch's hair for my trophy case."

They end the connection. A second later, I hear Gareth's boots on the ladder, scaling the oil derrick.

I stand up as quietly as I can, staying out of sight of Gareth as he climbs. The platform is small. The world seems to sway around me. I feel like I could topple over and fall right down the middle. My stomach clenches.

I take my SIG Sauer out of its holster. I slide my finger inside the trigger guard.

One of Gareth's hands comes over the top onto the platform. Then the other. He hoists himself to where his head can swing over the ledge.

"Hold it right there, Gareth," I say, aiming the gun at the bridge of his nose. "Make any sudden moves and I'll drop you off this tower with a hole in your skull."

He looks at me and laughs. His eyes are covered by sunglasses, so it's hard to be sure, but his facial

expression indicates he isn't the least bit surprised—
or scared.

"You double-crossing son of a bitch," he says, as
if we're old pals and I just played a practical joke
on him.

"I only double-crossed you because I knew you'd
do it to me."

He shakes his head. "It was Dad's idea."

"I figured," I say.

He doesn't seem at all concerned that I'm about to
arrest him, which has me worried. Doesn't he know
he's beat?

His rifle is slung over his back and his pistol is
on his hip. He can't get to either one of them in the
position he's in, not before I get a shot off.

I tell him to climb up onto the platform, keeping
his hands where I can see them and away from his
gun belt. He does as he's told. I back up to give him
space, and he stands up, staring at me defiantly. Then
I tell him to slowly remove the rifle from his shoulder,
holding it only by the barrel, and set it on the metal
platform, the barrel pointed toward him.

Again, he does as he's told.

Keeping my gun on him, I pull my handcuffs off
my belt with my free hand.

"Now," I say, "use only the thumb and forefinger
of your left hand to unholster your pistol. Drop it off
the derrick."

"No," he says.

"Excuse me?"

"I got an alternate proposal," he says, grinning
like he holds all the cards. "How about we have that
old-fashioned shoot-out after all?"

CHAPTER 99

"THAT'S NOT HOW this works," I say to Gareth. "You're under arrest."

"Like hell," he says.

"Gareth," I say, "we're eighty feet off the ground, and I've got a gun aimed at your heart. You're about to go skydiving without a parachute. I'm not messing around."

"Neither am I," he says. "You ain't taking me alive, Yates. I'm going for my gun one way or another. The only choice is whether you give me a fighting chance. Come on, cowboy. Holster that gun and prove that you're quicker than me."

I don't want to take his bait. I would be stupid to agree. When we were out on the range, I missed the bottle on purpose, but he was still just as fast as me. Now we're less than ten feet apart, standing on top of an eighty-foot oil derrick — and I'm a much bigger target than a beer bottle. Even if I'm faster and more accurate, I would put myself at great risk.

I could get wounded.

I could get killed.

I could fall right off this damn oil derrick.

"I've got nothing to prove to you," I say.

"Come on, Ranger," Gareth says. "I know a part of you wants to do it."

He's right.

A part of me.

The hothead part that's always getting me into trouble.

But I'm considering his proposal. I hate the son of a bitch standing in front of me. I hate him because he killed Dale Peters and Skip Barnes and probably Susan Snyder. I hate him because he dated the girl I like and treated her like shit. I hate him because he was born into the kind of privilege most people can only imagine, and he's done nothing with it except hurt other people. I hate him because he's an arrogant, egotistical, chauvinist asshole. I hate him because he's a homicidal maniac. I hate him because, when it comes down to it, he's a bully.

But mostly I hate him because he killed a Texas Ranger.

Kyle and I had our differences, but at the end of the day, he and I wore the same badge. My mind flashes to an image of Kyle, coughing up blood with his last breaths, and I can't help myself.

The hothead inside me wins.

"All right," I say, keeping my gun on Gareth. "I'll give you a fighting chance. But first you have to answer three questions."

He looks hesitant. In my peripheral vision, I get the sense that we're being watched from the ranch house. But I can't take my eyes off Gareth long enough to be sure. Unless they have a sharpshooter as good as Gareth, we're too far for any of them to do anything. I think they're going to let this play out, confident Gareth can handle himself. Until I hear ATVs racing to get in range, I'm going to assume that's the case.

"If you're so damn confident you'll beat me," I say to Gareth, "then what does it matter? You're going to kill me sixty seconds after you give me your confession."

He shrugs, consenting to my questions.

"That was you up on the hill yesterday?" I say. "You killed Dale and Kyle?"

Gareth nods, grinning. Proud of himself.

"And you killed Skip Barnes and Susan Snyder?"

"Not Susan," he says, still smiling. "Poison ain't my style."

"Why'd you set up Ariana?" I ask. "You could have just made Skip disappear. Why the whole elaborate frame job?"

"It seemed like a good idea at the time. It almost worked. Once I kill you, it will work." He chuckles, so pleased with himself. "Besides, it felt kind of poetic after what I done to her daddy."

"What?" I say, surprised for the first time by any of these admissions.

"I set him up for selling drugs back when we were in high school," Gareth admits. "Stashed the bag in the janitor's closet. Got my buddies to tell the cops that he sold to them. That's what that little bitch gets for not putting out after Homecoming."

I'm on fire inside. I've never felt such rage. Even in high school, the depravity of Gareth McCormack knew no bounds.

"Who killed Susan Snyder?" I say, trying to subdue the anger in my voice.

"Sorry, Ranger. You're out of questions."

He's right. I should have made it ten questions, but I gave him my word that we would do this.

"Fine," I say.

I toss the handcuffs toward his feet. They slide across the metal and stop at his boot. Then I holster my gun.

I hold my hand at my side, six inches from my gun. Gareth does the same.

"Here are your choices, Gareth," I say. "Reach slowly for the handcuffs and you live. Reach quickly for your gun and you die."

He doesn't look the least bit nervous.

What a sight we must be, standing atop an oil derrick, facing off like a couple of Texas gunslingers from a hundred fifty years ago.

"Before you make your choice," I say, "know this. You're stronger than me. You're a better shot with a rifle than I am. You were probably a better football player than I ever was, and you were no doubt a better soldier than I ever could be. But there's one thing I do better than anyone. You want to test me on that, I'll see to it you wake up tomorrow morning in hell."

He smirks. "Nice speech. You finished?"

"Yeah," I say. "My conscience is clear. You've been warned."

"Good," he says.

And his hand flies as fast as lightning to his gun.

CHAPTER 100

IN A SPLIT second, he snatches his gun grip, yanks the pistol free, slides his finger into the trigger guard, and raises the barrel—all in one fluid motion. All at an unbelievable speed.

He's the fastest gunman I've ever seen.

But he's not fast enough.

My bullet punches a hole through his heart before he can get his pistol into a firing position. He takes a step back, his face filled with surprise. He tries to lift the gun to get off a shot, but his muscles aren't working anymore—not with his heart gushing blood from the hole in his chest instead of pumping it through his body.

I holster my gun.

His arm drops to his side and the pistol slips from his fingers, clanging against the metal. His knees buckle, and he topples forward into the big opening where the drilling equipment would normally be. He falls headfirst, his body spinning in a half somersault, globs of blood arcing out behind him. He lands on his back eighty feet below with a sickening thud.

I stare down at Gareth McCormack. His sunglasses have fallen off, and his vacant eyes stare upward.

There's no life behind his stare—I can tell that even from this far away.

"I told you once, you son of a bitch," I mutter aloud, not that he can hear me.

He was dead before he hit the ground.

I turn away from Gareth over toward the ranch house. A half mile is a long way to see with the naked eye, but I can make out a cluster of men standing in the grass by the ranch house. I assume Carson McCormack is one of them.

I see something else—Harris's police cruiser coming up the driveway.

I kneel down and grab Gareth's M24. I check to make sure it's loaded, then I pull the gun up to my shoulder and try to orient myself with the telescopic sight.

I get the scope into position in time to see McCormack yanking Ariana from the police car. He makes her face toward the derrick and he stands behind her, using her as a shield. He's quite a bit taller than her, but only his head and shoulders are exposed. In one hand, he holds a walkie-talkie. In his other hand, he holds a pistol.

He points it at Ariana's temple.

She looks scared, but more than that she looks apologetic—she thinks she's disappointed me.

A static crackle comes from eighty feet below, and I hear Carson say from the walkie-talkie still on Gareth's belt, *"Yates. Can you hear me?"*

I can't answer. Instead, I scan the other men. I count three others besides Carson.

Harris.

McQueen—aka Mr. Broken Nose.

And one more guy I haven't seen before.

Harris hasn't drawn his gun, but the two soldiers carry automatic weapons. The one I don't know is holding binoculars to his eyes, relaying to McCormack what he sees.

"You just killed the only thing I ever cared about," Carson says from below. *"How about I hurt something you care about?"*

I kneel and use the railing as a shooting rest. I put the sight on McCormack, but I can't keep the gun steady. The crosshairs float all over the place. A foot to his left. A foot to his right.

He knows I can't make this shot—that's why he isn't ducking for cover.

I might have been able to draw a pistol faster than his son, but when it comes to this rifle and shooting a bullet the length of ten football fields, I'm not in the same league as Gareth.

"I'm going to count to three, Yates," Carson says through the walkie-talkie on Gareth's belt. *"When I get to three, I'm going to shoot Ariana. If you want to save her, drop my son's rifle off the derrick before I get to three."*

CHAPTER 101

I TRY TO remember where my bullet hit the last time I fired this gun.

A foot high and to the left.

If I were sighting in the gun, I'd shoot at least three times, try to find a pattern, then adjust the sight. The problem is I've had only one test shot.

I aim at what I think would account for the difference—a foot low and to the right—and I find that the crosshairs are lined up directly over Ariana's face.

"One," Carson says.

I can't do this.

There's no way to know if the range is the same. It looks like a thousand yards, but I could be off a hundred either way. I'm shooting at a downward angle now—that changes things, too. And there's no real way for me to know that the one and only shot I've taken with this rifle was a good one. If I took one or two or ten more shots, it's doubtful they would hold a tight pattern around the first. I don't know if the adjustment I'm making is the right one.

I stare at Ariana's scared expression through the scope.

If I squeeze the trigger, I might kill her.

But if I toss down the gun like Carson wants, he'll kill us both.

Taking this shot is the only chance we have.

"Two."

My trigger finger itches—that damn rash!—and I try to push the distraction out of my head.

My father taught me there's a lot that goes into being an accurate shooter. There's your angle and trajectory, velocity and range, all that stuff—physics and math. But to be a truly good shooter, it's really about the feeling.

Muscle memory.

Knowing in your gut—not on a piece of paper—that you can make the shot. Especially when you're shooting at something more than paper targets.

I learned to trust my feeling when I was growing up hunting deer, when I'd shoot uphill, downhill, sometimes at targets bounding through the trees. And I learned to trust my feeling in the Rangers when the thing I was hunting could shoot back.

I tell myself to trust my feeling.

I line the crosshairs over Ariana's nose.

From the walkie-talkie below, I hear Carson say, *"Thr—"*

I squeeze the trigger.

CHAPTER 102

"—EE," CARSON SAYS.

Ariana sees the muzzle flash from Rory's rifle, just a tiny spark from atop the oil derrick. She knows she has a second or two to wait for the bullet and considers trying to dive to the ground. But that might disrupt where Carson is positioned and make Rory miss.

She has to trust Rory.

Carson must have seen the muzzle flash as well and doesn't believe Rory can hit him. As soon as the bullet zings by, she's sure the gun jammed against her temple will go off and she'll be gone.

She closes her eyes and waits.

I believe in you, Rory, she thinks.

There is a noise—*thwack!*—like the sound of a nail gun popping against a piece of plywood. The sound is so close and so loud that she's sure the bullet must have hit her.

But then the gun barrel jammed against her skull pulls away.

She opens her eyes and turns her head in time to see Carson McCormack falling backward, as stiff as a board. He lands unmoving in the grass, his python-skin boots pointing at the sky.

Her whole body feels numb. She lets out a breath she didn't know she was holding.

I can't believe I'm alive, she thinks.

And then she realizes this isn't over. Harris and two of McCormack's men are still crowded around her. Harris—her former boss, that son of a bitch—reaches for his pistol.

Ariana scrambles onto her knees and pries the gun out of Carson McCormack's dead fingers.

"Freeze!" Ariana shouts, pointing the gun at Harris.

He stops, his gun half in, half out of its holster. He looks scared for an instant, and then he realizes the odds remain in his favor. He grins.

"Ariana, sweetheart, you're still outnumbered."

Keeping her gun on Harris, she glances around quickly. The guy with the broken nose and the other man both have their AR-15s aimed at her.

She turns her attention back to Harris and sees that he's pulled his gun the rest of the way out. He hasn't raised it yet, but his body language tells her that he feels confident she won't shoot.

He's wearing a bulletproof vest, and although it's unlikely to fully stop a bullet at this close range, she's sure it's giving him extra confidence. She raises the gun so it's aimed at his face. Then, still crouched over Carson McCormack's body, Ariana reaches down slowly and picks up the walkie-talkie.

"Rory," she says into it. "If you can hear me, I've got Harris. Put your gun on one of the other guys."

Harris chuckles. "It's still three against two, sweetheart," he says. "And as soon as the shooting starts, your boyfriend ain't gonna be able to hit a goddamn thing. That shot against Carson was impressive, but we both know he ain't no Gareth McCormack with that thing."

"You'll be dead first," Ariana says.

"You've got to hit me for that to happen," he says, and he begins leaning his head from side to side, like a boxer bobbing and weaving. "The rest of us here, we've served in war zones. This ain't nothing new to us."

Ariana's arm begins to tremble. She can't help it.

She knows that if she pulls the trigger, she's dead. Even if Rory gets someone with his first shot. Even if he gets them all after the fact. As soon as the first shot is fired, she's dead.

"It's three against two," Harris says again, unable to keep from grinning. "Your call."

Ariana prepares to pull the trigger.

If she has to die today, she's going to go down fighting.

"Actually," she hears someone say in a nasal voice. "It's two against three."

She looks over and sees that the soldier with the broken nose—the one Rory had talked to at the gate that day—is pointing his AR-15 at McCormack's other man.

Harris looks like a gambler who thought for sure the three aces he was holding would be a winning hand, only to find himself penniless after his opponent dropped a royal flush.

Ariana glares at Harris and says, "Your call, *sweetheart*."

CHAPTER 103

I WATCH THROUGH the rifle scope as Harris and the other man lower their weapons and set them in the grass. Ariana, with the help of Mr. Broken Nose— or McQueen, as I guess I need to start calling him— makes the two men lie on the ground with their hands clasped behind their heads.

When I'm sure they have the threats secured, I sling McCormack's M24 over my shoulder and start down the ladder. It takes me almost ten minutes to walk over to where they are. When I get there, Ariana gives me a tight hug.

She was stoic through it all, but when she's in my arms and I can feel the tremble of fear in her body, I get a sense of just how scared she was.

"You saved my life," she whispers in my ear.

"I owed you one," I say, and then when we break the embrace, I wink and give her a smile.

I walk over to McQueen and extend my hand.

"I had a feeling about you," I say.

"I couldn't stand by and be a part of this anymore," he says. "I knew what we were doing was illegal, but I never signed on to hurt innocent people. I didn't sign on to kill Texas Rangers."

"You did the right thing," I say. "If most of your brethren in the armed forces are more like you—and less like Gareth McCormack—then America is in good hands."

"If the rest of the Texas Rangers are anything like you," he says, "then Texas is in great hands."

We both laugh. It feels good to laugh.

I ask McQueen if he'll help us until the cavalry arrives. When more law enforcement officers get here, I'll ask him to give up his gun.

"You'll be arrested," I say. "But I swear I'll do everything I can to make sure you're treated fairly. We'll need a cooperating witness to help us make sense of everything that's been going on here. If I have anything to do with it, you won't see the inside of any jail cell."

He considers my proposal.

"The other option," I say, "is you take off right now. You'll be a fugitive, but I won't stop you from going. Not today. I owe you that."

He shakes his head. "No. I'll stick around and do the right thing. Like you said, it's not too late."

I nod my head and turn back to Ariana.

It's been an intense forty-eight hours. Her hair is a mess. Her face is streaked with dirt. Her clothes are torn and dirty.

But she has a smile on her face that gives me butterflies.

"What now?" she says.

I nod to Harris, lying in the grass with his hands over his head.

"You want to do the honors?"

She smiles even bigger.

"With pleasure," she says.

She walks over and kneels next to Harris's face.

"Chief John Grady Harris," she says, "you have the right to remain silent..."

CHAPTER 104

THIRTY-SOME HOURS later, Ariana and I are at the Rio Lobo police station, talking through the latest in the investigation.

A lot has changed.

Instead of the two of us by ourselves in the cramped conference room, there are at least fifteen other people representing a variety of agencies: the Texas Ranger Division, the county sheriff's department, the FBI, the DEA, the ATF, and Homeland Security. Each has at least a few representatives here.

And this meeting is only the tip of the iceberg, just the epicenter of the investigation tornado. Out and about in Rio Lobo, there are two dozen Rangers—not to mention at least twice that many other law enforcement officials—doing investigative work. Most of them are at McCormack's ranch, searching the buildings and the property, bagging evidence, scouring the hills with cadaver dogs, excavating hidden graves. At least ten people are just inventorying all the cocaine and illegal guns we've found. Other investigators are interrogating town officials. We don't yet know how widespread the corruption was and who all was in on it, but I feel certain that the arrests we've made so far—Harris, his right-hand man Hank Humphreys, and fifteen of McCormack's soldiers—won't be the last.

The town population has probably doubled in size overnight if you add all the law enforcement officials and all the journalists who have converged on this little map dot, vying for rooms in the motel, which was vacant a day ago and is now filled to capacity, with the overflow bunking in RVs or tents set up in vacant fields. Every major newspaper in Texas is here, not to mention all the national news channels. Reporters from CNN and *Today* aren't too famous to wait sixty minutes for a restaurant table. The town's two stoplights can't tame the street traffic.

I've been told that what happened in Rio Lobo is the top story on every news network. This won't go down as the biggest drug bust in US history, but it will certainly make the top ten.

Not that I've seen the news myself. I've been working nonstop since I climbed down from the oil derrick, with the exception of about two hours of sleep and the time it takes to shower and put on clean clothes. The El Paso company commander brought me new pants and shirts since everything I had burned up in my truck.

McQueen has been a big help, explaining McCormack's operation, pointing us to where Kyle and the others were buried, showing us the stockpile of drugs McCormack had on the property. McQueen is currently housed in Rio Lobo's one and only jail cell, but if I have anything to do with it, his incarceration will be temporary.

Every hour or so a new bombshell of information drops in front of me.

Earlier today someone found a cardboard box hidden under the floorboards on McCormack's property that contained a variety of items, ranging from Middle Eastern clothing to Kyle Hendricks's badge, Dale Peters's familiar Dallas Mavericks cap, and Skip Barnes's cell phone. Skip's phone revealed texts from Gareth assuring him that the McCormacks would buy his silence and asking him to meet Gareth by the old shed out by the oil derrick—a trap luring him to his death.

We suspect the box holds keepsakes of some kind from all or most of Gareth's victims, and we've got people trying to figure out who once owned the rest of the items. The fact that the box contained a belt buckle Ariana recognized as belonging to the former police chief has led us to believe that Gareth killed him to put Harris in power. That's a new arm of the investigation. What happened with Ariana's father, who is now in the final months of his prison sentence, is another new aspect.

Despite how busy we've been, Ariana was able to make a tearful phone call, telling him that for the first time in her law-enforcement career she could finally help him and apologizing for ever doubting his innocence.

Cadaver dogs also sniffed out some hidden gravesites on the property, and we now believe that the employees who used to work for McCormack, the ones he supposedly bought out and sent on their way, were probably killed. That would include the lead singer Dale and Walt used to play with. We're waiting on DNA testing of all the bodies. I haven't had a chance to talk to Walt yet about Dale. I'm sure he's heard—everyone in town knows—but I'm going to have to break it to him that his other friend was also murdered.

When I first met Harris, he bragged that Rio Lobo hadn't had a murder in over a decade. Turns out that was far from true.

After a long time of spinning our wheels in this investigation, it feels good to finally get some answers. Ariana and I have been going on adrenaline and caffeine, but I can feel my body needing to crash. All I want is to crawl back to my little apartment over Tom and Jessica's garage and pass out.

But before we call it a day, Ariana and I—and the rest of the team leaders—are talking about a mystery we still haven't solved.

The death that started all this.

Who killed Susan Snyder?

Gareth admitted to me that he killed Kyle, Dale, and Skip, but he denied murdering Susan. He said poison wasn't his style, suggesting that she *was* killed. We just don't know by whom.

"Did you ask McQueen?" a senior special agent from the FBI asks me.

"Yeah," I say. "He swears he didn't know about their involvement. Like everyone else, he was still fooled into thinking the McCormacks were bad, just not *that* bad. Drug dealers but not murderers."

We speculate about whether Harris knows anything, but so far he hasn't been willing to cooperate. He and the others are locked in the jail at the county seat.

"After all that's happened," Ariana says, shaking her head in disbelief, "we're back to square one on the murder that started it all."

Ariana has circles under her eyes and looks as tired

as I feel, while somehow remaining as beautiful as ever. Like me, she was able to get a shower and change into clean clothes. She's back in her signature jeans, white T-shirt, and boots, with her hair pulled back.

It's been a pleasure to work with her. We make good partners.

I can't help but think we might make good partners off duty as well.

As I'm looking at Ariana and thinking this, I realize a hush has come over the crowd in the station.

"Is that who I think it is?" someone says.

I look up from my daze and see a familiar face standing in the lobby.

Willow.

When she sees me, she rushes through the crowd of people, wraps her arms around me, and gives me a big, long kiss on the mouth.

Someone starts applauding, and then the whole station joins in, laughing and smiling in a setting that has been nothing but grim and serious since investigators started arriving in Rio Lobo.

Willow breaks our kiss and hugs me tight.

"I came as soon as I heard," she says into my ear.

I hold her close, but I catch myself looking over her shoulder at Ariana, feeling like I'm cheating on both of them.

CHAPTER 105

INTRODUCING ARIANA TO Willow feels surreal.

Part of it, I think, is just how sleep deprived I am. But on top of that, seeing the two of them shake hands feels like two worlds colliding.

Or maybe two alternate futures.

The expression on Ariana's face portrays contradictory emotions. She seems genuinely happy for me that my girlfriend is here to support me. But at the same time, she seems subdued, saddened by the reminder that I have a girlfriend. When I explain that Ariana saved my life, Willow is effusive in her gratitude.

I tell Willow that I have a little more work to do before I can beg off from my responsibilities, but Ariana tells me to go ahead and call it a day.

"Go get some sleep," she says, pushing me playfully toward the door. "You deserve some R and R."

"You do, too," I say.

"I'm right behind you," she says. "I'll be out of here in fifteen minutes."

"If anything comes up, call me," I say.

"No," Ariana jokes. "Turn your phone off."

I realize that in all the chaos of these hours, I never recharged my battery. It's still as dead as a doornail.

"Give yourself one night of rest," Ariana says. "Then we'll hit it hard again tomorrow. If I really need to find you, I know where you'll be."

Willow and I walk to her rental car, which she picked up at the El Paso Airport. The streets are so crowded that she had to park several blocks away. It would be faster to walk straight to Jessica and Tom's, but her stuff is in the car. Besides, it's nice to walk with her. The sun is setting, and the landscape looks picturesque. Willow takes my hand and intertwines her fingers with mine.

When we arrive at Tom and Jessica's, I carry Willow's bag and her guitar case—like me, she never goes anywhere without it—and Jessica spots us and rushes out to greet us. She gives me a big hug and then beams at Willow.

"I've heard your song on the radio," Jessica says. "I love it!"

She asks if we want any dinner, but Willow ate a sandwich on the drive and I've been living on whatever food arrives at the station. Tonight it was cold pizza. Again.

Jessica offers to make us breakfast, and I consent, telling Willow that she makes the best pecan pie I've ever had.

"How's the intrepid reporter doing?" I ask.

She says Tom is okay. His nose looks like hell, but he hasn't complained about it. He's spent almost as much time at the paper as I've spent at the police station, putting out a special edition of the *Rio Lobo Record* and then being interviewed by every major network that sent a news van to town.

"This is his fifteen minutes of fame," she says jokingly. "He gets to be a big-time journalist for a while. No bandage on his nose is going to stop that."

Willow and I retreat to my little studio apartment. I unstrap my gun and put it in the safe, honoring Jessica's wishes to keep it locked up. Then I strip off my boots and sit on the bed. I'm so exhausted that I almost don't want to go through with the conversation I know I need to have with Willow.

She stands by the window, looking out at the arroyo and the desert hills. She's wearing blue jeans and boots with a red blouse—nothing fancy, but she still looks like the gorgeous country star that she is. Her golden hair catches the light, and I can't help but stare. The picture I'm looking at could be her album cover.

Am I really the fool who is going to break up with this amazing woman?

She turns, her face full of worry, and says, "I've got something to tell you. I've met someone else."

CHAPTER 106

IT'S HARD TO describe how I feel about this.

Relieved.

But also hurt.

"I haven't slept with him," she says, coming forward and kneeling in front of me. "But I like him and he likes me. I hate telling you this after all you've been through, but I wouldn't feel right if..."

She trails off, but I know what she means.

"I like someone, too," I admit.

She has an expression that tells me she's feeling the same as me — relieved and hurt all mixed together.

"It's that pretty detective, isn't it?" she says, smiling knowingly.

I nod.

"Nothing's happened," I say. "Not so much as a kiss."

She sits next to me on the bed.

"I wasn't sure what I wanted to do about it," I say. "It's just been hard living apart."

"I know," she says, leaning her head on my shoulder.

We talk for a long time, but there's really only one conclusion we can come to. It's time for us to split up and go our separate ways. Neither of us is sure it's the right thing to do. But neither of us feels that staying together is the right thing, either.

We apologize to each other. Willow cries, and I think I would, too, if I wasn't so numb and shell-shocked. Some police officers go their whole careers without ever firing their sidearm—I shot and killed five people in the past several days. It will take a long time to process the emotions associated with all that's happened. Getting over Willow will be one part of healing emotionally from what I've been through. But tonight it's all too much for my brain to handle.

Once we talk through everything, we're unsure what to do. There are plenty of songs out there about couples having sex one last time before they break up, but neither of us feels right about that. Even though we're not with other people—not yet—it would feel like cheating. And making love might make it too hard to go through with the breakup.

But there is something we can do together that feels intimate and still feels right.

Willow opens her guitar case and pulls out a nice Gibson acoustic. She lets me play the guitar, and we sing some of our favorites. We mostly play fast songs, fun ones. Juice Newton's "Queen of Hearts." "Chicken Fried" by the Zac Brown Band. "Fishin' in the Dark" by the Nitty Gritty Dirt Band. As I watch Willow and listen to her voice, I'm overwhelmed with sadness that we weren't able to make it work.

The first song we ever played together was "Mammas Don't Let Your Babies Grow Up to Be Cowboys," and when we play it again tonight, neither of us says it, but we both feel like it's the perfect song to end on. It was the first song we sang together, and now it's our last.

Willow closes up the guitar case and tells me she wants to give me the guitar to replace the one that was destroyed. I accept it with gratitude.

Then Willow goes into the bathroom and puts on what she's used for a nightgown ever since we started dating: my old high school football jersey. I strip down to my boxers and T-shirt, and we climb into bed together. I turn out the light and put my arm around her shoulders. Not in a way that will lead to anything sexual. Just friendly. Comforting. She takes my arm and pulls my embrace tighter.

Sleep comes quickly.

My last thought before drifting off is how I forgot to plug in my cell phone and how I need to make sure to do it first thing in the morning.

CHAPTER 107

I AWAKE TO someone knocking on the door. It's a polite knock, just enough to stir me from my slumber. I sit up, surprised that so much sunlight is pouring through the window.

Willow is already awake, sitting in bed reading an Emily Giffin book. She rises and goes to the door, still wearing my football jersey. Jessica is at the door, holding a breakfast tray.

"Am I too early?" she says. "Tom told me to wait until y'all came down, but I couldn't. As soon as he left for work, I started whipping up breakfast."

Willow, always polite, tells her to come in.

"What time is it?" I say, my voice hoarse from sleep.

Jessica says it's eight, and I suddenly feel panicked that I need to head to the station. I hadn't meant to sleep this late. I tell Willow and Jessica that I need to get going, but Willow asks me to stay for a few minutes and eat.

"You could use a good meal to start your day," she says.

I discreetly pull on my pants over my boxers and join Willow and Jessica at the small table in the corner of the room. Jessica is smiling widely, and I can see that she plans to stay while we eat. She's so thrilled to meet Willow that she can't help herself.

"I heard y'all playing last night," Jessica says. "It was pretty muffled by the walls, but it sounded great. Any chance you can play a few songs for Tom and me tonight out in the garden?"

"Sorry," Willow says. "I need to head back to Nashville today."

"Oh, that's too bad," Jessica says.

I drink a few sips of coffee but realize I've had too much of that lately, and what I need now is a good meal, not more caffeine. I devour the french toast and poached eggs in front of me. Then I go for the pecan pie. Willow isn't as hungry as I am, but she drinks every drop in her cup of coffee. I insist she try the pie.

"It's delicious," Willow tells Jessica, eating a couple of bites and setting down her fork.

"I sure am glad I got to meet you," Jessica says. "Tom and I have really gotten to know Rory. We're going to miss having him around."

"This is my home away from home," I say, feeling a little queasy from eating too quickly.

"Whenever y'all get married," Jessica says, joking, "I expect an invitation to the wedding."

Willow and I exchange a look, unsure what to say.

Jessica looks horrified. "Did I just put my foot in my mouth?"

"It's okay," I say. "Willow and I decided to take some time apart."

I'm not sure why I say it this way. Maybe to soften the blow. Maybe because I'm not quite ready to say what we've really decided, to break up for good.

Willow yawns—she must not be as awake as she

seemed—and explains to Jessica that we love each other very much but that our lives are going in opposite directions. Jessica apologizes profusely, sounding truly embarrassed, but I find I can hardly listen. My stomach is cramping up, and I feel like I could vomit. I let my body run on adrenaline and caffeine for too long—I'm afraid a big breakfast was too much for my system to handle.

I excuse myself and go to the bathroom, and find that my legs are unsteady as I walk across the room. I have trouble walking in a straight line, like I've been drinking beers instead of eating breakfast. The light coming through the window is especially bright, and a headache appears in my skull out of nowhere. When the first responders came to town two days ago, the EMTs wanted to put Ariana and me on IVs after the dehydration and exhaustion we'd experienced. We both refused, feeling like we had too much work to do.

Now I wish I'd said yes.

Once I'm in the bathroom, I feel like dropping to my knees and vomiting into the toilet, but I'm afraid Jessica would hear. She's already mortified from the comment about the wedding. What would she think if I puked up the breakfast she made?

My stomach cramps worsen. I try to urinate but can't. My skin is clammy with sweat. I cup water in my hands and notice how inflamed the rash on my fingers has become. I splash the water on my face and look at my pale reflection in the mirror. My pupils are gigantic, black pools nearly as big as the irises that encircle them.

This isn't right.

Something is wrong.

I yank open the door of the bathroom and charge out. I freeze in my tracks. Willow is unconscious, still sitting upright, but with her head slumped down to where her chin is practically resting on the jersey. Her bare legs are splayed out, her hands dangling limp at her sides. She looks like a passed-out drunk who, at any second, will fall out of her chair.

Jessica stands next to her, aiming my own SIG Sauer directly at my chest.

The safe she asked me to lock the gun in sits in the cabinet with its door wide open.

CHAPTER 108

ARIANA PULLS HER Harley Davidson into the parking lot next to the police station. Normally there are plenty of spaces, but now, with the lot full of vehicles from various law enforcement agencies, there's nowhere to park a car.

Luckily, Ariana only drives a car when it rains.

She squeezes her motorcycle onto the sidewalk near the door, shuts off the engine, and saunters into the station. The place is already bustling with various officials from various agencies. She expects to see Rory but doesn't. For a moment, she's glad that he's getting some extra rest. Then she pictures him having an early-morning make-out session with his gorgeous country-star girlfriend, and she feels a little sick to her stomach. She tells herself to put the thought out of her head and focus on the work in front of her.

As she passes the front desk, Liz, the dispatcher, says to whoever she is on the phone with that she'll check to see if Detective Delgado is available. She puts the caller on hold and looks up at Ariana.

"A guy named Freddy Hernandez is on the phone," she says. "Says he's the medical examiner from Waco and he's been trying to get ahold of Rory."

Ariana almost says to tell him to call back in an hour. She doesn't want Rory to think she's poaching information from his sources. But Rory wouldn't think that. She would trust him to take such a call meant for her—he would do the same, wouldn't he?

They're a team.

"I'll talk to him," Ariana says.

"I'll transfer it to the chief's office," Liz says, giving Ariana a look that says, *You're the chief now. Even though you don't have the title yet, you're in charge.*

Ariana nods, touched by Liz's unspoken endorsement, and she walks into Harris's old office. It feels strange to be in here knowing the chief is in jail.

Ariana picks up the phone.

"I've been trying to get in touch with Rory since yesterday," the medical examiner—and also Rory's childhood friend—says through the phone. "My calls keep going to voicemail."

She says that Rory will be in soon, but if Freddy has information, he can tell her and she'll pass it along. There is quiet on the other end of the line, and she gets the feeling that Freddy doesn't want to talk to anyone but Rory.

"I can just have Rory give you a call when he gets in," Ariana says, ready to hang up.

"Wait," Freddy says, as if fearing that his message will get lost. "This is important. Rory asked me to have a second look at the blood samples from Susan Snyder. I think I've figured out what killed her."

Ariana's heart pounds, as if the organ is suddenly pushing twice as much blood with each beat.

Freddy begins talking scientifically about the blood containing evidence of tropane alkaloids—whatever those are—and how this caused him to do some further investigation. Most of what he is saying is over her head, mentioning secondary metabolites and bicyclic alkaloids. Ariana interrupts him.

"Freddy," she says, "you can explain all the science stuff later. Cut to the chase, please."

"I think Susan Snyder was poisoned by a plant called belladonna," Freddy says. "Also known as deadly nightshade."

CHAPTER 109

"STAY RIGHT WHERE you are," Jessica says.

I'm not sure I could move if I wanted to. The cramping in my stomach seems to be spreading, and now the muscles in my legs are tightening. I don't think I can take another step forward, let alone try to rush Jessica and wrestle the gun away from her.

The sunlight is gushing in the window, and I have to squint to protect my wide-open irises. Jessica's face is in extreme focus, but everything else around her is blurry.

"You killed Susan Snyder?" I say, my words slurred.

She nods. Her demeanor has changed from the starstruck fan she was pretending to be a few minutes ago, but she still has a half smile on her face, as if she's enjoying this.

"Why?" I ask.

"For Tom, of course." She says it as if the answer is obvious. "It's the twenty-first century. Journalism is dead. That newspaper would have folded ten times over if it wasn't for Carson supporting it."

I squint, trying to make sense of what I'm hearing. Tom never said anything like that.

"Oh, Tom doesn't know," Jessica says. "Carson bought advertising through intermediaries. Lots of businesses in town put ads in the paper. Carson was the one actually paying for them."

I remember what Norma at the motel said about how Rio Lobo would crumble up and blow away if it wasn't for McCormack subsidizing most of the businesses one way or another. Still, I'm having trouble making sense of all this. If McCormack's been subsidizing the paper for years, did Jessica owe him? When he called to collect, was the murder of Susan Snyder the price she had to pay?

Jessica answers my question without being asked. She explains that she and Carson go way back, all the way to high school, and that they've been doing each other favors for years.

"I helped him out once a long time ago," she says. "And since then he's helped me keep Tom's business afloat. Taking care of Susan was the first favor he'd asked for in a long time. And since I'd done something like that before..." She trails off.

I'm having trouble focusing my thoughts. I feel like a drunk who's trying to solve a puzzle that he's sure he could do easily if he was just able to sober up.

Then it hits me.

"Carson McCormack's wife," I say. "You killed her?"

She smiles. "When people didn't get on board with what Carson was doing, sometimes he could make them disappear. But other times it was best if it looked like an accident."

My legs are incredibly weak, but the pain from the cramping has subsided. Replacing the pain is a numbness spreading throughout my body.

I try to take a step forward, but instead I drop to my knees on the carpet.

I feel like I've been given a sedative, and no matter how hard I try, I won't be able to keep unconsciousness at bay.

"You won't get away with it this time," I say. "No one will believe that Willow and I both died of natural causes."

"Oh, you're not going to die from what I put in your food," Jessica says. "I'm going to shoot you." She gestures to Willow, whose unconscious mouth is drooling onto my jersey. "Then I'll shoot her and put the gun in her hand. Murder-suicide."

"No one will buy it."

She laughs. "Everyone in town thinks you're fucking Ariana Delgado," she says. "Willow even has a song on the radio about how girls shouldn't date a Texas Ranger. People will think she finally had enough and snapped. *Everyone* will believe it."

CHAPTER 110

ARIANA STANDS IN the middle of Harris's old office with the phone pressed to her ear, her heart racing. She knew Susan was murdered. Just knew it in her gut.

Now she has validation.

"So the peanut allergy didn't actually kill her?" Ariana asks.

"Not only did the peanut allergy not kill her," Freddy says, "I think it was used as a decoy. A distraction."

"I'm not following," Ariana says.

Freddy believes whoever killed Susan Snyder gave her food that was laced with both peanut oil and belladonna. The person would have known she'd use her EpiPen, so the peanuts would not be enough. But anyone examining the body would assume that her allergic reaction to peanuts was what killed her. No one would bother looking deeper and noticing there was another toxic substance that actually did her in.

"Belladonna isn't the kind of poison a medical examiner routinely searches for," Freddy says. "If the body shows symptoms that point in that direction, a medical examiner might check. But in this case, whoever looked at her would have been distracted by all the swelling and redness of the skin. Belladonna actually causes a paralysis of muscle function. She probably died because her lungs stopped working. Or her heart."

He explains that every part of the plant— seeds, roots, stems, flowers— is toxic. The berries are sweet and could be used in sugary desserts. The plant itself is dark green with either purple or yellow flowers and berries that resemble blueberries.

"Apparently," Freddy says, "just brushing up against the plant can cause a terrible rash for some people. It's that noxious."

Ariana thinks of the rash on Rory's hand and how they assumed he'd had an allergic reaction to something out on McCormack's property. Maybe he'd brushed up against this deadly nightshade, not realizing what it was. She tries to remember if they saw any plants with berries or purple or yellow flowers when they were walking that path through the trees.

"So this grows naturally in West Texas?" Ariana asks.

"Oh, no," Freddy says. "Absolutely not. It's way too dry there. But someone could grow it—legally, I might add—in a greenhouse or garden."

Ariana's breath stops in her chest.

"You're looking for someone who would have known about Susan Snyder's allergies *and* is a skilled gardener," Freddy says.

But he's talking to an empty line.

Ariana has dropped the phone and is sprinting through the police station to her motorcycle.

CHAPTER III

I'M ALREADY ON my knees, but I can't even keep myself upright. I slump back against the wall. None of my limbs seem to be working. The viselike cramps that had gripped my muscles earlier have eased, and now I feel only numbness. Meanwhile, my heart is racing like a thoroughbred being flogged by a maniacal jockey. I try to take deep breaths to keep up with the oxygen intake my heart is demanding, but for some reason my lungs just won't work fast enough. The room was so bright before, but now everything seems to be in shadow.

I'm close to passing out.

"What did you give me?" I mutter.

"I put deadly nightshade in the pie and the french toast," Jessica says, smiling as if proud of her craftiness. "The sweetness of the berries blended with the other flavors. Just like in Susan's cookies." She gestures toward Willow. "I also roofied the coffee. I'm glad I did because she hardly touched the food. She ingested some of the poison," she adds, unable to keep from grinning, "but not nearly as much as you."

Jessica goes on to explain that a medical examiner might find benzodiazepine in Willow's system, but he'd just think that she took something to calm herself before killing her cheating boyfriend.

"I'm sorry, Rory," Jessica says, raising the gun and aiming it at my chest. "I need to make sure the bullet kills you before the poison does. That *would* raise some red flags during the autopsy."

"You said you hated guns," I sneer, suddenly mad about that betrayal on top of all the others.

She laughs. "I said I *loathe* guns. It's true. I much prefer poison."

She puts her finger inside the trigger guard.

"Good-bye, Rory," she says. "I really did like you. I just wish you and Ariana had eaten the damn food I gave you the night you left."

I remember the grocery bag of food she'd packed that was in my truck when it burned. It was only luck that Dale had brought pizza that night. Otherwise, we all would have died of poisoning out there in the desert hills.

But it looks like I only delayed my fate. I'm tempted to close my eyes and welcome death from the darkness behind my eyelids. And if it was only my life at stake, I might. But Willow is going to die, too, and I can't stop fighting for her. My body is useless. The only thing working is my mouth. I have to talk Jessica out of this.

"Let Willow go," I say. "Let the poison in me run its course. She'll wake up sick but won't die. Don't make her pay for what I did."

"Sorry," she says. "It has to be a murder-suicide. Otherwise, the autopsy will—"

She stops, cocks her head, listening.

I hear it, too: the rumbling sound of a motorcycle.

Jessica smiles. "Good," she says. "This is even better. Now I can make it look like Willow killed you *and* your lover."

CHAPTER 112

ARIANA ROARS INTO Tom and Jessica's driveway and slides to a halt in the gravel next to the garage. She looks around and sees no one. Jessica isn't in the garden, nor is she looking out any of the windows of the house. No one is peering down from Rory's apartment, either.

She tells herself that it's possible Jessica isn't home. Or maybe Rory and Willow went to get breakfast before he planned to come into the office. There are perfectly rational explanations for why no one noticed her racing into the driveway on a loud motorcycle. But she tells herself to follow her gut.

And her gut tells her something is wrong.

She dismounts her bike, draws her gun, and starts toward the stairs on the side of the garage. She sees the rows of berries and spots one plant with dark berries and yellow flowers. Rory must have brushed it with his hand.

Ariana takes the steps two at a time, but before she gets to the top, she hears Rory cry out, "Jessica has a gun! She killed Susan—"

"Shut up!" Jessica snaps.

Ariana freezes a few steps from the top, unsure how to proceed.

"He's right," Jessica calls out. "I have a gun. I want you to come on through the door, keeping your hands where I can see them. Any sudden moves and the country singer dies."

Ariana holsters her gun and moves slowly up the stairs. She eases the door open and walks in with her hands raised over her shoulders.

Jessica is kneeling behind Willow, who is unconscious on a wooden chair. Jessica is holding a gun—it looks like Rory's pistol—against her head and using the woman's body as a shield.

Rory is slumped against a wall, and, for a moment, Ariana thinks he's been shot. His entire body is limp—the kind of dead weight that comes with death. But his eyes are open and he's looking at her. He's not dead.

Yet.

"You killed Susan?" Ariana says to Jessica, hoping to get the woman to talk so she can have time to think.

Jessica laughs. "That's not all."

Ariana takes a moment to understand what she's suggesting, but then it occurs to her. Besides Susan's murder, what is the one other piece of the puzzle they haven't solved yet?

"You stole my grandfather's gun?" Ariana says. "You took it out to Gareth McCormack? After he shot Skip, you took it back and put it under my bed?"

"You're good, Ariana," she says.

Ariana realizes something else. The morning Harris came to the paper and broke Tom's nose and hauled Ariana out to McCormack's ranch, the chief hadn't shown up because he saw the truck out front.

"You called Harris and told him I was looking for Tom," Ariana says.

"Yes," Jessica says, "and I wish he would have shot you on the spot instead of pistol-whipping my husband. If Carson was still alive, John Grady would answer for that."

Ariana looks over at Rory and sees his eyelids struggling to stay open. Whatever Ariana is going to do, she needs to do it fast.

"You can't get away with this," Ariana says.

"Rory said the same thing, but you're both wrong," Jessica says, shifting the gun away from Willow so it's pointed directly at Ariana. "It's simple. Willow found out you and Rory were screwing around and then she killed you both before turning the gun on herself."

Ariana can't believe what's happening. She's known Jessica since she was a teenager going to the pharmacy to pick up prescriptions for her parents.

"Why are you doing this?" she asks.

"Because you two couldn't just let things go. You came in and screwed up everything in Rio Lobo. You know the town isn't going to survive without Carson's money. The newspaper will fold. The pharmacy will fold. A year from now, Rio Lobo is going to be a ghost town."

"The people of Rio Lobo make this town what it is," Ariana says. "Not Carson McCormack's money."

Jessica begins arguing with her, but as she is talking, Ariana remembers watching the video of Rory in the bank. He dropped to his knees, drew his gun, and fired on the men before they could shoot him. She needs to do the same thing now.

Only she doesn't have a clear shot at Jessica. Jessica's head is sticking up over Willow. If Ariana misses, she might put a bullet through the top of the singer's skull. Then she thinks of the shot Rory made to kill Carson

McCormack—how he took the shot even though Ariana was in the line of fire.

In everything that happened in the last few days—in the open space and out at McCormack's ranch—Ariana didn't shoot anyone.

She's never shot anyone.

But Rory told her she had what it takes to be a Texas Ranger.

Now it's her time to prove it.

CHAPTER 113

I WATCH FROM the floor as Jessica is about to shoot. I can see it in her body language, the way she steadies my pistol, tightens her finger over the trigger. I want to shout to Ariana to warn her, but I can't. My mouth is as paralyzed as the rest of my body.

All I can do is watch.

What happens next takes only a couple of seconds.

Three at the most.

Ariana drops down right as flames shoot from the pistol in Jessica's hand. Wood splinters explode from the doorjamb behind Ariana. Ariana folds into a crouch and yanks her gun from its holster just as Jessica lowers the pistol, trying to get a second shot.

Jessica is using Willow as a shield, and I want to scream for Ariana not to shoot.

But she does.

Jessica's head jerks back as blood mists the wall behind her. She leans back, her gun arm still extended, and crashes onto the carpet. She keeps her arm stiff for a moment, pointing the gun at the ceiling, then loses her muscle function, and her arm falls to her side, limp.

Willow's body slumps out of the chair onto the floor.

She's still unconscious, but the bullet never touched her. It passed inches over her head.

Ariana runs to my side. She pulls out her phone, calls 911, and shouts, "Texas Ranger down! I've got a Texas Ranger down!"

She yells into the phone what our location is, then turns her attention to me. Her eyes are filling with tears.

"You're going to be okay," she says, cupping my face.

I stare at her, wanting to tell her how much she means to me, how proud I am of her. I want to tell her that she'll make the best goddamn Texas Ranger this state has ever seen.

But I can only croak out two words.

"Save...Willow."

She stares into my eyes for a moment—just a moment—then leans down to kiss my forehead. She runs over to Willow and lifts her flaccid body in a fireman's carry. I watch as she squeezes through the door, and I listen as her footsteps bound down the staircase.

My eyes close, and I feel a mixture of relief and sadness.

Relief because both of the women I love are safe.

Sadness because I'll never see either one of them again.

CHAPTER 114

ARIANA STANDS AT the edge of the Rio Lobo cemetery, watching Tom Aaron out among the gravestones. He is kneeling.

Weeping.

She's been dreading this moment, but she feels she needs to face it. She walks along the pathway, passing several new grave markers. One for Dale. One for Skip. One each for the other bodies they found on McCormack's ranch. They were all given big funerals. Practically everyone in town came out to see them laid to rest.

But no one came to the funeral today.

No one came to see Jessica Aaron interred.

Except for Tom, of course.

Even their kids, in finding out what Mom did, wouldn't attend. They drove back from their colleges to take care of their father and mourn. But they refused to honor her passing.

Ariana finds Tom hunched over the fresh dirt, his back heaving. He is shaking all over, shaking more than when she was staring down the barrel of the gun that Jessica aimed at her.

"Tom," she says softly, and his body stops convulsing. "I just wanted to tell you how sorry I am."

She wants to say that if there had been any other way, she wouldn't have squeezed the trigger. But now she's crying, too, and she's afraid she won't be able to speak. Tom rises and turns around to face her, his eyes red. The splint on his nose is gone, but some of his skin is still black and blue, which makes his bloodshot eyes even more menacing. He takes a deep breath.

"I don't blame you," he says to Ariana.

She sobs in relief.

They hug and cry, and then, afterward, they walk back through the cemetery, talking. It's a beautiful morning. The heat will be unbearable later, but now, walking among the freshly cut grass, the temperature is pleasant.

"You know," he says, "when I was looking through the old yearbooks, I told Rory about the picture I saw of you and Gareth. But I found an even older one, from when Jessica and Carson were in high school, that made me suspicious. She'd never talked about him, but there they were, standing in front of a line of lockers, smiling like they were the best of friends. Carson was a senior and Jessica was only a freshman, but they looked as thick as thieves."

He says the picture gave him a bad feeling, but he pushed it away. Then, after his nose was broken, Jessica rushed to the medical center, and when she saw him, she said, "I can't believe they did this to you."

"It was the way she said it," Tom explains. "Like she felt betrayed by someone she'd had a deal with. I pushed it out of my mind then, too."

"Don't blame yourself," Ariana says. "She fooled us all. And if it's any consolation, she did everything for you. I think she really did love you."

"It's not a consolation. It actually makes it worse. I feel like I'm to blame somehow."

Tom explains that all his life he'd fancied himself a good journalist, but he'd been blind to what his own wife was hiding. When he and Jessica had the opportunity to purchase the pharmacy, she suddenly inherited a big chunk of money. Now he realizes that money came from Carson—as did a lot of the advertising revenue that kept the newspaper in the black all these years.

Ariana says, "You're not to blame at all. In fact, if it wasn't for your help, this case never would have been solved."

She doesn't mention that if Tom hadn't helped, he likely could have gone on forever under the illusion that his wife was who he thought she was.

"I never kept a secret from her," Tom says. "It turns out that all she did was keep secrets from me."

They arrive at Tom's Land Cruiser, which is a little more scratched up than it used to be, thanks to Ariana stealing it and taking it out into the open space.

After they hug good-bye and Tom drives away, Ariana climbs aboard her motorcycle. She rumbles into town and heads straight to what has been quickly renamed the Rio Lobo Medical Center. As she enters, one of the nurses at the front desk intercepts her and says, "Miss Dawes checked out this morning. She wanted me to give you this."

She hands Ariana a handwritten note.

Dear Ariana,

I can't thank you enough for everything. You have a friend for life.

Willow

Ariana smiles. She unfolds the page farther and sees there's a postscript.

P.S. He's all yours.

Ariana laughs.

When she pushes through the door into his hospital room, she finds Rory sitting up in bed, reading a John Grisham book. He looks pale, a little on the thin side, but still handsome as hell.

"How're you holding up?" Ariana asks.

"The doctors say they're not ready to release me," Rory says, "but I'll tell you what: I'm ready to get the hell out of here and get back to work."

She can tell it's taking all of his willpower not to yank out the IV and strap on his gun belt. One of the reasons he hasn't is because Ariana keeps assuring him that everything is under control. In a few days there will be a big memorial for Kyle Hendricks in Waco, and she knows Rory won't miss that no matter what the doctors say.

She sits down next to him and fills him in on the latest in the investigation.

When the EMTs found him, he had no heartbeat. They had to zap him with a defibrillator. And even after that, his chances were touch and go for a while as they waited to see if the decontamination treatment would take effect.

His family drove in and waited until he was awake and stable before heading back to Waco. His former lieutenant, Ted Creasy, kept him company for a while. Willow, who recovered quicker, having ingested a smaller amount of the poison, hardly left his side.

The first time he saw Ariana after waking up,

he said to her in a weak voice, "You saved my life. Again."

"Well," she said, trying to make a joke out of it. "You'd wiped the slate clean, so I wanted you to owe me again."

"I owe you double," he said. "For me. And for Willow."

CHAPTER 115

ON MY FIRST day out of the hospital, Ariana and I go down to the river to have lunch under the big oak tree. We watch as workers take down the MCCORMACK COMMUNITY PARK sign and begin installing a new sign that says SUSAN SNYDER MEMORIAL PARK. When I first got to town, there were three guys—Alex Hartley, Skip Barnes, and the chief himself—all claiming they'd had affairs with Susan. It turned out all of them were lying. I have no idea if she was promiscuous or not—and I don't care—but what I do know is that she really cared for this community.

She died to bring out the truth. The least they can do is name the park after her. I hope they name something after Ariana. She deserves it, too.

I'm not sure why, but along with our lunches, Ariana also brought a cardboard box with her. It's about eighteen inches by two feet, and I have no idea what's inside.

I still feel a little weak, but I'm getting better every day.

Most of the various agencies—not to mention the journalists—have cleared out, and Rio Lobo seems to be getting back to some semblance of normalcy.

Several Rangers from the El Paso office remain, and they've pretty much taken over the investigation. When Kyle first sent me to Rio Lobo, he told me the El Paso company couldn't cover it because they were working on a big trafficking case. Turns out the drug dealers they were looking for all along were the ones in Rio Lobo. Now that the two cases have merged, they don't have much use for me. This was never going to be a long-term job. But it's bittersweet to know I'm leaving soon. I've come to love this little town.

Ariana and I watch the reflection of the sunlight on the water. There's so much I want to say to her that I don't even know where to begin.

She does it for me.

Ariana holds up a note Willow left her and says, "Rumor has it you're single."

"I am," I say, grinning sheepishly.

I stare into her dark eyes. She looks as beautiful as always, but I know her well enough to tell when she's guarding her emotions. There's something she's not telling me.

"How about it?" I say. "Want to join the Texas Rangers and maybe date one while you're at it?"

Ariana gives me a sad, sympathetic smile.

"I'm sorry, Rory. I can't. Last night the town council voted to make me the new police chief."

I try to appear stoic, but my heart is breaking.

"Congratulations," I say. "I mean that sincerely. You'll do the job better than anyone else could."

"I hope you understand," she says. "This is my home, and it needs me. Now more than ever."

"Trust me," I say. "I know the importance of home."

The problem is I'm not sure where home is anymore. The town of Redbud has always been home.

My parents' ranch has always been home. But my little house on the property—that was something I shared with Willow. Even though she was in Nashville more than she was there, I still thought of it as *our* home.

I've known for a long time that I was going to be starting over. But for a while I thought I might be starting over with Ariana.

Not starting over alone.

Now I think about how strange it's going to feel going back to Redbud, trying to step back into my old life as if I'm the same person. I don't feel like the same person who drove into the town of Rio Lobo only a month ago. Ariana says she needs to stay in her home, but for me, for the first time in my life, I feel like maybe I need to find a new home.

Ariana picks up the cardboard box and hands it to me.

"Something to remember me by," she says.

I open the box, and a big grin fills my face. Inside is a brand-new ivory-colored Stetson. I take out the hat and set it atop my head.

"How's it fit?" she asks.

"Perfect."

And it does.

Without another word, Ariana leans over and puts her lips against mine. She gives me a long, passionate kiss.

Then she breaks away and says, "Come on, cowboy."

As we walk along the river, I can't help but smile, thinking about what a great first kiss that was. And then a feeling of sadness rushes through me like a cold breeze.

Not only was it our first kiss—it was also our last.

EPILOGUE

I STEER MY brand-new Ford F-150 through the crowded parking lot of Isleta Amphitheater, a fifteen-thousand-person concert stadium south of Albuquerque. On the passenger seat next to me is the new Stetson Ariana gave me. On the floor, leaning against the seat, is the guitar and case Willow gave me.

The parting gifts of the two women in my life.

After I park, I walk through the crowds of people, make my way through the long line at the gate, and find a place to sit on the lawn, which overlooks the empty stage and the rolling desert hills behind it. It's a beautiful venue for a concert. Everyone is decked out in cowboy hats and country music concert T-shirts. All I had to do was take off my badge, belt, and tie, and I fit right in. I might seem a little overdressed, but I don't think anyone will notice. If anything makes me look unusual it's the fact that I'm carrying around an old high school football jersey.

This morning, when I got into my truck—which my company commander had delivered to Rio Lobo yesterday—I had every intention of driving east toward Waco. But then I realized what day it was—

checked and double-checked the date to make sure I was right—and I headed west and north instead.

I'm not really sure what I'm doing here. I told myself on the drive that I just want to see her perform, that I'm here to support a friend. But I think the truth is I'm just not ready to go home yet.

Willow will be the first opening act. After her, Brandi Carlile will play a set. And then the headliner, Dierks Bentley.

Willow has her work cut out for her. As the first act, when she comes onstage, people are still filing into the stadium. Half the people aren't paying attention. But she doesn't let this stop her. She struts out onstage as if she's played to crowds this big a million times. From where I sit, she looks no bigger than one of the action figures my nephew, Beau, plays with. But even this far away, her stage presence is unmistakable.

She gets the crowd's attention right away by playing a Shania Twain song and following it up with one by Taylor Swift. Her band is fantastic, and I know I'm biased, but I think her renditions are just as good as the originals.

Maybe better.

After she plays the cover songs everyone is familiar with, the crowd is hooked, and she segues into some of her own songs. No one in the audience has ever heard them before, but everyone—in the chairs up front and at the back of the lawn—is standing up, moving to the rhythm of the songs. People clap their hands and, once they get the hook of the chorus, try to sing along. As Willow prances around onstage, the sun sets behind her, casting a beautiful reddish glow over the hills.

I'm overwhelmed with emotion. I can't express how proud I am of Willow.

How impressed.

It's just a matter of time before she's the one head-lining shows like this.

Toward the end of the set, Willow says to the crowd, "Have y'all heard my song 'Don't Date a Texas Ranger' on the radio?"

The crowd erupts in cheers and applause.

"You know I was dating a real Texas Ranger, right?"

Again, roars of approval.

"I've got some sad news," Willow tells the crowd. "We broke up."

The audience gives a collective "Oh" of surprise and dismay. Willow tells the audience that in real life her ex is a terrific guy. She only wrote the song for fun, and her boyfriend had been very supportive of her releasing it.

"He knew it was going to be my first hit," she says.

As she's talking, her band discreetly leaves the stage. A roadie carries out a wooden chair and sets it in the center of the stage. Then another brings out an acoustic guitar and hands it to Willow.

"I hope you don't mind," she says, sitting on the chair with the guitar across her lap, "but I'm going to do the song a little differently tonight."

With that, she starts to pick the strings. It's the same song, only much slower. The version of the song playing on the radio is a fast-paced boot stomper. This version is slow and melancholic. The lyrics, when performed this way, are more haunting.

She sounds heartbroken.

Tears spring to my eyes.

The audience loves the performance. People in the crowd hold lighters and cell phones in the air, illuminating the darkness. The only light onstage is a single spotlight on Willow.

She sings the lyrics exactly as I've heard them before, but when she gets to the last chorus, she changes them, saying in an almost conversational voice,

> *Take it from me, ladies,*
> *I should know.*
> *If you ever have the chance,*
> *You should definitely date a Texas Ranger.*

The crowd goes wild, laughing and clapping, as Willow strums the last notes of the song. She stands, bows, blows a kiss to the crowd. And she walks offstage.

I applaud like a madman. Tears stream down my cheeks.

That's my girl, I think.

That was *my girl.*

As the stagehands are setting up for Brandi Carlile, I walk down through the crowd and find a security guard standing in front of a backstage door.

I ask him if there's any way he can give the jersey to Willow.

"Are you that Ranger she was singing about?" the guy asks. "I seen you on TV. Man, you're a freaking hero. Mad respect to you, my friend."

He offers to take me backstage to see Willow, and I consider it for a moment. But I'm afraid what might happen. Seeing her onstage—seeing what a star she's going to be—I know I need to let her go. Dating me is only going to hold her back from her dreams.

"Just make sure she gets the shirt," I say, handing over the jersey she inadvertently left at the hospital. "She'll know who it's from."

I push through the crowd as Brandi Carlile begins

to play. I consider staying for her set and Dierks Bentley's. I'm sure they're great. But I'm emotionally drained.

I climb into my truck and head off into the darkness.

I drive through Albuquerque and travel east for a while, but I suddenly get an urge, and I decide to turn off the highway. I find a dirt road that stretches into the hills, and I park somewhere in the middle of nowhere. I sit on the tailgate and look up at the stars. I take out the guitar Willow gave me and pluck at the strings.

I play "Mammas Don't Let Your Babies Grow Up to Be Cowboys," singing about how cowboys are never at home and they're always alone. But as I play under the canopy of stars, without another soul around for miles, I don't feel sad about being alone, starting over on my own.

I'm alive—that almost wasn't the case.

And I can't help but feel that Willow or Ariana— or maybe both of them—will be a part of my life again someday.

ACKNOWLEDGMENTS

Special thanks to Captain Kip Westmoreland of the Texas Rangers.

ABOUT THE AUTHORS

James Patterson is the world's bestselling author and most trusted storyteller. He has created many enduring fictional characters and series, including Alex Cross, the Women's Murder Club, Michael Bennett, Maximum Ride, Middle School, and I Funny. Among his notable literary collaborations are *The President Is Missing*, with President Bill Clinton, and the Max Einstein series, produced in partnership with the Albert Einstein estate. Patterson's writing career is characterized by a single mission: to prove that there is no such thing as a person who "doesn't like to read," only people who haven't found the right book. He's given over three million books to schoolkids and the military, donated more than seventy million dollars to support education, and endowed over five thousand college scholarships for teachers. For his prodigious imagination and championship of literacy in America, Patterson was awarded the 2019 National Humanities Medal. The National Book Foundation presented him with the Literarian Award for Outstanding Service to the American Literary Community, and he is also the recipient of an Edgar Award and nine Emmy Awards. He lives in Florida with his family.

*   *   *

Andrew Bourelle is the author of the novel *Heavy Metal* and coauthor with James Patterson of *Texas Ranger*. His short stories have been published widely in literary magazines and fiction anthologies, including *The Best American Mystery Stories*.

ALEX CROSS ENTERS THE FINAL SHOWDOWN WITH THE RELENTLESS KILLER WHO HAS STALKED HIM AND HIS FAMILY FOR YEARS.

TURN THE PAGE FOR A PREVIEW OF THE NEWEST ALEX CROSS THRILLER

FEAR NO EVIL

COMING IN NOVEMBER 2021.

CHAPTER

1

Washington, DC
Late June

MATTHEW BUTLER COCKED HIS HEAD to one side, considering the big-boned blonde in front of him. She was handcuffed and shackled to a heavy oak chair bolted into the concrete floor beneath bright fluorescent lights.

If the woman was anxious about her predicament, she wasn't showing it in the least. She was as chill as the yoga outfit she wore. No sweat on her pale brow. Beneath her warm-up hoodie, her chest rose and fell calmly, each breath measured. Her shoulders were relaxed. Even her eyes looked soft.

Butler adjusted the strap of his shoulder holster.

"I know they've trained you for this sort of thing," he said in a voice with the slightest of Western twangs. "But your training won't work against me, Catherine. It never does."

A fit, balding man with a hawkish nose, Butler had workman's hands and wore black jeans, Nike running shoes, and a dark blue polo shirt. He crossed his thick forearms when she smiled back at him with brilliant white teeth.

"Whoever you are, you are going to be destroyed for what you're doing," Catherine Hingham said. "When they find out—"

Butler cut her off. "You know, in my many years as a professional, Catherine, I have come to rather enjoy the delicate process of breaking into hearts and minds. They are very much interlinked, you know—hearts and minds—and I have found that one is almost always the key to the other."

"Langley will annihilate you," Hingham said, studying Butler as if she wanted to remember every line in his face.

"Your operators won't help you today," Butler said, gesturing at a pile of blank paper and a pen on the table before her. "Tell me the truth and we can all move on with our lives."

"I'll say it again: You have no jurisdiction over me."

Butler chuckled, gestured around the room. "Oh, but in here, I do."

"I want to see a lawyer, then."

"I'm sure," he said, sobering. "But we're talking about a serious threat to our national security, Catherine. A few rules of engagement can and will be broken in order to thwart that threat."

"I am not a national security threat," she said evenly. "I work for the Central Intelligence Agency, with the highest clearances, in support of my country's freedoms. Your freedoms as well."

"That's what makes your traitorous actions so hard to understand, Catherine."

Her face reddened and she shifted in her chair. "I am no traitor."

Butler took a step toward her. "The hell you're not. We know about the Maldives."

Hingham blinked, furrowed her brow. "The Maldives? Like, the islands in the Indian Ocean?"

"The same."

"I have no idea what you're talking about. I have never been to the Maldives. I've never even been to India."

"No?"

"Never. You can talk to my case officers about it."

"I plan to at some point," Butler said, taking another step toward her. He reached down to touch the back of her left hand before letting his finger trail across her wedding band and modest engagement ring. "Does he know? Your husband?"

"That I work for the CIA?" she said. "Yes. But he has zero idea what I actually do. Those are the rules. We play by them."

Butler sighed as he gently took hold of her left pinkie with his leathery hand, thumb on top.

"Do you know the surest way to sever the connection between the body and mind, and therefore the heart?"

"No," she said.

"Pain," Butler said. He gripped her little finger tight and levered his thumb sharply downward until he heard a bone snap.

CHAPTER

2

CATHERINE HINGHAM SCREAMED IN AGONY, fighting against her restraints, then yelled at him, "You cannot do this! This is the United States of America and I'm a sworn officer of the Central—"

Butler broke her ring finger, then waited for her to stop screaming and crying.

"You have eight fingers left, Catherine," Butler said calmly. "I will break them all and if you still do not tell me what I want to know, I will have your five-year-old daughter brought here and I will begin breaking *her* tiny fingers one by one until you confess."

The CIA officer stared at him in disgust and horror. "Emily has cerebral palsy."

"I know."

"You wouldn't. It's...monstrous."

"It is," he said and sighed again. "And yet, because there is so much at stake, Catherine, I will break your little girl's fingers. But only if you make it necessary."

The CIA officer continued to stare at him for several moments. He gazed back at her evenly until her lower lip trembled and she hung her head.

"The costs," Hingham whispered hoarsely. "You have no idea what a child like Em…" She could not go on and broke down sobbing.

"The heart wins again," Butler said. He pushed the pile of blank pages in front of her. "Start writing. The Maldives. The numbered accounts. Their connections. All of it."

After a few moments, Catherine Hingham calmed enough to raise her head. "I need witness protection."

"I'll see what I can do," Butler said and held out the pen to her. "Now write."

The CIA officer reached out with both handcuffed hands shaking. She took the pen. "Please," she said. "My family doesn't deserve what will happen if—"

"Write," he said firmly. "And I'll see what I can do."

The CIA officer reluctantly began to scribble names, addresses, account numbers, and more. When she'd moved to a second page, Butler had seen enough to be satisfied.

He walked behind the CIA officer and nodded to a small camera mounted high in the corner of the room.

A gravelly male voice came through the tiny earbud Butler wore in his left ear. "Mmmm. Well done. When you have what we need, end the interview and file your report, please."

Butler nodded again before moving in front of Catherine Hingham. She set her pen down and pushed the pages across the table at him.

"That's it," she said in a hoarse voice. "Everything I know."

"Unlikely," Butler said, using the nail of his index finger to lift up the first sheet so he could scan the information she'd provided on page two. "But this looks useful enough for now. It will give us leverage. Was that so hard, Catherine?"

She relaxed a little and said, "Okay, then, I've given you what you wanted. Now I need a doctor to fix my hand. I need witness protection."

With his fingernail, Butler scooted the confession pages to the far right of the table. "You're a smart woman, Catherine. Well educated. Yale, if I remember. You should know your history better. We don't protect traitors in the United States of America. From Benedict Arnold on, they've all had to pay the price. And now, so will you."

The CIA officer looked confused and then terrified when Butler took a step back and drew a stubby pistol with a sound suppressor from his shoulder holster.

"No, please, my kids are—" she managed before he took aim and shot her between the eyes.

CHAPTER

3

FROM THE TIME WE'D MET as ten-year-olds, John Sampson, my best friend and long-term DC Metro Police partner, had been stoic, quiet, observant. Since his wife, Billie, had died, he'd become even more reserved and was now given to long bouts of brooding silence. I knew he was still wrestling with grief.

But that late-June morning, Big John was acting as wound up as a kid about to hit the front gates of Disney World as he bopped around my front room, where we'd laid out all our gear for a trip we'd been talking about taking for years.

"You think we'll see a grizzly?" Sampson asked, grinning at me.

"I'm hoping not," I said. "At least, not up close."

"They're in there, big-time. And wolves."

"And deer, elk, and cutthroat trout," I said. "I've been studying the brochure too."

Nana Mama, my ninety-something grandmother, came in wringing her hands and asked with worry in her voice, "Did I hear you say grizzly bears?"

Sampson glowed with excitement. "Nana, the Bob

Marshall Wilderness has one of the densest concentrations of grizzlies in the lower forty-eight states. But don't worry. We'll have bear spray and sidearms. And cameras."

"I don't know why you couldn't choose a safer place to go on your manly trip."

"If it was safer, it wouldn't be manly," I said. "There's got to be a challenge."

"Glad I'm an old lady, then. Breakfast in five minutes." Nana Mama turned and shuffled away, shaking her head.

"Checklist?" Sampson said.

"I'm ready if you are."

We started going through every item we'd thought necessary for the twenty-nine-mile horseback trip deep into one of the last great wildernesses on earth and for the five-day raft ride we'd take out of the Bob Marshall on the South Fork of the Flathead River. An outfitter was providing the rafts, tents, food, and bear-proof storage equipment. Everything else had to fit into four rubberized dry bags we'd use on the river after he dropped us off.

We could have signed up for a fully guided affair, but Sampson wanted us to do a good part of the trip alone, and after some thought, I'd agreed. Six days deep in the backcountry of Montana would give Big John many chances to open up and talk, which is critical to the process of coping with tragic loss.

"How's Willow feeling about our little trip?" I asked.

Sampson smiled. "She doesn't like the idea of grizzly bears any more than Nana does, but she knows it will make me happy."

"Your little girl's always been wise beyond her years."

"Truth. Bree liking her job?"

Thinking of my smart, beautiful, and independent wife, I said, "She loves it. Got up early to be at the office. Something about a possible assignment in Paris."

"Paris! What a difference a career change makes."

"No kidding. It was like the gig was tailor-made for her."

"Maybe we should think about going into private-sector investigations too."

"Pay's better, for sure," I allowed.

Before he could reply, my seventeen-year-old daughter, Jannie, poked her head in and said, "Nana says your eggs are getting cold."

I put down my dry bag and went to the kitchen, where I found my youngest child, Ali, already finishing up his plate.

"Morning, sunshine," I said, giving him a hug. He ignored it, so I tickled him.

"C'mon, Dad!" He laughed, then groaned. "Why can't I go with you?"

"Because you're a kid and we don't know what we'll be facing."

"I can do it," he insisted.

Sampson said, "Ali, let your dad and me scope it out this year. If we think you're up to it, we'll bring you along on the next trip. Deal?"

Ali scrunched up his face and shrugged. "I guess. When do you leave?"

"First thing in the—"

My cell phone began to ring at the same time Sampson's chimed.

"No," John protested. "Don't answer that, Alex. We're supposed to be gone already!"

But when I saw the caller ID, I grimaced and knew I had to answer. "Commissioner Dennison," I said. "John Sampson and I were just heading out the door on vacation."

"Cancel it," said the commissioner of the Metro DC Police Department. "We've got a dead female, gunshot wound to the head, dumped in the garage under the International Spy Museum on L'Enfant Plaza. Her ID says she's—"

"Commissioner, with all due respect," I said, "we've been planning this trip for—"

"I don't care, Cross," he snapped. "Her ID says she's CIA. If you want to continue your contract with Metro, you'll get down there. And if Sampson wants to keep his job, he'll be with you."

I stared at the ceiling a second, looked at John, and shook my head.

"Okay, Commissioner. We're on our way."

JAMES PATTERSON RECOMMENDS

JAMES PATTERSON

TEXAS RANGER

& ANDREW BOURELLE

THE WORLD'S #1 BESTSELLING WRITER

TEXAS RANGER

So many of my detectives are dark and gritty and deal with crimes in some of our grimmest cities. That's why I'm thrilled to bring you Detective Rory Yates, my most honorable detective yet.

As a Texas Ranger, he has a code that he lives and works by. But when he comes home for a much-needed break, he walks into a crime scene where the victim is none other than his ex-wife—and he's the prime suspect. Yates has to risk everything in order to clear his name, and he dives into the inferno of the most twisted mind I've ever created. Can his code bring him back out alive?

THIS BOOK
WILL MAKE YOUR
JAW DROP
INVISIBLE
THE WORLD'S #1 BESTSELLING WRITER
JAMES PATTERSON
& DAVID ELLIS

INVISIBLE

When I started writing *Invisible*, it seemed like every other TV network was telling the same kind of police stories, robberies, and crime twists. So I wanted to tell a different kind of suspense story, one that would really make your jaw drop. In the novel, Emmy Dockery is a researcher for the FBI who believes she has stumbled on one of the deadliest serial killers in history. There's only one problem—he's invisible. The mysterious killer leaves no trace. There are no weapons, no evidence, no motive. But when the killer strikes close to home, she must crack an impossible case before anyone else dies. Prepare to be blindsided because the most terrifying threat is the one you don't see coming—the one that's invisible.

And don't miss Emmy Dockery's second mystery, *Unsolved*, available now.

JAMES PATTERSON

THE FIRST LADY

BRENDAN DUBOIS

THE WORLD'S #1 BESTSELLING WRITER

THE FIRST LADY

The US government is at the forefront of everyone's mind these days and I've become incredibly fascinated by the idea that one secret can bring it all down. What if that secret is a US president's affair that results in a nightmarish outcome? Sally Grissom, leader of the Presidential Protection Division, is summoned to a private meeting with the president and his chief of staff to discuss the disappearance of the First Lady. What at first seemed an escape to a safe haven to get away from the revelation of her husband's indiscretion turns into a kidnapping when a ransom note arrives along with what could be the First Lady's finger. It's a race against the clock to collect the evidence that all leads to one troubling question: Could the kidnappers be from inside the White House?

JAMES PATTERSON

AND BRENDAN DUBOIS

*Her family is missing.
She'll do whatever
it takes to bring
them home.*

THE
CORNWALLS
VANISH

PREVIOUSLY PUBLISHED AS *THE CORNWALLS ARE GONE*

THE CORNWALLS VANISH

There's nothing more terrifying than coming home and knowing that something is wrong. Army intelligence officer Amy Cornwall experiences that when she finishes a tour filled with haunting sights and she walks in the front door to find her home empty. She receives a phone call with very specific instructions, and failure to complete them will mean the death of her husband and ten-year-old daughter. Now Amy has to defy Army Command and use every lethal skill they've taught her to save her family. There's no boundary that she won't cross in order to find them, because without her family, she might as well be dead.

NEVER

IN THE NEVER NEVER, NO ONE KNOWS IF YOU'RE DEAD OR ALIVE

NEVER

JAMES
PATTERSON

CANDICE FOX

NEVER NEVER

As tough as Alex Cross. As smart as the Women's Murder Club. The brilliant, fierce Detective Harriet Blue. She's a tough woman who can hunt down any man in a hardscrabble continent half a world away. My newest detective, Harry, is her department's top Sex Crimes investigator, and she'll need to use all her skills when her own brother is arrested for the murder of three beautiful women. And clearing her brother's name under the watchful eye of her new "partner" is anything but easy. She has to delve into deep dark secrets, and failure to solve the mystery may mean she never makes it back.

For a complete list of books by

JAMES PATTERSON

VISIT
JamesPatterson.com

 Follow James Patterson on Facebook
@JamesPatterson

 Follow James Patterson on Twitter
@JP_Books

 Follow James Patterson on Instagram
@jamespattersonbooks